Cry Not For Me...

Enosh Sunny Lazarus

ISBN: 978-0-692-79597-2 (Hardcover)
ISBN: 978-0-692-84340-6 (Paperback)
ISBN: 978-0-692-84144-0 (eBook)

To my sister for her undying belief in me.

꧁꧁꧁

Part I

꧁꧁꧁

Chapter One

ço ço ço

"Let them burn all the way to hell, what do I care?" I said a little vexed at the sound of a gasping fire truck that came blaring across a sinuous trail through the outskirts of midtown, awakening countless haggard souls as far as the cacophony could permeate the dormant city. It wasn't much astonishing to sight a few windows light up, concerned possessors of those enclosures appearing beyond a cover of draperies and vinyl blinds to witness the ingress of Engine 54 and another deafening roar of a horn.

Just another false alarm! This blatant ruckus in the calm of the night is nothing but a nuisance; a thought emerged from a dark, cynical concavity of my mind. As this dissonance disrupted my protracted stare into the dark void of my bedraggled sublet unit, it also instigated me to interrogate the site of incident by contributing myself to the roster of fifty other spectators identically glancing through the glass panes squinting for a better view, trying to ward a momentary visual impairment against a burst of red flashing lights.

As I watched irately the situation unfold, I saw a band of fire fighters all equipped from head to toe with protective gear and suits prepared to take on the worst the insouciant world has to offer. I looked closely again, suddenly imbued in disgust as I had espied the source of smoke and all this commotion was only to douse a smoldering cigarette that had steamed off a little more than it should have and singed a garbage bag left to be sanitized on a Friday night causing smoke to emanate from it along with a small flare. It wasn't the first time I had seen an utter waste of time and resources and it wouldn't be the last I assumed. But I undoubtedly would seek to murder the numskull who made the hazard call. Only if people were more enlightened with certain criteria established by the Fire & Safety Department to evaluate specifics of a situation before making the panicked decision to report to 911, I'd say we would be accorded a sweet full night's sleep all of us yearn for. To assume some social responsibility wouldn't hurt any of us, or maybe it would, I couldn't say.

Well, I couldn't say much about anything for the moment as misanthropy had forced me down an entirely wayward path that led nowhere but desolation of my soul. But nearing fifty-seven in age, life had given me some wisdom, if not much, to differentiate between right and wrong. Right was to stay alive, live hard through tough times, down to the knees, up again and journey on. Wrong was to open up this window and let myself go all the way, plummeting down six floors into the concrete sidewalk below. Tonight was a long, pensive night. It was a dark night. My initial plan entailed a ten dollar Old Crow bottle of whiskey, some cigarettes, and suicide. Didn't I just toss a cigarette down the window before this ordeal began? Hell, it couldn't be me causing all this commotion. Well, maybe it was.

I leaned back on a chipped armchair eyeing the cracked apartment walls, a cupular ceiling, a squeaking metal bed frame that bore a torn, age old spring mattress and a plate of spaghetti on the bedside savored by a horde of roaches. Better to do something than sitting idle eating spaghetti, I thought and puffed on another cigarette. Though, I meant that for the firefighters, not me. I took another inhale of the deleterious miasma into my body and flicked the singeing cigarette butt out the window. Closed my eyes, tried to sleep, never actually succeeding at that.

༺ஒஒஒ༻

Night had drowned in despair and ache of desire. The city had awakened to a turbid veil of fog that hung around the eightieth floor of Empire State Building. It was an overcast but frigid dawn, and the tranquility of darkness had transmuted to a diurnal turmoil of machinery and men. I had treasured my fourteen dollars worth night long stay in the luxury of my rickety enclosure and it was time to depart the seven floor apartment building with each room individually and illegally sublet to people with little money like me, charging per night or as long as each stayed. The guy who operated this *personal* business stood knocking outside my door very early, around seven, and held out his hand for me to turn over the possession of the room and its key to the rightful owner. Well, I hadn't developed any sentimental attachment to the gilded furnishing in there like the squealing bed or the jagged armchair, so parting wasn't at all challenging.

Dank morning breeze washed my face anew as I came out the building entrance. As much as I intended to eschew the sight that befell me now, I couldn't; Humans. Overwhelmingly overabundant. No one I knew, but all seemed somewhat kindred spirits in the journey of life through a relationship elusive enough but comfortably grasped with just one prolonged intrusive stare into their eyes as their hearts and minds unfolded before you like parchments of an antiquated scroll. A relationship of longing and desire, of sorrow and misery, of unrequited love and unanswered prayers. Was there a soul in view that appeared replete with pleasures of life? Not many, at least not to me. Call it a lack of perceptivity or a trenchant ability of true discernment, I couldn't find one. But all of them sought and attained the strength to survive one more day, just one more.

Last night had given me a similar strength, strength to make another arduous journey, possibly the last of the kind. A voice called out to me while I slept. I didn't sleep too well, or my sensory receptors wouldn't have heard anyone or anything let alone a name call in the din of the night. But this voice had always interrupted my scraggy decision-making process and deterred me from that set course of action I resolved to every time I reached a conclusion. Last night it hindered my attempt to commit a suicide and advised me to embark on another journey. A two thousand seven hundred ninety - five mile journey to Hollywood, California. No, I wasn't going there to try my luck at Hollywood splendor, I wasn't that personable. Neither to see the city for one last time, I was never the itinerant type. Just a common, age old reason; nostalgia. Can't seem to forget the years of my childhood that were spent in the bliss of Hollywood Hills, but that is another story. Right now I had to figure out how I plan to gather the leftovers of my life savings to make the bus fare that charged approximately two hundred seventy dollars for the troublesome travel of almost three days. But when the Voice calls, all you can do is obey. A gold wedding band had lounged on my finger for a very long time, so long that I had almost forgotten the reason it was there. About time I put it to some good use.

"What can I do for you?"

The pawn shop wasn't all glitter and charm, and a balding store owner with a beer gut and grotesque teeth looked up at me suspiciously. He cleaned the crevice between his anteriors with his pinky and burst into a question in a low pitched voice.

I headed up to his counter and without a word placed my ring upon the glass. He eyed me dawning with an assumption that I had stolen the piece of jewelry, and then took an appraising look at it. Even though, the assessment didn't last for long, he came up with a splendid response to my silence.

"Give you one fifty for that," he said.

I was elated at the sound of his words, not too much for the spit sputtering mouth though. A nod came from me following the offer. He reached for his register and took out a stack of cash. An outpour of seven 20 dollar bills, concluded with a simple Hamilton. He collected his treasure as I did mine and headed off after a handshake completing a pleasant transaction. Next stop Port Authority.

Chapter Two

ૐ ૐ ૐ

I approached a block long queue that meandered even longer with successions of luggage between the waiting travelers. The ticket windows were inundated with expectant passengers on December twenty-first as the big day waited around the corner. Motley of families, couples, singles and children hastening across the swarming terminal in their sweat soaked sweaters and frigid palms, attempting to assimilate the Christmas spirit to their best capability. But the troubles of travel overcome all. I was an exception amongst this horde. No hurries, no worries, my demeanor was as cold as the weather. But I applauded their holiday effort and observed their exuberance in anticipation of imminent family reunions and gatherings to relive and revive the forgotten memories, antique homes and ancient people living in them. Some excited smiles across young faces to meet their grandparents after years or even for the first time, with a curiosity to actually discover the true sight of withering skin in folds. Unsettling hesitation in young women who accompany their boyfriend or fiancé for that one onerous task of meeting the family. It was vice versa in some cases as well. Exhausted mothers securing their children, counting heads time after time, making sure all are accounted for. Travailing fathers with glares and frowns as they haul heavy luggage crammed with gifts and presents. All in a haphazard bustle that brings joy, maybe discomfort and weariness at times, but all overlooked in hopes of meeting loved ones and family.

Good for them, all of them. Hope they do realize what a privilege having a family could be. I, on the other hand, had a different intention behind making this trip. It was solely to find an end to my aching self, and what place could be more appropriate for this caprice than the one where it all began. I couldn't find the courage to accomplish my longing for demise in New York, but I hoped I would there. I hoped.

The boarding process commenced and wasn't any different from the bustling terminal itself. The bus aisle inside was jammed with settling passengers, attempting to fit their oversized luggage into the compartments above the seating. And amidst that turmoil a faction of kids screaming and shuffling up and down the constricted space. I'm certain some parents would have contemplated dumping those imbeciles along with the luggage in the trunk and have a moment's peace. Only a passing thought, jest intended. I perched on my window adjoining seat number 31 and without any intention to stay awake, rested my head against the closed window and shut my eyes, hoping to stay reticent for the rest of the travel.

"Is this seat taken?" A voice sounded.
Then again I had almost forgotten the incessant streak of my crappy fate. I opened my burdened eyes to behold an elderly face leaning excessively close to my own. Though unwarranted, I had noticed there was no sense of personal space in people from "*that*" time. Or perhaps the people of "*my*" time were not comfortable getting close to each other, even the ones we trusted. I shook my head blankly in response to her question. She gave a splendid smile, or so to her rejoice, and took the seat. I stirred to make space for her on the armrest which she gladly accepted and enfolded herself in a sweater that even smothered me around the peripheries of my limbs. While all this went on I silently thought, didn't they actually have seat numbers on bus tickets nowadays? Mine did, so I was safe to assume hers would bear one as well. So, why did she ask in that case? Gone were the days when you could just take any seat without a slightest concern and could get away with it out of mutual respect and understanding. These days an imminent threat of aggression and possibly a fistfight were included as consequences of grabbing the wrong seat. I prepared myself for the impending argument and the lady's eviction. Though, it didn't

matter much who sat next to me, what mattered was that no one did. A young couple moved matching seat numbers to their tickets and finally found their destination. They were split by the aisle and both shared seats with strangers. The young man kept his bag on the seat across the aisle while the young woman was supposedly on the one next to me, which now had been illegally occupied by the old lady.

"Am I in your seat, sweetheart?" The old lady leaned forward looking up at the beautiful blonde.

"I think you are!" She exclaimed with a smile.

"Oh no, honey, I know precisely what I'm doing." She rummaged her handbag and retrieved her ticket. "I'm supposed to be at 31D, but when I saw you both at the ticket window I realized you two had just gotten married and were visiting your in-laws for the holidays, am I right?"

They shook their heads suspicious of her intrusive nature.

"Well, I thought why not grant you some private time together and let you two create some more moments of love and memory out of this pleasant journey. I'd hate to split you two, so I took this seat and that side is all yours."

The young couple looked in disbelief. The woman took the old lady's hand in hers and thanked her earnestly. The old lady was all smiles as she watched the couple settle in their seats.

"How beautiful is young love, isn't it? How long has it been?" the old lady asked.

"Two months," the blonde replied.

"God bless you," the old lady wished with a deep breath. While they were getting blessed, I actually cursed the old lady within because by the looks of it, this journey would be far from quiet and peace for me.

Her attention now diverted from the young loving couple to a miserable man on her left. She glanced at me with a smile, but it soon faded when she received none in response. Her trembling, arthritis stricken fingers brushed against my arm as she again wrapped herself in a sweater which had rolled off of her during her recent excited conversation with the couple. But it wasn't until the conductor had announced the particulars of the trip and all necessary details that she had settled herself completely in the seat. I observed her from the corner of my eye out of curiosity, possibly to know how I'm going to be fifteen-twenty years from now. I noticed that she listened to the conductor with extreme enthusiasm that kept her riveted for the duration of his speech and she switched between two pairs of glasses that hung down her neck, one for reading and the other for everything else. It surprised me the way she could concentrate at this age, when I completely ignored the resounding announcements and why wouldn't I? We all knew where we were going, how long it would take for us to reach there and where we must get off. This guy just junked 6 minutes of his life and ours being redundant which wasn't much appreciated by anyone in the bus except the old lady next to me. Her interest was thorough and enjoyment ardent.

Our journey had commenced, the crowd had settled in, the bus lurched forward and slid down the interlaced nervures of Manhattan. There was a monotonous mumbling in the air as everyone spoke merrily to one another. I eschewed that instinct. The only thought that filled my mind was simple; two days and seventeen hours wasn't a short duration to be spent in a moving cubicle. Well, a break here and there and a stretch of legs at bus stops wouldn't count as respite. How I planned to spend this lifetime on the road even I didn't know. I peered over to my right and found the same withering face gazing down at a photo album, perhaps years old. A sepia colored picture quivered in her unsteady hands. There was a tinge of joy in her eyes to ogle the handsome, groomed man who looked right back at her. I don't know how, but she discerned that my gaze was fixed at the picture as well.

"That's my husband," she said leaning towards me. "1952, the year this picture was taken." She smiled and glanced over, this time I did manage to lend her quick one because she had just given me an idea on how to spend long travel hours without getting bored. I wasn't sure if it would bring me pleasure as it did to her, or sorrow as it did to some. But I was willing to take a chance for one reason only; I knew it will last just as long as this journey. Maybe even outlast it. So, just like every other person on this bus I was about to go down the memory lane to reminisce and reflect and it took me right back where it began, in fact two and a half days earlier than I had hoped. The bliss of Hollywood Hills.

Chapter Three
ೞ·ೞ·ೞ

I surely couldn't go as far back as 1952, but I could speak about the 60s out of my personal experience. Back then life was surprisingly simple. You lived and you passed on, and the part that came between the two phases wasn't as complicated as it's made to look like today. I can say that because I have been through both times and I've observed the people change into machines. I've seen them become beasts of burden and vulnerable. I've found them hurt others and themselves. The so called game of success wasn't much participated in back then and satisfaction wasn't just externally visible, but internally felt.

I was 7 at that time. It was a warm summer day of August 1964 when a white Rolls Royce rolled inside the massive wrought iron cathedral gates of a baronial property that was erected in the heart of Beverly Hills. Everything about this structure was awe-inspiring. A mile long, treelined driveway led to a four tier marble fountain pool, landscaped frontage that stretched for acres that even had a hedge maze which I was never able to navigate entirely in all the time I had spent there, as it wasn't much. Yes, I will say "I" because it did belong to me, or my father actually, but I believe it was the same thing. I watched this looming grandeur from the rear seat of the vehicle but my view was partially obstructed by an outline of a human head topped with a crisp white chauffeur's hat.

Frank was our chauffeur at the time and I always used to question him, not about his driving skills, but why every other chauffeur there is happened to be named Frank? I personally knew three other chauffeurs named Frank driving my father's wealthy acquaintances. Then I discussed with him that how they would, if they ever meet, converse with each other? Would they title each other Frank one, Frank two, or rather use their middle and last name initials along with their first names, like Frank G N, or Frank Z Q, or in his case Frank B L. Or maybe they would like to categorize each Frank into an age group, like Frank 30s, or for our Frank, Frank 50s. Even he would laugh at the idea of how their first meeting would be like. All four coming across each other saying "I'm Frank, me too." He didn't have an answer to my queries, I guess it was just a common human mistake to categorize a name with a profession, but that was only a passing curiosity. I went on living.

My diurnal activities were no different from any other kid my age. Mornings began with a decent breakfast and school, afternoon with a lunch and solitude, evenings with homework, supper, and isolation of my enclosure for the rest of the night. And yes, I did have parents as well. Mr. Vincent Frederick Bailey, my father and Jeanette Flora Bailey, my stepmother. That's about all I knew about them, their names, never insisted on discovering any more than that. But I knew one thing for sure, I wasn't even on their minds. My mother had passed away when I was three years old. She died due to a prolonged illness that I later came to know as cancer. Well, it hardly left anyone alive they said, my mother was no exception. My father wasn't that much moved by her passing as he had married Jeanette some weeks later, sooner than I could go to sleep at night without soaking my pillow in tears, and I was just three. His relationship with his new wife was not too elusive; she was young, ambitious, and audacious, he was aged, balding, portly but rich. There wasn't much communication between them or us. In fact, the only time we would get to see each other was at the dining during supper. It was pleasant, if you'd consider clatter of gold-lined silverware in silence of a lavish room with three wealthy souls mute as a dead duck as pleasant, then it was. But if you'd rather take a tumultuous family desirous for long conversations asking each other how their day was, dining on leftovers from last night at a food and word scattered table, then you're at the wrong place. We were rich with a social circle as multitudinous and affluent as the senate, but had nothing to talk about. We were decent enough to surrender our plates to the waiters and leave table even when hungry. And we were considerate enough to resolve our troubles and difficulties with our own reasoning and capabilities without any assistance from family members. Then again it wasn't a complaint, it was just a lifestyle. The only thing I loved about my life was that I got to visit the most beautiful place in Hollywood every night of the week. My father's theater called The Blue Crescent.

I was driven to the theater every night some moments before the whole place lit up in lights like a Christmas tree. Now that is one thing I always appreciated of my old man, he had given me an inspiration to seek out a meaningful profession. A life in theater. I wasn't much against it. After all, it was the show business that attracted me the most. The beauty of it was fascinating, the idea of stardom was infatuating. Speaking of infatuations, I came past the hallway into a corridor that led to multiple green rooms, but just before I could knock my father's office, she came out.

She stood before me like an angel had descended from heavens and taken form in flesh. Labeling her beautiful or gorgeous would be unjust. The concrete walls radiated silver with her resplendence and even that is merely a justification of her sublime appearance. She was a paragon of divine exquisiteness, she was the sweetest of all beings ever created, she was Audrey Gaskins. She walked towards me and winked at me with her beguiling smile as she always did. She moved forward and tapped my head passing me by, "missed you yesterday, what happened?"
She didn't stop for a response and wouldn't have done any good if she did because she would receive none. I was just in awe of her voice suitable for lullabies in paradise. I stood there paralyzed until Frank nudged me to continue, it was only then that I was revived out of my reverie. I finally had fallen in love.

There was nothing as sad as unrequited love, and I realized that the hard way learning that my father had an extramarital affair with Audrey since the day she was discovered by his casting agents who were not as much excited to introduce her as the new leading talent of our theater but acceded to my father's will and authority. I also

- 14 -

came to understand the true reason behind Jeanette's indifference toward me and my father, and I couldn't solely blame her. Even though, I didn't know of the circumstances that instigated such distance between them, but I guess you cannot applaud with one hand; you need two to create the sound and this sound was grave. I watched them drift apart day by day, minute by minute, and it wasn't strange for me or my father to notice that Jeanette had begun to seek attention elsewhere. It didn't come to me as a surprise to find strange men leaving our mansion early afternoon upon my arrival from school and waving to her a long goodbye from their steaming Ford Cobras and Chevrolet Corvettes. She wasn't much interested in the theater, so she kept herself from interfering in Vincent's matters. But she cherished the company of the people involved in the business. After all, it was her lifelong desire to greet the stardom of Hollywood and the men thereof with open arms. If she hadn't married my father, I think she wouldn't have failed at that. But due to a demanding stipulation enforced by my father which was the basis of this marriage, Jeanette was asked to abandon her aspirations and become a housewife. Though, it wasn't a contractual agreement, but gladly accepted in hopes of living it large as the wife of the most prominent theater baron in all California. If she ever flipped through the parchments of her past life, I'd say this was the biggest highlighted, underlined mistake written in bold capital letters she'd ever made and it came with consequences she was struggling with now.

For my father it seemed like a pattern he went with. His marriage with my mother lasted five years which ended in her death, and was followed by the current, disastrous second marriage he was going through for the past three and a half years. Now his sight was set on a third blunder which I clearly knew wouldn't go much longer. Somehow, witnessing this debacle of relationships for the most of my life and finding so many people hurt, it created a profound dislike for the word "marriage" within me. I never thought this word could bring so much dissatisfaction, pain and suffering in the lives that were a part of this relationship. I decided to go against this relationship and concluded that I will never marry, and if I ever do get married, it will only be once in my life and will last forever. Little did I know that true desires are hard to pursue.

It was just another day when I returned from school and discerned some distressed voices emerging from behind closed doors. I didn't make an attempt to investigate as I had been instructed against it by my father many times before. I went on straight to my bedroom, closed the door shut and sat in silence.

I didn't realize I had fallen asleep until the moment when my door was loudly knocked and opened, stirring me from a sound dreaming state. It was Jeanette who stormed in with traces of sweat upon her face and urgency to her movements that demanded my attention.

"What's the matter?" I rubbed my eyes to get a proper view of the situation.

"We have to go to the hospital," her response reeked of trepidation.

During my question she had managed to locate my jacket and had put me into it. She dragged me out of my bed and the room.

Our car charged through the streets of Beverly Hills at a velocity I had never felt in the back seat ever before with Frank driving. By the speed of our travel, I intuited something was wrong and my deepest fears surfaced upon my face when my eyes fell at the corner of the street far down. The site encompassed by a massive crowd of firefighters, police officers, journalists, photographers, spectators and the unfortunate employees of our theater.

The Blue Crescent was up in flames!

Chapter Four

❦ ❦ ❦

We drove past the site of devastation in utter despair and shock, and a dreadful feeling of loss had crippled my limbs as well as my mind to contemplate any possibility of something good that might have been spared that night. For the rest of our trip the foremost worry that troubled me was the safety of my father. I had also considered this mishap to be an outcome of a muffled altercation I had heard in the afternoon. It wasn't until I was taken to a muted third floor hallway of a hospital that I finally breathed some relief into my stifled self. My father was admitted in a private ward and was tended by two nurses around the clock. As I watched through a little square glass opening in the door, I saw a doctor reviewing the case file and conversing with Jeanette and desperately trying to alleviate Vincent of some unknown misery that befell him. I was unaware of his suffering until my eyes shifted a little below his knees and noticed that the sheet was creased to a plain surface without any impressions of legs or feet following down in their humanly order. My sight constantly shifted from my father's lugubrious visage to his amputated legs and the more I did, the more I commiserated with his dire streak of fate. I turned away from the vantage point and fell into a bench with tears streaming down my face and trembling hands that were not mature enough to bear the responsibility of a broken family, that were not large enough to draw in heaps of cash to maintain a wealthy lifestyle, that were not withered enough to declare an undisputable reputation in a social jungle. I was just a 7 year old kid with a lot of feelings that night.

My father arrived home about three weeks after it all happened. His arrival wasn't greeted by many but only a few which included Jeanette, Frank and me. He was on a wheelchair now and had to push himself around the house to reach places, and sometimes even that was rendered unachievable due to restricted spaces and passages. I saw him limit his wandering within a home he had built himself. His troubles did not end there and I came to learn the employees of Blue Crescent suspected Audrey of setting the theater stage ablaze which came in response to another affray that took place between her and my father not too long before the fire, and her disappearance after the whole incident only strengthened that suspicion. It also came to our attention, which particularly shook us all financially unstable, that Vincent had obtained a considerable bank loan to gift Audrey an upscale apartment in San Diego about a year ago with our home proposed as collateral and it was personally kept off the books to keep Jeanette from discovering the affair and the truth. These predicaments came one after another and I was surprised that Jeanette still remained by his side even three months after. But my commendation came to an abrupt end when one morning Vincent discovered a letter on a pillow next to him which usually bore a sleeping Jeanette every now and then. It was inevitable, Jeanette had left us both.

Our lives had changed, our living had changed, and soon our home would be changed. An estate that swarmed with two drivers, a chef, a waiter, a butler, a gardener, a doorman, seven housekeepers, and three security guards, was reduced to just Frank. A theater that employed five writers, eighteen production crew, three directors, numerous actors and uncountable laborers was now reduced to ashes. Our four cars were gradually sold off to cover our daily expenses which caused Frank's separation from our lives. Though, he was quite reluctant to leave our side until it was most essential to do so, but the responsibility of three children and a wife couldn't be compensated with a meager paycheck of what we could afford. It was a tragic departure as I saw tears in Frank's eyes for the first time since I knew him. He had conversed with my father for a very long time while I listened from outside the room. The conversation included his gratitude for the time he was given employment when the rest had rejected him and the years that followed. It also included his commiseration and offer of service whenever it might be needed, be it the late hours of night or any of the day.

Jeanette had bailed out at the right time as my father declared bankruptcy just a few days after Frank's and Jeanette's exit from our lives. And so the largest looming threat to our existence came in the hands of a district court employee who bore the notice of eviction and property auction, posting it to our gates. We had a hundred and fifty days to pay off the debt that with interest summed close to one and a half million. I had also gathered in this time that the price tag of the gifted apartment was way below that and the rest of the money had been prodigally spent by my father on Europe and Caribbean vacations with Audrey that took place over the course of a year, maybe more. The San Diego apartment had been sold off by Audrey without his knowledge about a week before the incident at a very low price, almost half of what it was worth. We were out of a retreat as well. So, the number of days dwindled, a million and a half to return, an insurance claim that would go under investigation for a long time due to the suspicion stated by other employees and a disabled, wheelchair dependant father who was shattered within. If I were to weigh in the possibilities of putting an end to all of this, I'd be an idiot, a criminal, or a coward. I was too young to be any of those. I decided to be strong and I counted days as the day of auction approached. I knew I would have to leave this house and the luxuries within these walls soon, so I made sure I toured the grounds and inside the mansion for a few hours every day until the end of the deadline to absorb the memories from every cobblestone road that led from one end of the lawns to another, every path that meandered amidst the maze and other forgotten parts of lavish acres, each room that accommodated some, if not a lot, of the things that I owned and every inch and corner of the walls that still resounded with my mother's voice, my father's scarce laughter, and countless chattering that I conducted with myself.

I watched, as the day drew closer, the prodigious man plummet from the pinnacle of his stature to the lowly state of misery. He would ring the phone all day long to people he once knew as contacts, helped as humans, befriended and acquainted within his social surroundings, seeking any kind of aid he might elicit from them, but failed woefully. He would sit alone in the deplorable darkness of wretchedness and brood, brood in silence for hours. He was proceeding toward his demise, and I was able to see it in his eyes. I pitied the man I saw before me, though, I was too young to understand that feeling, but I was disinclined to impute the fall of our family to him. All I saw was a disabled man who implored to his best ability to be extricated from his misfortune at any costs. Too bad he didn't have anything to cover those costs with. If he were at least able to ambulate and support himself into a living, I would have had different feelings toward holding him culpable for all that has happened. But I couldn't, not to the man who suffered, even if it was due to his own failures, I simply couldn't. Amidst these trying times approached the day I usually waited for the whole year. My birthday was in two days, and as much as I doubted that it will be celebrated this year, I still had a flickering hope in my heart that my father might surprise me with something, maybe something as little as a cupcake. Two days later as I woke up as an eight year old that morning, I found nothing but profound silence around the house. That wasn't what I would observe on my birthday for the past seven years or I'd say for a couple that I completely remembered. It was always a birthday song involving all the house help, Frank and most of the time my father and Jeanette. Well, it was just my father left in the house now and he wasn't there to bless me or kiss my forehead wishing an adventurous year ahead. That gave another fact a concrete assurance that possibly it was Frank and other household help that remembered my big day instead of my father and stepmother. As I made my way across the hall and found him on his wheelchair right at the main doorway staring at the porch and the property beyond, I knew he didn't remember. But someone did.

Frank came to the house later that afternoon with a small bouquet and a red 1950 Jaguar XK120 model toy car. I was elated to accept the gift and then thanked him for being so kind. He responded hinting towards his indigence and that was what he could afford, but I said to him that it meant the world for me to have someone remember my birthday and he was the only one who did. He then inquired about my father's health and left after an hour long stay. I cherished his visit and the presents for a very long time.

Finally the day came and the objects that were once in our possession began to leave our ownership with a tag dangling from them, one by one. There came a group of people accompanied by the officials of the court that visited the mansion and assessed every nook inside and out evaluating our home. It was an early but a great experience for me at the young age of eight to witness the true nature of mankind which dismissed any or all regard for the feelings and emotions of two souls attached to this structure who were still living inside of it and that money outweighed any or all codes of conduct when a bankrupt man, no matter how influential he was in the past, was on the other end of the scale. All we could do was just stand and watch them put a price on everything and take it along. They didn't seek permission or even a little acknowledgement as they emptied our home.

My father literally begged his insurance agent to make him a deal with the insurance claim investigators, utilizing what was left of his influence to its extremes, to settle for a pittance below expected. He ended up with seventeen thousand dollars for a claim that was assessed around seven hundred thousand dollars but would have taken at least ten more months to process. In two days, it was time for us to vacate the house and as we trudged farther away from gates of our once prized dwelling, I saw tears slipping down my father's eyes.

"Son, you see that? If you ever get into one of those again, be sure you make it on your own. Trust no one, especially women. They are just an object of your need." That day was the last I heard any words come out of his mouth and those words were wisdom for me for many years to follow.

Forcibly or gratefully we took that money and in hopes to begin a new life departed the bliss of Hollywood Hills, California.

Chapter Five

క్రిక్రిక్రి

Life hadn't gone as planned and it seldom did. Not only I, but every single soul in the world could corroborate that fact. But I didn't need their affirmation, my own experiences were enough for me to trust my judgment. I watched my father lean against the window of a moving bus as rain pelted the glass. His eyes were still and open, overwhelmed with emotions of all sorts; sorrow, grief, loneliness. I sat right next to him holding on to his folded wheelchair that was parked safely in the aisle. Looking at him I realized life isn't always what it seems to be. One day he was rich, wealthy, surrounded by admirers and lovers, he had authority over so many people, influence over the rest. He manipulated the law to his will, that's how strong he was. And today he was just an amputated, disconsolate man with no hopes of future happiness, name, fame or anything that he previously possessed, not even fake love. All he had was an eight year old kid, who in return was prepared to spend the remainder of their days together in his company. Our destination was unknown to me, but by the looks of our path and scarcity of other fellow travelers it gradually became evident that we were headed for isolation; perhaps from this world or the people who existed within. Or maybe even ourselves, to make memories out of our past that eventually could be eradicated. We had just crossed into Ohio as a passing signboard welcomed me to the state, a sudden realization dawned upon me that Vincent actually belonged to that state. His birthplace was a small village called Dresden located near Muskingum River and if I wasn't wrong, we were headed to his home where he grew up until the age of 17. I'd never been told if I had any grandparents. If they were alive I would be excited to meet them, if they weren't then I'd be a bit more excited to see how an abandoned house looks like.

It was abandoned all right. I just beheld a huge countryside cottage nearing a creek and a stretch of unkempt land as far as the eye could reach. We were dropped off by an old, squeaking pick-up truck at the side of the main road that lay a couple hundred feet from the house. I unfolded my father's wheelchair and assisted him to settle upon it, pushed him all the way through a jagged pathway that was laden with crevices and ditches and overgrown bushes to finally rest under the shadow of colossal beech tree that was pitching left, sporadically brushing against the ground in the breeze. We acknowledged our shared misery and just like the looming, rickety structure, we also held on to something. I had assumed the distaff responsibility for our survival without my father asserting on it, though I was indeed a neophyte at such affairs. I decisively took a step further and sighted an unhinged mesh door that could tip off to the floor any moment now. A deep sigh followed, I had a lot of work to do.

There wasn't much ground to cover as far as grooming of the interiors to a habitable domicile was concerned. There was a wrap-around porch that was rather tidy and usable with the aid of Mother Nature itself with wind working as broom and the rain as mop. There were two rooms inside, out of which one could be considered a living room due to its location in the center of it all which also bore a hearth. There was another one inferior in size and comfort which I labeled as a bedroom for my father, a bathroom that adjoined it and a kitchenette that opened into the living. The walls were brick I suppose as they had no signs of water damage or dampening even after years of endurance and the floor, I was certain, was cold concrete and uncarpeted. A few articles of furniture were abandoned in a utile condition, but the rest was a detritus after ages of depletion which could come handy if I could get the fireplace burning. Of course, I had to get the plumbers over to fix the bathroom functionality as well as the water supply in the rest of the abode. In this matter I was fortunate enough to meet my neighbors and seek assistance in finding feasible labor.

The neighbors had actually visited with a fruit basket and introduced themselves as Benningsons from across the street. Well, I didn't sight any houses across the street but there must be one concealed behind those elephantine trees and a barricade of hedges, and they must have had some sharp eyes to sight us over all that distance. Just a regular married couple about late 40s, no child, no immediate family, good acquaintances of my grandparents and it was through them that we came to know the last to pass away of our elders was my grandfather at the age of eighty-eight, three years ago. My father didn't know that, didn't bother to inquire.

Benningsons said they had expected us to return one day and kept paying taxes on the property to keep it from being confiscated. Though, only a pittance in amount, my grandfather had left them with all his savings to conserve the property as long as they could in hopes of having his son return to his hometown one day. It was almost as if my grandpa had seen the future and knew what was coming, or maybe just knew life all to well and the way it deceived people. Benningsons said they still had about six hundred dollars left from that amount and gave it over the next day. I had lost trust in people after what I witnessed against my father and even myself, but somehow our neighbors made me realize that in this world humanity is never pervasive rather scattered, but not lost.

I had always dreamed big. I don't know whom I should blame for this as my father was equally a part of my conviction and there was one thing he always insisted upon no matter how much of distance there was amongst us or his indifference towards my upbringing, but he impelled me to be a part of the show business. Well, maybe not after he was spurned and banished himself, but before it all happened, he did encourage me to learn about it all. And I did develop an ability to write, even though it was never validated by opinions of others as I never submitted my works for reviews, but I had a personal belief that I was exceptional at it. It also dawned upon me that it might have been just a passing enthusiasm towards authorship as it did dwindle away during the years of my endurance in our little cottage, but it was never forgotten. I began attending a school where most of the townsfolk sent their children to be educated. For me it was just a way to get through. I was never a popular student in terms of having the whole class as my social circle or scoring grades that even my teachers struggled to in their times, but I was renowned in drawing awkward stares and hushed whispers. I used to spend my evenings by the river, sometimes writing, other times writing and thinking. It wasn't always that Benningsons would bring in a casserole as courtesy, and when they wouldn't, it'll be my dexterous capability paired with my father's silent skills that we'd come up with some good supper.

I had nothing to complain about throughout those years. There were many like me in that village, that town, the city, the world, who didn't have a mother, had a disabled father, a humble dwelling and just enough money to drag through. Well, in most cases it would be either one or maybe even a combination of two, but I had the whole bushel. As I reached completion of high school and the age of seventeen our household was running out of capital, the insurance money we had. And it was about time I took responsibility of our survival. I had requested the manager of the garage where I worked part time, polishing and buffing cars, for a regular shift. He wasn't going to find many high school graduates ready to work for a meager seven dollars a day, so he agreed. My added job responsibilities involved everything, and I was literally sweating all day long. No matter how much I wanted to leave that town and the strenuous work, with my father's obligation I was shackled to that place.

I had seen my classmates depart the abject confines of our town one by one, and they were right to do so as the town evidently didn't offer much to furnish our raging aspirations and a hopeful future. There were only a few jobs that were still being held in quivering clutches of moribund seniors, and those that were too arduous for the elders, were given to a handful youths including me. Time went by as my yearning to leave the town surged and waned and it was one fine day I came to realize that some times your longings are granted in the most outrageous manner perhaps, but they are. That afternoon I returned from work around 4 and as I sauntered my way across the curving road and onto the little pathway that led through the guard of the woods, I saw a pack of humans surrounding my porch. As I approached the cluster of mumbling strangers, I sighted the Benningsons amongst them and his wife softly whimpering. I went in further as my neighbors drew nearer with a countenance replete with empathy, holding me by the shoulders and leading me on inside the house. I entered and sighted a shrouded body stretched upon the floor, and it struck me hard that I had just lost the last bit of family I had in this world.

My father was dead!

ᔕᔕᔕ

"Where're you headed?" The sound of these words resonated through my auditory perception as I was revived out of the abstract rumination I was drowned in for possibly two hours and I realized I was back where I left off; the bus. As I glanced over my shoulder I saw a familiar face of the elderly woman occupying the seat next to me. I was amazed how she had gone without uttering a word for the past two hours, but it also appeared to me that she might have slept soundly for all that time. And now that she was awake and restored to her former chattering self, I might be in for some long hours of vexation.

"Where are you headed?" she asked again, "I'm sorry, if you don't feel like talking, it's all right. By the way, I'm Louise. I couldn't help but introduce myself as we've been sharing this seat for more than 2 hours now without sharing a word." She expected an answer, I could tell by the glint in her eyes. What I didn't know was that whether she was actually trying to get me to talk out of pity or she actually couldn't zip it up. She looked away a bit crestfallen.
"George." And I offered a handshake with that. "George Frederick Bailey," Louise instantly accepted my hand for a delightful shake.
"Nice to meet you, George."
"You as well," I responded.
"Where are you headed?"

"California." I answered this time.

"To see your family, I suppose?"

"Not exactly, no."

"Visiting someone?"

"Nope, I don't have anybody there."

"Oh... I understand. Tired of this terrible frigid cold, aren't you? A warmer place for a blissful time. I agree."

"I hate to tell you this, but my travel does not relate to the weather or Christmas or New Year's or any other holiday we might encounter in the upcoming weeks."

"Recreation then?"

I gave up and went on with a splendid, waving nod. She fell back on her chair peacefully with satisfaction to her prying nature. But just before I could drift off back into the state of nostalgia, our bus pulled into a rest stop and with our arrival I came to realize that we had already reached Philadelphia, Pennsylvania and I must have missed the hoardings on our way. I also commended Louise for keeping a precise track of time which she mentioned to me earlier, though, we were fourteen minutes late to our first stop.

The bus emptied gradually as only a few sound asleep souls remained inside. I leaped out the wheeled box along with many others and stretched preparing for another long travel to follow. It was quite an elongated stop spanning forty-five minutes. I thought it was more than adequate for someone to grab a bagged meal and a trip to the restrooms. But most of my fellow passengers believed otherwise. I took a seat at one of the picnic tables set to the exterior of the restaurant while everyone else hastened inside into the comfort of warmth, except for a couple of children who were frantically running around chasing each other and having the most merriest of Christmas holidays. I espied Louise amidst one of the queues at a KFC counter. She was famished, I could tell as her hands tapped her folded elbows in extreme urgency and she tipped upwards to take a peek at how many were in line before her. I, on the other hand, was intent on being parsimonious for the duration of my travel. I was holding 18 dollars and some change scattered through my pockets that could only defray the expense of two dinners and two lunches for the following two days. I knew I would be out of money when I reach Los Angeles, but I had avoided any thought pertinent to the matter. I glanced at my watch and saw that I had a lot of time, plenty to think and to contemplate on the past events of my life. And so my mind drifted once more back into the years of my freedom, my independence and the years that led to long awaited prosperity and success.

Chapter Six

ഔഔഔ

It was a sizzling hot summer of 1975 when a red Buick convertible drove into our garage. I emerged all dingy and greased from underneath the chassis of an obsolete Ford model at the nudge of my colleague, Kirk, who ogled the wheeled beauty with wide eyes. I sat up looking at the all glimmer seamless body of the convertible, but as I rose up to my feet, I realized my co-worker's sight wasn't fixed on the car, but the person who drove it. I had heard for a long time that our boss has a daughter who was sent to Miami to complete her High School in the guardianship of her aunt. I had also heard for a couple of days that she had returned to the town recently and was the only sight to behold on the streets of Dresden. As the driver's side door opened and a pair of legs slipped out, my peer next to me almost swooned at the sight we saw. She came out in towering block heels, blue denim shorts that scantily covered the creases of her butt-cheeks and a mid-riff baring tank top that just waited for a malfunction hanging by her shoulders. Now, I knew that big, urban cities did render people with an extreme sense of autonomy and liberty, but what baffled me the most was that how such individuals are completely forgetful of their conservative hometowns and the populace that resides within, and the most ignorant quality of these returning youths was that they stood proud of their flagrant and obtrusive demeanor.

"Would you look at that!" Kirk said with a lick of his lips. I looked but didn't think of it much, but his drooling and stargaze were to continue for days to come as the boss' daughter, Casey Rivetton, would accompany her father to the garage every day.

It was just another fine day when she strutted into the garage alone and headed for the office passing a smile and wink on her way down. Kirk wiped his forehead of the sweat trails that had just given him a cold shower and we both receded to our work. Within a moment the call bell rang, I was summoned inside. I took the trip through the cars and knocked on the door to the office. After permission I entered and watched a young woman display her body like a piece of discounted jewelry at a pawn shop.

"Daddy ain't here, ya won't mind if I took care o' business a lil'?" She asked nibbling on a tip of a pen.

"It is your garage, miss, do as you please." I insisted.

"I'ma glad ya know who owns it. If I'ma run dis place, I wanna know names of all dat workin' for me, and while ya're here, let's starts with you? What does people call ya 'round here?"

"George."

"Georgey boy?"

"I haven't been called that yet."

"How lon' ya work'd here?"

"Three years."

"How old are ya?"

"Eighteen. I worked here part time through high school and then joined in full time. And Kirk, right there, he's been here for a very long time, I'd say seven years probably."

"I didn't aks ya 'bout him, now did I?" She struck a piercing gaze at me. "He a kid, I ain't interested in him. It's not the age I'm talkin'bout. So, ya like it here? I mean how lon' ya plannin' on workin'ere?"

"I wouldn't say I don't have aspirations, but as long as I can."

"They says there ain't many boys who stay this town afta' schoolin', or at least not the ones I likes to see. But I see every town got exceptions, highlights. Ya know any good joints to go 'round here?"

"This isn't my hometown, I think you'd know it better than me."

"I've forgot, how about ya refresh my memory? Lookie here mister, I ain't goin' stay here too long, ya know. I'ma leavin' in three weeks. So, if ya make this time fun n' games, ya won't regret a thing."

She stood up, came extremely close against me and rubbed her hand across my crotch and went into the adjacent powder room

- 30 -

pulling down on her denim shorts revealing the scarce thing she called underpants that was wedged between her buns. I remained there motionless for a long moment in ambivalence, and finally decided to give in.

I exited the office!

It didn't come to me as a surprise the next day when the call bell rang again, only this time it was not Casey but Mr. Rivetton himself. I stood before a scalding, bulging personality who went on to bestow upon me a bellowing tirade that was a consequence of my failure to entertain her daughter's business related inquiries and an overly rude behavior. As he went on with the censure, I listened in silence and did not counter his accusations with any contradiction because I knew if I did, it was either my job down the drain or my dignity along with hers. I could let go of my job but not my dignity. And with a cleared account for the days I worked, subsequently I was given the news that I was fired. I took my money and walked away, without regret, without a complaint. I saw Casey stand by the office door with a smirk on her face that delineated the outcome of denying the boss' daughter, and I wish it had affected me in a way, maybe change my outlook to match the kind of world we're in, but it couldn't and I was happy with that.

That evening I sat back on a broken couch and nibbled on some self cooked drumsticks and spinach salad and it dawned upon me that my days in this dreadful town were about to come to an end. I was determined to leave the confines of this dilapidated cottage and liberate myself perhaps in a densely civilized, prolific, urban city that has to offer more than a begrimed garage and a credulous ex-boss. New York City was the first place that lit up in lights in my imagination and I was willing to take that leap of faith. The next day I had gone to the Benningsons to discuss a possible sale of my property and found them quite optimistic about the idea. I wasn't going to wait for long, so I transferred the responsibility of selling the cottage to Mr. Benningson and headed off to New York with a hundred and twenty-one dollars in my pocket and a little thing called trust for they had given me their word to wire all the funds over once the sale is complete.

Chapter Seven

❧❧❧

New York City welcomed me with a cold draft and sporadic snow showers on the eve of November 25th. I was in awe of the grandeur of the city that never slept, and they were, beyond any doubt, spot-on with their observation whoever titled it so. I had never beheld such a sublime sight of vivid luminance of a metropolis firsthand, nor had witnessed a multitude that appeared like a ceaseless stream of undulating heads against a backdrop of asphalt skyscrapers and their coruscating facades. A horde of honking, steaming vehicles with their incorrigible swerves and turns across lanes and traffic lights. I took another swirl in profound veneration of the city around me outside the Grand Central station. My heart was palpitating with excitement on the thought that I had finally arrived to the land of my dreams and the measure of enthusiasm to commence my life on my own was boundless. The only provision I required now was a roof to shelter my drenched head.

I never thought I would come to realize the true meaning of the title 'The City That Never Sleeps' this early in my struggle, to be exact, only three hours into my arrival. It was well close to midnight and I had traveled from midtown to downtown in search of an affordable lodging for the night and I was soaked and exhausted as my aching legs couldn't bear me any longer. The glistening lights, the grand edifices, the bustling crowds and even the red flashing Coca-Cola hoardings were nowhere to be found here. I was now at the corner of a dark street with scarce luminance, infrequent pedestrians, lined with buildings that were architecturally identical and elderly in appearance. It dawned upon me that I had just been pushed farther away from my destination, which was the heart of the city, without a single intentional shove anywhere along the way. I just acquired a new learning from my experience which was quite clear and simple; to survive in New York you might lose a night's sleep to get where you want to be, in my case a couple of nights' sleep. As I said, it was a great observation by whoever titled this city so, but this was too small an obstacle to hold me back. Midtown was my destination, money was my aspiration and I was ready to hunt both down.

New York City is where I would say my life began, or to be more precise my personal life. I had no responsibilities except my own, I had no matters to worry for or contemplate. I was fresh as morning dew just waiting to drip down the tip of a green leaf. I began with the most odd jobs I could ever think I'd possibly get, but it was an acceptable start and I was in no situation to complain. It also happened to be by chance that for three subsequent years most of the employment I had obtained were customer service or sales related positions. I wasn't a manager or administrator of any kind and I wasn't under any misconception of becoming one anytime soon for I knew that I wasn't saturated with opportunities, nor did I have any laudable qualification or set of skills or expertise to receive them. I was taking the ladder one rung at a time, and it was best for me to ground my feet on that rung for stability before I could ascend to the upper one. There was a time I was doing three 6 hour shifts at three different places to get me through, but as my struggling phase mollified, I reduced that to two stable jobs spanning seven days, one through the week and the other over the weekend. I rented a comforting studio apartment that was adequate for my budget and ample for the space I required. It was all as planned and I was loving it.

I was setting up the display windows at my day job just below the awning that read Roland Novelty Gift Shop. By the name one would judge it to be an ordinary, conventional, your average go-to gift store for the eleventh hour shopping ideas, and they would be right in their conjecture. There was nothing special about it. The season was nearing close to Christmas day as there was an air of festivity encompassing us all and trinkets, ornaments, flashing lights and trees all over midtown. As our entrance door jingled, I watched an elderly couple enter and scan the store for their perfect buy. I had kept my eyes on them as they browsed through the displays and were assisted by one of the associates but only for a fleeting discussion. They must have decided to leave as they proceeded to the door. I quickly jumped in on them to try my luck at pleasing them into a transaction.

"Good Morning, sir, ma'am. How can I be of assistance today?" I said as I approached them both straightening my tie. The elderly couple shifted their attention to me and the man responded.

"Oh no, young man, we have already spoken to one of your sales associates. We have nothing of our interest here."

"Sir, now what's the use of me being here if I can't produce one thing out of this massive storehouse to spark your interest back again? It will be my pleasure to assist you in any way possible in exchange for a little bit of your time."

The man glanced back at his wife as she insisted on giving me another chance, he conceded.

"We are looking for something exquisite to gift our son this Christmas."

At the strike of their demand I knew they were at the wrong place, but being a faithful employee of the company I was bound to ensnare the customer by smooth prevarication and lead them into a purchase.

"What a wonderful thought, if I may say so. After all, the children must be pleased now to be obliged by later in time, isn't it?"

"Isn't that the truth?" the woman responded with a slight smile.

"True indeed, married?

"Oh, thirty-six years now." She said again with a coy look this time.

The man nudged her uncomfortably and transmuted to a harsher voice. "He means to ask about our son."

The old woman was mortified and effaced herself behind her man.

"Come, come, I would have asked you the same, ma'am. Now, you don't look a day older than thirty-six yourself."

She smiled again, but refrained from replying.

"So what do you have young man? And yes he is married, just recently."

"Yes sir, thirty perhaps? I mean of age."

"Quite close, thirty-one."

"Purely delightful, now by observing the glint in your eyes, I will allow myself to presume that you're willing to surprise him with a higher value item than just an everyday, common product of regular use, which might also attract his newly wedded bride towards your benevolence. Am I right?"

"Well, of course, we would like to surprise him in the most positive manner possible." The woman spoke again. This somehow drew in the elderly lady towards me, more as a customer which was keenly noticed by her husband.

"Just as I thought, would you please follow me here?"

I allured them into a purchase of a 14 karat gold tie pin that was embellished with a cubic zirconia in the center. Little did I know that the person I was attending actually hadn't come to buy anything, but to evaluate the sales capability of his competitors in the novelties market, and he marveled at what he saw. That man owned a similar gift shop three blocks down from this one and a job offer came along.

I was quick to accept the furtherance that came towards me as I wasn't in any way sentimentally attached or morally obligated to my current job and employer. My new workplace was much more exquisite, had a commodious showroom, larger work force, and a higher pay rate, and I was indeed attracted to especially the last incentive. I was diligent, scrupulous, disciplined and prudent, qualities that were acquired with time and learning but were indelible from my character and were impartially appreciated and rewarded over the course of next two years. At the end of those two years I was on my way to be the head salesman and the floor manager, accounts for that particular store also came under my supervision. But I knew my aspirations weren't just confined to being a salesman or even a manager, it was aiming for that little room at the rear of the warehouse, all glass and air conditioned from where one man could articulate his arbitrary decisions and declare unto a group of submissive subordinates to follow as revered regulations. That little room was the owner's office, and a high back, button-tufted all leather chair was calling out to me.

I always kept an eye out for better opportunities, and when they came, I was swift and strong enough to take my chance and pursue them. The part in which I was divinely blessed was that I never had to quit or got fired from a job. It always ended in polite, unhostile conversations and harmonious understanding. I received a kind farewell from all my colleagues and employers and was let go with a stunning recommendation letter that could even fetch me a job at the White House if I tried, but I knew the boss' chair in the White House could never be mine, so I didn't even try. I had moved over to Gardon Corporation as a sales executive which was a manufacturing and suppliers company and dealt in the most expensive and exquisite jewelry and rare artifacts in all New York. Within 6 months of my stable employment there I had my own cabin and a telephone to receive orders. I was able to rent a small apartment on 2nd Avenue in midtown and had savings of eleven thousand dollars. I was on the top of the world, but I was just about to fall, fall in love that is.

Chapter Eight
ço·ço·ço

There are certain times in one's life when your beliefs and views held stable for so long are suddenly shaken and altered, and there occurs a forced change of mind and opinions due to some situations, circumstances and the people attached to them. It is in human nature to change with time and I wouldn't be the first to apply that principle. I'd held on to a belief of autonomy and singlehood since I saw my father's debacle years ago, and I was determined never to falter from my path. But that was back when I had someone who reminded me of that path day after day, be it an oblivious father who wasn't there for me at all, but still I had a family member who suffered because of it. But when I reflected on his past, I couldn't find anyone but him to blame for all that happened in his life. As much as I wanted to impute his collapse on his love affairs and the women in his life or even his second wife, none of this would have happened if he didn't make the mistakes he did. That thought continued to haunt my mind and made me believe the one true fact; if a man commits to his family, there isn't much that can go wrong.

I had breathed in the loneliness for quite too long and it was about time I breathed in some unscented fragrance of a companion. A change from the monotonous routine of work, coming home to isolation and watching boredom take over the night. I was never the partying type, so socializing was not an option for me. I preferred a few but close friends, and right now I only had one. I wanted someone I could talk to, associate with, share things I couldn't with a friend. I needed someone more than a friend. I wasn't warding myself from any romantic relationship anymore as I was more than eager to belong to someone, to be hers and call her mine. It was a simple desire of a twenty-five year old working, settled man kicking in. Now, I wouldn't say it was entirely the fault of the stars or destiny as there was willingness on my end as well, but what is to happen, happen it must. That night was such a night. I was about to plummet into the green, picturesque valley of love and beauty and it was so abrupt that I didn't even have a moment to contemplate my retreat.

I was galloping down the street trying to stay under the awnings to save myself from a downpour. But no matter how hard I tired, it always got me. I just turned around the corner and suddenly collided into someone who just made me realize that one split second diversion from your path could lead you into... paradise. It was a woman I could tell, with her long dark hair now sodden in rain, she'd already kneeled to the sidewalk retrieving the scattered remains of some printed sheets that were soaked and possibly inutile now, and she was overcome with deep alarm and frustration.

"Could you just watch where you're going?" She spoke in the most mellifluous voice I'd ever heard, even though her tone was truculent, I would have loved if she repeated herself. "Oh, no, no, no..."
I crouched along helping her in gathering the soggy documents, but my intention was to grasp a glimpse of her face which was still veiled behind her raven black hair. She finally looked up at me with her green eyes and a furious countenance and I came to realize if there is such a thing called paragon of beauty in its perfection, it was right in front of me. I had admired only one other woman in a similar manner before. The woman I met at The Blue Crescent, and somehow she reminded me of her which drew my attention even deeper. It naturally evoked a smile across my face while she quickly sheltered the saved work under the awning of the storefront.

"Look what you've done! It's all gone." She said holding the soaked papers in utter defeat. "What are you smiling at?"

I was shaken out of it, as it was the most incongruous expression to the situation. I urgently changed it to a commiserating one. "No, I'm sorry. I was just coming in a hurry and wasn't looking, I should have."

"I wish your apology could dry these off, unfortunately it can't. Anyway, can't hang you for it. It's just that I'm going to be out of a job tomorrow morning."

"Was this really important?"

"No, I just carry these around for fun. What do you think?"

"You look quite disappointed right now. What is it, if I may ask?"

"Something really important."

"Can I do anything about it?"

"Hardly, these are my company's annual account reports. I have to submit these at work tomorrow, it's the deadline. Now I can't, thanks to you. I can already see myself at the far end of a long queue for food stamps at the unemployment office. That's what it is."

"Now, I wouldn't give up on it so soon. We can definitely work something out."

"I don't think so. You can hardly see what's written here, can't do much with this now. It's over. I'll have to redo everything and pay another one fifty for copies, for which, I'm a dollar short." She rummaged her handbag.

"Do you live around here?"

Her poignant glare just pierced my heart as she looked at me with a frown.

"You pervert." She began to leave, disgusted.

"Oh, no, no, you've got me all wrong. I didn't mean for it to sound that way." I came around in front of her, barred her way.

"Look mister, it doesn't matter how good you sound, I know where you're going with this."

"I don't know what type of a man you've mistaken me for, but I can assure you I'm not the kind you think I am."

"They all say that, don't they? This is exactly what it starts with. Next thing you know, there's an offer for dinner and drinks coming your way, isn't it?"

"I wouldn't dare to do that. Look, I live close by here. I don't know how often you come around this neighborhood, but I can offer to straighten this out for you."

"Really?" Her voice reeked of sarcasm.

"You see, I'm well conversant with accounting and other works related to it. I've done it in the past. I know how to do what you just lost here. I could do the damaged work overnight and return it to you by tomorrow morning if you can make another trip here. It'll be like an apology for my mistake, that is if you accept."

"You will work all night on these reports just to apologize?"

"I think just a verbal apology wouldn't suffice, it never does. It'll make me feel better, save my integrity."

"You aren't working for any of my competitors, are you? Just trying to get you hands around our numbers?"

"I don't even know where you work. It's nothing planned or premeditated, you don't have to worry about that. So, do you live around here?"

She remained hushed as a windless night. I had to break that awkward silence.

"Okay, how about we meet right here in the morning at eight. I hand over the papers to you, you make sure everything is complete and ready, and submit them over at your job. Sounds like a plan?"

She just gazed blankly at me.

"Look, I know people these days don't trust each other so easily, but I can assure you wouldn't be disappointed if you make an exception tonight. This whole ordeal does sound a bit strange, but I prefer to make it up to the people I've inconvenienced. So, if you would, trust me. You have nothing to lose here, miss." I stretched out my hand and grabbed the sheaf of papers from her, she was wordless. "I wish I could stay here and continue the staring game, but I have to return home and get to your work."

"I'm sorry." She shook her head.

"Now remember, tomorrow morning at 8, sharp. Is everything I need in here?"

She nodded her head, "my hand written notes are in the middle."

I took up the job and hastened down the street, but before I could fade from her sight, I stopped and turned around once more.

"My name is George. What's yours?"

"Audrey... and you better watch where you're going."

With that said, she turned around and went down the dark street fading behind a wall at the bend and I just stood there watching the most beautiful moment in my life pass by. Just as she uttered that name, I knew it was a sign for me to just let go and give it a try. And honestly I wanted to, so I did.

Chapter Nine

The next morning I waited around the same corner at the exact square inch not to be missed by any chance. The world was in a bustle around me through which I saw the most mesmerizing sight my eyes could ever accommodate. Audrey strode towards me in a royal blue dress that outlined her tall, slender figure splendidly. Her eyes sparkled with tranquility, her sharp nose, wider at the tip, settled graciously over her crimson lips that were shaped like a cupid's bow, and a square face that bore a strong jaw line, high cheekbones and nothing that wasn't divinely symmetrical on there. Her hair tied up in a bun and a ravishing smile that could linger on for ages. She sipped from her coffee and approached.

"I didn't think you would actually come," she uttered.

"Good morning to you, as well."

"Morning."

I handed her the bundle of papers all neatly clipped together which did impress a bit out of her.

"Now, there were a few errors I took liberty of correcting myself, hope you don't mind. You would have caused your employer three hundred and forty-seven dollars if you turned in the previous version."

"Are you trying to imply I don't know what I'm doing?"

"I didn't say that, anybody can commit an oversight. There you have it. I kept my end of the deal."

"Was I supposed to do anything in return?"

"No, not according to our agreement last night, but I was just thinking if you would honor me with your company this afternoon and have lunch with me?"

"I thought you were doing this out of courtesy, to apologize?"

"I am, that's from my end."

"And from mine?"

"A little appreciation, that's all."

She smiled again, the most heavenly laughter followed and she began to recede, distancing herself from me.

"Last night I was afraid I'd be fired for not bringing these in, now I might get fired for showing up late. If we are destined to meet again, we will." She said tauntingly.

"That we are." I replied confidently.

"We shall see." She turned around and went down her way. I was left alone with a warm titillating sensation that accompanied thoughts of a future George who couldn't be without her.

For the remainder of the day it was smiles and delight gleaming from my visage and wishful daydreaming that surged within my freshly ensorcelled heart. I was on the phone when a familiar face popped up behind the parapet of my cubicle, an officious one but always welcome. The one friend I had, Harry Sherwen. I had known him since the first day I stepped into this office quivering with nervousness as a new employee. This was the only guy who shook my hand following a flippant greeting, directed me to wrong cubicle and had me sit on somebody else's desk until I was thrown out of it. He did apologize for that after a long uncontrollable laughter and finally, by the end of the embarrassing day, instructed me on how to use the telephone for the calls. That ephemeral humiliation subsided and eventually grew into a close-knit friendship that was one of the most encouraging assets of my lonesome existence at that time. But his bantering nature couldn't be suppressed as even after years of routine usage of that telephone, he could still make it sound like I'm a tyro and teach me a thing or two that I had learned and forgotten ages ago. He was an honest soul, lonely deep down but wouldn't let the anguish reflect in his persona. I guess the fact that drew us both into the bond of friendship was that we both were alone, but we cherished each other, maybe not always, but in the unfathomed depths of our emotions, we were related as brothers perhaps.

"Yes sir... very much so... you are exactly right. Anything that does not live up to the customer's satisfaction is a waste of time." I spoke on the phone as Harry leaned inside my cubicle trying to get his hands on my concealed jar of mixed nuts in the first drawer. I hit his hand with my gel pen, but he persisted.

"What... oh yes, sir. I entirely agree with you. And on that note I'm willing to offer you a product of your choice from our catalog at no cost. In addition to that, I will personally make sure there are no charges for expedited shipping on this order. Compliments of The Gardon Corporation. Yes sir, you too, sir. Thank you... goodbye." I kept the phone down. "Would you get your own nuts for once in your life?"

"I could, but then you wouldn't bring any coz' you hardly eat them."

"Thank you." I said a little annoyed and averted to my register.

"Do you know what you just did? You just cost our company a lot of dough just to save your ass." He commented.

"Really? I didn't know that."

"Assuming he orders the most expensive item from our catalog, you're going to give to it him for free?"

"He runs a toy store, the most he can order would cost us a little over one hundred dollars."

"Oh... but what if he orders something else?"

"He can't. He has a corporate account with us, which limits his establishment to purchase fixed inventory items that are listed in our agreement. If he wants to order out of that contract, he'll have to initiate a new DBA. Now you don't want me to pull up his contract, do you?"

"No, I believe you." He said, quite impressed. "And I see that you're learning fast. Well, of course you will, it pays to have a mentor like me."

"Mentor?" I asked doubtfully.

"People can be so ungrateful at times, but I've learned to live with that. Can't expect appreciation from all, can you? Besides, I strive to give and receive nothing in return. That's my goal." He said munching on nuts.

"That's divine thinking, o holy master. I'm not capable of that."

"I know. There are only a few born with such magnanimous soul. So, what's stirring about your miserable life, anything new?"

"Nothing worth mentioning, except that I think I'm beginning to like someone."

"What?!" He was goggle-eyed. "Who?"

"A girl."

"Well, of course a girl. I know the drift when it blows, but you ought to know a little more than her gender. What's her name?"

"Audrey."

"Full name, you dumbass. Last names tell a lot of tales."

"I have no idea."

"She didn't tell you, or rather you didn't ask?"

"Both."

"You know what? I knew you were a bit twisted upstairs, but never figured you for a moron. Where does she live?"

"I don't know."

"Well, are you going to see her again?"

"I can't say if we ever will."

He shook his head in disbelief. "What are you gonna do now, print out pamphlets? A hundred dollar reward to whoever informs of her whereabouts?"

"Let's see what happens." I said with a shrug.

"Nothing's going to happen. That's the most obvious trick women play on men, give 'em their first names and have 'em search around for the rest of their lives like some desperate dog in search of fried chicken leftovers. And the worst thing about it, our sniffers are shit compared to theirs."

"Sniffers?" I asked.

He tapped his nose and went on, "and they're off living their lives with some rich son of a bitch spending his money on caviar and trips to Belize."

"Quite an observation."

"Yeah, you can bet on that. Take my word for it, I've been there and done that. When did you meet her?"

"Last night."

"You're kidding me, aren't you?"

"Nope."

"And you like her already?"

"Love at first sight."

"More like lust at first sight. I hope you're not in for a heartbreak. These women I tell you..."

"She's different."

"Time will tell. You coming to the game tomorrow?"

"Nah, I have to go to work."

"Tomorrow is Saturday, you know that? How about a day off?"

"A day off is a day lost. It's my weekend job."

"You know you don't have to go around killing yourself, no wonder she only gave you her first name."

"Harry, right now I'm just an employee and my aspirations do not stop at that. It takes two jobs to change that into an employer. You just wait and watch, I'll be hiring you one day."

"Yeah, I can't wait for it. But not without a raise." He drowned behind the cubicle wall.

"And Harry, she said if we're destined to meet again, we will. And I know where she works." I said with a smile.

In a moment, I saw an emerging outline of a human head one more time.

Chapter Ten
ဖော်ဖော်ဖော်

A couple of weeks had passed and the world had come around another new year with revived hopes, resolutions and aspirations. But I crossed the festal eve with one adamant desire instilled in me from the past year. I endeavored to fulfill that desire quite a couple of times and had gotten very close to it, but each time my attempts were deluged by my diffidence. No, it wasn't a wish to be one of the most respected dignitaries of the city, though, it should have been the primary focus. It was Audrey. I had attempted to approach her many a times, but just as she would get close enough to sight me amidst the crowd, I would hide myself or turn away fading into the crowd searching for more courage. I was terrified of being spotted by her. But I will say that adventure, lasting for an hour or so, of anticipating someone just to get a fleeting glimpse of her face was very fulfilling. I knew where she worked, now I knew what time she left work, but I wouldn't follow her like a stalker all the way where she lived. I couldn't afford to frighten her away, so I gratified myself with just one glimpse a day and it was enough to get me through the rest of the time until we met again. I always wondered if she ever took a moment out of her eventful life to ponder over someone as insignificant as me. If she ever sat down on a couch after supper and thought whatever happened to the guy who did the reports for me. Well, it was just a part of the report, but I did have my share in it. And if she did, she could have done better to inquire about me and at least express her gratitude. I wasn't that hard to find, I was just around the corner.

I sat in the courtyard of a corner cafe sipping from my cup of coffee and reading from a newspaper. It was a silent Sunday morning, I guess people preferred their Sunday morning coffee in bed, and even if they did travel all the way to the cafe for it, no one would be caught dead sitting outside at the tables in freezing twenty-eight degrees temperature and arctic wind chill. But my preferences were always contrary to the conventional population. I guess it was out of choice and a bit of liking as well. But then I suddenly realized that there were some other demented people in this world that were quite analogous to me.

"You wouldn't mind if I share this table with you?"
I looked up at the person who stood before me bearing a congenial love for the cold. And just as I looked up, I was entranced as Audrey smiled down at me and waited for a response. I was frightened to acknowledge the fact that I was beginning to imagine her not only in my dreams, but now in life and in-person, be it an illusion. I chuckled and swung my head right to left amused at my own hallucinations but then the voice sounded again.
"I think you would." Her smile had faded by then.

It was a striking realization and I arose abruptly, staggering to my feet while the newspaper slipped through my fingers.
"You!"
"You just reacted like you saw a ghost." She said with a smile.
She was indeed there, standing before me. A miracle had occurred in my life, and it was the most welcome and anticipated one.
"No, no, I just couldn't imagine you being here." I was confounded.
"Why not? I do drink coffee just like everyone else, if that's what you're thinking," she said perching down on the chair right next to me.
"Oh... that's nice... right, coffee is good, for everyone, or rather most of us, some of us. Why don't you sit down?"
"I think I am."
"Oh, I'm sorry. You are. I'll sit down." I sat trembling in nervousness. We sat there in silence. She waited for me to talk. "Would you like some coffee?"

"Well, I could sit out here without one but by the end of it you might have to warm me up on a grill."

"Yeah... that's funny. I'll get one for you."

"Thank you."

I went into the cafe and emerged with a seething cup of coffee and laid it down on the table before her.

"Wouldn't you sit down?" She asked.

"Oh, yes thank you." I settled back on my chair. Following that, I literally stayed wordless for two minutes and seventeen seconds which I could tell exactly due to my constant glimpses at the wristwatch.

"Do you need to go somewhere?"

"No, no... I don't."

"No, you keep looking at your watch, so I thought you did."

"My watch? Oh this, just an old thing, nothing fancy."

Her brows converged as my state of restiveness entered her intuition.

"I'm sorry if I startled you, I didn't mean to. I just saw you from across the street and thought of saying hello."

"Hello!"

"Yeah, exactly. Actually, the reason I came over is that I wanted to thank you for what you did the other day."

"What did I do?"

"The reports?"

"Oh, that."

"Yes, they were tremendously well received. I was actually promoted and I guess I must thank... well, you for it. You corrected some mistakes in it, so thanks for making it impeccable."

"It's perfectly all right, I had to do it."

"So you do live around here, don't you?" She asked gazing into my eyes. "I mean who'd come out here for a cup of coffee in this frigid weather unless it's really close."

"I like their coffee and I like the cold. I don't know why, but I do. And yes, I live just over there, around the block."

"Right..." she took a swig from her coffee and finished. "I think I should be leaving now." She began to fish her wallet for the tab.

"No, please, I got it."

She halted, smiled. Began to leave. Stopped and turned.

"You know you could come and say hello if you want to, don't have to hide every time I come out of the building." There was longing in her eyes as she said that. I was completely taken aback that she knew. "And yes, I do live around here as well, not a block, but not that far either."

She walked down the street leaving me in suffering. I slammed two dollars on the table and hastened after her. But returned to tuck the money under the cup and then rushed back. I approached her at the end of the block and barricaded her way, gasping for air. I finally straightened up and looked at her and uttered the most flagrant gesture I had ever made toward a woman in my life.

"Can we meet again?"

There was no verbal reply that I got from her, but her glorious smile said it all.

As I sat within grey coated polymer walls of my cubicle with heaps of imperative workload strewn across my desk, all I could do was fancy Audrey in the most fascinating dreams of my imagination. She came into my life like a bright, sunny day after years of continuous downpour. A perpetual misogyny that devoured my mind throughout the years of my adolescence was inexplicably effaced by the ingress of this beautiful being. I was indeed infatuated, I was in love and just as I was about to enter another one of my reveries with just the two of us in profound isolation, a familiar face popped up behind the partition from the next cabin.

"Hey, what's going on?" I asked somberly.

"You tell me, you're the one who looks enchanted." Harry said raising his brows and flexing his forehead to eyeball me from above his glasses that tipped at the brink of his nose.

"Enchanted? Haven't heard that in a while." I responded shaking my head in fake disbelief to ward his further inquisition.

"There are two things in the world that no matter how much you try, you can never hide."

"Really? What's that?"

"Love in your eyes and increasing waist size."

"What? Now, I'm going to pretend I didn't even hear that. I'm busy with work, please bother someone else."

"Yeah, I know what kind of work you're busy with. The same girl, isn't it? So you finally met her again?"

"And how do you suppose it is the same girl?"

"You're not the type to be sniffing around every manhole, I know."

"Why do all your similes have to be related to dogs?"

"Man's best friend, easy as that. Now keep coming with the details."

"All right, I give up. I told you about the little favor I did for her. Well, she found me and thanked me for it. I asked her if we could meet again, and..."

"And she refused right to your ugly face?"

"Yeah, something like that."

"Friday night, 7:30, a small but decent Italian eatery, or maybe even Chinese?"

"You know, if you quit this job and became a psychic, you'd be very successful at that. Palm reading and tarot cards, you know?"

"Don't counsel me on how to harness my gifted ability of clairvoyance, peasant. Tell me where you're going?"

"She said she likes Chinese." I shrugged.

"Tell me, are you a chocolate guy or flowers guy?"

"I never liked chocolate since I was a kid." I answered honestly.

"You don't have to make a spectacle of your dumbness all the time. I wasn't concerned about your penchants, but hers. Aren't you going to get her anything?"

"Well, am I supposed to? Aren't gifts usually for later on?"

"Gifts? A bouquet of flowers, you consider that a gift? That's the reason I keep telling you to go out on dates, so you can get some social sense into your brick head. Those are not considered gifts, wise guy. They are more like a token of appreciation for the lady who agrees to accompany your lame ass to a restaurant and spends 3 hours of her precious time listening to your crap. It's something that constantly reminds her of you after you've left, in your case maybe just once or twice. It's something that compels her to consider if you are the guy she's been waiting for all her life. Nothing you would know of you self-centered, thoughtless, careless-"

"Okay, okay, I got it now. Thanks for your input on the matter. Sorry, I'm not a pro at this."

"Look, you need something to make an impression on the lady when you go out with her. You don't have a car, so you'll probably be walking her home. You obviously are not going to take her to a grand hotel for the dinner, which clearly indicates your stingy nature. The only option we're left with is gratitude, to show her that her time is invaluable. This is how you show it. Believe me if you don't keep them riveted, women drift away. They need something to remind them of you. How much you like to be around them, how much you think about her. Doesn't have to be extreme, but subtle and sweet."

"How about jewelry?"

"No, no, no, jewelry is a possible relationship builder. This is the first time you're going out with her. Who knows if you'd even want another date with her or not, so let's keep it down to flowers only."

"Right." I took a deep breath of relief.

"Now you don't want to know what happened three years ago when I went out with Ginger. You know the girl I once told you about? Frizzy hair, facial breakouts, grandma eyeglasses."

"Oh no, I definitely wouldn't want to know about that."

"Well, I only strive to educate young men like you with no experience on the matters of love. Anything else, you know where to find me."

With that he descended into oblivion beyond the cubicle parapet and I thanked the heavens for saving my ears of another protracted exhibition of experience in failed relationships and despondent date nights.

Chapter Eleven
ଓଡ଼ିଓ

I was quite excited to make it home early that night, attire myself with the best of my closet and parade down the street with a bouquet of red roses in my hands to pick Audrey up for an evening I've been dreaming about for weeks now. It was finally to come true. And I did just as planned.

My wristwatch ticked close to 6:15 and I marched through an array of passing pedestrians down a row of brownstones finally reaching the address of my destiny. I stood breathing in long inhales of cold air in front of a flight of steps that ascended up to a ramshackle threshold. I managed enough courage to charge head-on into the unknown horrors I may encounter beyond that door. But come what may, I was determined and willing to see this process of trial and assaying until the end. The thought of Audrey's smiling face and her mellisonant laughter and most importantly her companionship for life dwarfed any tribulations that may befall in my effort to gain her affection and love. On that note, I took the stairs one step at a time and finally pressed the buzzer and knocked once with my trembling index finger. As I stood awaiting a response to my knock, I heard faint sounds of laughter from inside, apparently children maybe adults but hardly all of them. My first supposition was that Audrey possibly belongs to a large family with many younger siblings, or maybe they shared the duplex with some other people. I was just halfway in contemplation, when the door was suddenly opened ajar and a woman appeared peering through. This was indeed a woman of grand stature not only figuratively but physically as well. I could imagine her to be in her early 60s, graying hair by the roots, plausibly discontent, seeming so especially by the countenance, which I couldn't intuit if it was an outcome of long years of unpropitious circumstances or just the sight of a stranger at her doorway. She glared at me from the hairs to the soles and it finally dawned upon me that her obtrusive disgruntlement was in fact due to my presence there.

"Good evening, I'm here to see Audrey." I spoke in a quivering voice.

She fumed through her nostrils and went back into the house calling out to someone in a strangely unfamiliar language. To attempt a guess, I thought it was Italian, but I couldn't be too sure. In a moment Audrey strolled down gracefully to the door and welcomed me inside with a smile.

"Hello George, how are you? Please come in."

I nodded and stepped in following her into a small living room which wasn't populated much, but on the other hand, it couldn't afford much crowd in there either. There were two young children in there, probably 10 and 9 at the most. They were neatly groomed and dressed and well-behaved.

"Hello kids." I said with a fake smile.

They sat together silently upon a corner chair staring back at me without a word.

"I'm sorry I'm not ready yet. I just returned from work not too long ago. I'll be only a moment." Audrey spoke eyeing the room for any inconsistencies in a confused manner.

"Please take your time." I said reassuringly.

"Thank you."

With that said, she went around the adjoining kitchen speaking in her native language to her mother. Their conversation gradually diminished to whispers. After a moment, just as I sat down, Audrey's mother passed through the living room again glowering on her way forward and I sprung back up on my feet trying to pass a frightened smile, but rejected. My throat dried, I sighted a glass on the table and looked for water. I found a round pitcher on a sidetable under a lamp and poured myself a drink. Just as I gulped down the first swig, the children pointed to the pitcher right from their seat.

"That's for fish." One of them said blankly.

I spluttered a mouthful right back onto them, showering them wet. They lurched back, soaked. I abandoned the idea of water and went back to the couch and drowned into it wiping my mouth with a handkerchief.

There were sweat trails down my forehead as I watched Audrey's mother wipe off the two kids while mumbling to herself, which obviously wouldn't be in much of my approval. Audrey entered the room in a shimmering red dress that complimented her subtle simplicity even more than I could imagine. I remained speechless but stood up feeling relieved now in her presence. Her mother turned and embraced her, but began another tirade to Audrey's displeasure.

"Mother, we don't have to talk about this in front of a guest." She beseeched her mother.

"All I say is be home before ten." Her mother finally spoke a sentence in English in a heavy Italian accent.

"I will be." Audrey responded and kissed her mother goodbye.

Audrey looked at me and nodded to proceed. I stepped on at her behest and came to her mother.

"Thank you for letting your daughter come with me, Mrs... Mrs... I'm sorry, I actually never asked your last name."

"Gallo." The mother said in her demanding voice.

"Mrs. Gallo. Thank you." I was just about to leave, but returned with something.

"This is for you." I handed the bouquet of roses to her.

"You bring this for me, red roses?" She asked, annoyed.

"For... for her actually... I'm sorry." I snatched the bouquet from her hands and gave it to Audrey.

"For the home." I said and ran off to the door.

I could hear Audrey giggle at this while I waited by the door. She didn't take long and joined me at the stairs.

"Shall we go now?" She asked with a warmest beam of divinity across her face.

I took her hand in mine and we both came down the steps together. Our eyes never left each other.

An attendant brought dinner to our table and served in the most comely manner possible. We sat incongruous amidst a crowd of Asian diners in a decent Chinese restaurant, but I was glad to see that it didn't matter much to Audrey and that she was determined to have a good time instead of judging me on the monetary aspect of my life. She laughed and laughed as I sat a bit mortified after divulging the story of fish water down my throat.

"My mother cleans up that pitcher and changes water for the goldfish twice a day, and while she does that, the fish is in a bowl." She said taking a sip of green tea.

"And I had to feel thirsty right in the middle of it."

"I'm so sorry." She tilted her head earnestly.

"No, it's not your fault." I brushed the embarrassment off. She laughed again, but this time it didn't make me uncomfortable, in fact I just went on to admire her beauty even more.

"You're beautiful."

Her laughter waned as she grew a bit conscious of herself and erubescent.

"Who were the kids?" I swiftly changed the subject to make her easy.

"My mother babysits some evenings for neighbors, if they're working late or going out at times. Makes a little on her own, helps the family."

"That's good. That's what a family is, right? Helping each other out. So, it's just you and your mother?"

"No. I have a sister, she works as a waitress in Brooklyn. She's a single mother. We're all she's got."

"Your father?"

"Passed away when I was four."

"I'm sorry."

"You don't need to be, he caused his own death. He was an alcoholic, died of liver failure. Our mother took our responsibility at a very young age. She carried us through a lot. She still does and never married again for our sake. Once was enough for her, I guess. I hope you don't mind the way she acted today with you showing up and taking me out."

"No, not at all. I guess every mother is like that towards her daughters."

"It's just that she feels very vulnerable and unprotected with just three women in the house. She doesn't trust men now, after what happened with my sister, she says it's better to stay unmarried than be heartbroken, and God forbid with a child. She'd say sometimes she wish she had a son, a man to take care of the family. She'd say it bluntly to my face, if I were a boy she'd be happier."

"I'm sure she doesn't mean it."

"Yeah, me too. I know why she doesn't trust people anymore and following in her shadow, sometimes even I begin to think identically. But then I alter my thoughts inclining towards a more sublime feeling that comes to humans naturally, love. Maybe that'll be true for me someday. Even though, I haven't witnessed it, but I hope." She finished holding my gaze for a long moment. "Well, that's enough about me, how about you? You didn't tell me anything about yourself?"

"I'm not that interesting to know." She laughed at my remark.

"Well, you got to know about my past, now it's my turn to get to know yours."

"Okay... if you insist. I come from California, that's where I was born. My father was extremely wealthy to begin with, but it didn't last very long. Well, at least not after I was born. I was only eight when he had an accident at his workplace and his legs had to be removed. There was a great fire at the theater which he owned and whilst he lay crippled on his bed everything slowly came to an end. My mother had passed away when I was three and my step mother eloped with someone after all this happened, I was the only one left with him. Forcibly, we had to leave California and settle in his hometown where my grandparents had lived. I grew up some more and when he passed away I decided to start somewhere new, somewhere I hadn't been before. And that brought me to New York. So, now I've stayed here a long time and in that while no family at all, no responsibilities, free as a bird, never been in a relationship before, managed a small social circle and only one friend. That's me. Not much of a story is it?"

"That is sweet."

"What?"

"A man with a small social circle dedicates a lot of his time to his family. It's natural."

"Well, I never thought about it, but now that I do, you're right." I took a moment to begin again. "Audrey, I'm sorry if I ever made you uncomfortable by showing up outside your workplace. I don't know why, but I couldn't convince myself otherwise. And if you don't like that, I wouldn't anymore."

"I would appreciate it more if you'd approach." She answered with a warm smile.

Our conversation continued for the subsequent hour until we finished our dessert and exited the restaurant. I stepped up checking my watch as Audrey stayed close. I began waving to hail a taxi when she caught me by the arm.

"What are you doing?" She asked softly.

"Calling for a cab." I responded with converged brows.

"What for?"

"Your mother asked me to bring you home by ten, and I have no intention of disappointing her."

"I'm sure she can give us fifteen minutes on top of that."

"Look Audrey, I'm going to be very honest with you, I know people try to impress their dates with dinners at big hotels, taxi rides, gifts and... all those things. But I don't do much of that, much of anything. The least I can do right now is to get you home safely in a cab."

"But who said that attracted any of us? Look, I've come across a few men in my past, but never went more than a mile with them because I suddenly realized their true motives within thirty minutes of our conversations. No matter how much they try to hide it, their personality, their true intentions always slip out of their lips. Yours did too, but for the first time I can say I've come across a good man. Now, I'm still not certain if my judgment is right about you, it would take a few more dates to find out, but I think I'm not wrong. Whether I'm right or wrong, proving that is up to you. Besides, taxis are a faster way to get home, I was thinking if we could take a walk, unless you're trying to get rid of me."

At that moment I realized my affection towards her was reciprocal. She took my arm and we began walking down the street silently, but exuding intimacy.

We came to stop outside a corner store that was being held for lease.

"What happened?" She asked.

"I used to work here, some time ago. It was run by a very kind man."

"What happened to him?" She showed her concern.

"He died, some time after I left here. You know sometimes you think this world and the people living in it are so evil and all they want is to harm you, hurt you. And then people like this man come around and completely reverse your outlook on humanity."

"I know exactly what you mean."

We sauntered further from the storefront and onto our way to her apartment.

"It's pleasant outside tonight. I hope it stays like that for the rest of the night." She exclaimed with a gleam in her eyes.

"I hope it stays like that for the rest of our lives." My response made her curl up closer to me.

"Sometimes I do believe in all that, wishes and desires and miracles. Wish upon a shooting star or toss away a coin in a pool. Do you?"

"I believe in nothing that hasn't come to pass."

"Oh..." she looked down the dark path ahead of us.

"But I do believe that miracles happen, or I wouldn't have found you. Do you remember what you said to me the second time we met?"

"If we're destined to meet again, we will."

"And here we are. There had to be something more than just a coincidence behind it. A little push from my end and bit from yours, we made it work. I don't know how many times I must have come down that specific part of the street where we collided, but that was the night, that was the time. So, I do believe that."

I stopped and stood before her looking deep into her sparkling eyes.

"I don't know if I have ever seen a woman more beautiful than you. And I mean not just your appearance, you're beautiful within, I just discovered that. Looking at you makes me believe that there is something called love. I did not trust it since the day my stepmother left my father. I believed it was just an abstract excuse people use to get closer to each other and once done with their intentions, it's over. You changed my mind, my thoughts. You changed me as a man. I'm beginning to fall in love with you."

Standing in the middle of the sidewalk, all we could see was each other, drawing nearer every moment as it passed. But our blissful proximity was suddenly disrupted by a loud familiar voice originating from three houses down the block. It was pure Italian, but I understood the concept of that utterance, which was clearly to part us both.

"I'm coming ma." Audrey responded then turned back to me.

"She doesn't like me at all, does she?" I asked and we both burst into laughter.

"No." She replied plainly. "But I do."

Her words echoed within my body like a resounding declaration made amidst towering pinnacles of a mountain range. And with her simple but explicit statement, she turned and walked away from me going up the stairs of her dwelling, waving a sweet goodbye and shutting the door close. I almost jumped in elation, but quickly restricted my jubilance within and strode down the street a man in love.

Chapter Twelve

❦❦❦

We had just pulled out of Pittsburgh after an hour long hiatus and I was beginning to experience the effects of lethargy due to discomfort concurring with hunger. I glanced down at a small bag of chips and regretted having spent fifty cents on something that hardly assuaged my grumbling stomach, but it was all I had for the moment and that was all it took to devour what I had.

"Would you like a sandwich?" A voice erupted from the seat beside me. It was my good neighbor, Louise. "I bought two, but I'm in no mood to eat them both. Actually, I don't like the taste of it."

"No, that's all right, I'm okay." I managed a fallacious answer.

"Well, I guess this goes to garbage then."

"You're going to throw it away?" My concern deepened.

"I told you, I don't like the taste of it."

I extended my hand and took the brown bag from her. I ruffled the contents of it and emerged with a wrapped Philly cheese steak sandwich and took a huge bite of it.

"This isn't that bad, you know." I mumbled with mouthful of beef and cheese.

"We all have our taste buds, don't we?" She sounded off and went back snuggling within her blanket.

"Where are you going?" I asked her. This somehow stirred the old woman out of her slumber and into a conversation which, by the looks of it, had been long awaited by her.

"I thought you were never going to ask." She responded with a smile. "I get off at Grand Junction, Colorado. My son lives about six miles from the stop. He'd be coming over to pick me up."

"Grand Junction comes after Denver, right?"

"You're correct."

"Is a long way from now."

"Yes, I believe we have a lot of time to talk then."

"We surely do. Do you visit him often?"

"Every alternate year, I switch between my son and my daughter. She lives way up in Maine. Though, she is closer to me, I still give my son a visit every other year, so he doesn't forget his mother."

"Married?" I asked to inquire further.

"Oh yes, both of them. My son has two children, twelve and seven. Beautiful girls. My daughter just got married, quite late in my opinion, but she was younger of the two. She just had a baby, I was there with her throughout. As much as she wanted me to stay a little longer, I couldn't. I love them both equally."

"And you live in New York?"

"Yes... New York is where my husband settled after our marriage. We began our journey there, then our children came and time just flew out the window. Our bodies withered, my husband parted from me and left me to care for his home, our home. My son went to college in Colorado. He was more familiar with that area, so he decided to get married and stay there. My daughter actually had to move with her husband all the way to Portland. He's a writer you know, and he says he only finds his solace in seclusion. She had to move with him. It's me that's all left now."

"You stay alone?"

"It is that time of age when you are left alone, sweetheart. You will realize when you get there."

"I think I realize now."

"You are married, aren't you?"

"I was, a long time ago."

"I could tell, that indentation of a wedding band is still fresh. What happened?"

"It's a long story."

"Well, when two people are bored to death in a moving bus, all they need is a start, the rest of the conversation paves its own path. And as I said, we have a lot of time, don't we?"

ഗ⁀ഗ⁀ഗ

Time was passing, days raced by splendidly like a draft of crisp breeze that chills your cheeks and shuffles your hair. Audrey's arrival into my life was just as welcome as daybreak after a rainstorm. For the course of next eight months, we met each other almost every day. Sometimes she would find me leaning against a corner lamppost by the side street glancing at my watch, waiting for her to lighten up my day and save me from a routine ennui. And sometimes I would find her perching silently in the foyer at my workplace, looking out at the rushing bustle of the world through the glass facade and brooding in silence, which would be interrupted as I would come down the elevator and take her hand in mine and kiss it gently. She would be all smiles after that. Our meetings transmuted from formal dinners to weekend getaways and movie nights, and our affection grew even more. It grew up to point where she admitted herself to a promise that no matter how far I went to secure a future for a prospect family, or how long I took to bring my proposal for our union to her mother, she will wait. Her belief in me was strong and unwavering, and I suppose through her belief, fate turned in my favor as well.

I was overcome with delight when I received a wire from Benningsons and the news it bore. My father's property back in Ohio brought in a businessman who was willing to concede a hefty amount in order to purchase the site that suited his commercial interest. I was in no condition to delay in finalizing a deal and wanted to get rid of the old house as swift as I could. Within six months and a couple of trips back and forth, the paperwork was concluded and I got my hands around a large sum of money, three hundred and fifty four thousand dollars to be precise. I thanked the Benningsons for all they had done for me throughout the years with a gift of ten thousand dollars and also took Audrey to meet them once. Though, they were not interested in accepting any money for their favors, but they couldn't refuse when Audrey insisted with her becharming smile. I was finally done with my past on that day and was ready to move on. My goals had altered, my abilities improved and my financial status enhanced, and that Audrey became the reason for such extreme streak of luck in my life, my next few moves were inevitable.

Sitting idle in my cabin, I had sometimes glanced up a flight of steps to a glass separation on our floor which was the manager's office. James B. Gosham, our divisional manager, was a man in his late 30s, proud, demanding, contentious and alpha in ridiculing his subordinates. We hadn't ever met since the day I was hired and introduced to him by his assistant, but now I was in plans to see him personally. No one could elevate their voice up to the owner's and board of directors' floor without getting it scanned through his ears. And the matters that went through him and reached the proprietor's desk were most of the time personally beneficial for him more than the company. Due to that inconvenience, I was bound to come in contact with him. Though, I didn't know it would turn out to be the catalyst to everything that followed.

"May I come in, sir?" I asked as I peered through his glass door after a knock.

"Come right in." James responded hardly taking off his eyes from a sales ledger.

"Thank you for seeing me, sir. You don't know how much it means to me." I said taking a seat.

"Do you know what you just did?" He asked.

"No sir. What did I do?"

"You just wasted time. Every minute is valuable, there's a reason people invented the expression 'cut to the chase' and that's exactly what I want you to do. Besides, what is it that you wanted to bring to my attention? Your colleague giving you a hard time, or you made a commitment to a customer you can't keep up? Or even better, you just cost the company a couple because of some ignorant mistake? I know every employee coming up here has problems like these, so what's yours? I intend to leave office exactly when I'm supposed to. Be quick."

"I'm sorry, sir. I... the reason I wanted to see you today was that I have a business proposal for this company that I wanted to discuss initially with you and perhaps with your seniors consequently." This finally riveted his attention to my talk.

"A business proposal? You?" He questioned taking off his glasses and glaring at me.

"Yes, sir. Being the divisional manager of our corporation, I know you're responsible for presenting novel ideas and proposals pertaining to development, marketing and furtherance of our company to our owners for their consideration."

"Stop narrating my job duties and tell me why you're here."

"Sir, I have worked for this company for some years now, you obviously have been here longer. The products of Gardon industries we're selling here are unquestionably inimitable in quality and content. But I wish to promote this company one step further by bringing it out into the open, available to the people. What I believe is that due to the lack of our actual presence amongst our customers we're not exposed to a larger variety and numbers of buyers that we deserve. Gardon products have tremendous customer base and loyalty out there. Our advertising campaigns, telemarketing promotions are great. But we're only available through catalogs and telephones."

"What are you trying to say?" He demanded with more uneasiness.

"I want to change that, sir. I want Gardon products to be made available to the customers in person for the first time. I want to open up the first brick and mortar store for Gardon products."

After listening he responded to my proffer with a mocking laughter. "You're going to do that? And you expect them to agree to this?"

"Yes, sir. If we are all intent on our employer's betterment and expansion, we all should have a similar outlook. I can guarantee this will be as lucrative as they expect it to be. I have the capital set for a roll. I have a venue I'm negotiating for. I'm ready to go. All I need is you to convince the board of directors and get this idea sanctioned to advance. Gardon Industries wouldn't lose anything even if the idea collapses. It'll be my capital that goes to waste, not theirs. I build the store, they supply, that's all. If I lose everything, they still get their merchandise back safely."

"What makes you think we haven't discussed the possibility of a physical store before?"

"Well, if it is in talks, I would like to extend my services to the development."

"Yeah, you're the next millionaire, aren't you?" Another wry smirk emanated from him.

"I have enough for a store, sir. James, I need you to understand my thoughts as clearly as you can. This is nothing personal and you haven't spoken to them. I'm taking a chance of a lifetime. This is going to make their products available in the city, it's nothing harmful. We'll have the company's name imprinted in every shopper's mind. All I'm asking for is a ten percent discount on wholesale prices which would turn out to be my profit. I don't want to be more expensive than our catalogs just because it's a store. The business is going to go the same as before, just a new showroom for the people to buy in person if they prefer. Same prices, same quality, just the added convenience of customer service and availability on demand. They wouldn't have to wait for shipments to reach their door which usually takes two weeks in some cases. This is a win-win concept."

"You really don't get it, George, do you? That's your name right? You are an employee in this company, stay an employee as long as they keep you to be. Don't try to outsmart any of your superiors. I don't know where the hell you got all that money from but you better save it. Because you will need all of it very soon when you're kicked out of here if you continue to pester me with your ludicrous proposals. You're just a salesperson who sits in a four by four cabin all day long taking orders and listening to customer grievances, that's all you're made to do. Anything more than that is beyond your understanding and your paygrade. So, don't try to get on the other side of this table because it's already taken. Now, get out of here."

I took in a deep breath. But I wasn't finished. "How the hell did they hire a dumb fuck like you on that chair?"

"What did you say?" He was enraged.

"I said just wait and watch. A salesman like me is going to make you beg. You think I came in here to plead? You think the moment I step out of here I'm going to burst in tears like a six year old because you turned me down? I have contacts. I know people. I can get things far better than what we... you sell here for a price you wouldn't believe. And as far as firing me is concerned, I quit this job right now before I do something crazy like kicking your ass six ways to Sunday. So, shove it up where it all came from." I arose infuriated, and made for the door. But stopped and turned for one more comment before exiting. "Remember, there will be a time when I sit on that side of the desk and you'll be standing before me. I guarantee you that will happen and when it does, I'll make damn sure I remind you of this day." With that said, I left the office and the company, never to look back again.

Chapter Thirteen

ço-ço-ço

I had quit couple of jobs before but always out of mutual understanding and respect and never with such hostility. The event of being unemployed is frightening for everyone, capable of crushing them within. But I was feeling the liberating air of freedom permeate my soul as I stepped out of the stifling enclosures of subjugation and enslaving restrictions and for the first time in my life, I wasn't saddened by the decision of leaving a job and the friends and acquaintances along with them as there were none except Harry. I was prepared and willing to enter the brutal world of business with my unyielding desire to plunge as deep as I could in the pool of wealth. Though, this initiation would only be peripheral, but the edge of the bubble is where the needle needs to be to penetrate through. I had been trained since a very early age, if not officially, with the basics of commencement of a new venture and the first rule that applied towards it was to never use the money you have on hand to start even the most smallest of establishments. You hold the money you have and use the capital that is available to be borrowed, and what better place to begin with than a friendly financial institution conveniently located right around the corner of a neighboring street. Commercial banks welcomed proposals of all sorts and were quite malleable especially if you had a huge balance in your savings account. I was greeted exceptionally well by the branch manager and was offered a lunch and coffee twice through the duration of our discussion. After three subsequent meetings spanning the following two weeks, we finally shook hands over the terms of the agreement. Even though, the amount approved was a little less than I had proposed for, nearing two hundred and fifty thousand dollars, it was sufficient for me to begin. I was ready to proceed.

I called the Realtor for an appointment to view the store that was up for lease and as I went into that store, I revived the memories of those wonderful years that I had spent working within these walls as an employee, now I viewed these walls as an employer. I was right on track. The rent was suitable, the place and setup was familiar and it was situated at one of the most crowded streets of the city, there was no reason for me to delay in signing a ten year lease.

With the capital and venue all setup, the only challenge that remained was the most important thing called inventory, and indeed this was the most arduous of them all. I knew I did not have enough time to proceed at a modest pace as I wasn't interested in paying rent for any period of time I wasn't using the store. I accelerated and expedited the process of searching for suppliers and dealers within two and a half weeks which would have easily taken a month for any person to acquire. I traveled the entire stretch of east coast and secured forty-one dealers to my supplier's roster which included direct manufacturers and subsidiary agents of jewelry and exotic items. Gardon Corporation wasn't one of them. I did play a hand at subtle treachery and cozened most of these suppliers into providing me with one sample of each item I was supposed to sell at my store, and within six days I had enough shipments to embellish my store from floors up to the ceiling. It was all ready to roll and the grand opening day was set for Friday, November 4th, which also happened to be our anniversary. It had been two years since I met Audrey on the street in a rainy night that would change me forever, and her companionship since then had been the only force giving me strength enough to go all the way with my dreams and ambitions.

I couldn't be any happier as I brought in the only two people that I loved the most or rather who actually loved me back. I opened the doors to let Audrey and Harry inside a glittering bright gift and jewelry store that now belonged to me, to us. The grandeur of the shop baffled them both into a speechless stance. There were crystal chandeliers reflecting off of checkered granite floors and coruscating glass showcases. Stands of sparkling jewelry and ornaments, expensive gifts of all types and sorts. I took them further into my office as they stared in disbelief at the button-tufted leather chairs, carpeted floors, velvet lined framed walls. I took Audrey along and made her sit on my chair, the owner's throne.

"How do you like it?" I asked leaning over.

"This is wonderful! I think I'm in heaven." She said holding her pounding chest.

"It's all for you. And Harry, what do you say?" I walked over to him.

"Um... I'd prefer black leather for the boss, but brown still works." He ended up bursting into laughter. We followed. He came over for a brotherly hug. "This is amazing, George. Simply stunning." A smile emerged upon his face that was accompanied by increase of water in his eyes, that day I saw the true meaning of friendship.

"Harry, I want you to join me here. I wouldn't be able to do this all by myself." I asked holding him by the shoulders.

"You don't need me here, George. This place is too much for me."

"Not for both of us. We begin tomorrow and I need you to take the keys. I entrust you with this responsibility." I handed the keys to him.

"You sure?"

"Always."

"This calls for a celebration!" Audrey exclaimed jumping off the chair. "And George's paying the tab."

"It'll be my pleasure."

I took them out for a fun night out.

೫ೀ೫ೀ೫ೀ

The inauguration was profound and exulting as we all opened the doors to our new future. Harry took the role of an overly meticulous and fractious supervisor and began the day by instructing three young, amicable women on the essentials of customer service to which all three listened intently on their first day of work as sales associates. I leaned against the office doorway and watched a frequent horde at the store windows who marveled at the contents on the other side of the glass, but none of them came inside to take them home. The wait to see a customer enter our doors extended into late afternoon as I was beginning to wonder whether my decision to quit work and open this business was sensible or not. It wasn't just my life that depended on it, but Harry's as well, as he had quit his job without a single question when I proposed to him to join me and be a part of this venture. I saw him stand there with a low face and creases of concern on his forehead. The three ladies were given their lunch breaks one by one and after their return they now just stood clustered near the empty cash register and conversed in whispers, sometimes admiring the sparkling artifacts and exotics secured inside the glass displays, and sometimes discussing their family and personal issues with each other. Impatience grew within us all. I could see it on every face in here, but exceedingly insurmountable in my mind as I had no idea how to overcome losing, if I ever do, two hundred and fifty thousand dollars in a failed enterprise. I was at the verge of trembling with fear and nervousness, when suddenly I sighted a familiar face jostling through the crowd of spectators outside.

The door opened with the chimes signaling ingress and Audrey stepped in with a reassuring countenance that rendered me hopeful.

"Afternoon, afternoon, afternoon everyone," she greeted and strode in with some donuts for all and landed a kiss on my cheek. "How are we doing?"

"Terrible," I replied shaking my head. "I was expecting at least some of those people out there to come and give us something to work with. Maybe for a look around, but they haven't so far."

"Well, that's going to change in a moment." She was as sure as one could be.

The chimes rang again and this time an elderly customer sauntered in eyeing the entire floor full of glitter. Harry gestured one of the girls to attend her, she proceeded quickly.

I went back inside the office with Audrey and shut the door close behind me.

"See, what did I say?" She sat down on a chair and sipped her coffee.

I went over and crouched by her side kissing her hand, "you bring fortune in my life. I don't know what will happen to me without you."

"I guess we'll never find out," she smiled.

"How come you're early?"

"I took the rest of the day off from work, I couldn't miss this."

"I was going to wait for tonight, but now that you're here... I need to tell you something." Audrey stirred of unease with every passing moment. "Look Audrey, I don't know what you think about this, our relationship and the time we've spent together. But I cannot go on like this any longer. I think it's time for us to leave each other... or get married. The decision is yours."

Audrey almost trembled as I finished and when I ended, she was blank and stiff as a stone as if she'd seen a corpse come alive.

"I earnestly hope you choose marriage over separation."

I retrieved a velvet case and opened to reveal a glimmering diamond ring and placed it right between us. She first hit me on the shoulder and tacitly complained, but then covered her gasping mouth with her hand while her tearful eyes did the talking.

"Will you marry this despicable, irritable, hard to understand, hard to deal with creature and show him how great life in love can be?"

"Now I know it's you we're taking about." We laughed at her remark. She nodded and permitted me to slip the ring on her finger making it an official engagement.

"Thank you. And I really mean it, for allowing me to spend my life with you. I love you."

"I love you even more." She wrapped her arms around me and rested her head against my shoulder. "Do you know what my mother always said about you, about us? She never trusted this relationship and told me so many times to stay away because you were going to leave me once you find someone better, once you're done. But I wanted to prove her wrong, just for once I wanted to show her that my judgment could be right as well. You don't know what this means to me."

"More than it does to you, it means to me. I will love you always."

Just then Harry appeared at the door after a knock. He brandished four twenty dollar bills with a joyful gesture. "The first earning of the day." But just as he saw the ring on Audrey's finger after she flashed it to him, he had a whole another reason to celebrate.

Our marriage wasn't a grand event. Handful attendees at a modest ceremony that took place exactly six months after the day of our business inauguration. As I watched her come down the aisle between the chapel pews all attired in white, looking enchantingly beautiful, I knew something gracious was nearing my dormant fate step by step, moment by moment, and I wasn't wrong. I found this union of two souls strengthening and our business thriving for the next year and more. Within that time we changed two apartments that escalated in lavishness and affluence each time we moved, corresponding to the furtherance in our social status and distention of my bank figures. In three years I had expanded our small gift store to a massive thirty thousand square feet emporium that had three separate departments accommodating our catalog of exquisite gifts, diamond and platinum jewelry, and high value exotic collectibles that ranged from a few hundreds to eighty thousand dollars. I had loan transactions with many banks by that time and finally after some more flourishing months and a staggering upsurge in sales, I could begin to fancy my deepest ambitions and desires to be revived after a prolonged slumber.

I took my family and drove them to the Bay area of Long Island and entered the gates of our new haven. A long treelined driveway led up to an awe-inspiring, baronial mansion which was laden with every conceivable feature and luxury one could think of harnessing to use. Audrey was spellbound as she stepped out of our Mercedes convertible and gazed upon the majestic structure before her, and to my surprise, the reaction wasn't any different on any other face that I saw following hers, which included her mother and Harry as well.

"Oh my God, George, is that ours?" Audrey asked trembling with excitement.

"It's all yours." I said as I led her inside the engraved twelve feet tall brass doors.

The house came entirely furnished and all we had to do was move in. Of course, the obsolete things we possessed had no place in our new, opulent dwelling, so everything from the past was either discarded or given away. Except for Audrey's goldfish called Gogo, which she brought along and introduced her into a commodious, much more habitable aquarium. The goldfish was elated at first to be transferred from a pitcher to an actual fish tank that gave her more space, but as she began to sight the company of larger fishes, she cowered in the corner and stayed there.

Chapter Fourteen

ৎৡৎৡৎৡ

I had woken up early with intentions of touring the house which I hadn't explored entirely even three months after moving in. I stood by the wall-sized windows deep in thoughts, staring at a pleasant day with two acres of mowed lawn and a pool in sight. I owned a successful venture. I began to experience the advantage of a growing influence which helped me along the way and continued to expand with every passing day. I had a name quite renowned in the industry pertaining to my business. I had one of the most expensive residences in the area and I had the most demanding personality which proved obligatory for success in a city like New York. I was finally a man I wanted to be, just as someone I once knew, my father. And I... I almost forgot, I had a wife... I have a wife. Work had kept me away from home for quite a while now.

Two fragile arms wrapped around me and fingers entwined together. I leaned back a saw a familiar face behind me.

"Morning," Audrey said softly.

"You're up?"

"Come back to bed." She pleaded. "What are you doing here?"

"Looking down... from up here. Doesn't it feel strange?"

"Strange? I don't know. Why?"

"A couple of years ago, I could only dream of living in such a place."

"Well, you worked hard, you worked a lot, and you worked clever, that's what got you here." We kissed. "You did overlook one little thing in all this, but it's all right."

"What's that?"

"Me!"

"I'll have to leave in a couple of days for some business meetings. I don't know how long it will be, but three days at least."

"Again? Is everything all right?"

"Yeah, nothing to worry about, just a word with some suppliers. Their costs are going up too high and too fast, I need to bring them down to the ground from up there."

"Can I come along?" She asked childishly.

"If you want to be bored, maybe. I'll hardly be there the whole day, so..."

"Then I won't."

"Audrey if you feel lonely why don't you have your family come here for a while and live with us, maybe for a few months? If they like it here they could stay, otherwise, go back. You'll have a good time, you won't feel all alone throughout the day, and you'll stay occupied a little."

"Really?" There was a sparkle in her eyes.

"I wouldn't mind."

"I thought about that, but I couldn't ask you."

"Hey, this is our home. Your family is my family now. I don't have anybody on my side, you can have here anyone you like. You don't have to ask me."

"I love you."

"I love you even more. Now let me get dressed, got to get to work. You want to come?"

"No, I'll stay here. Explore the undiscovered floors of this massive maze you've bought me." She landed a kiss as I went into the bath.

"Make sure you don't get lost."

ೞೞೞ

Over the next couple of days I was able to manipulate my suppliers into lucrative deals and curtailing their rising costs back to feasible numbers by threatening them to completely abandon their products and also ensuring that my personal acquaintances of similar interest did the same. It only took a matter of minutes to conclude an agreement, and it was a harmonious one. After returning from that successful campaign, in just a few months I had gotten used to seven figures sales and a huge customer base that was to go a long way. With massive amounts of revenue rolling into my accounts, I had come to terms with the fact that money made every material thing malleable and the true meaning of wealth was intimidation and manipulation to your own advantage. My father had known that truth all his life, while I was just beginning to gain that knowledge. But there was a harsher side to this dark ambition. I was beginning to weigh everything around me in the balance of wealth that even included the people I once loved. Maybe I still loved them, but I pushed myself beyond the boundaries of admission. I did not realize the dreadful path of emotional imperviousness I had taken unintentionally, but I guess every man who has come in possession of wealth too swiftly or undeservedly is always accused of the same at some point in his life. I wasn't accused as of yet, but I was guilty nonetheless. But in all this trade I had forgotten that some things cannot be exchanged for money or status. I was neglecting Audrey and not only she but I could attest to that. There was some madness driving my mind that I couldn't overcome. At times I knew I was wrong, but then I was so unemotional and callous that I never attempted to change myself. I had begun to seek affection in wealth and influence. I began to distance myself from home and from the woman who waited in that house all alone. I didn't realize this shallow rift would rupture so deep the roots of our relationship that we might even fail to recognize each other. The only contact we had with each other, be it physical or spiritual, was in the bedroom and even that was becoming quite prosaic. Our intimacy was lost and it was just barely a union of two bodies, however, that's what I sought. The last string of esperance Audrey held onto for staying happy was having her mother stay with us since I went to the suppliers' meetings. She had left work and taken full responsibility of a housewife in expectation of making this brick and concrete mansion into a home. A home that I was eluding for unknown reasons. There was nothing lacking there, but I did. Her social circle was close to zilch as she had devoted herself entirely to this house and her man only to receive nothing in return.

"I thought you'd be ready by now." I walked into the bedroom and saw Audrey curled up on a couch next to a window wrapped in a blanket, seemingly afflicted with some anxiety.

"You're home?" She opened her eyes and gazed at me. That look in her eyes was inexplicable, and I had no intention of scrutinizing.

"I told you I'd be having some guests coming tonight."

"You did?"

"I called you."

"Oh yes, I remember now. It was an hour ago after you missed about twenty calls from me."

"I was busy at work, Audrey."

"Yeah, and I had nothing to do."

"I'm not around the phone all the time. Besides, what is it that you had to make twenty calls for? If it's so important you can tell me now."

"If you don't want to hear, I have nothing to say."

"Can I ask you get dressed then?"

"What for?"

"Do I have to remind you?"

"Thrill my memory, George. It must be really important that you remember it and I don't."

"I've invited people over for dinner, it's our anniversary."

"Is it? I'd almost forgotten."

"Well, you have twenty minutes to get ready before they start arriving."

"Do I really have to come, George? My mother is there to take care of things. My sister is coming as well. I'm not feeling like it tonight. I'm actually bored of parties now. Besides, they're not coming here to see me, they're coming to see you."

"They're coming to see the couple that's celebrating four years, not their mother or sister."

"Are we celebrating?"

"You're angry because I didn't give you a present, is that it? That you didn't wake up with flowers on the pillow next to yours? That you didn't have your breakfast in bed?"

"Yeah, you got me right there. That's exactly what I wanted."

"I'll get you a present if it's the only thing that matters."

"I'll be so glad. It'll be the best thing you ever did for me."

"I'm waiting downstairs. I hope you won't disappoint the guests?"

"But I am disappointing you, aren't I?"

I kept silent.

"The question is simple, George." She added.

"I won't answer that."

"You won't or you can't?"

Our eyes met and as we both held our glare at each other. One of us had to concede, I took leave.

The party wasn't grand in any respect, just a couple business acquaintances and three neighboring families. Harry had taken full charge of the preparations and there wasn't a foible in his management. He stood by the entrance of the hall and welcomed everyone inside warmly. Audrey's mother had also joined in along with Grace, Audrey's elder sister, who looked quite changed since last I saw her at our wedding. She arrived in a dark red imprinted evening gown and became the person of discussion amongst many men and women who were strangers to her identity. I was amongst them. We greeted and kissed each other and I went around introducing her to my friends, but my eyes were fixed on the stairs still waiting for Audrey to come down.

"How do you like the arrangements, buddy?" Harry pulled me into the corner and waved to the attendants to serve more guests.

"Amazing, Harry. Well done. And keeping this in mind I've decided to give you a little promotion."

"Oh boy, you're not going to hire me as your chef, are you?" Harry smiled expectantly.

"No, I'm sure you're a frightful cook. You better look for a floor manager for the store because from now on you're going to be my personal everything, from assistant to advisor."

"A pay raise?"

"Absolutely."

"You know what I hate to say in friendship; I appreciate it. But today I really mean it." He shook hands with me. "And I took the liberty of inviting a guest at my discretion, and you're going to thank me later for it." Harry took me toward an aging man who seemed aloof and withdrawn from the crowd.

He stood with a glass of bourbon sipping from it, scanning the hall with his prudent eyes, possibly trying to evaluate the things he saw. He was very lean, not very tall, a chiseled face that had seen much and balding, which was quite premature. "This here is Mr. Marcus Jacoby and it's my genuine pleasure to introduce you to Mr. George Bailey here, my good friend as well as employer."

We shook hands.

"Mr. Jacoby is a diamond merchant based in Cape Town, South Africa. He deals in some of the most rarest of antiques in gems, jewelry and collectibles. In fact, one of his recent discoveries and auction of a three thousand year old Egyptian crown was ranked amongst the most hefty transactions of the year in the world. Quite respectable in his nation's regard, he seeks to expand his business here in the states. And I was thrilled to invite him here for further discussions on the matter. Mr. Jacoby, I can assure you are in the presence of the most generous man in all of New York right now. This here, my buddy, is the man you want to talk with for your business."

"How do you do, Mr. Bailey?"

"I think I'm suddenly overwhelmed by that introduction."

"Oh, he exaggerated a little."

"I'm sure everything he said was close to accurate."

"Well, if you insist, I'll take the credit." He said with laughter.

"Did you just recently arrive in New York?"

"Not too long ago. I'd say two weeks perhaps. It was a mere chance that I met with your friend here, but he impressed me immensely with his prowess to influence the people around him. The strength of tongue, that is something my enterprise relies upon. I needed someone like him. However, talking to him for some time gave me the knowledge that his employer is even more distinguished in this skill. I couldn't help but show my interest."

"And your interest is greatly appreciated."

"I hope so is my business."

"What are your aspirations, Mr. Jacoby?"

"If you'd ask me to be blunt, I'd say money. You can never have enough unless you have it all, isn't that right?"

"I would somewhat agree with you on that."

"Let's talk a little while and we'll see that somewhat alter into a lot." We laughed at his remark. "Everything follows money, in my opinion. I believe it is the truth. Even your loved ones are nicer to you once they see all that wealth. Take my wife for example, there's nothing she wouldn't do to please me. That wasn't the case seven years ago when we divorced each other. Now she'd even please my girlfriends. She's a changed person now."

"A wife and girlfriends, now that's a lot of burden to bear," Harry commented.

"You should try it as well, both of you. It'll do wonders for your relationship." Jacoby answered. "But I think I've digressed from answering your question, Mr. Bailey. What I want is to set a base in the states for my discoveries to be displayed and auctioned to an exclusive circle of patrons that will benefit us both. You have the place, you know the people, and I bring the goods. Well, of course by exclusive I mean to say extremely prosperous individuals who can afford to bid handsomely on items that I produce. Whether you want to come along and be a part of this or not, I leave the decision to you."

"On that note, I'll let you two discuss this further while I go and check up on some other things. But you can be certain of one thing Mr. Jacoby, my buddy here won't disappoint you."

"I'm sure he won't."

Harry went on his way.

I began an extensive conversation with Jacoby familiarizing myself on how his enterprise functioned and was established, explaining to him similar things about my business. Through this talk I gathered that he was quite an itinerant type and had contacts throughout the African continent in dealings of diamond and exotic gems. He even invited me to accompany him on his next month tour from southern Europe all the way to Cape Town in hopes of securing some lucrative business settlements. He also hinted that along the way he would make sure that my time was well spent and replete with pleasures. I understood that he was one of the men who believed in carnal freedom, a lothario, and liked his escapades to be unrestricted. Before I could leave him to fetch myself a drink, his last inquiry stirred my attention.

"Tell me, Mr. Bailey. Not a business related question, but my curiosity is kindled. Who is that woman over there in the dark red evening dress?" Jacoby's intrigue heightened.

I looked behind me and saw Grace talking with her mother.

"We haven't been introduced so far." He added with a crooked smile. With this expression he wanted to convey a message that I intuited very well.

"Did you two get anywhere? Are we looking at millions or what?" I had just excused myself from Jacoby and Harry took me along.

"He's interested all right, but needs another six months or so to set up his exports. A lot of important people must be brought in order to bring in illegal items into the states. Once done we'd be rolling in cash."

"Can't wait for the day. Say, I don't see the talk of the town here yet?"

"What?"

"The apple of your eye?"

"Audrey?"

"Don't say that with a question mark in the end, come on."

"I asked her twice. If she doesn't want to be here, there's hardly anything I can do."

"Oh, let me give it a try. She might answer my plea."

"Go ahead, make my day."

"I'll be right back."

Harry went up the stairs and I joined the crowd again. Moving through and having random conversations with the invitees. I sighted Grace in isolation from the revelry along with her mother standing close to a doorway. I quickly approached with intentions of introducing her to Jacoby.

"Now, please don't tell me you two are planning to leave this early?"

"I won't lie to you, we actually were thinking about it." Grace had a slight inkling of a Brooklyn accent.

"Please, you can't do that. You sister's already angry with me and refused to come down. You're going to leave me alone as well?"

"You don't want us amidst those rich, wealthy friends of yours, George." She said with a mesmerizing smile.

"Now whoever said that, it must be a terrible misunderstanding. I'd love to have you stay a little while longer. Please Mrs. Gallo, I beg of you. And you as well."

Grace looked at her mother and then both nodded.

"Well, your sister's abandoned me tonight. You wouldn't mind if I took you as her replacement?"

"She not coming down tonight." I heard Mrs. Gallo speak this time.

"Yeah, I think she's upset at me for not bringing her a gift. I was hoping this gathering would suffice, but women, you know how they are." My eyes were still fixed at Grace.

"She no tell you?"

"Tell me what?"

"I think you hear from her, it is better."

"Please tell me, you're making me nervous. Is there something I should know?"

"She went to doctor today and they say she will have-" She conversed with Grace in Italian about something that came as a surprise to her as well.

"She means to say Audrey has some fertility problems." Grace translated.

"It is woman problem. She can have baby, but it hurt her, difficult for her to keep alive at birth. She cannot be a mother."

Chapter Fifteen

❧❧❧

"She didn't say anything about this to me." I was trying to absorb the news when I was interrupted again.

"Hey George, buddy, can I talk to you for a moment?" Harry stood behind tapping my shoulder. I turned a bit nettled at him for interrupting.

"I couldn't do it, you win champ. Audrey said as cold hearted a husband I have, I still love him too much to ask for a divorce."

I was wide-eyed for a moment.

"I got you there, didn't I? Just playing with you, man." This enraged me even more as he pushed closer to Grace and her mother. "And please Mother-in-law, don't even think about leaving before trying the chicken pot-pie, I specially ordered that for you. I know how much you like it. And Grace, I can't help but compliment you tonight, you look stunning. And I'm sure every man in this hall thinks so."

"Thank you." Grace smiled.

"How about you give it another try, buddy? Maybe with mother-in-law and sister backing you up this time? I know it is the most difficult job on earth to keep a wife happy, but I'm sure she just needs a bit of nudge out that door now. She's right at the brink of giving up and coming down."

"All right I will, get back to work now. Make sure the guests are comfortable." I lacerated his contentment with my words.

Harry frowned. He was wordless for a moment, then laughed. "You just got me there. I can never interpret when you're being serious and when you're not."

"You can be damn sure I'm serious right now."

The laughter suddenly faded from his face as he took a hard swallow. Grace and her mother took a small step away from us in certain embarrassment while Harry stood mortified. He began to recede.

I took him by the arm. "Don't get too comfortable around my house. And remember, it's Mr. Bailey or sir from now on."

"Yes, sir." His voice quivered as he uttered that word. With that he went on straight to the dining.

The mother-daughter continued their talk in Italian as I left their company in considerable shock.

People had left, the party was over. It was close to midnight. Harry packed up the leftovers and led the help out of the house going along with them. I sat alone in the massive hall listening to the sound of loneliness. I had hurt people tonight, a friend out of anger and a companion out of apathy. One of them indignant and the other dispirited.

I felt a moving presence of a living soul around me and as I stirred to look, I saw Audrey coming down the stairs.

"They're all gone, you're late." I spoke as I turned away from her.

"You're still here." She answered coming closer every step. "The others don't matter much." She stood near the couch and took a seat at the other end. "Did you enjoy yourself? I'm sure it was great, plenty to talk about, plenty of people to talk to?"

"I spoke to your mother."

"Oh, that'd be the last thing you want to do. You two narrowly get along. I can't get her to talk without her ranting in Italian, how did you manage?"

"You could have told me that yourself."

"That she's difficult to speak with?"

"You know what I'm talking about."

"Do you?"

"Yes, I do. And I never expected to hear something so important to the both of us from her."

"Is it important?"

"Goddamn it, stop patronizing me."

"That's my last intention. I'm sorry if I'm upsetting you, I can go back."

"Yes, go ahead and make a devil out of me. I'm the one who's wrong every time, isn't it?"

"No, George. This time I was wrong."

"So, you admit that?"

"I just did, if it makes you happy."

"You couldn't tell me this when I came to see you?"

"You came to see me, when was that? Oh, I'm sorry I almost forgot. You were in the room, weren't you? Telling me to get dressed. Yeah, I should have mentioned this in passing. It would have only taken a moment. I'm sorry."

"You know you're just impossible."

"I tried every other way, nothing seems to work."

I arose and stormed away from her. But I heard her whimpering and stopped.

"You didn't ask me, George. Not even once. You knew I was going to visit the doctor today. You knew why, but you never even bothered to ask once. I'm trying my best to change us into a family, but it's not my fault that I can't have children without complications. I know no family is complete without them, and I'm willing to die to give you a child. But please, try not to hate me. I can't bear another burden." She wiped away her tears and stood up. "Can't we make everything go back to the way it was?" There was yearning in her voice.

"I don't know, you tell me?"

She came over and took my hand in hers and caressed it. I cheated eye contact with her even then.

"I'm sorry for my faults, whether I committed them or not, it doesn't matter. If I upset you in any way, then I'm sorry. I just want us to be happy again. Can we do that? And I promise from next time on I would tell you things like these, not my mother. I don't want anyone to come between us. It's good that she's gone."

"She isn't. After what she told me about your health, I asked her to stay another two weeks along with your sister Grace. They're in the guest rooms."

She rested her head on my shoulder and smiled softly.

"Then you still care about me. The doctor said there's still hope. Miracles do happen, right?"

"Yeah." My response was bland, I looked away.

બ૰બ૰બ૰

A week had passed since the day I learned that I might not become a father ever. But every time I'd contemplate on the matter I couldn't find myself commiserating with my wife. In fact, I was searching for a way out, a way to get rid of my barren counterpart, a way to escape the clutches of an infertile woman and find someone who could bear me a child.

With that thought, I stood by the French doors of my den overlooking the stretch of my yard and a swimming pool that could possibly qualify as an Olympic swimming contest venue. But my eyes were fixed on someone who's been drawing my attention for the past week. Audrey sat back on a pool lounger with a book in her hands reading through the pages, her mother attempted a conversation sporadically. Her 8 year old niece, Claudia, performed a cannonball and splashed into the water. And then emerged a woman from the pool in a bathing suit that outlined her voluptuous body perfectly, dripping wet with silver droplets that slid off her hips and soaked the floor. Her tender shoulders were marked with tan-lines that grew wider reaching down to her bosom, and the lines also stretched horizontally across the top periphery of her thighs. Her face was a whole another wonder to speak about as her wide, strong forehead led to big brown eyes that were almond shaped and always alluring with a certain severity in her gaze. Her nose was straight with an upturned tip, and her delicate lips were downward shaped and forever dark red as if welcoming a man into the enigmatic world of her seduction. And it was all outlined by the resplendence of her red hair that just added to her exquisiteness. Even after being a mother and carrying the responsibility for the past 8 years, she had kept the appeal of a small, curved waist but broad hips almost as wide as her shoulders, large breasts and thick but shapely legs that completed her hourglass figure to perfection.

I had seen Grace and conversed with her but never drawn to her in such a way before this visit. She joined Audrey by the recliner chair and took a sip from a cocktail glass. As much as my heart instructed me to shift my concealed desires and sight from my sister-in-law over to my wife, my eyes deceived those commands. Suddenly, I heard someone come into the room and as I turned to look, Harry walked in with some files tucked under his arm. He stepped to the desk and opened them all in front of me.

"I got the monthly reports here. You want to take a look, sir?" His voice was stern and countenance irate. He sat down across my desk.

"Total sales?" I asked, disrupting my gaze from Grace and perched on the edge of my desk.

"Eight hundred seventy six thousand, four thirty-two and fourteen cents."

"We're down from last month?"

"Well, I'm trying my best to keep the *July tumble* as steady as could be. We got August coming, that'd be another downswing. But right back on track from September and onwards."

"Net?"

"Close to four fifty."

"Harry, I think I should implement your notion of expansion." I placed my thoughts before him. His disgruntlement suddenly expunged from his face.

"I keep telling you that. What're you thinking? Another site or more floor space?"

"No, we'll stay with one for now. But what would you say to the possibility of having our hoarding from one end of the block all to way to the other?"

"Entire block?" Harry thought scratching his chin. "I don't see many problems with that except one."

"So, there is one?"

"Yeah, the restaurant guy is okay. He's on a lease and old, almost retirement age. He wouldn't mind leaving with a little incentive, but the one right in the middle, the Laundromat. I don't know how long that guy's been there, seems almost like a century by the looks inside. He's refused to talk, I've tried before. That guy is stubborn as a tree."

"That doesn't mean he can't be cut down. That's why I have you."

"No, I think it's external pressure, an influential competitor perhaps. Why would he be so adamant otherwise?"

"Did you make an offer?"

"I tried. Not too long ago, a full appraisal of his inventory, assessment of his store's sale value, and a twenty percent on top of that."

"What's the estimate?"

"Comes around six hundred thousand."

"What can you do about it?"

"I think I can do something."

"Well then, I don't see a reason we should wait any longer. Let's get to it. Fix a meeting with the Laundromat guy. Let's see what he has to say. And Harry, don't disappoint me."

"Yes, Geor- sir."

I went back to my view of the pool while Harry left the office incensed at my remark which was the least of my concerns.

Two days later I returned from work early afternoon and came inside a silent home skimming the dining, the pool and everywhere around. "Audrey... Audrey." I called out to check if she was in.

As I returned back into the living, I heard a familiar voice calling out from somewhere close by.

"They went out for some shopping." Grace appeared in the kitchen doorway wiping off her hands with an apron that hung by her neck and tied around her waist. She tied up her hair and continued, "they'll be back soon, I'm the chef tonight." She went back inside.

I followed her into the kitchen and watched from the threshold her auburn hair that bounced off her shoulders as she moved. Her black stretch pants embraced the shape of her posterior and folded at the creases of her butt cheeks.

"Do you want something, to drink maybe?"

I heard her voice as it shook me out of my fantasies and looked up at her face which was with a warm smile, expecting an answer.

"No, no... nothing right now. They're making you do all the work, that isn't fair." I moved closer to her and even more, staring up and down the length of her back, she had turned away by then.

"Nah, I'm good with it. It doesn't hurt once in a while. Besides, I'm used to it. I do it all the time for Claudia." She bent down to retrieve something from the cabinet and I quickly eyed the cleavage but looked away soon.

"You know you two are so dissimilar, Audrey and you." I commented trying to gain her attention.

"I know, many people say that. She's the cute, pretty one. She's nicer, kind, subtle, and she's the one who went to college so there goes my verbal skills. You know the reason I stayed away from your guests that night? I didn't want to embarrass you in front of them. I try so hard when I'm around you two. Both of you speak so good and I... was I suppose to say well? See, there you have it. "

"I didn't mean your educational level." She looked around the counter for something. "What are you looking for?"

"A grater."

"Here..." I intentionally rubbed against her back as I reached for the drawer and gave her the needed. She didn't notice the act in such manner and didn't oppose to it. I got even closer.

"I meant you two are really different in ways that men usually find attractive. I was thinking if you and I-"

"George, there you are." Audrey jumped into the doorway and beamed. I swiftly receded, distancing myself from Grace to a couple of feet away. Audrey came rolling and landed a kiss, it was supposed to land on my lips but I averted and it marked my cheek. Claudia came running to her mother as Grace picked her up in her arms and rejoiced.

"Oh, I love you so much. You didn't bother your aunt too much now, did you?"

"Nope." Claudia responded softly.

"She was an angel." Audrey confirmed.

"Mom, come I'll show you what I got. Aunt Audrey bought it for me."

"Aw, Audrey you shouldn't have done that."

"Don't tell me what to do with my niece, mom. She's my niece, not yours." Both laughed and Claudia dragged her mother out. Audrey turned to me now. "How was your day?"

"Fine."

"Tired? How about you take a long, relaxing bath, me included?" She drew nearer to me and gripped around my chest in a tight embrace.

"I have work to do." I pushed her back and left her alone.

ဖော်ဖော်ဖော်

There were two things in life that I despised the most, waiting on someone who's late and someone being an impediment to my intentions. The man I was about to meet was both. My breaths were like fumes billowing from a dragon's nostrils as my office door was knocked and opened. Harry stepped in with an aging man who had no sense of personal hygiene and self grooming, ironically, he operated a Laundromat. He walked in with his belly jiggling upon a tight waist trouser that could give way any moment now, an undershirt and an unzipped jacket on top. His facial and head hairs were graying and receding, his smile was suitable for a tobacco advertisement. He came mumbling to himself a blend of expletives and glanced around trying to showcase his indifference and unaffectedness.

"This is Mr. George Bailey, Mr. Anderson." Harry introduced us.

There was no formal greeting as he took a chair and waited.

"So, it's you." Anderson said unable to hold my glare. "Done quite lot in these years."

I skipped the prelude and went straight to our point of discussion. I reached out for the drawers of my desk and retrieved signed check in the amount of six hundred thousand dollars and laid it down before him.

"You fucking kidding me?" Anderson's response to all the money.

"That is how much your place is worth." Harry said.

"Well, I ain't impressed."

I reached for something else and threw onto the table with the check. A stack of ten thousand dollars. Anderson looked down at it confused. I slammed another one on the desk.

"You think your lousy money will change my mind?" Anderson smiled and shifted back on his chair.

I tossed another bundle into the heap, and another one. This stirred him up to lean forward.

"You think you can force me to shut down?" Anderson was agitated and weakening.

Another two joined the pile.

"I'm not going to sell my place." He wiped the sweat off his forehead. With another one dropped in front of him, he wasn't going anywhere. "I'm not money hungry, you know..." Two more came his way.

"I don't know what to say, Mr. Bailey."

I put the final stack on the desk and began. "Final offer, this is a hundred thousand dollars, cash, tax free. Take it or get the fuck out of my office right now."

"The store is yours, I leave tomorrow."

He gathered the cash in his arms, pocketed the check and stormed out of the office. Harry looked down at me and winked. I smiled and leaned back on the chair in complete triumph.

Chapter Sixteen

❦❦❦

Some days had passed as my condemnable but fervent desire to have Grace was unrelenting. The distance in our marriage was growing moment by moment, and I suppose Audrey was able to intuit the reason behind it as her mother, Grace and Claudia had just left our home a day ago using fear of theft at their own house as an absurd excuse. I was enraged to be separated from my want when I gained knowledge of their departure. As I walked into the living the following night returning from work, I saw Audrey sitting by the window pensive and oblivious of her surroundings, staring out at the pelting rain against the glass wall. There was a poignant silence in the room, no presence of anyone else. My arrival stirred her up to her feet. She passed a smile and proceeded towards me relieving me of my coat, allowing me to sit.

"You're quite late, what happened?" She asked gently.

"Had some work to do." I replied bluntly.

"You know you've been working quite a lot lately. I thought once this business was up and running smoothly, I'd have you all to myself. It turned out to be the other way around."

"Running your own place is a lot harder than a job."

"I know that, but just... a simple thought of having you by my side more often."

"Well, don't we live in the same house? I always come back here, don't I?"

She delayed her response, trying to absorb mine. "Yes, that's all we do, live in the same house."

"What is it that you want from me? You want me to give up work and sit by your side gossiping about other women, jewelry and soap operas? You want me to stay home with you and feed the goddamn fishes, read fashion magazines all day long, cook dinner for you?"

"I've never asked you to do any of it, have I? Besides, it doesn't hurt doing that once in while, maybe not for me, but giving yourself a day's rest." She kept a comforting hand on my shoulder, but I could tell she was emotionally wounded.

"What is wrong with you?" I jumped away from her touch. "If I wanted a life like that I wouldn't have gone through all this trouble to be what I am today. That... would be possible with what I was."

"Yes, I now think so. What you were and what you are. I thought this was about us."

"This is for you. All I do is for you. I'm not going to take this wealth with me to the grave. What do you lack? What do you lack in life? House, jewelry, cars, money, clothes, what is it that you want I haven't already given you?"

"You haven't given me yourself in a very long time." There were tears in her eyes.

"You really couldn't pick a better time, could you? You know we were supposed to go out tonight. I specifically asked you to stay ready. But you aren't."

"I was waiting for you."

"Well, now I'm here."

Audrey held a long thought provoking gaze at me before leaving upstairs to change. I was so impervious to culpability that I failed to grasp what that stare intended to do.

I walked into our room buttoning my shirt and wrapping a bow tie in a knot and my eyes fell upon Audrey who sat at the vanity table concluding her facial make-up in a black satin evening gown that adorned her stunningly, but our recent argument still fresh in my mind denied me to disregard the affray and go in with a compliment to reconcile. Her eyes were still upon me as I came into view in her mirror. I reached for my jacket when I found something that I had brought for her. I retrieved a case from one of the pockets and went forward placing it on the table.

"This is for you." I walked away.

"I thought husbands were supposed to put it on as well."

It made me stop and come back to her. I unfolded the case and took out a shimmering diamond necklace from it. She shifted her hair to one side as I embellished her with it.

"I've never seen anything like it before." She was amazed by it.

"It's not every day you see women wearing something like it. It comes from a very wealthy acquaintance of mine."

"How much did it cost?" She shifted to look up at me filled with concern.

"Twenty-eight thousand." I finished hooking the necklace securely around her and went back to wearing my jacket.

"I don't know whether I should thank you for it, or ask you to return it." Our eyes met at this remark.

"You can wear it tonight, after that it is yours to do as you may please. Throw it away, I don't care."

She turned back to her mirror and wiped below her eyes, I stepped out of the room.

A multitude of dignitaries and high-end patrons marched down the red carpet and diffused into the amassing of entrepreneurs, businessmen and merchants. I joined this array of wealthy capitalists with Audrey barely existing by my side and moved along to the doors of a large banquet hall waving and acknowledging some acquaintances down the way. Our hosts for the evening, some executives of business association, welcomed us both inside. As I went in, my sight filled with rich, privileged industrialists and tycoons with their festooned and bejeweled spouses, and I felt honored to be counted amongst them. My only mission was to make influential acquaintances and profitable contacts tonight and I was willing to impress all these people with glib, ingratiating ability that I possessed imbued in some blarney without risking any diversion or humiliation of any sort. I met a group of friends amidst the crowd of prospects and joined them separating from Audrey, while she tried to assimilate the pervasive affluence around her. My attention did move toward my goal but my sight remained upon her.

While returning from the bar with a glass of scotch in my hand, I was accidentally introduced to someone whom I've hoped to stay away from to keep my temper in check.

"Mr. Bailey?" The voice compelled me to turn around.

"Yes?" I answered.

"Gardon, Ben Gardon."

My smile effaced, even though I had seen cursory glimpses of his face when I worked for him, but I couldn't recognize him at first. He was around the age of seventy, lean and tall, all white head with bushy eyebrows and razor thin lips. He was a little slouched due to years of hard work, but enjoyed the luxuries of wealth in his later years.

"Gardon Corporation?"

"Yes." He answered with elation.

"How are you?" I said uninterested in continuing this conversation.

"George, I'm not exaggerating even a bit when I say this, but it is a pleasure to meet you."

"I'm sure it is."

"I love to see a man driven with ambition and desire to achieve wonders through hard work. I'd always had an intention to expand our catalogs to a physical store, but you preceded us all. And look at you now, a small employee at our company, a sales executive, now one of the most successful businessmen of New York City. You can't measure the delight I feel, my boy."

I glanced around at the faces that were suddenly a part of our conversation and were fixed at me. I held my composure just as well as I held my smile, but I was enraged deep inside at the disclosure he's just used to belittle me.

"I think I can, Mr. Gardon. Your words directed toward my humble beginnings were quite explicit for the people around us to hear. But I'd suggest we keep such connotations on each other's pasts to ourselves, because if I begin to check down that long list of humbling details, there might be some facts you wouldn't like to be divulged before all these influential men. And if we so much as attempt to resolve our differences here tonight, I will suggest you begin by staying away from my block of competitors and not try to manipulate them against me, especially those I'm seeking to buyout. We can both be sure what I'm talking about because you just lost one, not too long ago. And you're precisely right that I precede you, do you know why? Because of your inept, incapable manager who needed to suppress an idea like this just because it came from a subordinate and not his own dumb mind. He caused you this monumental loss that you can't even imagine. And it wasn't just him, I wrote to you with this offer, but I guess that envelope probably found its place somewhere in a stack of unread correspondence on your desk. So, next time keep an eye out for people like me and save yourself the cost of losing one because if you still had me, *you* would be the biggest businessman in New York right now." I walked away from a stunned elderly face that was nothing but filled with regret and deprived of words and appeared even more withered with embarrassment.

I found Audrey distancing herself from the superficial conversations of other gilded women who surrounded her. I approached her and took her by the arm to a corner and yelled at her in whispers.

"Please try to make an impression, Audrey, don't just stand there."

"I'm trying my best." She responded dryly.

"Try harder."

Another voice interrupted our little affray, as I turned around I recognized a colleague from some years ago. This was Alex Boaster. A towering man at 6'4", and stocky, altogether a massive obstacle stood before me.

"Alex?"

"So you do remember old friends?"

"How you doing?" We hugged each other.

"Good and you?"

"Well, it doesn't get any better."

"That's certainly true, and who is this moonlit beauty, right here?"

"Alex, meet my wife Audrey. Audrey, this is a very old friend. The store that we own, when I used to work there, he was with me all the way." They shook hands.

"I never took you for the marrying type." He said jokingly. "But you can't refuse someone like her, can you? But one thing that baffles me, how did you fall for an ugly, wretched guy like him?"

"Love makes you do silly things," Audrey responded plainly.

"Well, that is amazing. I would like you to meet my girlfriend here, this is Helen. Helen, my very old friend, George Bailey."

Helen stepped up with a gorgeous smile and greeted us in a most sensuous accent I'd ever heard.

"Helen is from Poland, she just came to New York and we met only a couple months ago. I think you two will make best of friends, Audrey." Alex said forwarding her for a handshake.

"Hello Audrey," Helen's voice resounded within me.

I held her hand and admired her beauty without words, her blue eyes, defined facial features, blonde hair, perfectly tanned skin and a model-like figure. I ogled her from head to toe and was instantly desirous of her, and the acceptance of that lust was tacit. I read it in her eyes. It was some unknown fervent want burning inside me to have any other woman than my wife to quench my hunger for flesh and I was willing to give myself away to anyone who came in my sight worthy of one night. Alex was one of the rare men who took pride in his obtrusive conviction of sharing his belongings with his friends, which is a wonderful belief as long as someone as revered as you wife is not a part of that catalog. It was quite reprehensible in my opinion back when we worked together, but somehow the dislike I carried for such flagrant thinking was nowhere to be found in my mind now.

"I have heard a lot about you from him, Mr. Bailey."

"I hope all worthy of your interest." I still held onto her hand, she was in no hurry to let go either.

"Indeed, some even highly impressive."

"Really?"

"When will this be over, George?" Audrey cut in objecting our prolonged handshake.

"The party's just begun, Audrey. You're already looking to bail out?" Alex nudged her playfully. "Let's get you a drink, make you more relaxed. It'll take a lot of drinks before you get out of this. What can I get you?"

"Lemonade please."

"Lemonade? That's for hangovers dear."

"That'll do, please."

Alex went off to the bar and Audrey attempted to draw my attention toward her, I resisted and stayed around Helen.

"I love that song." Helen turned excitedly to the orchestra then back at us. "You wouldn't mind if I steal your husband for a while do you, Audrey?"

Audrey summoned a fake smile in response as Helen dragged me to the dance floor. Alex came along with a glass of lemonade and handed it to the lonely soul.

"There we are."

"Thank you, Alex."

"You are most certainly welcome. What's up with these two, already on the floor together?"

"I guess they both like to dance." Audrey said uncomfortably.

"With each other, that is." Alex enjoyed the view. "It is such a world we're living in, sweetheart, more than your own plate, you're always curious of what the guy next to you is having for dessert, and we all want a bite of it."

Audrey glanced up at Alex solicitously.

"That's the reason we don't mind anymore. Sooner or later we have to give it up and share, don't we?"

"I don't believe in that."

"Well, I can see why you're still sticking with lemonade. You'll get there with time. You wouldn't mind if I asked you to join me on the floor?"

Audrey considered then accepted his invitation and joined the couples on the floor.

As I moved around with Helen in my arms, I caught sight of Audrey with Alex but extremely distressed and distant from each other. He attempted to bring her to life with a comment here and there, but she refused to associate or answer avidly.

"You have to visit this resort in Belize, it gives you the most beautiful views you've ever seen in your life." Helen whispered in my ear.

"More than you?" I managed to make her laugh.

"Yes."

"I doubt that. When did you come to US?"

"About a year ago. I was modeling back in Poland, then I lived in Moscow for some time, then London, Madrid and finally here.

What better place to move to than New York City to advance my career."

"Quite an itinerant life so far."

"What can I say, I never found a man like you to settle down with."

"Are you looking carefully?" I joked.

"All the good ones are always taken. You being one of them."

"What makes you think I'm good?"

"You're taken. And believe me, I can tell a lot about a man by looking into his eyes."

"What do mine tell you?"

"You want me to be explicit or leave some details to imagination?"

Helen took me from the dance floor and we concealed ourselves behind a massive pillar in the corner of the hall. My mind wanted her, but my eyes deceived me as I kept watching Audrey and Alex from there which wasn't very far. It wasn't with the purpose to secure Audrey from Alex, or even defend her if something needless happens, but only to observe and ascertain that she carries out my instructions on propriety in such grand social surroundings.

"So what brought you into his life, Audrey?" Alex gracefully slid on the floor holding Audrey gingerly in his arms. His booming voice echoed as if through a thousand watt amplifier.

"A mere chance that we met. It does sound a bit unrealistic as they show in the pictures, rainy night, two people colliding into each other. But that was our beginning." Audrey answered.

"Fairy tales don't exist in real life, at least not for me."

"I guess you're right, all fairy tales come to an end sooner or later. But what breaks your heart is when you realize that you placed all your bets for a happy future on nothing but remote promises and false hopes."

"I keep telling the world but they never listen. Look, I'm a pragmatic soul, I live in today. I don't think about tomorrow, I don't reflect on the past. Life is a revelry, that's how it's supposed to be spent. Have fun, enjoy your days, celebrate your nights, they don't last too long especially the young and passionate ones. Make love, don't fall in it. Free love leads to a good life."

"I'm afraid we all can't think like you do."

"Well, you lose it then. A happy married life is a myth, an illusion. There is no such thing. And those who make it sound like it's the way of life, the pinnacle of companionship, the warmth of two souls, are just trying to throw you into that quagmire they've been stuck in for years and can't get out. It is either out of a pu rpose, a goal, or selfish conditions that two different human beings stay together, nothing else. Men have a reason to be there, which usually comes down to a woman's beauty, her body, the idea of having her in your life and your bed, and in return women a sk for financial security, social recognition and some freedom of mind."

"Wow, that's some misogamist opinion of marriage."

"As much as I hate this relationship, I love the kind that completes it. Womankind, can't live without them, can we? And I must admit George has a tremendous taste in his women. You as his wife, and now Helen as his.... I'm the one left alone, how about we change that?" He leaned in for a kiss but as Audrey receded, he only managed a peck on her cheek. They parted, Audrey's face was streaked with disgust and anger, but she contained her seething feelings well enough.

"I must find my husband, I can't see him." Audrey said, tipping forward searching for us in the crowd. "Where are they?"

"They'll be back, it won't take too long."

"What do you mean?" Audrey began jostling through the dancing pairs. Alex followed her.

"Now don't tell me you wouldn't know."

"Know what?" Audrey stopped to understand the meaning behind Alex's insinuating grin. "I'll go look for him." She disregarded the truth and went on searching.

"Relax Audrey, let them have their privacy for a while. If you want we can find our own." Alex extended his arm and held onto her elbow pulling her close.

"What?" Audrey cried.

"Well, if you are so intent on finding them, try the m en's room first, and don't forget to knock."

Audrey refused to believe that and came closer to the pillar behind which we hid.

Alex continued, "how about we take the one next to theirs? I have everything you can ask for, and I'm certain you'll enjoy every inch of that."

Audrey, in all her rage and consternation, landed a slap on Alex's face. A sudden silence swept the hall. I had heard all of this from behind the large column that was wide enough to hide Helen and me from the rest, but I never thought it would escalate to this. We both joined this hushed crowd. Alex stepped back mortified, Audrey in her own dismay stormed out of the gathering. Helen and I stood disconcerted and in utter disbelief.

Chapter Seventeen
❧❧❧

I had driven us home in foreboding silence, while Audrey's incessant whimpering sounded from the passenger's side. Still, my anger wasn't anywhere close to being mollified. We reached home and I charged up the stairs into the bedroom and she followed slow and heavy with sadness. The thoughts that permeated my mind were all but those that favored my wife. I was afraid of losing my high-class acquaintances including my friend and Helen. I was frightened at the inkling of being ostracized from the wealthy community I had worked so hard to be a part of and yearned for ages, and it was all because of that woman who had no sense of proper demeanor at such gatherings. I ripped away my bow tie and unbuttoned my shirt and in extreme anguish took a tabletop clock and hurled it at the mirror smashing it to fragments. Audrey entered the room in silence and came to my side as I sat on the bed flank.

"I'm sorry, I didn't mean to do it." Her voice trembled through her sobs. "I was looking for you all over-" she placed her hand on my shoulder but I arose furiously and stepped away from her.

"There was just one thing I asked of you tonight, just one. And you had to ruin it all for me."

"I'm sorry I couldn't-"

"You had no right to do that."

"I had no right? He was being disrespectful to me."

"Disrespectful? Do you even hear what you're saying? All those people over there, they were my competitors, my superiors, my colleagues, all rich and respectable people of New York city and I wanted to make an impression on them that could last and help us in the future. But you know what, you actually did help me do that, right? You did. All of them are going to remember me for what you did tonight for a long time to come. My wife, evidently too pompous for such gatherings and the people there, couldn't take a bland joke from a friend and landed a slap right across his face. Sounds really spicy, doesn't it? You ruined me tonight. You ruined my image, my reputation, the respect that I had garnered in all these years. It took you just one moment to flip it all around, to make me lose all of that. I'm so glad, you don't know how happy I am tonight. Do you even realize what you've done? Do you realize who that man is?"

"George, do you realize who I am? I am your wife. You took an oath to protect me. You married me. That man asked your wife to accompany him to the men's room."

"He was just trying to be friendly. He was trying to loosen you up a little, trying to make you laugh."

"Trying to make me laugh or trying to laugh at me? And more than that, at you. Friendly you say, by trying to force me to have sex with him, he was being friendly?"

"I shouldn't have taken you along. I made a big mistake taking you with me. I didn't know you would act like an ignorant nuisance."

"Well, maybe I am a nuisance, incapable of a lot of things. Incapable of attending your fancy, noble, rich people's social meetings. Incapable of presenting myself like an exhibition before your wealthy friends. Incapable of agreeing to spread my legs for them. Maybe I am ignorant, but at least I have my honor intact."

"Watch your mouth when you're talking to me."

"That's what he should have done when talking to me."

"You could have uttered a simple refusal in place of hitting him and making a scene out of nothing. This is business we're talking about here, these things happen all the time. We're not living in brownstones anymore, where people have no sense of ambition, no sense of association and socializing to reach their goals. This is the city, people need to entertain each other in order to resolve their purpose."

"What is your purpose, George? To have me put up on a display for your friends?"

"I'm your husband, if you were so much disturbed, you should have come to me. But you just went ahead and assaulted a man whom I call friend."

"My husband sends me in someone else's arms and fills his own with another woman? Well, I looked and I couldn't find you anywhere. It's a pity I have to apologize to you for protecting myself. It's a shame that I had to slap his face to bring him to his senses, when it should have been you."

"Me?"

"When I married you, I knew you for a person who would smash his face in the man who so much as tried anything lewd with me. Who would give away his world for one moment of my smile, who would melt at the sight of my tears. What has happened to that man I married?"

"I'm not a street thug to be behaving like an imbecile with no sense of etiquette. I'm not risking my status for something insignificant as this."

"Insignificant? Well, the next time someone comes asking me for it, I might as well charge them for the time. What do you say about that? I think they'll pay a good amount for someone like me, Mr. Bailey's whore?"

I charged forward and smacked her right across the face forcing her to stumble back and on the bed. Audrey held her cheek, then arose back up.

"That's exactly how I felt."

ৎৡৎৡৎৡ

The event that night was the signaling of a greater rift in our relationship and triggered a detachment of our emotions, feelings and love for each other. For the following weeks there wasn't any communication between us. I could tell we were drifting away as these circumstances were recurrence of a situation I had personally experienced before in my life, more than twenty years earlier. But I was so driven against the will of my heart and humanity to pursue the fulfillment of carnal hunger, that I completely suppressed the possibility of our reconciliation. And since that callous feeling had overtaken my emotions, I was inescapably trammeled within false and superficial confines of sexual desire and mortal sin. It began with casual dinner nights and lunches with Helen that soon transmuted into fervent trysts and inevitably a clandestine extramarital affair. I had Helen accompany me for business trips I was supposed to conduct alone. I was staying late hours at office using work as an excuse to spend countless illegitimate evenings with her. My relationship with Audrey was at the threshold of destruction and demise. Her presence meant nothing to me anymore. In fact it became a source of vexation now to see her face when I returned home after hours of torrid lovemaking with Helen. I had contemplated possibilities of a divorce and thoughts of separation had crossed my mind numerous times. I did not know what constrained me from proceeding on with it, but every time such thoughts traversed my mind, they were replaced by something more imminently gratifying like money or Helen, but it never exited my subconscious.

While I began seeking company elsewhere, Audrey resorted back to her mother's for most of the time during the day. I wasn't certain of the persuasions, feelings and thoughts that went in her mind, but all I saw in her was a stoic, ineffectual mannequin that lingered around me but never spoke unless enticed to answer. I never invited her to accompany me to social parties or gatherings anymore, and she never participated in the ones that were held at my house. She would lock herself up in the bedroom and remain there for the rest of the night. Her mother visited sometimes but their conversations were limited to her health and well-being. Our confrontations that grew in the recent time were now scarce and very brief, if they ever transpired, as Audrey opted to prevent engagement in any argument as soon as she would intuit one gaining ground. Her conduct brought our lurching world of marriage to a standstill. And that led to the day when I approached my counselor at the behest of my love, Helen, and instructed him to proceed with the preparations of an official separation.

I sat in my office reading the divorce documents as I received them after a visit from my counselor that morning. I was unaware that I was about to experience a whole another level of unfathomed satisfaction that noon out of a situation that was an absolute surprise to me. No, it wasn't the event when Audrey would accept our separation without contest or finalize the divorce with her signatures, I hadn't even gotten close to bringing her the papers. But it was to emanate from an entirely different person. Harry walked inside my office and I disrupted my gaze from the papers.

"Can I talk to you for a moment, sir?"

"Yeah, Harry?"

"I've brought someone to see you."

"Who is it?" I asked.

"James Gosham." My brows converged at the sound of that name, Harry continued. "I hope you remember him from our previous job? He's out of work right now, in fact since a very long time and quite beaten and homeless. He came to me last night begging for work and I promised him I'll look into it."

"Did you?" I stirred in my chair and leaned forward with excitement and anticipation.

"I told him about you and how you've become so successful. I know you're generous enough to consider his situation and give him some work, only a little to hold on to."

"James? Now, that is a pleasant surprise."

"Should I bring him in?"

"Yeah, please. I'd love to see him."

After a moment the door opened to the man who once insulted me and threw away my idea along with me out of his office. This time the places were reversed, but his appearance seemed even worse than mine when I stood across his desk imploring for assistance. He walked in as I shifted back on my chair with a wry smirk across my face.

"James B. Gosham, look what the wind blew in." I teased.

"George." He spoke in a hoarse voice.

"Uh-uh, my friends call me that, for you it's Mr. Bailey or better, sir."

James' effortful smile vanished from his face. Harry struck a glimpse at me.

"I think it's better that he leaves." Harry said indignantly.

"No, no Harry, let him stay. And you as well. The more the merrier to watch a proud man humbled, right? You know how glorious it feels when you accomplish something you once swore to achieve. Someone's humility for example. Take a seat, there's a lot to watch."

"I need to speak to you, sir, can I sit down?" James spoke never attempting to look me in the eye.

"No, you stay right where you are. I want to relish this sight and I also want you to take a look around yourself and realize how it feels to be on the other side of the table and be humiliated by someone who doesn't have any idea what consequences it might hold for him in the future."

"Can we forget all of that, please Mr. Bailey?"

"Forget? Forget what you did to me? If it were up to you, I'd still be working in a 4 by 4 cabin answering phone calls, resolving grievances, right? Isn't that what you said?"

"I'm sorry."

"Now are you? With utmost certainty?"

"I mean it. I need a job. I desperately need a job."

"What happened? Mr. Gardon heard rumors of your grave mistakes and kicked you out of his company?"

"He fired me."

"Of course he did, your arrogance, your pride cost him greatly. Do you know where he heard it from?"

"I'll do anything you want me to, George... Mr. Bailey, cleaning, scrubbing floors, security, I'll stand outside your door all day long, but I need a job."

"Harry, look at him. He once used to be your boss. Today he stands before you as a beggar."

"Mr. Bailey-" Harry began, but I cut him right there.

"Shut up Harry, let him plead. I'm enjoying myself here, aren't you? Look at his face, he can't hold your gaze anymore. His back is bent, his pride is seeping out of him and I'll make sure there's not one drop of it left in him. Derive pleasure out of this, he has a humble request for us. But you know what? I'm a compassionate man. I will give you a job, but only if you do all that I ask."

"Anything you want."

"Get down to your knees and beg me for it."

"George..." Harry arose in anger. I discounted him.

"What?" James asked in tears.

"Get on your knees and beg for it." I stood up waiting.

James got up and slowly came close to me and staggered down to his knees as I towered before him. He joined his hands in supplication and began whimpering. "Please... Please...."

I laughed and enjoyed that moment of conceit and his humiliation. "Get this miserable man out of my sight."

Harry helped James up to his feet and took him out of the office as I stepped back to my desk in my triumphant, complacent glory and just when I was about to sit, I found Helen entering the store and waving to me on her way to the office. I greeted her at the door with a long passionate kiss and shut the door behind me.

"Oh wow, you're excited today. Who was that poor fellow?" She asked as she sensually positioned herself on my desk and crossed her legs allowing the slit dress to reveal her smooth upper thighs.

"An old adversary. I told you about him once. The same man who turned me down, now comes here begging for a job."

"And you made him cry? Poor guy, I didn't know you could be so cruel to people."

"You have no idea."

"I think I do." She referred to a bruise on her upper back that was inflicted some nights ago. "So did you give him a job?"

"I would never."

"No... that's not how you come back at your enemies, George. You should have given him a job and made him understand your actual worth. You should have him enter that door every day and address you as sir and wait for you to command him the rest of day's work. You should let him watch you day by day and realize and regret his mistake of misjudging your abilities. You should have him stand by your desk like an obedient pet, a dog and his master. That's how you avenge insult."

"You know, you surprise me with something new about your character every day. I have an obstinate penchant for heartless women."

"Well, how do you like it so far?"

"I don't think words can do justice to my arousal right now."

"Then let's try a different method."

Just as I leaned forward to kiss her and slipped my hand between her thighs, the office door swung open. Audrey stood at the threshold, her initial gaze changed into a glare and her composed countenance altered into an incensed scowl.

"Audrey, it is so nice to see you again." Helen quickly pushed my hand away and dismounted the desk to shake hands with her. "How are you?"

Audrey responded with a fake smile and glowered at me, then averted my impenetrable stare and left without uttering a word. Helen shrugged and walked back to me.

"She doesn't know yet?"

"I don't know and frankly, I don't give a damn. But you aren't supposed to be here. Maybe that's what made her angry." I replied lighting a cigar.

"If you want I can leave." She said innocently.

"The damage is done, and it's not you who will be leaving now."

I retrieved the divorce papers from one of my drawers and put them down before her. She excitedly came over, opened the envelope and began reading the documents.

"Is it true we're going to be together now?"

"Looks like it. But until then, you're just a customer, so behave like one."

"Very well, Mr. Bailey, what do you have for sale now?"

"I am up for sale, would you care to buy?"

"Absolutely. But you're priceless."

Chapter Eighteen

໑໑໑

I returned home that evening to encounter certain abandonment in the air that permeated the rooms through open windows and fluttering draperies. There was nothing but dire silence except for the whistling winds that went sweeping into the hall and fading into oblivion. Even though, I did not look forward to finding Audrey's presence anywhere in this house or around me, but I still personally searched the rooms and made sure she was away. I had hoped to hand over the divorce papers and obtain her signatures on them to free myself of this damned marriage and stagnant relationship, but due to her absence, my intentions of expediting this process were delayed. I assumed she might have returned to her mother's residence and reverted to a doomed life replete with indigence and desolation and drudgery. And if it were to be true, I would be the most exhilarated soul on planet earth tonight. I just importuned my fate to be in my favor for this one last time. As far as her signatures were concerned, I had decided to transmit the documents to her via Harry. He was to arrive in some moments to submit the daily sales report to me, which was his routine and final chore for the evening. As I moved towards the stairs planning to get dressed for the night, I stopped by the aquarium and looked at the bubbling water and the inhabitants within. I saw something missing and just as I examined closely, I saw Audrey's goldfish afloat on the surface, dead. I removed it from the tank.

I appareled and groomed myself for a small gathering of friends I had arranged for tonight which was to begin in a few hours. By the time I reached downstairs, I saw Harry stepping in with his reports and spreading them open for review on the table.

"Harry, you will do one more task for me before you're done for the day."

"Yes, sir."

"Here, I want you to deliver this to Audrey. You know where she lives, right?"

"She lives here, doesn't she?"

Our eyes met at his comment, mine exuded a storm of aggravation and his expressed a motley of empathy, sorrow, outrage and despair.

"Do you know where she used to live?"

"Yes, sir."

"You will deliver these there. Now get going, you can go home after that."

"Yes, sir."

Harry accepted the envelope but delayed for a moment and gazed at me filled with remorse and dismay. He attempted to burden my soul with culpability, but I repudiated any such endeavors that were thrust at me. He looked down at the envelope, shook his head and went away.

Within an hour I began to welcome my guests for the evening. They were only a few, but important nonetheless. I greeted them all with short but ingratiating conversations and waited impatiently for Helen to arrive. As she did, I rushed over to her and took her into a small concave near the bar and kissed her passionately finally surprising her with the news of my divorce. She was delighted at the mention of it. We joined the hall and others after a couple of intimate moments together as she joined me in hosting the night.

"Hey, how's my man doing tonight?"

I flipped to see right behind me. "Alex!"

"You son of a gun, you nailed the deal with the Harsons. You know what? I always doubted you, but after this, I might have to give it to you." Alex entered with another stunner beauty by his side and startled me with his convivial nature after all that had happened.

- 112 -

"I told you so. Thanks for coming, Alex. I wasn't sure if you would."

"Come on now, forget the past. Don't worry about it too much. Hey, take a look at this, meet my fiancée Dasha Ivanova. She's from Russia, doesn't speak much English, but boy is she a game changer."

"She sure is." I shook hands with her as Helen joined in and offered them Champagne.

"Oh, I see that you're using her well enough." Alex said while kissing Helen on the cheek. "So tell me how's life treating you?"

"Not too bad, in fact, just as I want it to." I replied with a pompous laughter.

"Let me move closer to the bar, one glass of champagne isn't gonna do much good here." Alex and Dasha began meeting other guests on their way to the bar.

I glanced around and found everything just as I needed it to be, Helen stepped closer and landed a kiss. Just as we parted, I caught sight of Audrey making an ingress. She was dressed for the night seductively in a black mini dress, as I had never seen her before. Her face was aglow and her eyes sparkled. My delight suddenly effaced and I hastened over and took her by the arm trying to shove her off back outside and away from anyone's sight.

"What are you doing here?" I asked pulling her to a corner.

"Well, you forgot to send me an invite, so I allowed myself in. Is that a problem?" She responded with a smirk. "Did I do something wrong showing up like this?" She gestured at her dress.

"It would have been better if you didn't show up at all."

"Yeah, sometimes you realize that. But by the time you do, it's quite too late. Do you remember? A dark, rainy night, two people coming around the corner of the street, different ends? I just wish you didn't show up at all."

"I made a mistake."

"Good, you realize it. But quite too late, don't you think?"

"You need to leave, right now."

"What's the matter, don't you need a hostess tonight? Oh, I understand, you already have one. Never mind, I'll try to be a guest for the night, how about that? A guest in a house that I thought was my own. Isn't it a great feeling?"

She yanked away her arm from my clenching hand and amalgamated into the socializing invitees. I stayed close to her to make sure nothing unwanted is instigated. She joined the bar and met with Helen and Alex.

"How are you?" Audrey sounded pouring herself a drink.

Alex seemed a bit uncomfortable at first but then started with a smile. "Um... good and you? George's wife, right?" He answered trying to remember her name.

"Well, at least you remember who I am, Mr. Boaster."

"You remember my name?"

"Yes, I'm not that ignorant to forget the people I've met in my past, and especially those who've left a lasting impression on my life. I'm not that rich either to manifest my narcissism by forgetting names, am I Helen? How is my husband treating you? Must be good, why would you stick around otherwise?"

Helen and Alex were both speechless. I interrupted and pulled her away from them.

"What are you trying to do?"

"I'm trying to be friendly, see, am I doing well? I know I'm a work in progress, but we'll get there." She took a swig from her glass of scotch.

"When did you start drinking?"

"I always wanted to see what difference this makes. Why people so willingly fall for this little thing? And what does it do to change them so much. I do know now."

"I need you to leave."

"Come on, the party's only started, let me enjoy for a while. All I'm trying to do is entertain your guests. After all, I might get to sleep with one of them tonight. I'm sure the women are queuing up for you."

Audrey made her way behind the bar and poured herself another glass.

"You're out of a drink. Allow me to make you one." She poured champagne into Dasha's flute. "Anyone else? Helen, you seem to be avoiding alcohol. What is the matter, big plans for tonight?"

"How are you, Audrey?"

"Well, you tell me about that, I guess you know better about my situation than I do. Look at the progress you've made, few months ago you were just another slut wrapped around his arms. Today the sides changed and the man's changed, but you're still the same slut, aren't you? What's the next move, few months later another man perhaps? Do you see anyone eligible around here?"

"That is enough Audrey." I steamed in anger.

"Relax George, it's just friendly talk, isn't it Helen?"

Alex lighted a cigarette and puffed smoke.

"You might want to douse that, Alex. You don't want to hurt a mother's womb with all that smoke."

Everyone around that bar went silent, Audrey stared at all the shocked faces.

"Smoking is detrimental to an unborn child's health."

"What are you talking about?" I asked demandingly.

"Well, if you can't tell a woman apart who's three months pregnant, that's your problem, George."

"You're pregnant?" Helen inquired.

"No congratulations, not even from the father? Anyway, do continue drinking, that is hardly damaging."

Alex quickly put off the cigarette in the ashtray. I was as shocked as anyone else around that bar.

"George, I believe we all should leave now," Helen said.

"Oh no, don't spoil your sport because of this insignificant detail. I have something to make your night even more delightful. Here..." Audrey went for her handbag and rummaged for an envelope kept inside. She placed it on the tabletop. "Here we are. That calls for a celebration, doesn't it? After all, George's all yours now. How does that sound?"

Helen receded and scrambled away leaving the hall.

"Come on now, this is a night befitting revelry, wouldn't you agree, Alex?"

"George, I think Helen was right, we must leave you two at it. Be seeing you."

Alex took his fiancée and hinted the rest of the guests as they all began to depart at the inkling of escalating hostility between the host and his wife. The hall emptied. An everlasting silence between us.

"I didn't mean to ruin your celebration in any way, your guests were so important. If you want I could apologize to them. I definitely wouldn't want you to go to sleep all alone in a cold bed." Audrey said teasingly.

"You're pregnant?" I asked bluntly.

"Yes."

"Three months?"

"A little over."

"But you said you couldn't."

"Miracles do happen, right? I told you hope wasn't lost. And yes it is your child, don't you dare think otherwise. You came home drunk plenty of nights to find pleasure in the arms of your lovers, but unfortunately you ended up sharing the bed with me every time. You just couldn't recognize who lay under you."

"And this is how I come to hear about it?"

"Well, I made the effort of telling you myself this time as promised. You didn't tell me the manner in which I should inform you, so I didn't know how else to tell. Doesn't make a difference, does it?"

"It does to me."

"Since when, George? Since when?"

"Since right now, because that is our child."

"Nothing is ours, nothing. You just don't put it that way. This is my child, not yours. And you just asked for it to be only mine with this..." Audrey threw the envelope at me as the divorce papers were strewn all over the floor. "It is your money, it is your house, your wealth, your status, but this child is mine. You have nothing to do with it. Look at you, rich, esteemed, respected... arrogant, self-centered, alone, the poorest man I've ever seen. I pity you, I pity you. The day I entered your life I vowed never to leave you until I drew my last breaths with your name on them. I promised you love and I gave every bit of it I had. I tried every day, every hour to make it right between us but how... how could a man change so much? How could a man be so blind to everything around him? What madness had taken over you for you to regard love as evil and sin as good? In your depravity, you've ruined our lives. You've destroyed everything you and I had. I loved you, I loved you like no one else. I gave you everything, but not this time. I will never let you close to my child ever in my life. You wanted a divorce? There's your wish. Rejoice all you can, but don't ever call my child yours. "

Another moment of profound silence followed.

"Then get out of here." I said after a brief moment of hardening and a sigh. "I don't need you, I don't need anyone. Go back to that hole I took you out from. Go back to the filth you are so used to. I want you out of this house and out of my life. And listen to me, " I held her by the shoulder and pressed her close against me, "no matter what happens, don't ever come back and show your face again. Not yours and not your fucking offspring. Get out." I pushed her away.

Audrey braced herself, took in a deep breath and with tears streaming down her face, she ran off departing the hall, the house and my life forever.

Chapter Nineteen

❧❧❧

"Mr. Bailey... wake up... wake up..."

Such faint noises gradually gained substance in my dozing senses. I was awakened out of a deep sleep and introduced to a throbbing hangover by Harry who stood leaning by my side and shaking me up.

"What are you doing here in the middle of the night?"

"It is actually the middle of the day." The response came from him.

I had slept in my den upon my office chair and was still in my clothes from last night, crinkled and unkempt. I realized I held onto a bottle of bourbon which had rested placidly upon my stomach for all this time until it slipped and crashed on the floor. I sat in here last night thinking about a lot of things, a lot of mistakes I had made, a lot of words I had said. Harry took his chair right across the desk and waited for me to rekindle my consciousness while I massaged my aching head.

"I just came here to get these checks signed, some miscellaneous payments need to be made. And I'll be off right after." He cut right to business.

"Have a seat, Harry. Talk to me for a while." I implored.

"I am seated, sir. But I have to return to work, the store needs to be opened."

"What? It isn't even 10 yet?"

"No, sir. But for me it is the middle of the day."

"Sir? Mr. Bailey? What is the matter? I used to be your friend."

"Yes, you used to be my friend. Now, you are my employer."

"And that changes anything?"

"It changed you." His gaze at me was stern and unyielding. "Please sign these and I shall leave."

"Even you wouldn't want to spend a moment with me? Listen to what I have to say, tell me where I went wrong? Just for once?"

He fell silent following my supplication. Then finally took a deep breath and leaned toward me.

"What is the matter, George?"

"Audrey is with a child, my child."

"That's wonderful news. Where is she? I need to congratulate her."

"She's left me. The papers you took to her place last night were annulment papers."

"No George, she didn't leave you. You made her leave."

"I know it is my fault..."

I poured myself another drink and took a swig from the glass as Harry watched in utter silence.

"George, I've watched you ruin your life in the past years like a mad man. I don't know for what reason, but you have destroyed your family, your relationships, your soul and everything you loved. You've done it yourself. You aren't the man you used to be. And that woman, your wife, was the only thing that kept you from taking your adamance, your arrogance, your crazy behavior too far. Now that you've lost her too, you won't survive for long. Audrey loved you. Without conditions, that woman loved you. She still does. She's carrying your child inside of her, what else do you want from her? This is your personal life and I shouldn't be prying in such matters but for someone like Helen, you left her? Helen's never going to be yours, ever. You're just a rung of a ladder she needs to climb. You're just a part of that plan. But Audrey will remain your wife no matter the things you do to her. Bring her back. You cannot afford to live without her and she can't survive without you. You need her by your side. Bring her back."

"You think she will talk to me again, forgive me?"

"I'm sure she will."

Abruptly, the phone rang. Harry stretched out to pick the receiver to answer.

"Hello? Yes..." Suddenly his eyes grew wide in shock. "What are you talking about? How the hell did that happen? No, no, we're going to be right there."

"What happened?" I asked solicitously.

"There's been a burglary. Everything's gone."

Harry and I hastened to the city and after dangerously speeding and a couple of reckless turns, we finally reached our store. There was a crowd of police officers securing a perimeter around the front entrance sealing the sidewalk with yellow barrier tape. Pedestrians continued to move but glanced in curiosity. We swiftly jostled through the lines introducing ourselves as the owner and manager and entered the store. The interior was completely ravaged. Destroyed shelves, cabinets, closets, counters, with shattered glass and ornaments strewn all across the floor. All the valuables missing, some abandoned in urgency. A complete devastation. The store employees who were already there were being questioned by a detective. I stood in disbelief upon the ruins of my life right before my eyes. A detective moved toward me.

"Are you George Bailey, the owner of this establishment?"

"He is." Harry replied in my stead.

"I'm detective Grant and I have a couple of questions for you if you may..."

I staggered away from him stepping further to view the desolation of my dreams and future.

"I can help you with your inquiry, detective." Harry responded commiserating with my stunned soul. "But can we delay this for a while, just a little bit?"

"Take your time."

Harry came with an alleviating grasp around my shoulders and took me inside my office. He made me sit down and sighted the open safe under my desk.

"They didn't leave the cash either. It's all gone. I'm going to phone our insurance, and ask them to send somebody over right away. George, don't worry about anything, it will be all right." A reassuring smile spread across his face. He gave me a glass of water.

"It won't be all right, Harry. It's all over." I said stoically.

- 120 -

"Hey listen, I'm going to call some people and I'll be right back. Just don't give up, not yet."

"It is my fault."

"Nothing is your fault, it's just bad time that does this to people. Just stay here, okay?" Harry exited the office and returned after some time with the detective accompanying him.

"Who usually closes up here?" The detective asked.

"I do. And just like any other day, I closed the store last night at 7pm and left with the keys in my pocket, which I still have."

"Anybody else would have access to the keys beside you?"

"Well, just the owner, Mr. Bailey himself. Just two set of keys. I open and close this place, no one else."

"Well, I don't know if you are aware of this, but there were no signs of breaking in. The door and the lock were not even tampered with."

"But how is that possible?"

I stayed wordless and watched them both converse sitting down before me.

"I was hoping I would get that answer from you."

"There is no way a duplicate copy of our keys could be made. I secure and guard my keys with my best intentions, detective."

"I do not mean to imply any allegations at this point, sir. I'm just trying to do my job, and a part of it is asking questions and finding possible suspects. So, if you would cooperate, it will be appreciated."

"Yes."

"Have such occurrences of theft or tampering happened in the past?"

"None."

"Are there any indications of doubt that you might have observed, that may involve any other employee that works here?"

"No, I trust all of them. They all have been here for a long time."

"No such interrogation would be necessary, detective. I think I have an answer to all your questions." An alien voice interrupted their conversation.

I looked up to find our insurance agent being accompanied by a man whom I was introduced to at the initiation of this store. This was a claims inspector appointed by our insurance company. He walked in a smirk across his face, our agent was wordless next to him.

"And you are?" The detective inquired.

"I am a claims investigator, employed at Hartfield Insurance Inc., here's my card. This particular business comes under my, in your language, jurisdiction. I believe I'm stepping in quite early into the matters than I'm supposed to, but what can I say, I couldn't resist."

"What do you have to tell us?"

"I was thinking maybe Mr. Bailey was willing to cooperate with us and walk us through what happened last night."

I shot a look at him.

"Mr. Bailey? What are you talking about?" Harry cut in defensively.

"After all, it is a matter of fault and liability, isn't it, Mr. Bailey?"

I stayed but a torrent of emotions arose within me, I was incensed as well as guilty at the same time.

"Shall I go ahead then? Very well, detective, you might have noticed the door and its lock was in an unusually decent and unagitated condition which is quite unlikely and implausible in such situations of intrusion, trespass, vandalism and above all, grand larceny. On the contrary, it is mostly noted that such crimes involve forceful breaking and entering and sometimes even destruction of the outer walls which in this establishment are just glass, therefore, easier to break. But no such force was implied at all. Why is that? Mr. Bailey? Oh, come now, it is in our best interest to know the truth, and a monumental claim of fifteen million dollars, one answer is the least you can elicit for such a handsome reward."

"I will kill you, you fucking bastard." I lunged at him with wrathful intentions to tear him into pieces. The detective and Harry distanced me from him.

"Our guilt surfaces in the form of violence. Unfortunately, that wouldn't help you here much. The truth is Mr. Bailey had left the door of his storefront open from midnight until the time the crime was committed."

"Open?" Harry was astounded.

"Open, unlocked, unsecured, unattended, call it what you may like, but he entered this shop late last night and left without closing the doors to protect his business from this unfortunate incident."

"How dare you say that?" Harry stood up demandingly.

"I have a video tape to prove that Mr. Sherwen. What did you think Mr. Bailey, a claim worth fifteen million and I wouldn't afford a closed circuit camera across the street? Our company takes good precautions when such high stakes are involved. So, when would you like a viewing of the tape, detective?"

"As soon as it is made available." Detective replied.

"Follow me."

"That still doesn't make a difference, we will file our claim." Harry insisted.

"You may do as you like, sir. But there is a liability clause in the agreement that your employer signed, and it clearly states the responsibility of the superintendent to secure the workplace, without any exclusions, specifically lock and secure the storefront in order to file a claim in the event of a forced break-in and burglary. This tape gives an entirely different story. And just between the two of us, what if I was to insinuate the detective on the possibility of a self staged theft. You know that is crime, don't you? We're not catnapping with our heads on our desks, not anymore. But I must applaud your endeavor, it was a nice try. Just before I leave, it's usually a rather protracted, onerous procedure to ascertain if you are found guilty of fraud and deception but I will personally make sure it isn't this time. I believe my work here is over. It was nice seeing you gentlemen. Goodbye now."

The detective led the insurance workers out of the office as Harry and I remained thunderstruck inside our enclosure. He fell back on a chair, disconcerted. I pushed my desk in rage and toppled it over.

"What did you do, George? Why did you come here?"

"I needed some cash, Helen asked me for it. She said it was something important. I was drunk, I came and took the money from the safe and left."

"Left without closing the door? Left without locking? This is New York City, every little gang of hoodlums would have known you left this door open. What were you thinking?"

I stormed out into the shop and frantically threw things around and smashed the remaining erect cabinets and shelves to the floor. Harry quickly came out and restrained me, my anger subdued. The three attendants looked alarmed and aghast at my actions. I kneeled down and exploded into tears.

"I'm sorry, everything is finished. You all are out of work because of my stupid mistake."

"We can still come out of it unharmed, okay?" Harry leaned by my side and tried to alleviate my pain.

"Unharmed? What do you think this is? A game? A fucking game? This isn't a game..."

The front door opened and Audrey slowly stepped inside witnessing my hysterical condition. I was infuriated.

"What are you doing here? Who called you here?" My voice resounded in the demolished ruins.

"I called her." Harry replied.

"What happened?" Audrey asked in tears and concern.

"Don't you see what happened? I'm finished, that's what happened. Aren't you glad? There you have the moment you've waited for. It's time to laugh at me, humiliate me. Go ahead, I'm nothing now. I can hear your laughter all around, great job, Audrey. Really."

"I'm sorry, George." Tears ran down her face.

"You're sorry? Oh, that'll make everything right. Aren't you glad to see all this? Look around yourself, you've won. That is what you wanted right? To teach me a lesson, that's what you wanted? Oh, you must have prayed for it with all your heart, didn't you? Well, have a long look at your triumph."

"George, she's just here to help you." Harry came forward.

"Help me? I don't need her fucking help. Not anymore. Tell her to go away. She left me once, it shouldn't be that hard. Get the fuck out of here, all of you, right now." I charged out of the store and slammed the glass door shut behind me.

I drove that entire afternoon until day descended into the womb of darkness just as my fate had drowned into the quagmire of misery and misfortune. I had contemplated resorting to a distracting company of a lover, but as I approached Helen's dwelling, I was informed by her maid of her indefinite travel to Belize with a business associate who was someone she had acquainted with last night. Those details, which I didn't ask for, ignited my wrath to an extreme as I recklessly sped away from there forever. I decided to return home and retire into barren solitude of my existence hoping to efface myself into oblivion and never be found again.

I came to a screeching halt and exited my vehicle, defeated and wasted. As I entered the grand mansion, soon to be relinquished, I heard muffled voices emerging from the dining. I made my way to the doorway and the conversation became more discernable to my befuddled senses.

"He's shattered inside, Audrey. But he needs you right now." Harry insisted.

"I don't know if he wants me here." Audrey responded in tears.

"I know he does, he just wouldn't admit it, that stubborn son of a bitch. You know how he is."

"It's been five hours since he left, I'm worried, Harry."

"I'm afraid if he comes to know the truth, he might do something foolish." Harry announced in a concerned manner.

"What truth?"

"I don't know if I should tell you, or anyone. Promise me he'll never come to know about this."

"Is it something about the theft?"

"I went to police to see the video footage from last night. I did see George leaving the place sometime after midnight and then three masked men, the perpetrators, came in. But before them, I saw someone else."

"Who?"

"James Gosham, passing down and looking inside the store as if he was there to do something, something wrong. This is the same man who affronted George at Gardon Inc. and this is the same guy who came asking for work that day and George insulted him quite blatantly."

"You think he did it?"

"There is a possibility. I haven't told the police about him yet, but I think so."

"What if George knows?" Audrey suspected.

Chapter Twenty
୧⁓୧⁓୧⁓

I drove downtown and swerved onto one of the streets in some hardscrabble neighborhood and sought the address of the man I wanted to question. All the houses lined down the street were dilapidated and lacked collective sustenance scattered in an inconsistent, disorganized construction pattern. This was no way near a planned neighborhood. I asked a couple of young men that dallied in the shadows of a corner store for Gosham's place and they pointed to the fifth one on the left after long, suspicious stares. I pulled over right outside and retrieved a baseball bat from the trunk of my car and headed off toward one of the rickety structures. I stormed inside after kicking open the swinging door and with a veil of madness enshrouding my reasoning. I looked for James with the most deadliest of intentions in my mind. James came into the room and stopped dead in his tracks, stunned and terrified. Without a word, I slammed the wooden bat on the first thing that came in my way and it was small dining table placed in the corner of the room. The wallop crushed a plate underneath and rattled the table. The impact sent two glasses flying into the air and plummeting to the floor shattering to fragments.

"What are you doing?" He demanded fearing ramification.

I took him by the lapels and slammed him against the wall leaving an indentation in the pitiful construction.

"You fucking son of a bitch." I landed a hard whack into his abdomen. "You planned this for a long time, didn't you?"

"What are you talking about?"

"Don't you play games with me, you dumb fuck. You thought I wasn't gonna know, you thought you could get away with it?"

"I don't know what you're saying." He implored.

"What the hell were you doing outside my store last night? You waited, didn't you? You fucking degenerate. Now where you gonna go? Did you enjoy yourself while you gloated over my destruction?"

"I didn't do it, George."

"You lying bastard. I'm going to finish you." I shoved him down against the couch. "Where's my stuff? Here's what I'm going to do, you give me my stuff back and I let you go. You aren't going to ruin me, you know I can't file an insurance claim, you know that. So give me my stuff and I let you live. Give me my stuff!"

"You're making a mistake."

"You're the one who's making the mistake, don't mess with me. Don't lie to my face. Right now, where is my stuff?"

"I don't know anything about it."

"You know there's one thing I despise the most in this world. That is when people like you try to act innocent because you're not. So, show me where it is and I let you go, right now."

James thrust forward and pushed me back. As I stumbled but regained my ground, he took off running toward the door. I grabbed the bat and swung at him hurtling it across the room. The bat hit him in the back as he tripped and fell right against a protruding edge of a chair. His head was smashed against it and a large open gash appeared spanning his forehead. He lay stretched out on the floor unconscious and bleeding uncontrollably. I was aghast. I did not mean to kill him. I slowly moved over and watched his lifeless body. Just as the thought of escaping this ramshackle place before any incriminating charges associated with this incident might begin to develop entered my mind, the door opened once again. I turned and saw Harry enter in surprise and marvel at my presence there. He stood there thunderstruck as the pool of blood expanded on the floor soaked all in its path, at the body that lay motionless, and his friend who was just about to be labeled a murderer.

"What did you do, George?" Harry walked closer with fear in his eyes.

"I didn't mean to kill him, Harry. I swear, I didn't want to kill him. I came in here to do it, but I couldn't. This was an accident. He fell and hit his head."

"Let's go, George, we have to get out of here. Right now. We need to leave."

Harry grabbed me and the weapon I brought in and dragged me out of that room and possibly hell. We leaped into my car as he began heedlessly accelerating through the routes of downtown.

"I didn't kill him, Harry, believe me." I watched the passing buildings from my passenger side window.

"I believe you, the police won't. You have to leave the city, George."

"Leave, what do you mean leave? I can't run away."

"That's the best thing you can do right now. You were not in this city when James died."

"I can't go away."

"George, you're not thinking clearly, are you? A man is dead, investigations are going to link him somehow to the burglary and if they get a slightest idea that this wasn't an accident, they are going to come after you. He was there last night, and he's in the tape. There's enough evidence of hostility between the two of you, I will not be able to do anything if that happens. You must leave. I'll take care of everything else."

"But where am I going to go?"

"Someplace far from here. You left this afternoon for a business meeting with some of your contacts, that's all. You will be back after some time. Stay there for a while, I'll be in contact."

Harry drove me across New Jersey to a small town. We waited at a bus stop in the middle of an isolated highway inside a grungy waiting area with only a handful of passengers awaiting the bus. He bought me a ticket and handed it over to me, I didn't even look at my destination. He also brought along a bag of eatables for the trip. He took a seat by my side and attempted to strengthen me as I went on in arrant hysteria, quivering with fear.

"Don't worry about anything here. I will take care of it all. He probably won't even be recognized. I did not tell the police about seeing him in the video. They wouldn't know to link his death to the theft. Even if they do recognize him, there are plenty of ways I can turn this around and make it look like a gang feud. They stole from us and fought each other off for the money."

"Then why do I have to leave?"

"Just for some time, in case if anything goes wrong, in case if they do find out. I want you to be as far from an accusation as possible. Once everything is settled, you come back. All right?"

"What about... Audrey and... our child?"

"Well, you're going to meet a newborn when you return. She'll be fine. I promise. That's my responsibility to take care of her."

A bus came into parking outside. People began to rise and board.

"There we are. I'll stay in touch, anything you need, money, clothes, let me know."

"You've done so much for me, Harry. How can I repay?"

"You don't. That's the thing about friendship, there are never any dues."

"Do one thing for me, tell Audrey, I'm sorry."

Harry smiled at this, "she'll be glad to have you come back home."

I ascended the vehicle, went up to my seat and glanced at him through the window.

"Take care of yourself." Harry said with a wave of his hand.

The bus began to move down the road. I waved to him and then shifted back on my seat to look forward at the looming darkness ahead of the road, devoid of light, devoid of destination. I glanced around, watchful for any eye that might be fixed upon me, but there were none. Most of the passengers opted to sleep for the remainder of the night, their resting heads against the cushion of their seats and placid faces caused a surge of unease in my mind as I envied their peaceful slumber. But I knew I couldn't close my eyes even if I wanted to as the burden of guilt was too great, and not just of the recent incident with Gosham, but many more, and those images fleeted before my eyes one after another reminding me of the faults, mistakes and errors I had committed. So, I sat back with eyes wide open and permitted them to criminate me all they wanted as we rode on into the night.

Chapter Twenty-One

ço·ço·ço

I had been away for quite some time now, perhaps five months, I had lost count. Within this time I was driven to change the towns and the motels I stayed in. I was instructed not to remain at one location for too long, and while a constant supply of capital arrived my way in face of a money order nearing about a hundred a week, I had no reason to dally. As my prosaic life continued, I stayed in touch with Harry via brief telephone calls in which we refrained from mentioning names, but conversed mainly about each other's well-being as well as Audrey's health in her toilsome condition. I was content to hear positivity time after time as I inquired, while a hidden fear of losing her at the time of childbirth still lingered in my mind. More time began to fly past as I traveled like a nomad from town to town and with all the spare hours to do nothing but sit in the shadow and reflection of my incommutable past, I began to despise myself. As much as I attempted to avert such thoughts resulting in self-hatred, I couldn't barricade them from entering my mind and leaving me to feel more abject as they departed. The things I had done, the people I'd hurt, and most of all, I had failed those who had loved me in return. I had lost everything I had put together. Our insurance claim was annulled due to evidenced failure of the possessor to ascertain measures to protect property from harm, our home and other valuables were auctioned to settle the debts of our suppliers and outstanding purchase orders. The store was eventually relinquished and the savings, or I shall say what was left of the accounts after my profligate splurges, came to a total amount of thirty-seven thousand, which was transferred to Audrey's possession upon my requisition and it was the only thing that went according to my liking. Through this onerous process I was fortunate to have Harry settling things down with a legal power of attorney to act in my stead and make decisions on my behalf. Though, they were always consulted. But bearing in mind that I had just lost every single material thing I owned down to the last penny, it was now safe to assume that my life was yet again over.

I was a free man, free as a bird that had nothing to lose anymore, neither to gain. It was almost as if I were a newborn, only that I wasn't a child anymore. It was the kind of life that was appreciated by many, but I despised and hated the very possibility of being subjected to it. That very idea of being stationary in purpose and never moving forward frightened me to the core, but that's where I was headed. Thoughts would dance in my brain one after another, and most of them would be self-destructive, but as it is said that nothing lasts forever whether it is the delight of happiness, or tears of sorrow, both are transient.

I came across news of becoming a father which was like a streak of hope in brutal darkness. For a moment all my ills were mended, all my sorrows alleviated, my life had come across a welcome change that was to be a new dawn in my misery. I was desperate to see my child, our child, but I was told Audrey hadn't returned home from the hospital for two weeks after facing some complications during childbirth and there was no one else to be imputed for her condition but me. I had given her too much pain to bear along with this child and I was guilty of that. I also had to wait until Harry deemed it safe for me to return and reunite with my family as the case of Gosham's death was still pending investigation. For the first time since I left New York I was eager to return and that eagerness was boiling to a point where I began to count days and hours in impatience and restlessness. All I could think about was my wife and my child. Whether I was sleeping or awake, their faces filled my eyes day and night. I kept asking Harry if I could come back and see them both, but he'd always delay and tell me to wait a little longer. But when I couldn't bear it anymore, I decided it was time for me to go back home with or without Harry's consent.

I rushed to leave that monotonous routine that had kept me afar from my family for too long now. I showered and attired myself in a newly bought jacket from a thrift shop. I paid up my balance at the motel and hastened to a railway station boarding the next train back to New York and arrived at Penn Station at 7:30 in the morning. My destination was an address provided to me by Harry which was a new home he'd helped Audrey mortgage up in New Hyde Park with the savings money she was left with. My excitement was inimitable, my happiness at the summit as I rode in a taxi cab after picking up a bouquet of roses from the corner flowery. I finally arrived and requested the driver to stop a couple of houses away. I paid the fare and alighted consuming the fresh and familiar air. I gathered enough courage to finally see my wife and child after months and began walking towards the house. I suddenly stopped and concealed myself behind a tree. It was back again, the innocuous mind and its troubling thoughts.

"Where am I going?" I thought to myself. "Look at that place, finally a home full of happiness, laughter, a newborn child, only because it's not yours, because you've stayed away from it. If you enter their lives once more, it wouldn't be any different than before or any other home you've been a part of. All you can bring with you is ruin, misery and devastation. And even if you do see them, live with them, your contentment is always momentary, isn't it? Don't you know yourself? What will happen when you should leave that house and seek wages? Will you go back to the city that shrouded you with disgrace, humiliation? The people that ridiculed you, made a criminal out of you? Will you be able to work amongst them who once showered you with honor but now shall look down upon you with disdain as a mere employee, a worker?"

I saw Harry stepping out of the house glancing at his watch, Audrey accompanied him to the stairs with a newborn in her arms. I managed a long look at the heavenly face of our child and I knew it was a girl as she was wrapped in a pink blanket, wore an ornate pink headband and had big brown eyes like her mother's. I then glanced up at Audrey who was beautiful as ever and glowing. There was an aura of delight that surrounded her. Harry kissed the child and conversed with Audrey for some time before leaving in his car down the road. Audrey scanned the entire block with her anticipating eyes and then stepped back in shielding the baby from the cold. I watched all this secretly and marveled at my cursed fate.

"Did you see her? She's content, she's happy after such long years of sorrow and sadness. Did you see that child? Will you give her all the love she deserves? Do not destroy their lives once more, because destroy you will. Go back, that child deserves a better father than you, Audrey deserves a better husband than you. Leave and never come back. Let them spend their lives in happiness, don't take it away from these innocent souls. You are damned to bring ruin upon all who love you. Do you know what will happen when that child grows? She will see a man who abandoned her mother, she will see a man who lost everything he had to his rage and pride. She will find out that you never wanted her. And she will see a man who killed...."

I looked away disgusted with myself.

"You want her to be called the child of a murderer? You want her to face that disgrace for the rest of her life? You are nothing but a coward, a man who ran away from his family, his responsibilities, a man who should be in prison. Go back, they don't need you anymore. Harry will take care of them. Remember what Audrey once said to you, she will never let your shadow close to her child. They have what they need, and you are not a part of it. Go away. Go away now."

I did not know if it was the right decision to make, but I...

PART II

Chapter Twenty-Two

ↄ·ↄ·ↄ

Light drizzle had quickly altered into heavy sleet as we moved past the hoardings that welcomed us into Indianapolis. Traffic was scarce and speeds were slower due to a fear of skidding into the mouth of mishap. I watched the frozen droplets pelt the window with a faint, continuous crepitation. It was very late at night, in fact well after midnight, and the bus was in a dire need of a respite after gurgling down the highway for almost four hours which soon became a concern for the driver. Just as we pulled into our stop, he took an initiative to inform the passengers that some minor engine repairs are required and will be taken care of at this stop which could take a little longer than expected. Hence, our departure might be delayed as a consequence. This elicited a unanimous hiss of deep breaths and sighs as some of the passengers had no intention of leaving their seats, or for that matter, their sleep as most of them had planned to spend the rest of the night, even this stop included, in their world of dreams. They couldn't be blamed for it as they already had their dinner stop few hours ago and no one was planning to have a midnight snack, except one. I hadn't eaten at our last stop and hoped I could outlive the night on the steak sandwich that I was given by Louise earlier that evening, but I was proving my gut feeling wrong as I was famished by now. As the bus came to a lurching halt, everyone was asked to exit the bus and find comfort in a small rest stop that had two food stalls and numerous sets of tables and chairs that were instantly occupied by haggard passengers, most of whom were still in slumber and hadn't disrupted their dreaming. But out of the few who were still awake and in good senses, there were two who still hadn't let this ordeal interrupt their conversation.

"Was that the last time you saw them?"

We took a table near the glass window from where a nice view of the dark parking lot, now soaked and gleaming, filled my sight. I looked back to my progressing conversation with Louise who just gazed back at me with the most probable appearance of empathy she could muster across her creased face.

"Yes, it was. Though, as much as I wanted there to be one more time, for that one last look at them maybe just a glimpse, I never went back to New York. I was glad that Harry had taken good care of them both. He had managed to gather up the remains of our business holdings, property and stocks and everything that could be liquidated and provide a future for my family. Audrey had a home in a safe neighborhood with some savings that could feed them both for quite some time. I was happy to see that. That was the most anyone had ever done for me, probably more than I could do for them under the circumstances. He was a true friend, the only friend. And I had hurt him a lot. I had hurt everybody."

"We do make mistakes, we all do. Always distrusting the right people because of our failure to differentiate them from the rest. But realizing that mistake is enough for those who love us."

"I wanted to return to them, apologize for my faults and ask for their forgiveness. I just couldn't go. It frightened me, the idea of looking into their eyes and standing before them, it scared me."

"I understand." She took a mouthful of peanuts and crunching them to bits with her dentures she revived me out of my despondency. "Was that the end of it?"

"That was the time when I finally decided to move on and let them be. But it wasn't the last of my misfortune. There was a lot more to come."

A sudden announcement shook everyone out of their lethargy as the driver leaned inside the door and declared that the damage was a negligible one to the front wheel bearings which caused the vehicle to make noises and that it was fixed now. He added that if everyone agreed the bus was ready to depart to which all heads nodded and all bodies stormed out towards him exiting the lounge and filling up the bus again. I quickly made a trip to the Chinese food stall and ordered myself a Chicken Entree. They wrapped it up almost instantly as I picked up the bag, paid for it and joined the horde with Louise by my side.

"You're hungry, aren't you?"

"Yeah, you never know what memories might depress you into binge eating late at night, especially when you're moving cross-country on four wheels."

"Make that six."

"See, even worse."

"Hmm... as they say, shared sorrow is half a sorrow."

Chapter Twenty-Three
ço·ço·ço

Some months had passed since my visit to New York and since I had seen or heard any of those I left back there. I knew there was nothing that could efface their memory from my mind, but I matured and grew to be fond and appreciative of my decision. Although, the scarce repository of my funds almost depleted, I continued to travel as farther away from Audrey and our daughter as I could, distancing them from desolation that followed my fate and afflicted all those who involved themselves in my life. I would never forget them no matter how far I went or how much I tried. That part of my life will always accompany and remind me and it almost seemed that I had left a little bit of myself or rather my soul back there, with Audrey and my daughter. At times I would curse my conscience in seclusion of my damned life, but then forgave myself for being considerate of other existences around me. I banished my mind from reflecting on the past as I traveled halfway across the country and was now somewhere in Nevada, in a small town that didn't even have a name or maybe I just failed to notice. I had taken up a job at a local motel, the only one around, as a housekeeper. The employers, an elderly couple now unable to handle chores on their own, preferred a female prospect for the work, but concurred with a unanimous decision to try out a male for a change. Especially after I counter-offered to work for minimal wages, 15 hours a day, performing all job responsibilities to perfection along with some added strenuous work of loading and unloading of supplies, upkeep of the building, and painting of the rooms, which is what largely swayed my interviewers from their inclination to hire a woman. I had been in this town for two weeks and I was beginning to like it. Whatever time I was left with after work hours, I would either spend them in a tavern across the street, ruminating on life if it had been any different, or spend the remainder of it in my bed still pensive.

It was just another night when I sat at the bar drinking from a glass of scotch watching a game of pool from afar, finding a gang of bikers placing dollar bets on their inaccurate shots. A game of darts was in session on the other side of the joint, a couple of women in enticing clothing and personas playing, titillating smiles and excitement pervasive across their countenance. But there were only a few as hopeless and abject as I was. Suddenly a loud exclamation had every pair of eyes in the bar staring back toward a phone booth.

"You know what? Tell that fucker to shove his offer up his ass. I'm not up for that dumb shit, and I don't fucking care about him or the people he knows. You tell him that."

As I joined the spectators and glanced behind following the rest of the gazing crowd, I noticed a woman slam the receiver on the telephone inside the phone booth, swinging at the ajar door and storming out, charging towards the counter barking at the bartender.

"Give me a shot, Frankie." She said retrieving a cigarette from her handbag and lighting it up.

This woman was suddenly the center of attention which really didn't bother her much. She was probably in her late twenties with a certain gothic inkling to her appearance with dark make-up around the eyes, gel-hardened straight hair, a filigree cage bracelet with gunmetal crosses dangling from it and a black velvet choker with a green pendant attached to it. She was entirely attired in black, with high heeled shoes that gave her lace dress a classy look.

Frank tardily walked up to the counter and stood there staring back at her, heedless to her request.

"You know that phone don't come for free."

"I put my quarter in." She answered nonchalantly.

"I ain't talking about the quarter. The phone could'a broke."

"Well, it's working fine. You can go and check if you want, after my drink, of course."

"What did I tell you last night?" Frankie demanded impatiently.

"Come on Frankie, I know you weren't being serious." She looked up at him with converged brows.

"You think so?" Frankie stood there with his arms folded.

"Frankie, I work my ass off and come here after a week's hard work and this is what I hear from you? Do I have to beg you for one drink?"

"The only thing that looks to benefit me out of all this is that you returned. Now, that you're back and you're workin' hard, how about you show me some due respect and money?"

"I wasn't going to run away."

"Well, I thought differently. Look, I'm runnin' a business here not a goddamn charity. You pay all the past dues, you get a drink. You don't, you get the kick. And it ain't a small amount we're talkin', it's three hundred and forty-seven dollars. I ain't that rich to just let it go."

"Is that it? Is that all I owe?"

"Yes, that's how much you owe. And I still don't see no cash in front of me still."

"Can I write you a check?"

"Do I look like a fucking bank? You pay cash around here."

"In other words I should leave?"

"No, no, don't leave. Get the hell out of here."

"Hey, I got it." The two contentious faces turned towards me.

"What did you say?" Frankie questioned in surprise.

"I said I got it, now give her a drink and stop that blabbering."

"You mean the whole thing?"

"Not the whole thing dummy, what are you stupid or something? He means to buy me a drink." The woman cut in.

I reached for my wallet and put a five dollar bill on the countertop. A long stare followed from the bartender, but he receded with the money and poured her a shot. The woman was equally startled but continued to gaze at me even when I had looked away.

"Thank you." She said with a smile drawing my attention, but I was far from impressed. I nodded and turned back to my drinking.

"I know it's usually followed by a response, but I'm sure you'd want to hold that back, wouldn't you? Because if you did say you're welcome, you might be at risk of buying me another one."

"You're welcome." I said stoically.

"You're new around here? I haven't seen you much before?"

"I've seen quite a lot of you in the past week on the streets."

"Maybe I wasn't paying attention to my surroundings. What's your name?"

"Doesn't matter."

"Quite some name you have there, first name doesn't, last name matter?" She intuited I was disinclined to talk but persisted. "That's a nice way to begin a conversation, buying a lady a drink and refusing to tell her your name?"

"What makes you think I want to begin a conversation with you?"

"We live in a world where people fight their guts out for twenty-five cents at a Laundromat or a parking spot. You don't just buy anyone a drink without reason. I know your kind very well. You're one of those overbearing, complacent types who just can't get enough of themselves and treat every woman around them like a dumpster. What comes after this? Another one of those friendly invitations for "good times" which actually gets you to unleash all the dark, demented desires of a sex-crazed maniac that you are? I've had my share of dealings with men like you. I don't need all of that anymore. Thanks for your initiative, but I don't need any favors tonight. Frankie, return this gentleman's money back to his account and keep my watch here until I pay my stub. I'll be back tomorrow."

"George Bailey." I whispered loud enough for her to hear. She turned back to me and again wondered about my character. Frankie walked up to the counter reaching out for her wristwatch.

"Give me that back." She snatched her accessory back from him and planted herself back on the stool.

"George Bailey, yup, that's definitely not from around here, is it?"

"Nope."

"I thought so. I'm Marilyn McLord, nice to meet you." She shook my hand with an enthralling smile. As I looked intently at her, I discovered she hid years of endurance behind her eyes and that inviolable personality was just a shield to guard her from hostile and harsh environs in which she existed. But something about her read that it wasn't her true self.

"You too."

"Where are you from?"

"New York."

"Oh, how long have you been here?"

"Three weeks."

"I hope you don't mind whatever I said, I was just trying to get you to talk."

"Really?"

"Or you can say I badly needed someone to talk to me. Your refusal just sparked all that anger I was saving for that uptight bastard I was on the phone with some time ago. I'm sorry."

"You are quick to rant and regret."

"That's me, but what brings a city person like you to this forsaken town?"

"Time off."

"Time off, here in this hole?"

"I needed a vacation."

"George, this town literally spans three miles. All that you can possibly see here is located up and down a single street, and that's nothing more than hardware stores and thrift shops. What could possibly interest you here?"

"Sometimes you find peace in a lonely room."

"Oh, so that's the kind of time off we're looking for." Her eyes were more and more intrusive into the depths of my soul and vulnerability. "I totally mistook you for the wrong person. You're not that kind."

"Maybe I am."

"Then are you going to ask me to your room?"

"No, I don't know you. Who you are, what you do."

"I make people happy, especially those who buy me a drink."

I gazed at her as she laughed off her failures deep inside her heart.

"What do you do?" She asked wiping off a look of defeat from her face.

"Nothing much at the moment."

"Welcome to the club, but that doesn't surprise you anymore when you've lived here long enough."

"How long have you lived here?" I inquired.

"Long enough. You might want to keep this watch until I pay you back for the drinks tonight."

"I think you'll pay in time. I don't need to keep track of it, I don't need a security."

A smile emerged on her face, and countenance exhibited motley of emotions toward me, but her mouth stayed silent this time.

"I'll see you around then?" I gave her an affirmation with a nod. She walked off and out the bar into the drizzling night outside.

Frankie strolled over to me and leaned in for a quick talk.

"Look sir, I think you're a family man and it'd be better for you to steer clear of that woman. You don't know her yet, but once you come to realize what she does and how she makes her livin', you will regret havin' anythin' to do with her."

"What makes you think I don't?"

Frankie shrugged and walked away leaving me to a much desired state of mind - alone.

Chapter Twenty-Four

I was working hard at my day job, and even at nights my mind would travail in dire thoughtfulness of my estranged life. But it changed and a time came when I didn't give much thought to anything anymore. What I was doing, where I was going or supposed to go. I stopped making plans for the future as I knew it was futile wasting your time and brain to structure something that had no guarantee of being constructed. I had stopped burdening my head with these unnecessary, meaningless determinations. The present was my objective; there was no past or future for me anymore. I was living in today. Some night responsibilities at the motel had kept me from returning to my evening hot-spot for some days. But after a few, I did return to the bar one night with clear intentions of getting drunk and wasted. I was halfway there perched quietly upon the last stool across the bar when a strong hand landed before me clutching a twenty dollar bill and firmly slapping it upon the countertop.

"If you think I'm up for charity, you're wrong." Marilyn took a seat next to me glaring into my eyes with her erratic personality at question once again. "I'm not up for that, you know. When I say I will pay you back, I mean it."

"So you did, but it wasn't charity." I responded as coolly as I could.

"You don't just disappear like that. There are some of us trying to return favors here, and if you think you're all that rich to just give away your money spending it on women to impress worship out of them, then you chose the wrong one."

"It was an attempt at friendship. I was looking for one if you didn't notice."

"Well, I was waiting for you the whole past week to return what you paid for my drinks that day. I thought you went away, I thought you weren't coming back." A hint of honesty reflected in her eyes. "You don't know the urge I had to battle not to spend this money on make-up or shoes."

"Shoes?"

"Thrift shop. You can get good heels for twenty around here."

"Oh..."

"Where were you?"

"Thinking, and when I wasn't, working."

"I know where you work."

"You do?"

"I checked with them three days ago, they told me you had gone away."

"Not permanently. You know the moment when you suddenly realize after reminiscing for hours and hours that everything you've done in your life so far was nothing but a mistake, and you could have just completely turned it around if you kept your head in the right place. I just outlived that moment."

"Been there, done that, welcome to my world, George. What happened, girlfriend? Wife?" She took a swig from my glass.

"It's all over."

"Did she leave you heartbroken?"

"Let's just say she's better off without me. I don't want to talk about it anymore." Frankie refilled my glass with a wave of my hand and glowered at Marilyn on his way back. "You haven't told me anything about yourself, so far. I guess that how friendships begin."

"Yeah, that's the usual process, but why should I? You haven't, and I just asked you."

I took a long moment and sigh before I spoke again. "I had a wife and I left her because of some things I had done. She doesn't know where I am, but I know she is well and so is my daughter. And my very good friend has made sure of that. There you have it."

"That fucking asshole, your friend."

"What? No, you don't know what he's done for me. All the times he's stood up for me."

- 149 -

"And he finally rear ended you. Is your wife beautiful?"

"Indescribably."

"Well, there you have your reason why he stood by your side all this time. I know these types of men, the so called friends, it's nothing new."

"You have no idea what you're talking about. I'm fortunate to have him in my life."

"Okay, that's your take on it. Let's forget what's forgotten us."

"Right, now it's your turn."

"For what?"

"I've asked you before, where do you come from? What's your story?"

"When did you ask me that?"

"About a moment ago, and you dodged that pretty admirably."

"See, I'm so good at it, but there is something I'm so bad at, carrying on conversations. I don't even remember you asked me this just now. Conversations are so tedious, you know. Were you in New York the days you went missing?"

"You still haven't answered my question."

"What question?"

"No."

"Is that a question?"

"You asked me a question and I answered it. Did I go to New York, no I didn't. Where do you come from? Let's hear your answer."

"I wanted to go to New York once."

I had grasped that she wasn't open to talk about her past so I gave up my attempt to persuade her anymore.

"I know what you want to know, George. So here it goes, I'm a stripper and a prostitute and the good thing about that is my first profession is just part time. After all, I only spend about three hours taking off my clothes myself, the rest of the time it's the people taking off my clothes for me. Now, you have an option to offer me fifty for the night and you get to go berserk while you're at it, or disappear on me once again just like you did."

I waited for her to catch her breath. "Why didn't you?"

"Why didn't I what?" She asked.

"Go to New York?"

"Life had me going in loops. I couldn't make a straight trip there."

"And you thought I didn't know?"

"That I couldn't go to New York?"

"That you were a... dancer."

"Then why did you ask?"

"Is that what I asked?"

"That is something that usually attracts men toward me, or draws them away. Honestly, you seem like a man I could speak to, talk to, probably see every evening for a drink or two. By telling you the truth I might have lost you and I didn't want to start off with lies. People around here don't have a good opinion of the work I do, but they definitely enjoy it. There aren't many gentlemen around here who would offer to pay for my drink without asking for something in return. I don't think you have that on your mind. You seem different and you're still here. I was happy to gain a friend, which I haven't had in a long while. But I don't mean to impose upon you in any way. I possibly can't force someone to be a friend."

"Yeah, you can't."

"But I think we are, aren't we?" Her question was full of earnest imploration and eyes in honest pursuit of it.

"Maybe, if you buy me a drink."

I gestured at the twenty dollar bill that still lay on the countertop. She smiled and waved to Frankie for the tab. I stood up and left the bar.

I had walked off a good fifty yards from the tavern when I heard sounds of four inch heels tapping the wet concrete sidewalk behind me. Marilyn caught up in a moment and began to accompany me down my long walk home.

"Why did you do that?"

"I don't like to be thrown out of bars on my good days, and if I did have another drink, I would have passed out."

"Not that. Why did you pay off my account with Frankie?"

"Who said I did?"

"The bartender is an ass but he's at least honest. You paid in full, why did you do that?"

"I don't have a bank account or many places to spend. I put it to good use, better than just let it lie around in my motel room."

"For someone you don't even know."

"Well, I can't say that now, can I?"

"George, why did you do it?" She held my arm and stopped my stroll.

"It's a new start, to a new beginning."

Our eyes met and acknowledged each other.

Chapter Twenty-Five

It must have been over ten months since I began working in this town and nothing much had changed, neither in my life nor of the town's. We both were similar in a way, stagnant. The difference was that this town was bound by nature, whereas I was bound by disinterest. I didn't care anymore if I grew old in this town and was buried somewhere in the nearby cemetery or even cremated as no one would bear expenses for my funeral. It didn't matter to me if my dead body would rot in a studio apartment for days or even weeks following my passing and be discovered only after neighbor complaints of an unbearable stench emanating from inside. Heck, I didn't even care if I could afford a studio to die in or be found in some garbage dump on the street side. There was a time when I despised sitting idle and not endeavoring to advance my career or better my social reputation. Now I had neither, and I fathomed being a nobody was going to be just as tiring as being the talk of the town. But I also realized that I was wrong all my life. I was actually relieved of many burdens, many anxieties. I had run away from this lifestyle, I had avoided being labeled a no one all these years, but I found out it wasn't too bad. You don't always have to stress and overburden yourself to be someone because sooner or later you will tumble from that pinnacle and if your fall is short and sudden just like mine, there will be a lot of hurt, a lot of suffering and a whole lot of regret waiting at the bottom. And I can guarantee you wouldn't have a single ledge to hold on to save yourself. Once you reach the lowest, it is never pleasant to acknowledge your humble surroundings once again and that sight shatters you to pieces.

To get away from that troubling sight of the nadir, it was usual for me to make that perfunctory trip to the tavern. A stay that sometimes stretched more than three hours until my stomach could bear no more of that rotgut and my limbs began to shudder from that intoxicating poison. I would get to see Marilyn some of the nights there, only if she was able to make it to the bar after her work hours. But I was certain by the looks of her arrival that she strove to reach there before I left, as she entered the place gasping for breath and rubbing off her aching toes constantly after grabbing a chair. I guess it was just an honest effort from her end to converse with someone who wished to talk rather than impose, who wished to listen rather than receive, even if it was just a few minutes, she still tried. I couldn't blame her as somewhere deep inside my soul even I waited for her to come by and talk to me, I was just as guilty. But all I wished for was a basic exchange of words that would make us both feel our existence, and nothing extravagant or irrelevant. A reminder that we belonged to the living world and that we still were a part of it. Loneliness silently withers people within, I guess we both knew that all too well. And for the nights she wouldn't show up, would turn out to be most lonely and nostalgic for me.

Our conversations were very ordinary, mundane for most ears. She would talk about movies, clothes, a lot of celebrities and her preference in men and women she likes to see on screen. At some instances she would mention the insane customers she would get to encounter through the course of her workday. We would discuss world problems, but not too much of them as our own were enough to fill our platters. I joined her in thoughts, contemplation, laughter, misery as all of those were plentiful in our relationship. I never thought I would ever call this a relationship, but neither of us realized when this companionship imbued in affinity and solace had escalated itself into our attention and impelled us to consider it such. It had been almost a year since our sporadic meetings transformed into intentional, frequent rendezvous. But it only began as an honest desire to communicate, bond, relate to someone who understood or maybe just tried to understand. It had matured since, and it had grown vast.

It was a cold mid November weekday when I reclined back upon a grained covering that spanned a mile long semicircle edging the stretch of a scenic view of Lake Tahoe that loomed before me. It was a day off and Marilyn had long wanted to come to this site to enjoy the vast greens and waters of this beautiful place. We had gone out in the recent weeks to the movies, parks, diners, but this was the first time we actually involved ourselves romantically with each other. The glistening surface of the water was suddenly agitated and through that rippling expanse of blue emerged Marilyn, swiftly brushing off the frigid droplets of the lake that remained on her pallid, freckled body a little longer than she had wanted. She gleamed in radiant, unhindered daylight and stood for a moment allowing the golden rays to warm her up. She turned and glanced back at me with a subtle smile and showered me with the resplendence that exuded from her. She joined me upon the coverlet that I had laid down for her to lie upon. Our eyes never broke that gaze, but they spoke nonetheless.

"What are you looking at?" She asked coyly.
"Red suits you." I pointed to her red polka dot bikini.
She lightly dismissed that remark with a short laughter.
"You had a good swim? The water is cold?" I asked.
"Yes, it is."
"Well, I better stay away from it. Don't want to catch a cold on the way back. You should have stayed clear as well."
"Cold is so much better than hot you know. When water gets hot, it could hurt you at the touch. But when it's cold and you're quick enough in and out, it doesn't hurt you, it just... cleanses you, washes away your fears, your impurities, your failures. Have you ever let yourself drown in it for a few seconds? It doesn't kill you, but when you come out of it, you're... relieved, revived, renewed. I do that occasionally, when I'm tired of myself, when I have doubts. Have you noticed a sudden shiver go down your spine at the touch of cold, maybe that's just something to shake you out of your made-up world back into reality. Heat's just a reminder of what we're

supposed to feel in the afterlife. A human soul scorched in the flames of hell, eternally singed and stifled."

I listened intently as she lay back on the blanket and brooded over her own words.

"Do you believe in Heaven and Hell, George? That in afterlife each one of us is bound to be restrained in either one of them? Too much of anything is considered bad, right? Whether it's good or evil."

"No, I don't believe there is Hell or Heaven in the afterlife. Not there, because it's here on Earth and we're living right through it. Our judgment doesn't wait that long to happen, consequences of our acts are right here before us. I'm the living example of how people survive in hell and I have seen people who've lived their life as if they were in heaven. Free of greed, lust, false pride, lies and envy. We pay for what we've done, good or evil, we clear our accounts right here, not... not there."

My response compelled her to reflect on my perspective even more profoundly.

"If that is the truth, then I'm definitely bound for hell in life, aren't I?" Her eyelids fluttered at she spoke.

"Well, that's the beauty of it. You never know which way you're headed until you're actually there. And the best part is, even if you are on the wrong path, one good deed is enough to completely turn you back and over."

"Do you think so?"

"I hope it is the truth, because if it isn't, we're all damned."

We drove down Route 50 in a rented 1972 Oldsmobile convertible replete with an immense feeling of appreciation for each other's company. It had been over five hours that we'd been on the road but surprisingly I wasn't tired at all. Marilyn shifted up on her passenger seat and stretched her arms aloft feeling the crisp breeze through her fingers and stayed there as long as the drive continued. After an hour of that gratifying sight, being next to me with her eyes closed and face devoid of any thought or trouble, I pulled over right next to a small, grungy food truck that suddenly jutted into my view amidst the everlasting desolation. There was another vehicle parked a bit further and a family of four had occupied a picnic table with fries and burger trays before them each, and it assured me that truck was still operational. We ordered what was available on the menu as the choices were scarce and utilized the hood of our convertible as our table. As we ate I realized that after a very long time of despondency, I actually felt liberated of the restraints that had me chained to my past, my failures and shortcomings. For the first time after incessantly running away from my existence, I felt I could stop now. I could stop and forget the past, as it had forgotten me by now. And as I sank in such thoughts, Marilyn noticed my sudden despair and jumped off the hood of the car and began to enact some part of a play that I hadn't come across in my life. I leaned back on the windshield and watched.

"Poison, Poison, I see, hath been his timeless end. O churl! Drunk all, and left no friendly drop to help me after? I will kiss thy lips; Haply some poison yet doth hang on them, to make die with a restorative."

She stepped closer to me and kissed me gently on the lips.

"That's tomato ketchup." She exclaimed tasting the red off my lips.

"It still works." I said with an impressed gesture.

"Thy lips are warm." She said as she stepped back with a plastic fork she had obtained from the pack of free cutlery. I chuckled.

"Hey... improvisation okay, now back to the play. O happy dagger, this is thy sheath, there rust and let me die."

She stabbed herself in the chest and poured some ketchup and oozed blood out of her wound through her hand. She dropped to the ground and lay dead as I went over and joined her upon the dusty earth and lay dead right next to her. We laughed hysterically but then regained our composure.

"And who am I supposed to be?" I inquired.

"Romeo."

"And he died as well?"

"Yup, you don't know this play?"

"I have heard of it. Never read it, though."

"Do you know what this story basically means?"

"Tell me."

"A simple misunderstanding followed by a hasty, impulsive decision can separate even the most devout lovers from each other."

"Yeah, I know the feeling." I was yet again reminded of my past.

"My stage director once said that."

"You used to act?"

"Nevermind," she hauled herself out from her past, "they are supposed to be like this." She shifted herself across my chest and then closed her eyes.

"End to a love story." I said lightly caressing her hair. But that remark suddenly waned the smile from her face and she sat up looking away from me and gazing at the weakening streaks of daylight. An orange and gilded sky welcomed the night.

"What happened?"

"Isn't it always beautiful, the sky in fading sunlight at the end of the day? As the sun drowns into darkness, but just before that, the skies changes so many shades of color, from one to another just as we do through our lives. And then it sinks behind the horizon, completely disappearing, dead."

"But there is a difference. We don't get a second chance at it like he does."

She leaned in for a kiss. I averted from her intentions. She looked up at me and her eyes were full of questions, full of doubts, full of humiliation.

"Marilyn... I'm not someone you would want to fall in love with. There's nothing you could gain out of loving me."

"Are you sure it's not the other way around?"

"You're a beautiful woman. You can have any man you want. You can let go of your past and start again with the right person."

"And if that's you?"

"It cannot be. I have already ruined a woman's life. I can be no different again."

"People change."

"I haven't seen any."

"I have. I am looking at him."

I took a long moment to read her eyes, then replied. "Let's not talk about it. Some things are better left to time."

Chapter Twenty-Six
ɢɢɢ

I had driven another hour and a half back into the snares of a detached town and disgruntled lives and although the trip had been pleasurable as long as it lasted, there was a plaintive glimmer that imbued both our minds as we anticipated the moment of separation from each other yet again. Even though, we both knew the disjuncture would span just another day or so and our union was inevitable at the tavern perhaps the next night, but it still elicited a dolorous pain in my heart, and I was certain about hers as well. I came to a stop outside a dilapidated three storey apartment building that stood ground only due to its strong concrete foundations that were laid ages ago by guileless and scrupulous builders. It did not have the strength to maintain its stature otherwise with a deplorable upkeep it had to endure.

"Here we are." Marilyn sputtered lifelessly. Then turned and looked into my eyes. I held her gaze as long as she wanted me to.

"That's a nice place to live."

She instantly intuited my sarcasm and chortled.

"Would you want to move in?" She teased.

"If the rent's affordable."

"Trust me, you can get away without even paying for a couple of months."

"I'm sure you tried that." I said trying to ease her up with laughter.

"Yeah." She came back as honest as she could. "I know you're going to refuse, but I'll still make a fool of myself and ask you because we both are going to go home and order some shitty

Chinese food and watch television until we fall asleep. So, how about we order that same shitty Chinese food and instead of watching television, why not talk ourselves to sleep? Together."

"Okay, when do we do that?"

"You're such a dummy, you know that? Obtuse, that's the right word for you."

"I wish I were."

"So would you visit my crummy apartment and have shitty dinner with me?"

"Would love to." I had no intention of turning her down anymore.

Marilyn led me through a creaking hallway with battered apartment doors in successions on either side and up a rickety, stifling flight of stairs to the second floor. She stopped outside another one of the resembling doors and rummaged her handbag for the keys. It took her a moment to recover them, but it took longer for her to wrestle the jammed door to open after unlocking it and it dawned upon me that the doorframe was inflated due to the weather and a bit out of structure. She welcomed me inside a small, ramshackle one bedroom dwelling that had evident trails of indigence scattered throughout, but nonetheless, it was a home. The walls hadn't been painted in ages, the ceilings were damp and were randomly showering the floor of deteriorating paint and debris. The floor was a motley of discolorations and appeared frazzled around the corners. She approached a begrimed window and lifted it forcefully as it parted the sill with a squeal. As I went past the door to her bedroom, a cursory glimpse of her clothes cluttered lair filled my sight. I proceeded to a couch that had stacks of magazines that were swept off to the floor by Marilyn to make space. There were empty bottles of beer and liquor on the table right in front of the couch, which triggered her to quickly clean up the mess.

"I'm sorry for the mess. I hadn't had anyone come up here in a long time. Hell, I haven't been here in a long time myself. Let me clean this up."

"A home isn't a home without the mess, it's a hotel room. Besides, I've seen worse."

"I have never heard that before."

"It's the truth, and the truth is hardly heard these days. It's all about the superficial veil of false pretense."

"You just quoted my instructor there." She said dumping the garbage.

"Which instructor?"

"Nevermind, it was a long time ago, and this probably is the only thing I remember him saying. You wouldn't mind if I disappeared for a moment and took a shower, I have sand all over me."

"Take your time. When do we order that shitty dinner?"

"Whenever you're ready."

She scuttled into her room and pushed the door ajar. I began an expedition around the living shuffling through old photographs on the mantle and some scattered obsolete stuff which included a 16 hole flute in a hapless condition and a tattered personal journal that hadn't been used in months. I blew into the flute and dust muffled the notes, it was better for me to let it rest in peace. I turned the pages of her life but kept myself from intruding by reading any. I harnessed a towel in the back of the couch to swipe clean the glass of a photoframe in which a younger Marilyn stood part of a graduation ceremony. There were a couple more pictures of her with an aged woman whom I presumed to be her mother and there were several photos of Marilyn in various outfits and attires that hinted theater or stage performances. I gazed at all of them for a prolonged moment to construe the true intent of those disguises and wondered. Just when my rumination hadn't even reached halfway, I heard a distant voice coming from behind the ajar door.

"Did you order yet?" She shouted.

"I need a phone to call them and in all this chaos, I couldn't locate one." I responded, my voice equally elevated.

"It's right on the table next to the sofa, might be under some magazines."

I discovered the phone right where she had instructed me to. I shuffled through my memory and dialed the number. Speaking on the phone and ordering fried wings, egg rolls and hunan chicken, I suddenly realized I did not have the delivery address.

"What's the address here?" I shouted this time.

"Address?"

"I need an address for them to deliver."

"Did they just ask you that?"

"No, but they are going to."

Marilyn opened the door and emerged in a loose shirt over something she might be wearing underneath, but the shirt reached well below her thighs. She took the phone from me and uttered her name with a loud greeting in Chinese. Then she hung up.

"They know me, it's an everyday thing."

"Was this an everyday thing?" I held up the picture frame in which she was dressed as a 17th century maid.

"Where did you find that one?" She asked with a chuckle.

"Right here."

"It's so old I don't even remember it."

"It doesn't look that old." I contested.

"You should have let the dust of time stay upon it."

"No, I just wiped it off."

"I see that."

"You said you wanted to know about me, why I ended up here? Well, I don't talk to strangers."

She smiled and that face said a lot.

Chapter Twenty-Seven
ల్లిల్లిల్లి

"There was nothing special about my childhood," Marilyn spoke softly.

It was well around quarter past midnight and the remnants of that shitty Chinese dinner sat quietly on a table in front of two familiar souls who reminisced and shared their lives to alleviate the burden of grief with reciprocated empathy. I had taken some good fifty minutes to narrate my life story to Marilyn and she had just recently begun.

"Just another girl living down the block. A shy child with only a few friends, mostly seen indoors, kind of creative but not exceptionally, but one thing dearest to her of all, she loved to dance. My mother was a single parent, raised me well, did all she could, worked two jobs, weekends as well to get me through private school and hoped for college if possible. As life continued and our expenses escalated, I knew I couldn't burden her with all the responsibilities, so I decided to lend a hand and began working at the age of 16. Just random jobs, grocery stores and Laundromats, nothing special." She poured herself some more wine as she went on. "I was a good student. My grades in high school compelled my mom even further to pursue college possibilities for me. She became adamant about it, I guess she wanted me to do things she couldn't do in her life. When time came she let me choose which way I wanted to go and I chose performing arts. That was the only thing I did, dance, maybe act as well, but I was never praised for my acting skills as much as I was for my dancing. Every person who ever watched me perform, my peers, my teachers, all remembered me for it. I couldn't have thought of a better profession. I began college and I loved everything, going there meeting with so many girls with a similar interest. It was all wonderful, almost like a fairy tale until it was time for fate to step in. I was twenty-three and just graduated, that picture is from that day. Mom was so happy, she almost cried when I dressed up in that black cloak and wore the hat. She hugged me so tight and I couldn't be any more proud of myself. She didn't say anything, she didn't need to. I knew it. And just two weeks after, she passed away."

A silence followed and I did not dare to disrupt that. She took her time to mollify her emotions and wiping off tears from her cheeks she began again.

"As if she was just alive for that one day, to see me become what I always wanted to be. I was all alone after her. I was independent enough as I had worked since an early age and it does give you a little something to hold on to, a certain confidence to make it on your own. But I never imagined my life without her. She was gone too soon. Maybe I made her work too much for my own interests, after all a person can only take so much. A seventy hour work week is not easy to endure. She wasn't supposed to leave me like that, and I didn't know what to do with me without her guidance, without her light. And as they say, once you lose the sheltering wisdom of an elderly you're bound to make mistakes. In my loneliness I was ready to give myself to anyone who'd even hint on loving me forever, though, their intentions might not be so. I went crazy and I got engaged to someone I'd only met three weeks earlier. Sometimes losing the only person you thought would never leave you turns you into something you can't even imagine, and this was an example of the most stupidest mistake I could ever make. It looked fine then, but everything that glitters is not gold. Our marriage was exactly like that. His promises, his affection, his love was all lies and I was trapped in his house for a whole year as his sex slave. He was rich, connected, influential, and a freak, and I finally understood the consequences of an impulsive, hasty, rushed decision to get married. I was abused day after day and not just by him, but for the amusement of his equally manipulative friends. I cried and cursed myself at first, I even resisted only to be beaten and thrown into unconsciousness. But then it became a routine for me. I didn't feel anything anymore, just simply trying to get over with it. That changed me, as a person, as a woman, and as an individual. When he was tired of me, he just simply released me. I was free to go wherever I wanted. I was given twenty thousand dollars as compensation for the pleasure and entertainment I had given, but I figured it was mainly to keep my mouth shut and I knew I had to keep shut because there was no use in reaching for the police or the law. The officials of both had been a part of those masquerades in which I was displayed and used at will. Surprisingly, I did not give up even after that, though, thoughts of disappearing and never be found again visited my mind frequently, but couldn't nest in there and I began ignoring them. But now comes the best part, my next stop was Hollywood. All that I went through for the whole year in my husband's apartment was nothing compared to what I faced there in the famous Hollywood hills. At least in his apartment whatever was done to me was done within the privacy of four walls, but in Hollywood, it is all done openly, isn't it? So, after years of struggles and denials, refusals to warm beds of old, balding people who can't walk a yard without help, and multiple casting agents, I finally gave up on that dream. And this is where I ended up, in this crummy town, with boring people, tired lives, and a job that sometimes reminds me of my horrible marriage. But the only difference is that strangers aren't permitted to put their hands on me until they pay more and I've had some offers, but I don't take that."

"And not to forget the shitty dinner." I raised a toast to the Chinese egg rolls.

"Yup, never forget that." She took a large bite of it. "People think I am a prostitute and I don't contest their assumption, their opinion of me, because it wouldn't make a difference. They can say what they want, but I don't do that anymore. I had enough of that in LA."

"Who the hell cares, right?"

"Right." She smiled but it soon faded. "But you can't be always unaffected, you can't go on like that. Being a human, living and breathing, you sometime desire to be appreciated, you desire to be treated well, I desire to be loved. I can't go on avoiding those fundamental feelings that, maybe not every day, but sometimes do get the better of me. At times I wish I had never been born. And it's the truth. What am I doing living like this? What is the meaning of my life? I'm not solving anyone's problems, I'm not capable of great deeds, I'm not making a family. The one person I wanted to do something for, to make her happy, my mother, and I failed at that too."

"You didn't fail, Marilyn, you lost her."

"Do you think she would be proud of what I am today?"

I remained silent, then changed my approach to her question. "We are never born out of our choice, but to live that life which is given is in our hands. Maybe you are born to be somebody, maybe your destiny still awaits. Who knows if you are capable of great things, great performances? Maybe you gave up too early."

"That sounds like another fairy tale to me now."

"Do you intend to go back? Try your luck differently this time?"

"Even if I do return, it wouldn't be any different than before. Luck is a rich person's disguise for favoring someone in return for amusement. Otherwise, there are no lucky people in Hollywood. None."

"What if you were given another chance, saying it might take some time and you would start right at the bottom and have to earn your way up. Would you take that?"

"I would accept any chance I get. I have loved the stage and screen since I could remember, and I had hoped by giving my honor I would at least gain some recognition. You know that feel of warm spotlight on you makes you forget the darkest mistakes you've ever committed. But the people I'd trusted to get me there, the so called defenders of humanity, esteemed dignitaries, philanthropists, social titans of name and fame were the ones most adept at veiling their black hunger for flesh behind a respectable persona. Though, I had dealt with similar people before, I made a fool out of myself yet again." She lit herself a cigarette. "It's not that I did not try to get a decent job. Being a stripper is no one's ambition, but there weren't many out there who would hire without a test trial. You know what I mean by that. And I was short on money, so I did what was right in front of me. A gentlemen's bar right across the street where I sat weeping and cursing at my life. All they wanted to see was whether I looked attractive enough to make it to the stage and if could I move my body around, I could do both. But why do you ask?"

I was in deep contemplation, "nothing in particular, just wanted to know if you still have it in you."

"The desire of stardom never fades even when you're on your deathbed. That last bit of applause and appreciation is always welcome." She added.

I took a deep sigh and stood up shaking on my legs that were numb after three hours of inactivity. "I should be leaving now, what is it, past midnight?"

"Yeah, way past that." She replied with a smile. "You know you're the first person I've talked to about my life since all this happened? I've never opened up to anyone like this before."

"I'm glad I am that someone."

"So am I."

ഇ-ഇ-ഇ

As I lay in my bed next to a window through which the neon sign, reading vacancy, intermittently flashed my face with red hue, I discovered myself sinking into a quandary that was far beyond my capacity to comprehend. It was a simple choice between forgetting a family and loving a stranger, only it wasn't quite simple for me or for any other person who could relate to the circumstances that had befallen me through the years. Forgetting a family to an extent where I was going to repress every memory of a woman who had loved me the most and a child that I had only caught a glimpse of to remember, and loving a stranger to an unforeseen situation where my affection could result in being unrequited and lead to a nebulous, lonely path upon which I am hesitant to travel. But no matter how hard I tried to eradicate a developing fondness, it pushed me down under to favor a more positive outcome from this relationship, friendship, companionship, heck I didn't even know what it was.

Call me crazy but just as the elderly have passed their judgments upon demented characters like me, I just couldn't keep away from forcing myself into another predicament from which extrication, as I knew well enough, would be a stinging one. I went on for a nighttime stroll through the neighboring town's most hardscrabble region with an intention of finding the only pawn shop in the whole area located there. After a good fifteen minutes of glancing around I finally came across a blinking awning that read in loud green neon, "Got Gold? Get Cash." As I passed a couple of young men who lingered in groups in the darkness of the alleys adjoining the stores and junctions, I knew I was being watched as there were hardly any people in town who could afford to enter a pawn shop and make a transaction, not a very frequent sight. Keeping a firm faith in my wrists while I prepared myself for an imminent ambush, I hastened across and entered the safe confines of the shop, or so it felt. A portly man looked up at me from behind the counter and with a flick of his eyebrows he questioned.

"How can I help you?"

I wasn't sure which seemed more salient in his appearance, his beer gut or his 100 gram gold chain that jangled and wrapped around his thick neck like a flashy dog collar.

"I'm here to sell something."

"Yeah, they all say that, you're not gonna pull out a gun on me now, are you?"

"No, but this..."

I unclenched my hand around my breast pocket that was almost sodden in sweat after a long tight hold at the thing I secured within. I retrieved a necklace that I had once given to Audrey. I had found this necklace hidden under a sheaf of documents in the drawer of my office desk and had kept it in my trouser pocket the day it all happened, as it was the only precious and valuable piece of jewelry the burglars left behind. I had carried it with me initially then secured it inside my motel room for a very long time, but now I decided to put it to some use.

As I lay my eyes on it, it suddenly reminded me of Audrey's inimitable beauty and how it adorned her the day our differences began. But the shop owner had different intentions as he ogled the sparking object in my possession which was soon to become his. He welcomed the necklace into his hands with a greedy countenance and a drooling mouth. He examined it for about half a minute and couldn't distrust the authenticity of the item. He looked up at me and took a longer time to peruse my character with his trenchant eyes.

"Look man, to come at you as clear as crystal, I don't trust you with this. I've never seen or done business with you before. You do have a genuine item right here and it's an expensive piece of jewelry all right. Now, I have seen goons and hoodlums in my life, but looking at you, I don't think you took this off of a woman at gunpoint who was leaving a fancy restaurant after a long romantic dinner with her man."

"No." I replied with a smile. "This belonged to my wife. She is... no more my wife. It's been around, finally put it to some use."

"Hmm... somehow I do believe you. So, I'll cut the bullshit and give you ten for it."

"Just ten? I bought it for a lot more."

"Hey, I said I trust you, but not as much to give you your asking price. Now, keeping in mind the depreciation costs and involvement in a possible larceny, the most I would go to is twelve, take it or leave it. Final offer."

"What if I put in my watch, it's good, rado."

He took the watch and stared at it. I interrupted.

"Look, I need fifteen thousand. Both of these things are yours, fifteen, final."

"Is that a fact?"

"I need the money."

He took his time. "You got it. Wait here, give me ten minutes."

"Sure, thanks."

I could almost break free in excitement that I negotiated my terms with a pawner. He faded into his dark enclosure behind the counter and I waited looking around the shelves at the other things he sold. He emerged from the room after a good ten minutes and appeared with a certain grin across his face that hinted on something.

"It's genuine all right."

"You have your expert appraiser back there?"

"Yeah... shut that door for me."

I moved back and lifted the door stop and let the door to a close. He cautiously removed a stack of ten thousand and loose bills to make up a grand total of fifteen.

"You might want to count that all."

"Nah, I trust you." I said with a stern gaze.

He bobbed his head and put the cash in an envelope.

"Be careful with all that cash on you. You're not in the most safest neighborhood, you know."

"Yeah, been here long enough to realize that."

"Well, good doing business with you. Anything else you want to sell, I'll leave that door open."

"I will, if I manage to buy anything worth selling." With that said, I parted the counter with a joyous smile and went on my way.

That jubilance was short-lived to only a block of fast strides as two masked men abruptly barricaded my path and forced me into one of the pitch black alleys that seemed like an imminent grave. Each of them held a six inch retractable blade brandishing them before my face and their voices were muffled behind their tight face masks, but intentions as clear as the gleam of their knives. One of them punched me right in the face which stunned me for a moment and staggered my stance down to the wet concrete.

"Give me the money right now or I open you up. Right now," said one of them aggressively advancing at me.

"I don't have anything." I put up my arms imploring for my life.

"Don't you fucking lie to me, you punk ass bitch motherfucker. You didn't go to that pawner to get your ass reamed, did you? Show me the money, right now."

"You'll have to kill me, I won't give it to you." I stood up stern and unyielding.

"Did you hear this dumb fuck, did you just hear him what he said?"

"Cut the shit out of him." The other responded nonchalantly.

Just before he could enact the requested course of action, another apparition appeared at the lip of the alley, holding something of great caliber aimed right at the two thugs.

"Now you two get the fuck away from that man or I blow your brains right here, right now."

With that voice I recognized him to be the pawn shop owner who had come to my rescue with a shotgun tightly gripped around the trigger. The knife bearing thugs were shaken off the ground as they took off running the other side of the alley and disappeared into the darkness.

I stumbled my way to my savior as he welcomed me with a series of repeat questions on how I was feeling. It was quite obvious how I felt at the moment, but I cleared my head and shook it positively.

"You're gonna have a black eye tomorrow."

"Well, that isn't the only thing that would have bothered me if you hadn't come."

"Yeah, I heard the way you stood your ground, it's foolish but valiant. I saw these men take after you right when you left my store. I knew they were after something. Let me drop you home, where do you live?"

"I'll manage, I don't want to trouble you."

"Hey, it's no trouble, I'm going to make at least ten thousand dollars extra off that jewelry you sold me, this is the least I can do."

"I live in the next town, leave me at the bus stop. I'll take a bus from there."

"You got it. Come on."

He led me to his car and as I entered the vehicle I suddenly realized that my perceptions of smell were still unharmed because I could tell the man was a great admirer of the scent of jasmine and fried pork chops. He began to drive down the road and I gingerly kept a handkerchief on the bruise around my eye.

"They could come back for you. You shouldn't have taken that risk because of me." I said looking back at him with one eye.

"No, they won't dare come for me. Let me ask you something, you know what's the most secure place in the entire block and its area? The pawn shop. Why? Because we're the biggest goons of all. We run this whole neighborhood, every crime and every criminal goes through us. They don't come for us, ever."

I was shocked to the point of speechlessness with his honesty and the revelation.

"Surprised?" He asked with a smirk."

"Yeah, quite much."

"Well, that's how it is. And here we are, that's your bus stop."

"Thanks once again."

I exited the vehicle and leaned into the window.

"As I said earlier, anytime. And whatever you're trying to do with that money, hope you get through with it."

I nodded to him and saw him drive back into the night, as I proceeded toward the queue of a handful passengers waiting to board the bus.

Chapter Twenty-Eight
ဇာၭၭ

"Did you sell that necklace for the reason I think you did or was it for personal financial stability?"

I was awakened by that question as I lay distorted on my seat while Louise was as fresh and lively as she had just hopped onto the bus for a fun ride. I rubbed my eyes after five hours of sleep and found the bus was yet again in a parking lot of a stop where people had gotten off to refresh themselves early in the morning.

"What do you think?" I replied in my jaded voice.

"Well, I'll find out in just a bit, but you better run off to the powder room before they take off. The next stop is more than two hours from here."

"Good idea."

I took off and entered the restrooms where I washed away the dinginess and weariness from my face and then borrowed some toothpaste from a fellow passenger and brushed with my finger as I didn't have a toothbrush or money to buy one. I came out into the parking lot and stretched my limbs a little as the call to board sounded some minutes later and I was back in my seat yet again next to the inquisitive, withering creature.

"Aren't you going to get something to eat?"

"Next stop maybe."

"Hmm... this new girl, Marilyn, what was she like? I don't mean physically, I mean as a person?"

"She was... I don't know, but something about her made me want to be with her. Maybe it was just a simple fact that she was the only person I could say I knew in that town. Or maybe our lives were, if not entirely, but somewhat similar. It had been a year since we both met, and I took all the time I could to... be with her, become a part of her life or rather have her become a part of mine. I took all that time to decide whether I should or shouldn't."

"So, you did sell that necklace for her then."

"I could have spent the years all alone, but when she entered my life, I don't know why but I had that urge to help her seek her destiny. Make sure she gets there. At first I fought myself to stay away from her, I knew I shouldn't get involved, but I lost. Maybe it was just the guilt of destroying too many lives that led me into believing that I could at least help with one, just one. Do you think I was wrong?"

"Would you take my opinion on this?"

"I will or I wouldn't have asked."

"Helping someone reach their purpose is never a bad deed. The question is, did you fall in love with her?"

"It wasn't love at first, and it wasn't intentional at all. But you know when you spend a year with someone, meeting them every day and talking and discussing everything, you do begin to have feelings for them. It took a long time for just that friendship to develop out of empathy. Then it did go to that point."

"Was she up for it?"

"I was about to find out."

The effect of last night's wallop hadn't subsided as I still couldn't gather a complete view from my left eye. While the other functional eye adjusted to the blinding luminosity that split through the open blinds, warmed my motionless body and awakened me from a deep sleep. But suddenly appeared before me a heavenly face, upside down, comfortingly smiling. I swiftly withdrew from that contiguity and sat up away from whom I recognized to be Marilyn after a second view. She stood there in a red dress, plausibly to spend the day out, stepped up closer to the bed and sat down with a laugh.

"I scared you, didn't I?"

"No I was just... a little... I didn't expect you here." I answered trying to compose myself for her company.

"Why? Were you expecting someone else?"

"No. I thought I was dreaming. You looked so..."

"So what?" she asked excitedly.

"Angelic."

Her impish laughter faded from her face and she crawled her way across the bed closer to me.

"What happened to your face?"

"Nothing."

She reached out for my swollen eye and touched it. I flicked her hand away in shooting pain.

"This isn't nothing."

"I got in a fight with some guys last night."

"At the bar?"

"No, they tried to mug me."

"Oh, what did they get away with?"

"This," I pointed to my injury.

"So you resisted?" She asked, evidently impressed.

"Yeah."

"What was so important that you wanted to save?"

"Some things are that important when your life depends on it. Sometimes more than one life."

"Is today your day off?"

"Nope."

"How come you're sleeping so late?"

"Am I?"

"It's nine thirty."

"Yeah, only that I just got into bed three hours ago."

"Oh... I'm so sorry, I didn't mean to disturb you."

"You didn't, I could hardly sleep. And now that you're here, I have something to ask you."

"Really?" She gave a sinister grin and stepped inches away from me, leaning closer and closer with every breath.

"What if I asked you to leave everything behind and come with me?" I gazed deep into her eyes.

"Come with you where?"

"Doesn't matter where we go, or what we do. The question is, would you?" My gaze was fixed at her. She took a moment and they looked up at me holding my gaze firmly with hers.

"Absolutely."

"That's all I needed to know."

"But what are we doing exactly? You know I hate surprises."

"This one will change that."

The following dawn I had arisen to a sudden urgency of removing myself from this town along with someone whose company I could cherish for a long time. I had given my employer a three day prior notice of leaving the job for which they decided to hold my two days wages in compensation for such pressing and short notice. I did not mind that at all as my mind and intentions were fixed upon the days to come, not the days left behind. I hailed a taxi from the bus stand and went to pick-up Marilyn who was still unaware of our destination. Her luggage was limited, I had none as we boarded the cab and were on our way to the nearest airport which was in the city about 40 minutes from us. Upon our arrival at the terminal and after passing the security checkpoint, Marilyn was quite surprised to find herself in a blindfold as I kept her from sighting or listening, with the help of earplugs, about where we were going. There were a lot of suspicious eyes that followed us as we walked further towards our boarding gate as they had never witnessed such an adverse event enacted before them. Marilyn was disinterested in being blindfolded for the rest of our travel, but I was determined to have her so.

"You know you're making a fool out of me if we're out amongst people right now." She said, hesitantly walking by my side.

"You can't hear me, can you?" I asked while holding her firmly with both hands so she does not stumble. She was silent, and I had the answer to my question. "Good," I smiled and took her on.

As we reached boarding gate number 3, the usher eyed us both questionably. I offered him the passports and the boarding passes but his attention was fixated on the blindfolded companion.

"It's a surprise for her. She doesn't know where we're going." I answered his muted inquiry.

"Oh..." a grin came across his face as his eyes turned sharp with pleasure. He tapped his ears to gesture if she could hear the announcements.

"Earplugs." I replied.

"Well done, here you are." He handed me the passes and I nodded to him before leading Marilyn onwards.

"I hope you're not leaving me next to a dumpster!" She detested this idea.

The journey to our seat number was replete with questions and my answers were identical to all who inquired. But there was no contempt on any face who realized the purpose behind the mischievous act. We finally reached our row and sat down, Marilyn still in her restraints.

"Now are you going to tell me..." I quickly placed my hand around her mouth as the volume of her voice was quite unsuited for an airplane. Some heads turned at me, but looked away with laughter. Somehow Marilyn grasped the meaning of muffling her voice and came back at me in a whispering note. "Where are we going?"

I removed one of her earplugs, "you'll find out soon enough." I put the earplug back and relaxed by her side.

"People must be thinking I'm crazy or something, the way you're carrying me around."

I placed my hand upon hers and she clutched it, giving herself courage to sit through another hour and half of embarrassment.

We landed around ninety minutes after we took off and it had given Marilyn an idea that we were flying somewhere, as she mentioned that while we spoke in whispers and was mortified to be amidst a hundred passengers who watched her board the plane blindfolded. After landing I led her out to the LAX terminal and finally stood her up against the glass walls of the terminal that overlooked a tremendous view of the Pacific Ocean. I removed her earplugs and the blindfold and she remained there rooted and speechless. With nothing been said for almost two minutes but just silent gazing at the waters and the land peripheries, I noticed a stream of tears just went down her right eye. I pulled up closer to her and held her. She turned at me and wiped away her tears.

"We're in Los Angeles?" She cried, her voice trembling.

I nodded in return.

"We're in Los Angeles!" This time she exulted and kissed me a bit longer than I had expected.

"Come on, we have a lot of things to do." I whispered to her as we parted and took off running to the airport exit with a lot of things in mind to be done next.

Chapter Twenty-Nine
❧❧❧

We drove through the open streets of the city laden with palm tress and replete with jovial faces, as a crisp sunlit day welcomed us. Our temporary stay was in a motel that was affordable and comfortable as well. It was almost dusk when we entered our accommodations, as we had taken gratifying liberty of traveling around and in the vicinity of Hollywood to get familiarized with the area, and it was a delightful travel as the cab driver was very enthusiastic in showing us around multiple celebrity houses and landmarks. The evening was wonderful and a tiring one. As we abandoned our luggage at the side of our room, I sank into the bed taking deep breaths and restoring my strength, but Marilyn walked to the window and looked out at the fading crimson light that imbued the Los Angeles sky. I went closer to her and enjoyed the view of her jubilant face in dying daylight.

"It is almost entirely different when you come to the land of your dreams with someone than being all alone by yourself. I have been here before, but never felt the way I feel now... with you. How long are we going to be here?" She questioned.

"As long as it takes."

"As long as what takes? You're here for some work?"

"Yeah, I have a million dollar deal waiting with a Japanese corporation, meeting is tomorrow. It's just a matter of time before we're one of the richest in LA."

"Come on, tell me." She hit me on the arm.

"Yes, we do have some work that needs doing here."

"We? What do you mean by that?"

"It's not just I who needs to shake a leg in order to get started, it's half your effort as well."

"My effort, what are you talking about? I thought this was a vacation."

"I can assure you, this is not a vacation."

Marilyn looked at me confoundedly. "Then what?"

"You've come here to become what you've always wanted to be. You're going to be an actress now. That's what we're here for."

Marilyn's brows converged in uncertainty. "I don't understand, George, why are you doing this?"

"I'm not doing anything, you're the one who's going to have to do all the work. I'm going to sit back and relax, watch you climb up the ladder of success."

"No... no... no, I can't... I won't be able to do it, not now after all these years. I've almost forgotten everything I knew."

"You never forget once you know and if you have it in you, you don't have to know much to dazzle the world. You just let yourself out." I tried to brace her failing confidence.

"Well, I don't have it in me." She was angered.

"That is something you or I cannot decide."

"Have you lost your mind, George? This is a joke, you're kidding me right?"

"Does it look that way?"

"How are we going to stay here? Who has the money for all this?"

"You don't have to worry about the money. I have plenty for both of us."

"I don't want you to do this, not for me. Look, we are not... we're not a couple. We're just friends, almost strangers. We will both go back and be on our separate ways, I have nothing to do with you, and you mean nothing to me. That's it."

I was deeply offended at this remark as I gazed into her eyes. I stepped back and retreated onto the flank of the bed. She softened and approached, sitting down by my side.

"I'm sorry, I didn't mean to say that. But George, look at me, forget about acting, I don't even look that appealing anymore. Who's going to give me a chance? There are no fools out there and I have no contacts, no references, no one to back my name, nothing. Maybe you don't know about movies that much, but I have looked at all of it from this close, it's going to be three years ago all over again."

"You're right, I don't know much about movies. I have no idea what goes on up there, but I do know some things about a place where all of them started. And that is called theater, that's called stage. And if you have the talent to make people cry and the ability to make them laugh, the guys from up that hill are going to make that long walk down just to carry you back up where you belong. And I will make sure that happens. You've followed this ambition avidly for years, but you didn't know where to start. Just because you failed doesn't mean you don't have that ability. I believe you do. I believe in you. Now you have to learn to believe in yourself. Don't hold back. Let's go and show them what you're made of. I know you can do it."

"What about our lives, our jobs?"

"What jobs? What lives? You haven't lived in years and that job wasn't for you."

"How are we going to pay for everything?"

"That's not important. I'll take care of that."

"Did you give something up? Did you sell something? George, why did you do that for me?"

"For us... for us. All you need to do now is prepare. Chip away at yourself to a performer you've always wanted to be. The rest is my responsibility."

"But George..." she went back to the window and looked through the blinds, "I'm scared."

"I know you are, but then what's the use of having me by your side when you can't overcome your fear? I'm right behind you."

"What if I fall?"

"Well, you'll have me to land upon. You just focus on your genius, leave the fear for me."

"How do you know about the theater? You never told me that."

"Well, that makes a good nighttime story." I gave her a wry smile and she kissed me passionately.

I had gained Marilyn's confidence in my belief and in my assurance to get her through according to my word after narrating to her about my childhood and how my father was one of the biggest names in stage and theater business. Now, my mission was to shuffle the options for her to commence her acting career and cull the best opportunity that would not only further but also retain her as a performer as long as she possibly needed before stepping up the ladder. Marilyn, on the other hand, was strictly prohibited from distracting herself with matters alien to her expertise. Her work was simply restricted to the study of her art that she began with attending numerous workshops, classes, seminars and group discussions at every level and opportunity she could. As I looked through a list of theaters in the vicinity of Hollywood and neighboring cities, one name suddenly caught my attention at the bottom of the paper which happened to be one of the least attended theaters in the past year. It was Durdawk Theater and that last name, presumably of the owner himself, struck a long forgotten memory back into my head and resounded in my brain chambers. If I wasn't mistaken, this man was one of the stage managers working under my father in his younger days and he must be quite old now. If it were to be a former acquaintance, I was very much fortunate. But there was still work left to be done, I couldn't just barge into his office and impose upon him to cast my girlfriend in his next show just because he saw me passing down the hallway at The Blue Crescent every day of the week. There had to be a different way to get to him, I needed to think of it.

I had learned from my father when I was five that the most dormant time of the day at a theater was the first show that usually began around eleven thirty and lasted a bit less in duration compared to the grand prime-time. I decided to give this theater a visit at that most unfrequented time of the day. As I sat there, I kept thinking uncrowded doesn't actually have to mean completely empty seats. There were no audiences except a sole ticket sold, and that was me. This was almost a rehearsal for the actors as I could distinguish a good performance from bad, but they didn't even care to impress themselves, I was out of that equation. During this perfunctory performance, I caught a glimpse of an elderly man peering from behind the curtains to sight any improvements in the number of attendees. There were none, and the distress of losing business drowned him. The last scene concluded and the curtains dropped. I refrained from applauding the performers as they were far from deserving any accolade, but I remained in my seat pondering the reasons behind the demise of this particular theater. I had the answer right before me. To fortify my assumptions, I made another trip to watch the horrendous performances once again in this theater at the supposedly most crowded time according to the stage experts, the Saturday night. The audiences were inconsistent and countable, far from a house full. No improvements or exceptions in the performances that I had hoped for, they were lamentable. Mr. Durdawk yet again stood in the darkness of the curtains smoking a cigar and peeking out at the aisles. Disappointed, he walked away. There were no expressions of reprehension or adulation as the play finished, but people just exited in indifference. I knew I had the right theater in sight, but I waited for the right time to introduce myself to the old, devastated owner and bring Marilyn out into the spotlight of stage life.

Chapter Thirty

ৡৡৡ

"What do you have in mind?" Marilyn asked distracting herself from an instructional article about dramatic impact.

I dried my face with a towel washing away the tedium after my second regretful viewing of the Durdawk theater show. "Hold the man where it hurts the most if you want him to scream out loud and surrender. Isn't that the truth?"

"Yes, but who, what, why, where?"

"You don't want to know, it's that bad, but we're going to change that. I have done my research. I've completed my homework, now it's time to show what we got."

"What homework, George?"

"Durdawk Theater. Used to be the place to go back when the times were great, but that's somewhat changed in the past. The place hasn't seen a house full in seven years. Not a single commendation from any critic in five. He's changed his female leads twenty-three times since. Twelve different plays, but nothing's come to avail him. He's in a desperate need of someone with an ability to make people laugh and make them cry. That's where you come in."

"Me? No George, I can't do theater. I don't know much about it. I'm not that good either."

"Trust me, the actors I've seen on that stage, you are. Besides, theater is not where you're supposed to act, it's the place where you live your character. And what better teacher than life itself, right?"

"If you say so."

"I've got it all figured out, the only thing remains is the moment of introduction. How do you leave an everlasting impression on someone? Indelible to a point where he trusts you with the most important decisions of his life?"

"You marry them?" She said blankly.

"Oh you're so cute sometimes, but no, not like that. The wise path to instill faith and trust is through empathy, in this case, acknowledge the failure. Once you've made that person realize that you have an equally keen eye on the failures and successes of his venture, only then he'll trust you completely."

"But why do we need him to trust us?"

"For him to believe that I know this business and what I would do with his would only benefit him at the cost of nothing more than what he's already spending. And... to get you there and jumpstart your career, breathe life into his theater one more time."

"How would that happen?"

"When we open up a new show in bright shiny lights, introducing first time on stage Marilyn McLord. And you win over the audiences along with every critic who tries to take you down. Get into their souls and touch their heart. That's going to be you."

"You seriously believe I would be able to do all of that, you think so?"

"I not only think, I know."

"Your faith in me has made me trust myself. So what are we doing next?"

ৡ৹ৡ৹ৡ৹

I was attired in a rented tuxedo and Marilyn was mesmerizing in her royal blue evening gown as I tended her sweetly into the rear seat of a taxi cab that I hailed at the corner of the street. I had come across an advertisement for a ticketed event, more like a convocation that brought together the giants of stage and theater to amalgamate with aspiring performers and their agents in order to find fresh and new talent. I would be an imbecile to let go of such an opportunity as I knew well enough that Durdawk is going to be there and it was clear to my senses that this was the time I had been waiting for to bring Marilyn to the attention of the right people.

"Now remember, all the contacts we can get." I reminded her for the twentieth time.

"I got it. How do I look?" She asked quivering with nervousness.

"You are the one they've been waiting for years. Now listen, don't let those nerves bother you, don't let it tremble your voice. A person who shudders while speaking doesn't belong on stage. It tells them you can't handle strangers which you must every day of work. Right now the only virtue you possess is self-confidence, if they come to realize that you're lacking in that aspect, there wouldn't be much attention around you and that is the last thing we need. So, let me see that smile."

She gave me one, a splendid one that warmed my heart.

"That's what I'm talking about. Now, you're a Swiss born, New York based performer. You studied ballet and dance in Europe, fluent in five languages."

"Five? I don't even know the one I speak entirely. Five, that's a lot of languages."

"Well, neither do any of them. You have stayed in Switzerland for the past two years to care for your ill mother and now that she has passed away you're here to impress the audiences of the world with your charm and abilities. And you're twenty-eight years old."

"Twenty-eight? I'm thirty-two."

"You know that, they don't have to."

"Hiding my age is hardly going to matter."

"Four years? You aren't doing anything that hasn't been done before. Besides, all the women you find in that banquet hall have been stuck at thirty since last ten years. They haven't moved an inch. That's the way it goes."

The cab came outside the stairs to the hotel building. I took a final glance at her and nodded in reassurance. With a confident visage, we both exited the confines of a taxi to step into the world of glitter and glamour.

The massive banquet hall was adorned in red with draperies, walls, floors, and everything in sight corresponding in color. The floor was clustered with tuxedoed men and their embellished spouses or dates and they all reeked of liquor and flattery to the extent of folly. The glittering Los Angeles grandeur gleamed in Marilyn's eyes, as she suddenly lit up at the sight of dignitaries and royalty and proceeded in awe to assimilate into the crowd. I was glad she didn't need another reinforcement from me this time. My intentions were fixed on Mr. Durdawk and my act to ingrain into his senses the endeavor to make him believe my commiseration to be genuine and for him to trust my judgment in leading him out of his failures and his business debacle was imminent as I had just sighted him and his wife amidst the crowd consuming a bit more space than a somewhat leaner counterpart. I moved across the floor warily to avoid any eye contact with them both in attempt to surprise them with a visit, but I kept watching their movements furtively. Mr. Durdawk was surrounded by other businessmen as well as some young neophytes who went on to allure him into hiring them as leads for his new show. He was a man in his mid 60s, still attractive in appearance, especially with his groomed facial hair. He was dressed in a three-piece suit, and smoked a pipe which complimented his personality like an intrinsic part of it. His wife was stocky, but still graceful in her black sequined ball gown. She had her hair up in a bun and was greatly fond of diamond hair pins that profusely crested her head set in such a pattern as to resemble a crown. As I reached closer, I switched to an inadvertent persona and slightly elbowed Mrs. Durdawk from behind. Facing away at the moment of impact, I quickly spun and reacted to the collision identically as Mrs. Durdawk.

"My apologies ma'am, I'm regretful I couldn't acknowledge your beautiful presence in a more decorous way." I leaned into a bow as I spoke.

"That's quite all right, young man. This wouldn't be the first time I've been nudged, but undoubtedly the first time I've been deeply impressed by an apology for the act."

"I'm certain they were beguiled by your resplendence, hence at a loss for words." She inflated at the sound of my ingratiating comment and strengthened her posture like a queen.

"Young man, as much as I would like to believe the words of your delusive flattery, I am quite certain I do not own a pair of magical sandals that alter my appearance in the eyes of others at such eventful nights. I am well conversant with my size and looks and could not be deceived at all in such matters at the age of fifty-eight. But I commend you on your etiquette, perhaps the first person in this assemblage I would actually love to speak with more than I must."

"Well, I'm greatly pleased and the pleasure would be entirely mine."

"What is your name, young man?"

"George, George Bailey."

"Have I met you before, George?"

"I'm afraid not, because if you had, that ring on your finger would have come from here." I took up her hand for a shake but instead, kissed it. She laughed hysterically which drew Mr. Drudawk towards our benign conversation.

"And what amuses you so much, my dear?" He asked.

"This young man right here has a preposterous sense of humor."

I extended my hand towards Mr. Durdawk for a shake, he responded with a smile. "And whom do I have the pleasure of meeting?"

His wife cut in before I could reply, "this is George Bailey."

"Pleasure to have made your acquaintance, sir, ma'am." I followed with more servility.

"Bailey? Now, I can swear by the heavens I have heard that name before." Mr. Durdawk contemplated tapping his pipe.

"Indeed you have, sir. I had the pleasure of watching you work the stage about twenty-seven years ago."

He strained his memory and suddenly lit up like a flash. "Are you the son of Mr. Bailey, Vincent Frederick Bailey?"

"You got me there."

"Oh my goodness to have met you like this. And sweetheart, look at this boy now all grown up."

"One of your employers, I believe?" Mrs. Durdawk inquired.

"Indeed, indeed, way back when I had only met and fallen in love with you. His father gave me the chance of a lifetime from which I still benefit, I am ever grateful to that man." He strengthened my position with his acknowledgment.

"Thank you, sir. He must have seen that keen eye for stage in you. But honestly speaking, Mrs. Durdawk, I have been an avid follower of your husband's theater since I can't even remember. I must say I haven't missed a single show at its premiere night since last three years."

"Is that true?" She questioned gladly.

"On my grave, I take an oath."

"Oh, I wish I had found an admirer like you some time ago, for now my theater is as good as a graveyard, none more than dead souls visit there." Mr. Durdawk expelled the truth, much to the dislike of Mrs. Durdawk. "But I think I have sighted you in my aisles recently, for there are not many faces to count there these days."

"You must have. But I can understand my face could easily be forgotten in the sea of other admirers, congratulations to you, sir."

"I'm inclined to distrust the sincerity of your remark there son. If you were regular at my theater you would know the circumstance of my hall."

"What can I say, it doesn't take long for fortunes to be reversed and I mean in all positivity, sir."

"I wish I could take that expression in exchange. Well, I must express my gratitude to such a loyal and ardent viewer, no matter how the shows turn out to be." His face grew dull and low. "Oh, but I loved the days back when your father and I used to work together. Second assistant director, that was my first position back in the 60s and the way I used to admire him and his performers, his shows. It was such a wonderful time. And you sauntering around, marveled at every sight that fascinated you. I still remember that kid."

"Those are the memories that refresh our souls, aren't they?"

"You have turned out to be wise, quite a likable quality and uncommon in young men these days."

"I have lived through a lot."

"Would you, my dear, excuse us for some time?"

"Certainly, dear. And I hope to see more of you." Mrs. Durdawk gestured toward me pleasantly, then took her drink and turned to others.

Mr. Durdawk pulled me over to a table and sat me down and ordered a round of drinks for both.

"Those were some good times, good people. I wish I could have your father with me to advise me now, help me through." Mr. Durdawk was as sincere as I needed him to be. "He knew this business in and out."

"But fate sometimes exceeds knowledge."

"Yes, it was an unfortunate event," he validated. "I wouldn't have left his side, if I hadn't had to support my own family. That was a difficult time for all who were attached to your father's theater."

"We all have our own responsibilities."

"But now I see what he must have gone through, in all that disappointment, in all that failure."

"I do not understand, sir." I acted obliviously to his plight.

"The splendor of my venture has somewhat diminished in the past, my audience has declined. I have endured a substantial collapse to my reputation as one of the best theaters in Los Angeles. Nothing is the same anymore. But why do you trouble yourself with my afflictions, it will pass. Just as good times, stressful times shall pass over as well."

"Then you have mistaken me for a stranger, if I am to disregard your worries and brush away from you into a more jovial circle of contacts."

"It's not that, George."

"I have seen the plunge in the numbers, Mr. Durdawk, I am aware of that. I did not desire to bring it up, for there is nothing more painful than probing an open wound. But now that we have made ourselves comfortable enough to share with each other the difficulties and delights of our experiences, I would demand to know more." My earnestness was evident through my eyes and he tapped my shoulder conceding to it.

"I am certainly glad to have met you, my boy."

"Then tell me," I pleaded.

"What shall I tell you? I cannot say anything with utmost certainty and I'm not a man to be blaming others for my failures, but I believe my audiences have lost their faith in my performers. I suppose I have, or more properly, my actors have failed to engage their emotions to delve into the soul of the characters and intrigue their audiences to elicit awe, as it once was some years ago. These new boys and girls, I tell you. You see when I was at the pinnacle of my strength, I was strong willed, I was deadly persuasive and I could emanate enthusiasm, but now I'm pushing sixty-five, I don't have that strength left in me. I wake up to a handful of medicines every day. I have to report to my doctor every two weeks. I don't see people that I can trust with the responsibility of my theater.

Even if I can offer incentives, that just makes things worse. That intent, that avidity, that spirit is no more. It's all about the money now. As soon as they see a higher paying opportunity, even if it means limiting their advancement, their education, their knowledge, as long as they get more money, none stay."

"I understand your situation, sir. There is indeed a dearth of responsible people these days. But I also believe that you may find the right person if you're willing to search unreservedly. What would you say if I offered to assist you in this matter to the best of my abilities?"

"I would say thank you and please. I would say God has answered my prayers."

"I have visited your theater in the recent month quite frequently and have seen your new play twice. When I have observed the audience and tried to grasp their feelings about your shows, personally and publicly, they, ingenuously speaking sir, do not approve of your female leads and your plays are entirely reliant on them. I don't know if this information has reached your ears, but out of all your performers, the most criticism received is towards your female leads. Now such kind of reproof can explicitly hurt the reputation of any institution of art, and we're not exempt. But fortunately, I think I have a way out of this for both of us. I would like to try my luck once at your theater. I would humbly ask you to entrust the responsibility of your next show to me. I would endeavor with all my strength to help you reclaim the grandeur, the glory of The Durdawk Theater. Trust me once, I believe it will be beneficial to both of us."

"I have trusted many unscrupulous people in my life, have gained and lost equally out of those mistakes. I don't see why I wouldn't trust an old acquaintance, more precisely, the cute, little friend."

"Just not cute anymore," we both laughed. "Allow me to shake your hand and drink to that."

We did as I asked and it was the start of a new beginning.

After our settlement and a gratifying conversation, I wished Mrs. and Mr. Durdawk a pleasant night and walked them to their vehicle that waited outside the building. I returned back in and jostled my way through the throng of drunk people toward the bar and sighted Marilyn as the center of attention amidst a circle of superficial and fake admirers. I wasn't going to disrupt her attempt to make as many acquaintances as she could, as I had instructed her to do so. I stood at the other end of the counter and ordered myself a drink. As I observed Marilyn, I suddenly came to realize that she did enjoy the company of such deceivers around her. A character quality that was completely contrary to mine or I must say, contrary to the personality I had acquired now. I was suddenly reminded of my time back when I used to be the same nature, which led me to destroy my own life, my own love. As the people began to dwindle in numbers, the crowd got smaller and a lot of new, inebriated couples made their way out of the hall staggering and trudging. Marilyn finally moved toward me with a delightful smile on her face. I welcomed her with a similar one.

"So... did it go according to plan?" She asked excitedly.

"What do you think?" I took a swig from my glass and turned to her. "We have ourselves Durdawk Theater to take care of."

"Oh..." she lurched at me and kissed me firmly. "You devil, how did you manage to persuade him?"

"That is called the trick of the tongue, my dear. You have a lot to learn."

"I'm sure I'll learn it soon enough." She pressed herself against me.

"That we will find out in some time, but for now, you need to prepare for the show of your lifetime."

Suddenly her laughter waned, "stage actors are so wonderful George, I don't know if I'd be able to do it."

"That is your test. If you're not able to do it, you don't belong here. But if you do, and honest praise comes you way, you're in for a long run."

"I can do anything if you're with me."

"I am there for you as long as you need me."

Chapter Thirty-One

ço·ço·ço

I waited another two days before showing up at the Durdawk Theater to hide my desperation, while I also needed to prepare myself mentally to man the reins of a business once again. When I reached my new place of work, I was greeted heartily by Mr. Durdawk and was introduced and acquainted with every employee of the theater. Though, the staff was limited, there was a subtle ingenuity that reflected in their personalities and were all benign and inviting towards the new delegation. I was made familiar with all the aspects of the theater for the following week and took my time to gain knowledge about everything before making any impetuous and unwarranted decisions. I wasn't there to impede the success of the theater, or be a hindrance to any person who strove there, as both of the facts might result in failure of my intent. I was to make congenial circumstances for everyone to accept a new face into their work-staff and assist her in getting through the most difficult time of her life, which undoubtedly is the commencement phase of a career. My initial step was to search for a script that had a strong female lead which suited and intended to impress the audiences and also highlighted Marilyn's ability the most. I went through a string of scripts that lay in dust in the shelves of the storage rooms and some that were offered for review by the current affiliated playwrights.

I wasn't hellbent on featuring Marilyn in something new as an old, establish story being revived on stage wasn't any trouble. With recommendation from Mr. Durdawk and some other seniors of the theater, I decided to give a read to a play submitted by an aspiring writer. It suddenly dawned upon me that this was the kind of talent I have been looking for the past week and it was in a moment that I made up my mind to forward this play into production. And when the matters came to the point of casting the play, I knew I had Marilyn in mind, but the others didn't. I went through two days of auditioning along with the casting director and Mr. Durdawk himself, but refused all who entered and impressed us in that room. I was guilty of deception and false reasoning that once as I went on to deny many great talents. But then reminded of the fact which instigated this, it was all meant to be for Marilyn's success and nothing else. I approached Mr. Durdawk and instilled within him a feeling of inclination to accede to my recommendation for Marilyn and I kept it from him the fact that I knew her at all.

I had auditioned Marilyn with Mr. Durdawk and his casting director alongside and she had managed to impress, m ore than me, the other two gentlemen who assessed her suitability for stage. I was finally relieved that my belief in her wasn't baseless and in our secret convocation it was the desire of the casting director to give her a chance with the new production. It was a response I had hoped for, and I was more than glad to accept it without hesitation. The following step was bringing Marilyn on board. The next couple of days were perplexing for Marilyn as she suddenly had to adapt to a new lifestyle and workplace. She didn't take much time to get acquainted with the personnel, but as the rehearsals began d uring the day, it became more and more arduous and tiring for all of us.

Marilyn wasn't the most experienced at stage, as there went on a torrent of censures and reprimands from the stage director that she had to endure, sometimes through tears and other through belief in herself. But I refrained from alleviating these critiques with aid of my position, or even secretly tending to her tears as I knew she must face the rejections and hindrances in order to become what I wanted her to be. It was brutal for her at times, I could tell, but through this furnace of test she will come to approve of herself, and I was confident that she wasn't going to give up or get replaced as the director had hinted that she is an awe-inspiring performer in need for some moral and mental sustenance and additional bit of discipline in order to be great. It was his way of conditioning her and I did not object.

Meanwhile, my relationship with Mr. Durdawk strengthened as time lapsed. He found immeasurable repose and solace when he spoke to me. Although, such instances were short and scarce, but I attempted to make them as frequent as possible by relieving myself of all work and distress and making time for him whenever he arrived or wished to speak with me.

He had surprised me that day when he had taken me to the storage and asked me to reach for a box that waited enshrouded in dust and wear of time, upon the top shelf of the far end wall. I took the step ladder and climbed onto it to stretch out my arms and remove the old box from its ancient grave and bring it into the light. I blew away the dust from and opened the cover to reveal some salvaged items inside, presumably from a devastation. I began to retrieve each item from the box and perused it closely.

"I want you to take a careful look at this and tell me what it is, or more importantly where it is from?" There was a deep excitement in Mr. Durdawk's eyes as he spoke.

I was taking my time to determine what they were, or where they came from. I saw two rolls of 16mm film, some singed burlesque masks, some rolled documents or as they appeared to be because the paper was thick, stock paper, and a battered manuscript. I unfurled the documents in the hushed silence of the storage room. Mr. Durdawk's eyes glittered and mine were just simply wide open in astonishment to discover a certificate of excellence and even more to read the recipient's name on it; Vincent Frederick Bailey. I realized that all these items were salvaged from the destruction that occurred at The Blue Crescent years ago. I looked up at Mr. Durdawk in kind acknowledgment of his benevolence to reunite me with some things that belonged to my father, as well as in amazement towards his effort to have retained and conserved all of these things to no avail, without hope of finding anyone who could relate to or accept them as their own, as a legacy on behalf of the family.

"You've kept all of this?" I spoke with utter surprise in my tone.

"Your father actually gathered all of these things, the last remains of his theater, but somehow left it in his office before leaving the city with you. I couldn't give this box over to be thrown into the trash. I had to bring it along."

"And all this time you just waited, hoping someone would come for it one day?"

"I had no hopes of finding you, but maybe you're right. I did believe, or you might even say suspected that someone would come claim it one day. But none can say I was wrong to keep it, now that you're here."

"Thank you, Mr. Durdawk. And I really mean it." I nodded to him.

"I know you do. Take a look at this masterpiece," he took possession of the manuscript from my hands. "Your father is the culprit here, and a brilliant one. This work is a piece of art, unfinished though, but wonderfully written. It is your responsibility to give it a conclusion. I wish to see this play put up in lights on the hoardings, exclusively at Durdawk Theater."

"I am not much of a writer, sir, but I will try my best if time allows." I assured him with a smile.

"Very well, so tell me George, when do I see your new play grace my stage?"

"I am hoping to be ready in five weeks, sir. Rehearsals are extremely important in my opinion. We do not need any weak performances on that stage."

"No, not at all, take your time with every aspect of the production. We will dazzle the audiences with performances they've not experienced in a long time."

"Yes, sir."

"Good, good, that's what I expect. I think I will head home now, bother Mrs. Durdawk for the rest of the evening."

"You enjoy your evening, sir."

I saw him trudge out the door and close it behind. I stayed there in profound silence with the remains of my father's desolation in my hands thinking if life had been different, if nothing had changed that day when our world ended. I couldn't think of an answer to that, no matter how hard I tried. There wasn't any. The human race has always been helpless against the intentions of time and fate, and it always will be.

That night I brooded in silence about life and its imminent uncertainties that encompassed us all. I mocked the brevity of every circumstance and laughed at its ability to expel us out of the clutches once it's had its sport by churning us through and breaking us down mentally and emotionally just to get us back up on our feet to face another one of its kind. It was a perpetual process, life was its name. I watched Marilyn as she fidgeted around the room and memorized her lines to perfection. She was so engrossed by the possibility of winning over audiences and critics for this one chance she had gotten in years, that she completely omitted the obligatory necessities from her routine, like food, rest, sleep, and love. And then I suddenly realized how Audrey must have felt when I abandoned her while at the peak of my business to leave her in dreadful solitude when she needed me the most. I managed to divert my mind off of any thoughts on the future, because that would be nothing but precious time wasted. I reached out for the old manuscript from the battered box, which was right next to a window, and began reading the work my father had left incomplete. As I went through the first couple of pages, it dawned upon me that he meant to write something that was relevant to human life as well. It was about a man who had just gotten married and suddenly faced the troubles and burdens of the new life. If I were to complete this work, I needed to make it my own, and I was beginning to give it a start.

Chapter Thirty-Two
ೲೲೲ

It was Friday night, the premiere night. Mr. Durdawk had harnessed his influential capabilities to rope in the best critics in the Los Angeles County from the biggest publications. He had also sent in formal invitations to his most respected guests and theater partisans. It was a big day for me as my word, my faith and my trust were at stake and I made my way through bustling corridors and passageways observing the nervousness across every face that passed my sight, which escalated my anxiety even more. I entered a brightly lit shared green room that was cluttered with urgently moving performers putting on costumes, make-up, final touches, one of them was Marilyn. She sat upon a chair being treated by a make-up artist, more for her waning confidence than for her appearance.

"It's going to be okay, honey. Just relax and do your thing," the artist said to Marilyn while she wiped off the sweat from her brow continuously.

Marilyn saw me and jumped up to her feet and hastened, clinging like a frightened child. She was frigid with cold hands, a trembling stature and almost tearful to which I objected or it would have washed away the attempts of the make-up artist.

"Marilyn, what's the matter?" I looked into her eyes and strengthened her.

"I can't do this, George. I can't do this, I'm so sorry. I have to go, I can't stay here." She tired to push herself out of this opportunity.

I took her to a corner away from the rest and abated her shivering shoulders. "You're not going anywhere. Have you seen how many people are out there waiting for you? They're not here for anyone else but you. Don't disappoint them, or me. You aren't just doing this for yourself, remember?"

"I can't go out there in front of so many people and perform. There are too many of them, I don't want to be embarrassed or humiliated."

"You think it will be less humiliating if you just leave right now? Leave this theater, me, Mr. Durdawk who's trusted you so much to put all of his money on the line for you. All these performers around you will probably lose their jobs. Do you want that to happen?" I paused for a moment as she began to cry. "Look at me, look at me," she looked up with tears streaming down her face. "There's always a first time for everyone, and believe me the best of them all went through the same fear just as you are right now. But they still went on the stage and that one step changed everything. There's no one out there who can do this better than you, because if they did, you would not be here. Believe in yourself, and believe the fact that I believe in you. Just go out and take them on, like you have for the past years of your life, meet them head on. This is the moment you have waited for all this time. Don't let fear or anxiety or nervousness overcome your true strength. Your strength is in your work, in your efforts, don't let it be defeated. It's too late for that. You listening to me?" She nodded in response. "Just remember one thing when you step onto that stage, you are better than everyone out there and I'm right there by your side. Okay?"

"Yes." She nodded as she gained her lost self-assurance. "I love you."

"I love you even more. Now go out there and shock the world."

I gestured the make-up artist to work on her face again and stood by her side for the duration of her preparation.

"How do I look?" Marilyn cried with the final touches.

"You look wonderful."

"You like the dress?" She pointed to her 19th century maid's costume.

"Love it, let's go." I held her hand walked her down the hallway and onto the stage and turned to her one last time before it all began. "Don't get nervous, and don't let it slip into your voice, ever. I know you'll get through."

I left the stage and receded into the left wing area with the rest. Marilyn assumed her stance, murmuring to herself words of confidence. It was time for the curtains to be lifted and so it began.

I effaced myself from the view of others and found a path leading through an empty passageway into a small opening of a room set apart for storage of lighting equipment and props. The voices were faint in this backstage area as I leaned against some metal railings and took a deep sigh, breathed slow and steady. As much confidence as I had exhibited just moments ago, fortifying every other person who seemed to be deprived of it, this was the time when I needed to fortify myself. I wasn't any different from the people out there, I did lose my courage here and there, but I kept others from perceiving it. I stayed and wondered if people would trust my belief in this production as much as I had. This was the sole chance I was going to be given. It was this end of the ocean or that, there was no sailing in the midst for me.

While lost in thoughts, I heard intermittent tapping of a walking cane and whispering footsteps that accompanied it. I looked up to find Mr. Durdawk coming closer with a warm smile across his face, something in his visage that acknowledged my present condition.

"I'm no stranger to that apprehension you're filled with right now, son. I have done many new shows throughout the years and I have witnessed myself tremble with the same feeling over and over again." He sat down upon a box in the corner and gazed at me.

"I was just a little... frightened of what may happen." I cheated my eyes from his.

"Aren't we all? That's what the premiere night is. The people on the other side of the stage, who probably have no idea what the people on this side go through, the phases, the rehearsals, all that hard work for weeks, pass judgment on our efforts with just one single sign of their reaction. Whether it's adulation or reproval, we have to take it. After all, that's what we travail for. We are at the mercy of the audience, day after day and with one minute of their, only a minute, that's all we ask for, one minute of their effort shapes our lives. The applause. If they give it to us, we thank them, if they keep it from us, we apologize to them. They win both ways, we're on the losing end. Right now, the worst thing for your performers is your absence from that hall. They need you, George. They need you to encourage them and when it's all over, they'll need you to approve of them. Because if they don't receive commendation from the audience, they're going to break inside. They need you out there, go and help them."

I managed to look up into his eyes and hold his gaze long enough to be vitalized. I stood up straight and went on my way to the stands.

I entered the left house section through the emergency door and stood at stairs in darkness observing the last act of the play. It was a story with perfect depiction of our social, common truth. The story of love and poverty crushed by the severity of wealth and pride of affluence. The story of a girl who had fallen in love with a man, but hidden the true fact of being impoverished while he represented the most reputable family in town. Of all the lies she had given just to keep him by her side and her love alive, the truth always finds its way. And when it did, it was time for her to lose. Lose what? Only the end could tell. The dialogue had poetic inkling, the setting was 19th century, and there were four performers on stage at the moment. Marilyn as the poor girl, the male lead as the rich man, and two others as his sister and mother. All of them at the summit of their dramatic ability.

"You had lied to me, o dear; for you are dearer to me no more." He said turning away from Marilyn refusing to see her face. "Did you not say you were as high as the sun that glisters, as pure as waters that come ashore? But why then did you lie? To you, I implore, say no more; for it has struck me like a squall. That you, whom beloved I call, belong to the lands beyond the wall, where nothing spawns but filth and brawl. Say you belong amidst us all in the land of wealth, where men rejoice and never crawl."

"And so you answer what you ask, my love." Marilyn pleaded turning to him. "For you assumed and never asked, my love. If you had, I would unmask, my love. Was I not pure as the waters in a silver flask, my love? Did I not glister like the sun to recover you of your worldly tasks, my love? Then how does this truth breach the tenderness of our love and stand you against me in my innocence of a dove? Was I not all you needed yesterday? Was I not all you asked last night? Then what brings the dawn of separation, then what brings the dusk of plight?"

"Do not pester my son, you wicked one," the mother stepped in. "For he is naive to the harshness of the sun. From lies driven and poverty stricken world you come. Keep away from him, your snare, your glum. With the false tenderness of evil beauty you allured him into a web, and wished his limbs to wither and his soul to ebb. And with thorns of your malice you infested his mind, to the extent where he affronts his own and stands an arrant blind."

"I thank the good intentions of the One who overlooks us all; for he kept him from drifting into darkness of deception and thrall." The sister joined in. "My brother, too late it is not for we come in time, to have you depart the clutches that appear intent on crime. Leave the woman and the shadow of her evil, for you know not how many she's ensnared and left feeble. The blood of indigence tutors its women to employ honor exchanged for gold and glitter; for they value more than honor and respect, their mirror and figure."

"Do not doubt my love, nor ridicule my honor; for I cannot bear your loathing against me any longer, for I will leave yonder and die and in my despair, wander. I am as chaste as the purity of light, and never in thoughts have I conspired to spite. A light I wished to be giving path in darkness. My love is like a sea and was never heartless. Love me, my beloved, then I leave in glee, but not with your hatred and not your hardness." The poor girl responded.

"Hear ye, my son, she intends to leave once done. She manifests her guilt and the lies she's spun. Your life holds value, but destroyed it can never be rebuilt, so her you shun, shun, shun. It is in the eyes of the poor, the glamour of wealth, their words are to tempt you in, their malice stealth." The mother cut in.

"I do not care for what the world perceives of me, but your faith is paramount, hear my plea. It is your love I desire, your company for life, you made a promise of true love, then why this strife? Poverty is not a sin, not a crime I've committed. Blame my ancestors to have brought me here when I hadn't permitted." Marilyn pleaded dropping down to her knees. "I have loved you and you only, before you I was just lonely. What of the words of love we had showered each other, what of the sweet songs we had sung together?"

"My son is no fool, he will smear not the filth of low to corrupt his renown. Go away cruel, stay the dank dungeons of your foulness, the dawn never met sundown. Forget not you're lower than low, and he is the crest of a crown." The mother held her son and pulled him away.

"I have come to your threshold, I seek forgiveness in love, sir. For the sins I've committed, even though they never were." The poor girl implored.

"There is no forgiveness for the sin of lies, I will speak to you no more, be gone unwise." The man replied.

"Say no not to me, my beloved clever. I will be yours, I promise forever." She held onto his knee.

"Go away to whomever." He pushed her away.

"Then you shall abide by your wealth and borrow and I shall drift to a world of sad and sorrow. The destitute is where I belong, where am yet not spurned and scorned but I was very well forewarned. What have I gained out of love, except for woe and disdain? Love for me has been my bane. The days that were once splendor, even the thorns of the field felt to touch tender. False were your promises, your fidelity untrue, for if this is true love, I would have it undo. Let no woman fall in love with a stone of a man. Return my heart to me if you will, or rather keep if you can. I will have no use of it anymore, its work is over, it cannot restore." The poor girl arose in tears. She began to cough, and stumbled back to her knees. "And all I ask of you, nothing more, to let me depart with one last kiss. I shall never come back, grant me my last wish?" She coughed up blood which dribbled to the ground from her lips.

"What have you done?" The man came to her and held her. She unfurled her fist to reveal a phial of poison. "Poison... but?" He's remorseful.

"My first and my last, oh, I remember the kiss, but this deceptive world couldn't bear to see us in a delightful bliss. I leave you now to your riches and gold, may you find a woman in beauty and love tenfold." She fell into his arms and more blood streamed from her mouth down her neck. "I loved you, I loved you with all my heart. And that truth, from this world, shall never depart."

She falls dead in his arms and the man repents. "No... no... no... my sweet. From me, do not part, do not part."

The curtain fell.

Chapter Thirty-Three

ço·ço·ço

There was a stinging, dreadful silence in the hall and it remained so for several seconds while my life was stuck in my throat. Mr. Durdawk joined emerging from the same door behind me and we both waited for so much as a flick of the audience reaction. I heard a couple sniffs here and there, and then suddenly a woman in the front row arose and in complete awe clapped her hands as strongly as she could. Following the echo of that lonely applause, the entire hall erupted in admiration with arms aloft and whistles. I realized those preceding sniffs originated from whimpering women scattered through the hall, who now reached for their husband's handkerchiefs and erased the trails of tears upon their cheeks. Mr. Durdawk gestured for the curtains to be lifted. The ropes were retracted and the cast stood the stage hand in hand, bowing to the extreme applause that thundered across and rattled the old walls of the theater. Critics were no exception, all of them deeply moved and appreciative of the show. Marilyn, especially, impacted by such boundless praise, was tearful and trembling. She finally caught my glimpse in the crowd as the exaltation continued and she nodded to me in gratitude. There was a smile on each face, a glimmer in each eye. We had made it through. We had come across just fine.

I went backstage and was greeted by countless joyous faces, all embraces and hugs and felicitations down the hallway. Everywhere was delight, a commotion of celebration, a joy of coming through the difficult times. I found Marilyn surrounded by fellow performers and peers being congratulated and extolled. I stayed and waited my turn but there was a surge of emotions within me that I could have lifted her up in my arms and kissed her fervently if I had no fear of being caught a conspirator, but I resisted that impulse and watched her silently. As the crowd around her diminished, I made my way and embraced her and she replied whispering in my ear, which were the sweetest and most honest words I've heard her say in years.

"I love you." We parted after that and gazed into each other's eyes for as long as we could.

A lot followed that streak of good fortune, a lot of acquaintances were made. A lot of hands were shaken and plenty admiration received. I had come across to meet, with the aid of Mr. Durdawk, the most respectable and influential names in the film business. There was an immense murmur favoring the chances of Marilyn landing in films sometime soon. Critics and spectators were equally enthralled and welcomed the cast with warm greetings as they entered the foyer to meet with the audience. Marilyn moved across the floor thanking and accepting acknowledgments and compliments and joined the circle of familiar faces amidst the throng.

"Here she is, the star of the night. Come, my dear, you have stunned us all, without a doubt." Mr. Durdawk exclaimed.

"Although, I hate to agree with him most of the times when he talks of young performers, but tonight I will second that, my love. You were fantastic." Mrs. Durdawk joined in, holding Marilyn by her shoulders and bussing her cheeks.

"I thank him for giving me the opportunity. If he hadn't trusted me for this part, I don't know where I'd be." Marilyn responded.

"Well, then I suppose it is the wrong man you're trying to acknowledge here. It's our new head of production, this man right here." Mr. Durdawk patted my back and brought me forward.

"And how can I forget him? He's the most important part of my career." Marilyn winked at me, it was quick enough to remain clandestine.

That night was the night we both made love to each other and by the end of it, we were in love with each other. As the clock ticked close to 2 a.m., I sat upon a chair looking at her sleeping soundly and breathing gently as her naked silhouette, outlined under a sheet in moonlight, undulated. I stepped over to the window and looked out at scarce life outside. A couple cars drove past, neons flickered, night sounds, nothing else. Suddenly, I felt soft hands slipping around my back and folding under my chest, her fingers entwined and she kissed the back of my shoulder.

"Hey, you're awake?" I asked arching my neck to kiss her on the forehead.

"No, you're not asleep. Come back to bed."

I turned around and looked down at her, she allowed me to. Then I lifted her up in my arms and took her back to bed.

ৡৡৡ

For the next eight months Marilyn had become the celebrity I had hoped her to be, and the star name that graced the theater hoarding radiant in lights. She had continued to be the lead performer in the two new plays that subsequently followed her first one, and was perpetually commended for her portrayals and her ability to master distinctly different characters. I was amazed myself at times to see her tackle the difficult parts so easily. I guess I had underestimated her capabilities when I had only met her, but did not doubt her anymore. But I was in fear of something that I had avoided so far but couldn't anymore. Marilyn was beginning to receive film offers, some of which were outright ridiculous, and a few worthy of consideration. I had thoughtfully weighed all the possibilities of her joining film, but I was still uncertain about a couple of facts. I knew if she went on to do a film, she would gain some quality and fame that reflects in her for the rest of her career and reminds the people of her name as soon as they hear of her. I wanted her to star in a movie that will create her legacy for the coming years, it was simple as that. Out of the offers that came her way, I completely ignored the producers who were renowned for their infamous reputation in the business. Those who valued private time and trips with their female leads more than any critical acclaim or even revenues at the box-office. There were some adult film offers that I would never allow her to do, and then there were some character roles that wouldn't give her the exposure and the stardom she deserved. I knew my failure to put her in the limelight would haunt her career forever, but I was in a predicament of choice and time. If I were to choose wisely, I needed time. And If I needed to act quick, I could err. The first impression is the last and that's all that matters. Marilyn was unaware of the fact that I had been relentlessly refusing, after deliberation, all propositions thrown at her and I made my decisions to appear as if they came directly from her. I was her manager, I was her assistant, I was her coordinator at the theater, and I was her man at home. None of it was going to change and I wanted to keep it that way. I wanted to protect her, to keep her from making a mistake she would regret for the rest of her life. I knew an artist at the summit of commendation is inclined to make bad decisions. An artist at the acme of success also tends to be overconfident. I tried my best to save her from both, but sometimes your good intentions are misconstrued for jealousy, envy and hatred.

Our relationship had thrived since our success concurred with the rebirth of Durdawk Theater. Although, it wasn't declared to the world that Marilyn was engaged or in a relationship, but people who were close enough to grasp our feelings for each other knew quite well that our companionship wasn't just professional and we did not attempt to hide it anymore. I did continue to oversee the operations at the Durdawk Theater, but now most of my time was spent managing Marilyn's career, or more precisely, refinement of her career. We had mortgaged a new home, not entirely into the hills area, but close enough to feel the air of limelight warm us as well, partially, but well enough. The two jobs that I had to juggle were a handful for me as my mornings were mostly spent at the theater and my evenings were expended in meetings and appointments with producers of all sorts.

It was a premiere night at the theater, before which I had received a call from one of the erotic film producers looking to cast Marilyn as their new face. I was already indignant at their courage to come up to me with such an outrageous offer, but I contained my temper and denied placidly. It was an hour before the opening and I was getting ready to leave for the theater when I heard a doorbell. I reached the door and opened it to two strangers. They were groomed and mannered, but unknown.

"How can I help you, gentlemen?" I questioned.

"May we come in for a minute? We won't take much time, sir." One of them answered.

I knew they weren't Mafia or anything. I looked into their eyes and intuited their intentions were related to business. I opened the door wider and welcomed them in. They slowly made their way to the hall and glanced around.

"Mr. Drake couldn't make it himself?" I commented which shocked them both. They were in utter surprise to witness my clairvoyance. "No need to be surprised, he's the one who sent you, isn't it?"

"I'm glad to witness such quality discernment, now that you are aware of our sender, I suppose you'd also be aware of our purpose."

"And that I am aware of both, I believe you are quite aware of my answer as well."

"It is just a gracious gesture, sir. Mr. Drake desires your friendship, your trust."

"I trust I made myself clear and quite direct when I said we were not interested in films right now. You're here needlessly."

"I would like you to reconsider, sir. Why would you want to keep her from films? Such a bright talent needs to be on silver screen."

"She will be. She will grace the screen one day when I see a suitable offer, but not in the manner your boss desires."

"I can assure you wouldn't find a better opportunity to introduce her to the world. We're offering a competitive paycheck, unreserved publicity, a wonderful film, what more could you ask for?"

"I have read your script, and no disrespect to your work, this isn't what I've held Marilyn back for all this time. It isn't, and it never will be. You have your audience, I give you that, but how many stars have you made so far?" There was complete silence from him. "I thought so. Your movies are like a quagmire that sinks actors to the deepest crevice of the business. None can relive on screen or stage after their disastrous decision to work with you. Their reputation precedes them, so does your boss's. So please, if you will excuse me, I need to attend a premiere. Thank you for coming. The door awaits."

I stood by the bar and watched the two men leave crestfallen, guttled a quick drink and left for the theater.

Chapter Thirty-Four

୨୦୨୦୨୦

It was yet another full house at the theater as some patrons were denied entrance due to lack of tickets and had to return unhappily to their cars. I watched the aisles from behind the curtains and saw a horde in a civilized frenzy to grab seats. I withdrew and went past the stage personnel as they urgently rushed to finish every last detail and overcome minute hindrances. As I went down the hallway, I saw a white suited chauffeur knocking the door to Marilyn's personal green room. I went further and noticed he was holding a bouquet of flowers with a card tucked in.

"She's quite busy at the moment, allow me to convey your compliments. I'm sure she will be glad to accept." I hastened over as I spoke and quickly barricaded the door.

"I have been sent by my employer to personally wish Ms. McLord well and carry a response back from her."

"I completely understand, but you would realize every moment is crucial just before start of a show and she has to be on stage in a few minutes. You may give this to me, I'll make sure she receives it."

"I have a message to deliver, and it's imperative for me to do so."

"You may deliver it to me and I'll channel it through to her. "

"You have no idea who has sent me, do you?"

"And no intentions of knowing, whatsoever. Goodbye." I snatched the bouquet from him and began to tear through the sealed envelope to read the card.

I entered the green room and found Marilyn all set with make-up and costume applying final brushes to her face. She turned and glimpsed the flowers in my possession.

"This comes as a surprise. You're finally beginning to learn what a woman likes." She sniffed at the fragrance emanating from the bouquet that had an assortment of Alyssum, Gardenia and Pink Roses. "This is the first time you've brought me flowers." She said smiling back at me.

"Twice actually." I cut right back at her.

"Really, I don't believe you."

"This is fake appreciation, it doesn't make a difference."

"Sometimes fake seems real."

"You'll be delusional to accept that. Besides, I gave you a rose once, at the premiere of Tears of Gold."

"Just one rose, yes I remember that."

"And then I sent you a bouquet on your first show's first night, anonymously."

"You did? Hmm... I didn't know that."

"It was anonymous."

"So you didn't bring these, did you?"

"Nope."

"Who are they from?"

"I will know if I can get this envelope opened." I couldn't put my finger through any gaps in the envelope and finally yanked at the sealed flap and tore away the covering and began to read the card. "Just as I thought."

"What is the matter?"

"Mr. Drake sends his compliments and his wishes to your success tonight."

"Who is this Mr. Drake."

"Another one of your admirers, hopefully a rich one. There's quite a crowd out there tonight waiting to get a glimpse of you. The only thing left now, if they begin chanting your name or probably hum like a mantra."

"I don't think any single person out there is honest to their opinion, their comments, or praises for me. I think they all lie."

"Why would they lie? They have nothing to gain out of lying."

"I don't know I just feel that way."

I stepped close to her, took her by the shoulders gazing into her eyes, "why do you say that?"

"Because the one man I think would give me the most honest, sincere review of my work hasn't said a word about my performances in the past 10 months, not a word. And has gotten me flowers only twice."

"And who is that man?"

"He's standing right in front of me as we speak."

"Marilyn McLord doesn't need flowers from this man to acknowledge her ability. She knows what she is capable of and is independent of any false praise."

"Doesn't she? I thought she was just another big eyed girl with dreams as huge as the sky to be a star. A hopeless dream."

"Well, she was, but not anymore."

"What is she now?"

"A star."

"You seem really proud of her."

"Why not, she's the only performer in years to have taken lead in three back-to-back acclaimed shows, especially at a theater that was contemplating bankruptcy some time ago. And tonight we'll change that number to four back-to-back shows."

"It's not just she who deserves all the praises and compliments."

"No, there are other performers as well, the backstage crew, the technicians, the director, Mr. Durdawk, and..."

"I wasn't talking about all those people. I was referring to someone who stood in the left wing every single show so I don't lose control. Someone who gave me courage applauding the loudest from way back next to the exit door on premiere nights."

"I'm proud of him as well."

"Really?"

"Shouldn't I be? He made it happen, he proved what he claimed, made a star out of a big eyed girl who had dreams as big as the sky."

I leaned in for a kiss, she placed her hand in between our mouths. "Make-up." I smiled and receded, a knock on the door distracted us. I went to the door and opened to see the coordinator quickly walking back down the hallway yelling "you're up."

It was yet another scintillating performance by not just Marilyn, but all the actors who worked that stage. It was a peculiar impact that Marilyn's public admiration and fame would combine to effectuate all the performers of Durdawk Theater and suddenly awaken the dormant actor inside them. Throughout the play, I continued to shift my presence from the left wing to the stands near the fire exit and I watched the show triumph over audiences just like any other that had graced this stage in the past months. But as I was enjoying the streak of good performances, I was abruptly distracted at the sight of two familiar faces that were in the second row with another gentleman who sat in the middle and whispered commands for them to jot down in their notes. This was Drake, the infamous millionaire who loved to label his exploitations as filmmaking. He had his eyes fixed upon Marilyn as I could almost smell the stench of his intentions from this distance. My attentiveness from the show gradually dwindled as my senses shifted to ward Marilyn from the inevitable attempt from Drake to obsequiously lure her into one of his films and possibly his bed. I was shaken out of my reverie by one of the crew members and realized the show had concluded and audience reaction was no different than any night before. There was a roar of applause in the hall and the people were on their feet including Drake and two of his leeches.

The backstage was teeming with actors who were now getting ready to meet the gathering of admirers in the hall downstairs. I took Marilyn towards her green room and kept from her the fact why I was hovering around her in a strange manner. I saw Drake and his men appear at the other end of the hallway, I swiftly guided Marilyn into her room and closed the door from outside and guarded it as they made their way toward me.

"If I'm not mistaken, I have the pleasure of seeing Mr. Bailey?" He asked while puffing on a cigar.

"Yes, Mr. Drake, I expected to see you as well." My response was dry and apathetic.

"Then our meeting is mutually desirable, I am quite relieved to hear that."

"I'm afraid I don't share the same eagerness."

"Oh pity, but perhaps due to my untimely visits. It was just in my good intention to find Ms. McLord at home before she left for the theater."

"Well, you never visited."

"I can assure you, if she were there, I would have. But I'd like to apologize on the behalf of my associates. They are novices at professional conversations especially with people superior to their intellect."

"I understood the nature of your offer, that's what they were sent for, isn't it?"

"Indeed, Mr. Bailey. I must admit I have failed this time in the art of persuasion and that is a rarity. But there are always other means to make people concur with your intentions, and I excel at that."

"I would hate to prove you wrong, sir, but I must."

"Enmity doesn't get us anywhere, does it? Maybe we started off on the wrong foot, why don't we head inside in a much cooler milieu and discuss in a more civilized manner? It is quite warm out here, which I believe affects our reasoning, our ability to negotiate."

"I think we're better off leaving now. Further discussion would just be a waste of time and nothing else. Marilyn is not an object that you may haggle with a seller and negotiate her price."

"You're shooting for the stars here, Mr. Bailey. Let us not forget that she after all is just an ordinary actress who's just beginning in this profession. She will need a lot of push to get where she wants to be, or rather, where you want her to be."

"She is perfectly fine where she is. And she doesn't need the push you're willing to give her."

"If I am to hear a refusal, it will be directly from Ms. McLord."

"She doesn't meet people I don't approve of. And you sir, I strongly disapprove."

One of his buffs stepped up to my face. "I'll break your face if you say one more word."

It didn't matter much to me, I was far from being intimidated. I had a crowd of my own people to back me up as they all gathered around belligerently. Drake and his men cringed without a word from me. The theater crew was ready to knock them down. But all of a sudden the door of the green room opened at the noise of this affray and Marilyn peered through. That was the moment that spiked my anger as I wanted to keep her from listening to all of this.

"What's wrong? What's going on guys?" She asked.

Drake quickly made his way forward and in an ingratiating fashion, took up her hand for a kiss. "I would like to offer you a lead role in my film, Ms. McLord. Mr. Bailey was just about to introduce us."

"Well, nice to meet you, Mr..." she said with uncertainty.

"Drake, Alfonso Drake."

"Mr. Drake."

Chapter Thirty-Five

§o§o§o

"I am a great admirer of yours, you wouldn't believe to what extent, Ms. McLord. Your performances have just shone of brilliance in the past few months. And if can remember, I have watched every play of yours at the premiere night." Drake flattered Marilyn with all his glib talk.

We were invited to the most prestigious restaurant in Hollywood Hills for a dinner three days after the incident at the theater. Drake was in full endeavor to attract Marilyn with his fallacious attempts, to wow her and have her question my discretion in keeping her from him and his films so far. Though, I was given a separate table away from theirs which I shared with his two goons who kept a steady eye on me, I still managed to overhear their conversation due to the hush in the dining hall, as everyone here spoke quietly in whispering soft voices.

"Thank you, sir." Marilyn was being callow in accepting his specious praise.

"Last I looked around here, the man on that table far left was the age of being referred to as sir, not me. I'm just an ordinary guy who loves the company of talented young women like you and strives to help them achieve the heights of celebrity they truly deserve. Alphonso, that's my name."

"Sorry, Alphonso."

"That's what I like to hear. My name uttered from the lips of beautiful women. Look Marilyn, I'm going to be very honest with you in terms of what I think you should do and why I'm here, and it never hurts anyone to be ingenuous. I believe a talent like yours shouldn't have to survive in the confines of theater. Theater is for little people with little minds. An actor like you needs to keep her progress consistent with the times. In our profession it doesn't take long for people to forget and that is the last thing you need right now. We all are aware of the pros and cons of stage. There is no fame in stage anymore, no future and definitely no money at all. Isn't it true?"

"You're not entirely wrong."

"Believe me sweetheart, I'm not wrong at all. I've seen everything this industry has to offer for the past twenty -three years. I wasn't brought up in this environment, you know, this isn't my hometown. But I had dreams, dreams just like anyone else and I came here and I saw and I conquered. It wasn't easy, none of it was. But when I see you, I'm enraged, I'm furious. Why would anyone who says he wishes the best for you keep such an absolute talent, a rising star away from prominence, from the silver screen for so long? I don't get that. You are holding yourself back. Think about the possibilities just waiting to be snatched out there in the world of films and TV. Be wise and be the one to take them away. They will not last, you will not last. The span of an actor's career in Hollywood is brief. Get what you can out of it as long as it's there."

"I have been thinking about it, it does sound interesting."

"Not just interesting, it sounds promising. What I'm offering here is a chance of a lifetime, maybe a shot in the dark. The first film is always so for a new performer. But I believe in you, I believe in your ability to entertain. I need a new face for my venture and you're my first choice."

"I'm thrilled to hear that."

"I wish we could discuss this in private, but Mr. Bailey there insisted that we meet in a public place. But I'm truly dying to hear your decision on this matter. Would you say yes to my film? There is nothing you have to fear, no contracts, no obligations. It's just a three letter word that will make my night, and your career."

Marilyn took some time as her eyes darted from Drake to me. "I will say yes."

"And there's no one you need to discuss this with?"

"No, I make my own decisions." She fortified her stance.

I caught him sneaking his hand upon Marilyn's thighs. She was instantly uncomfortable and slid away.

"We could have discussed this so much in details if were at a more comfortable venue like my office or my residence, without any interruptions." There was a lurid glow of lust in his eyes as he spoke. "But nevertheless, that could be arranged. Believe me Marilyn once you're onboard, there will be no looking back. It's just fame and fortune after that." His hand slipped around her waist, but Marilyn quickly withdrew and began rummaging her handbag to excuse herself and ward his flagrant advances.

I couldn't bear to sit through all of this harassment and opted to interrogate and stand against his obtrusive behavior.

"There are certain things that are better not-" He stopped as he saw me approaching but knavishly changed his tone as well as his words. "-disclosed before personal assistants."

Marilyn quickly jumped to my defense before I could reply.

"I think you're mistaken Alphonso, he's not my personal assistant."

"Oh, forgive me. The way he has been handling or managing you, I thought he was hired help."

"Marilyn, I think we should leave now." I ordered her.

"Does he dictate your decisions, Ms. McLord?"

"George, I think we can finish this conversation, I'll be all right." Marilyn pleaded.

"You think you can so easily ensnare her to fulfill your filthy needs with a false offer of a lead in the kind of films you make?" As my voice elevated, so did his two leeches from their seats.

"What kind of films do I make, Mr. Bailey?"

"If this was that kind of a place, I wouldn't hesitate a second to give you an explicit, in depth explanation of the milestones you've achieved so far. But this is a reputable business with honorable guests and customers who wouldn't like the honest truth said out loud. So, let's keep it that way and not break your heart."

"That is the thing about people from humble beginnings, they tend to get uncivilized so quickly."

"You haven't seen me uncivilized yet, Mr. Drake. And you pray you don't anytime soon." I was indignant.

"George, please sit down." Marilyn held my arm and contained me.

"Ms. McLord, I will disregard his conduct because of you. But if he's the one to answer for you, let me ask him this. How long do you intend to keep her from films and fame?"

"As long as it takes to find a proper opportunity that would help her career, not ruin it."

"I have made many careers, Mr. Bailey."

"Yeah, no doubt about that. I have seen so many of your fresh faces lined up outside gentlemen's clubs at night."

"This is an insult." Drake arose from his chair, his goons came close.

"George please..." Marilyn implored.

"You sit the fuck down on your chair, or I'll make you. Let's go Marilyn." The sound of silverware clatter suddenly stopped, the monotonous hum of light music abruptly muted. The dining hall was at a standstill with waiters converging and contemplating whether to intervene or not. I stomped away from that table, fervent with anger.

"I apologize on his behalf, I'm so sorry." Marilyn tried to settle things down as I waited steps away from her.

"You get rid of that man soon, Ms. McLord. He'll get you nowhere." Drake gestured his men to stay put. Marilyn collected her things and came after me.

Our drive home was dreadfully silent, but the flares of aggravation were exuding from both ends. As we reached our driveway, Marilyn stormed out of the car slamming the door behind and entered the house in sheer wrath. I delayed for a moment, contemplating the inevitable altercation. I finally exited the car and trudged inside the house.

I saw Marilyn at the bar emptying a snifter in two swigs. She eyed me as I entered, she was crimson at the moment.

"That was completely unnecessary." She slammed her hand on the bar counter. "What you did there was completely un-called for."

"I was looking out for you."

"For me or for yourself? What is the matter with you? You overreacted like a goddamn hoodlum off the street. That is one of the biggest producers in Hollywood today, George. The way you came at him was horrible, disrespectful."

"Disrespectful? You think I was being disrespectful when his hands were all over your body and you were faking that smile to keep him off? You think I don't know what he was trying to do?"

"I knew what he was trying, and he wasn't going to get anywhere because I know who I am and what I have to do to protect me."

"You're wasting your time with that man."

"Wasting my time? George, I'm desperately trying to give myself some options here. I'm trying a little harder to be what I've always wanted to be, for years. Isn't that what I came here for? And if that opportunity gets within reach, why not go for it?"

"You didn't come here alone, Marilyn. We did. And what do you think I have been trying to do for the past several months?"

"That's what I'm worried about, George. A year is a long time to be staying in one place and doing something over and over again. I'm not getting anywhere with this. I did not come here for theater, I was never a fan of the stage. You wanted a start, you have it. Now it's time to go forward."

"People spend their lives on stage."

"Well, I'm not one of them. You said start from the bottom, work your way up. If you see Drake's films as the bottom, why not let me start with him? I'll work my way up."

"That is not a start, that is a dead-end to your career."

"Can I for once make a decision about my life, my career? I want to do a film, George, I wasn't meant for theater. And he's made famous movies, he's one of the biggest names. Maybe he has done some poor ones here and there, but that doesn't mean he hasn't done his part in films."

"Films? You call his sexcapades films? When women are ensnared and forced on false hopes of becoming famous to be placed for a public display just for the viewing pleasure of a couple of perverts. You call that a film?"

"His personal life has nothing to do with us, George. I am going to work for him and that's the end of it. I have waited for this for very long and if I can find something to get me up the ladder, I will shoot for it."

"You have no idea what you're saying. You'll ruin yourself."

"Then let me, it is my life, my career and maybe I'll learn from my mistake for once. A start is all I'm asking, I can't wait any longer. I've been used before with nothing in return, maybe this time it will change. It is not a big deal to me."

"It is to me." I fell on the couch. A long moment of silence passed between us. "I'm asking you to not make this mistake, Marilyn. I have worked hard, you have worked hard to reach where we are now and this accomplishment isn't trivial. Don't end everything with one hasty, impulsive decision. I'm asking you to stay away from this man and his film."

"It's now or never, George. I have given him my word. I cannot refuse now. I never thought we would fight each other over something so insignificant. I couldn't imagine you will try to keep me from getting ahead. I know you have been denying other producers, as well. Why, George?"

I took a deep breath. "I have been running around as much as I can, making contacts, meeting with people, trying to promote your name. In one year this is what you've gathered. One year, a house, a car, a reputation that precedes you. People spend their lifetime looking for fame and celebrity. If you think what I've done so far is insufficient or scarce in any way, do whatever you want to do, Marilyn. This is your life, your career. I will have no interference in it."

"Oh George, it's nothing like that, I trust you." She came closer and sat by my side holding me by my arms.

"Do not talk about trust with me." I was enraged as I threw away her hands and arose in anger. "Do not talk about trust with me now. Out of all the women, I thought at least you would have that keen eye to tell apart perverts from good men. If you want to work with such kind of people, then go ahead. I will not stop you from sleeping your way to the top."

"George." She protested.

"I thought you would be a little different from the rest. But I was wrong. You are just another girl with big dreams of becoming an actress who'll spread her legs for anyone and let him have his way while he's at it. Well, that's your path, take it. Fuck your way to the top, if you can get there, and stay happy."

Marilyn was in tears, "so this is it? This is how it ends?"

I shook my head in disbelief, "I'll still stick around, if you need a personal assistant and can't afford one yet. I'll work for free, without expectations of course. But yes, this is how it ends between us. It's just you from now on, no more of us. If you still need me to handle your appointments with Mr. Drake and other professional contacts, fit your late hour rendezvous within your work schedule. I think I can manage that. I'll be around."

"I hate you, I fuckin' hate you."

"I'm sure you do."

Marilyn began to scramble up the stairs, but I stopped her again.

"I can phone Mr. Drake right now and apologize for my behavior. Maybe you can please him tonight and make sure you get that part he offered you."

"Get out of my life, leave...." she ran up the stairs whimpering and faded from my view. I sank into a chair and poured myself a glass full of scotch.

Chapter Thirty-Six
శశశ

The sky was yet indigo and dawn approached fast. It was an early wake-up call for me as I hardly slept the recent dark hours. A river of memories streamed my mind. There were feelings of regret mingled with pity. There were traces of anger mingled with despondency. I had come quite far to leave Marilyn just like that due to a single altercation. Our relationship meant more to me than pure ego and pride. I had let these destroy my marriage once before, I couldn't allow them to ruin me again. I knew if I wouldn't be mature enough to make amends, we would only drift further apart. I decided to surprise and reconcile with Marilyn by preparing and bringing her breakfast in bed. I placed the platter on the bedside and leaned in for a kiss that woke her up.

"Morning sunshine." My face lingered into her eyes.

"Mornin', isn't it too early?"

"Yeah, for your beauty sleep, it is. But sometimes you just can't sleep any longer, and then you bother your companion and wake her up to talk to you."

"I thought we were done with all the talking last night."

"Last night was a mistake, I said things I shouldn't have, and you..."

"What did I do?"

"You got furious and said things you shouldn't have."

"Did I?" Marilyn sat up, still wrapped in her comforter. "You sound changed now."

"Yes, you know the hardest gem in the world? A diamond. If we all stayed as adamant as that there would hardly be a difference between a human heart and a stone. I have changed my mind and my views."

"Good."

"But I'm still resolute in my opinion. It's merely a suggestion now, but I'm still with you even if you don't... if it doesn't matter."

"Even if it did, George, I have given him my word. I said I will do his film and I will. Now you can decide if you're there with me, or not?"

"I am. For now, I am."

Marilyn had made it quite clear that she'd decided to quit theater and join films as she refused to go for rehearsals or answer any phone calls received from the theater. She wasn't going to face the people there or Mr. Durdawk because she wasn't answerable to any of them, I was. They had trusted my faith in her and had come to meet her through me. She wasn't going to ask pardon for this abrupt absence and belittle herself before anyone now. After a protracted self doubt and dispute that rattled my soul within, I decided I couldn't possibly ask Mr. Durdawk to weaken their business or incur losses because of my failure. And I couldn't just simply assume silence and never return or face him again. I resorted to an easier approach, which was always beneficial to all parties involved; seeking forgiveness. The most I could ask of him, in the given situation while I sought his kindness, was cancellation of the show until further news.

I had already spoken to one of the directors on the telephone that Marilyn wouldn't work there anymore, and when I reached the theater there were some indignant glares thrown at me. They were wordless but exclaimed a world of anger and hopelessness. I stole myself from their frowns and went on into Mr. Durdawk's office and saw him brooding in silence. At my ingress, he quickly jumped out of his chair and welcomed me.

"Oh my dear boy, you almost gave me a heart attack disappearing like that. What happened to you? Is everything all right?"

"Mr. Durdawk, I'm extremely sorry for what I have done and it was utterly rude of me to not inform you of my whereabouts, but I have something to tell you."

"Go on, son." He grew intensely worried and took his chair.

"Marilyn has decided to... leave this theater. I mean leave stage entirely. She wouldn't be doing plays anymore. She needs to move into films now and she has made up her mind to join a venture. She wouldn't be able to come here any longer. I know her contract with this theater still has a couple more weeks to go, but...." I was at a loss for words after that glancing into Durdawk's eye. I was as apologetic as I could be.

"Hmm... I knew this was going to happen the moment that evil man stepped into my theater. George, you're a very good man. And one thing that you don't randomly find anymore is that you're a man of your word and wisdom. I do not own her. Well, according to the contract she had to perform here for six more weeks which completes her one year, but... even if I tried I couldn't overlook the honesty and altruism that you've shown us all. You brought my theater back to its glory, you have breathed life into us all. It has generated more revenue in ten months than it has in the past five years. Finding someone else is not a difficult task, but for her to leave the theater all of a sudden, I fear that she might be at a loss. She needs to learn a lot, ten months is nothing in this business. And if she believes what that man Drake has to say, then she will end up learning it the hard way and it wouldn't be very pleasant. You have waited so far, what's the hurry now?"

"Maybe she is right. Maybe I was seeking out for my own interest more than I should have. I was being too defensive."

"You were protecting her because you love her. This business is like a gold covered swamp. It's all glitter from above and nothing but filth and wretchedness underneath it. No one escapes it once you're stuck. All the talks, the promises, the hopes are all specious, transient. It'll vanish in a moment."

"I don't know, sir. If she wishes to do it, I will not stop her anymore."

"My theater has reared her like a child since the day she began. I cannot let her ruin her own life. Believe me, I have introduced about a hundred artists on that stage, but she had something special. There is still time, stop her."

"And you think she will listen to me? You think I haven't tried? She's gone too far now."

"So it is as I presumed. Well, I release her from my contract, you may fear no legal issues. You have my word George. Just for you."

"Thank you, sir. I sincerely promise to compensate for any losses in all this time."

"Do not shame me, George. I still can stand on my own. But why don't you stay with us. We could use you."

"I wish I could, sir." I rose up and shook hands with him. "Thank you, once again." I began to leave.

"George, she might not admit to this, but she will need you by her side. And for one last time she will look for you before it all ends. I hope you are there, for her sake."

"I will be there, sir." With that I left the office, the theater and a circle of most talented and honest friends I ever knew.

༺ༀༀༀ༻

I returned back home and went up the stairs lethargically after a grieving drive back from the theater. I knocked on Marilyn's bedroom door and entered to find her at the vanity in bright lights of the dresser, applying facial make-up. She glimpsed at me coldly in her mirror. I gazed at her thinking of all the moments that went awry in our relationship, there weren't many, but maybe I missed some.

"I don't mean to disturb you, but I wanted to let you know that I went to Mr. Durdawk and spoke to him about you leaving the theater before a year. He promised there wouldn't be any legal troubles to encounter, even though we have breached a contract."

"Good, even if he dared to sue me, Alphonso said he knew how to take care of such people. We wouldn't have had any trouble."

"Great, I was worried without a cause."

"How do I look?" She arose wearing a peach colored sheath dress, but before I could answer, she spoke again. "Hope they like it there. I don't want to make a lousy first impression at the office."

I smiled and remembered that there was a time when she worried whether I liked what she was wearing or not. Now, it was them. I took a deep breath and asked, "is there anything else I can do for you today?"

She turned and gazed at me.

As I grew uncomfortable I asked, "what happened?"

"What are you trying to do?" She questioned, a bit nettled.

"What?"

"This. Whatever this is you're doing. Whatever act you're trying to pull on me, stop it."

"Act? I thought that was your job. No matter how much I try, I could never act, even if I tried to."

"I think I'm done here." Marilyn got up and stormed out of the room, down the stairs and to the bar so swiftly, I could sense she was exasperated again. I followed her slowly down to the living.

"Are you coming or not?" She gulped a whole glass of bourbon in one breath.

"If you want me to."

"Whatever you do, don't make a scene there. That's the last thing I need right now."

"You have my word. I won't say a word."

She nodded and headed for the door. I came to the bar and calmly observed the empty glass, then headed after her.

We drove to Centre City which was the commercial hub of San Diego and fueled the economy of the surrounding areas. Our destination was a renowned commercial building where Marilyn had appointed to meet with Drake. We were catered by a valet at the entrance and continued into the shimmering facade of glass and steel to encounter a benign reception in the atrium.

"How may I help you?"

Marilyn took a step forward and smiled. "Drake Film Productions office, please?"

"Sixteenth floor, would you please sign the visitors register here, the elevators are to your right."

"Thank you." Marilyn signed the section and moved toward the elevators. I followed her keeping my promise of not uttering a word. We went up to the sixteenth floor and were greeted by another receptionist in the foyer. "How may I assist you today, miss?"

"I'm here to see Mr. Drake, I have an appointment with him at noon."

"Absolutely, and who shall I say is here?"

"Marilyn McLord."

"Just a moment, please have a seat and I'll ring him up."

Marilyn receded onto one of the couches as the receptionist began to work her telephone and attempted to intercom the office. She hung up the phone and responded with a pleasant smile. "He will be a short while as he's with some clients right now, Ms. McLord. Would you like something while you wait?"

"No, thank you. I'll wait."

We waited at the front for a good half an hour which I perceived to be intentional from Drake as he prioritized to belittle my dignity after the night of our verbal conflict. Little did he know that one must have dignity and honor to be stripped of as I had none at the moment or I wouldn't be here. I was there because I had made a promise to Marilyn to stick with her as long as she needed me. I wasn't going to break any more promises. Drake came out of his office with a grand smile from one ear to the other and welcomed Marilyn with a kiss on her hand and shot a glimpse at me with a smirk.

"How wonderful it is to see you both in my office. Why don't you follow me inside?" He said leading Marilyn to the door clutching her arm. "Get us some coffee." He ordered the receptionist before entering the office.

I followed Marilyn into Drake's lavish sixteenth floor lair and found it to be extremely impressive in appearance and grandeur. The walls were all glass with a spectacular view of the city behind, unnecessary for him to watch the weather news whoever possessed this den, as the glass gave a clear view of the skies miles to the west. He made Marilyn take a seat right across the desk and took a chair himself. I was uninvited, but treated myself to a chair.

"So sorry I couldn't attend you any sooner, Marilyn. I was with some investors for my next project. One must keep them interested with new ideas and possibilities. You always need the dough to make bread right?"

Marilyn laughed at his bland attempt at a joke.

"So, tell me what brings you here, or shall I speak to your manager perhaps? Oh, my apologies, I forgot you told me he's not your manager. If I can determine a term to name your relationship with each other, it would be quite unraveling."

"I am going..." Marilyn began to speak but I cut in.

"Mr. Drake, you may not trouble yourself with these trifling matters anymore. The good news is that Ms. McLord here is independent now, entirely capable of making her own decisions. So, you may directly converse with her about your future projects. There would be no disruptions from my end."

"Is that so? Glad to hear that, in fact, I would like to congratulate you, Ms. McLord, on your liberty from such stifling restraints. It is so lively to breathe the air of freedom, isn't it?"

Marilyn conjured a false smile. "Mr. Drake, I'm here to speak to you about the offer that we discussed."

"And it ended quite abruptly and undesirably due to some... misunderstandings or I shall say, deliberate hindrance?" He glared at me again.

"I am extremely sorry for what happened that night. But I am very interested in your proposal, Mr. Drake."

"You forget so easily, Marilyn. It's Alphonso for you, not Mr. Drake. That's for the girls who sit outside at the reception. You are so much more special than them."

"Excuse me, Alphonso. So as I said, I am willing to accept this challenge and hopefully I can perform to your expectations."

"I'm certain of that and in case if you don't, I know how to make people please me to the core."

I was lurid with wrath listening to this conversation.

"But I would still need you to reconsider, I mean sit on it for a while. Once you finalize your decision, we can move forward. I'm certain you would need some manner of approval from people who surround you in life, presently?"

"There aren't any so closely surrounding me at the moment, Alphonso." Marilyn retorted clenching her jaws.

"That is indeed good news, Mr. Bailey."

I shrugged with a wry grin. "I will be outside if you need me. I think there are some things that are better kept from people of no importance. I will wait by the reception, Mr. Drake, Ms. McLord."

I exited the office and charged down the hallway to the elevators with nothing more than a lonely heart, with which I started this journey, I ended it.

Chapter Thirty-Seven

❦❦❦

When a feeling of unvented wrath assuaged inside of me and I came back to the harsh reality of the world, I realized that I was alone, once again. Although, I had no intentions of abandoning Marilyn during these times which I knew were shaping to be very demanding, daunting and depressing in more than many ways, I decided to keep my distance from her as well as her work so that she might discover the true evil behind fallacious, compassionate personas and dissembled indulgences firsthand. I did not want her to get hurt, even after all that she had done and said, I did not desire any harm upon her. I was going to be around whenever she needed a hand of support, a shoulder to cry on. But there was something I knew for sure, it wasn't going to be anytime soon that she comes to unwillingly face the consequences of her choices and at that moment, if she does not find me, she will yet again destroy herself. She might not admit it, might not admit at all, but I knew. Maybe I was wrong, maybe I underestimated the strength within that petite frame, or maybe I misunderstood the hardened shell that had made her an unemotional woman, but I was willing to trust my first conjecture.

I took a long walk to the bus stop which I, after asking fellow pedestrians twice, found at the corner of the street about fourteen blocks down the main road. I stood in the queue and observed life around me which I hadn't done in a long time and as it went on in a prosaic monotony, I suddenly had the urge to be a part of it. It had been almost a year since last I had such disconcerting thoughts in my head, but now when they arose, I wasn't strong enough to repress them anymore. What is life? A journey that lasts only as long as you do, right? Well, as far as you are concerned, that's about it. And we all go around making it all the more miserable for ourselves as well as unintentionally for others. And that isn't just one man, or one family, or one community living a specific time period, it's the whole world. Man after man, generations after generations. And to top that cake with a cherry, even our depressions and delights, our woes and jubilations are the same. We rejoice our marriages, then despise our spouses with time. We can't live without our parents when young but can't bear to stay with them after our puberty and independence kicks in. We're excited at birth of our children, grieved at the death of our loved ones, glad upon our promotions and worried when laid off. We cry at our break-ups or hide it under a veil of celebration, we don't give a damn about others before our own interests. We derive pleasure from witnessing the failures of the people we hate. Not one aspect of this tedious life in which we differ from each other, is there? But there are some despicable rejects like me who cannot relate to some of these feelings because life hasn't come full circle. It has just tempted me at times and my inflated ego, my exaggerated narcissism and overbearance has done the rest of the ruining for me.

I got off the bus and began walking aimlessly down an unknown path. I didn't know where I was, and it wasn't the first time I'd felt like this. I came across a small children's park and perched upon a picnic table with a clear view of the slides and swings. A vivid happiness glittered from the faces of the little ones who toiled around the playground with no troubles to bother them, no worries to torment their minds. And the exuberance on their mothers' faces to see their children smile evoked a strange emotion within me. I was reminded of someone, someone I once knew, someone I wanted to forget but never could. My heart cringed to say her name, my lips quivered. I closed my eyes and imagined her face before me, that smile of hers that would take away all my fears, my failures. Those eyes, unfathomable, deep as the oceans of the world to drown my pain, my troubles. That face, enchanting to the extremes to render you euphoric with just one glimpse. Audrey.

I quickly wiped away that reverie from my mind and returned to the truth of my existence. I looked around myself and found nothing, no past, no future, no home to return to, no life to anticipate. It was just me and me alone. I didn't know if I loathed the idea of living a common life or despised my loneliness as my wants and wishes were cryptic even to me. I was ambivalent, uncertain, demented in my own perception. I couldn't demand from life anything more than it had already given me, but I still reviled it. I shouldn't have absolved myself for ravaging every joyous blessing life had granted me, but I still forgave. I didn't know where I was going or what I was about to do. I didn't even know if I wanted to live anymore, but I persisted.

I had wandered until dusk and sauntered through unfamiliar streets like a nameless spirit that wasn't acknowledged or even noticed by those around. I was invisible to all. But I continued to see, see all that went around me. Some of it replete with happiness, and some reeked of sadness. There were a thousand faces I had ambled past that day and none seemed the same to me. All of them bore a completely different perception of life, maybe similar to some extent, but not entirely. As night became prevalent, I came around the corner and spotted a dingy tavern. A meager joint partially lit by flickering neons. An old ramshackle place which drew me towards it, maybe to solace me in the times of despondency. I entered through a glass door that was covered in stickers of all kinds that have remained stuck there for years almost becoming a part of that door. I came inside, initially adjusting my eyes to sudden darkness that permeated the bar. I squinted for a better view of the place and in the red hue of the Budweiser sign, I sighted some jaded and jovial souls. It was a nice farrago of emotions. I made my way to the bar and ordered a beer listening to a "blue moon" instrumental on the stereo. The bartender brought up a bottle and tumbler, removed the crown cap with an opener and placed it before me. I took a swig directly from the bottle and glanced around at others. A group of bikers in Harley jackets, beards, and incessant obsession with tattoos and piercings, occupied a pool table in the far corner. Some other unkempt, haggard men scattered around in solitude listening to the prosaic tune and brooding, some at the brink of surrendering to slumber. A couple that took the table for two near the window, delighted with each other's company, kissing momentarily, smiling. They got up and the man paid the tab, leaving a tip. He clutched her hand and took her out of the joint. A group of teenagers playing a game of pool at the second table, as theirs were the only cheerful noises heard in all vicinity.

I glanced outside the window to my right and sighted the same couple coming to a stop right next to a black BMW convertible. He slid his hands right from the back of her neck onto her hips and leaned into her pushing her against the car and kissing her passionately before opening the door for her to enter and scrambling to the driver's side himself. He ignitioned the car and pressed on the accelerator while in neutral to show the power of the engines of his seventy three thousand dollar car. He slew out of his parking spot and raced down the road with no regard to safety or mannerism at all.

After two hours of aimless thinking about myriad troubles of my existence and six beers, the final subject of deliberation was something that every person faces by the end of the day; I had to go home. Home? Do I have one? And if I did, where was it? And finally if I did manage to inhibit my ego and pride and decided to return, another question arose; would I be welcome there? I had no answer to that, not even if I tried to flip through my memory to find one reason to return. I looked up at the bartender and understood that he waited for me to leave in order to close the place, as I was the last one in there. He maybe wanted to take a moment of relaxation in the back room, but eschewed saying it to my face. Was it because he commiserated with my current circumstance, or just simply because I had a tab of thirty-seven dollars still due. I rummaged my pockets for money and extracted two twenty dollar bills and put them on the table for him. He glanced down at the cash and nodded for the tip. I acknowledged him and then shambled out of the god forsaken place.

I came out into the brisk exterior called the world and joined in. With nothing more to do or say, or discover or resent, or curse or love, I walked all the way to the bus stop and with a couple of other people who kept to themselves, I waited. This diurnal activity of being lost and found became a routine for me as I didn't even remember how long it had been since the day I left Marilyn and Drake in that office and stepped out in the misery of my own world. Maybe a week or a month, but I certainly remembered to make wandering trips to strange far away areas of LA every day, sitting idle in parks and watching people in the afternoon and ending up in a bar and drinking to capacity by nightfall. Maybe it was simply to get away from the truth, so I wouldn't have to come face to face with and grasp the meaning of it, so I could just go to sleep drunk and return to my routine the next morning.

As I rode the bus that night, I checked my wristwatch and saw the time ticking close to midnight and it wasn't a surprise as I had traveled for almost an hour now and changed two busses to get back home. That's how far I'd come. Past midnight I staggered and stumbled my way to the front door of our small little heaven. I checked my pockets for the key but unfortunately couldn't find them tonight. I had no choice but to wake Marilyn up by knocking at the door and several attempts at the doorbell. I heard the faint sound of the door chain being removed as it jangled.

"Where is your key?" The words were hurtled at me instantaneously as the door swung open. Marilyn stood there in her robe seemingly aggravated, awakened from a deep sleep. It wasn't the best time to confront her.

"Did I wake you up?" My voice cracked, I hobbled further.

"No, I was waiting for you with dinner on the table."

"You were?" I couldn't tell in my fuddled state whether she was being sarcastic or truthful.

"God... what is the matter with you, George? I have to get up in the morning. I have rehearsals from tomorrow and I need to be there by eight to get started. I need my sleep."

"I did not know you were starting work tomorrow."

"Well, you have to be at home to know such things, which you hardly are."

"I'm sorry if I disturbed you."

"And you're drunk again. Great. Where did you disappear to this time?"

"I had a lot to think about."

"In this condition? Well, I hope you're done with all your thinking. I don't know if you want to come with me to the shoots, but if you don't, please refrain from bothering me anymore. I need no distractions, good or bad."

"Since when am I a distraction? Distractions are people that you need to attend, those who matter. I'm just as good as not being here anymore."

"You're drunk, and that's just as bad as not being there. Now go to sleep and we'll talk in the morning."

"Why does a person who speaks the truth is either called insane or drunk?"

"When you find out let me know."

Marilyn headed up the stairs and slammed her door shut. I knew I was sleeping on the couch without her having to say a word. I went to the bar, poured myself a drink, stepped over to the couch and sat by the window just watching the void black of the night skies above.

Chapter Thirty-Eight

ᎨᎨᎨ

The next day I had woken up very early with a throbbing hangover. Marilyn was still asleep as I helped myself to a cup of coffee and breathed in some morning air in our backyard. Minutes passed into hours while I stood and waited. I knew it was her big day, so I kept my grievances to myself and waited for her to dress and prepare and leave for the first day of rehearsals. She came down the stairs and joined me at the dining table not eating much, but trembling with nervousness. It suddenly came to my mind the way I had comforted her back in the day when it was her firs t night at stage. I wanted to do that again, I wanted to strengthen her once more but I was afraid this time, afraid of how she might receive consolation now. She stood up taking some long deep breaths and decided to leave. I wasn't beckoned, but I knew I had to tag along for a promise I had made.

We reached the studio and entered the gates to stage seven. A couple of trailers were lined up, one of them marked for Marilyn. A number of crew workers hastened around, some costumes being exhibited on a stand were rolled into the studio. Marilyn and I got out of our car and stood there absorbing everything for a while. We glanced at each other and nodded. Drake and some of his assistants came out of stage 7 and welcomed Marilyn with loud greetings.

"Ms. McLord, finally the day has arrived. We begin our new journey together. And let me assure you of one thing, this isn't going to be the last one."
"I'm sure it wouldn't." She replied gladly.

"Let me welcome you into your trailer right here."

I stayed behind to let them conclude their superficial exuberance and talks, as the door was shut and they stayed inside for a while. One of the script consultants came outside the trailer door and knocked, there was no answer from inside. He found me nearby and stepped close.

"Do you work for her? Marilyn McLord?"

I took a moment to answer him, "yes."

"Would you give her this script? Tell her it's scene number eleven we're rehearsing today, page nine."

"Sure." I took the clasped script from him and nodded. I began to go through the outline as I realized this wasn't the film that Drake had initially offered Marilyn. I was unaware when the project had been switched and quite uncertain all over again.

Drake exited the trailer and went on his way into the studio and I slowly reached up to the steps and inside the trailer. I saw Marilyn was already holding a copy of the script and going through it. She gave me a cursory glimpse then went back to memorizing the dialogue. I examined the trailer and assessed it to be neither superior nor inferior to a standard star wagon. There were enough amenities for a day shift, comfortable sized space, in fact commendable for an actress on her first movie role. I kept the script on the side and stood there waiting for Marilyn to address me again with just a glance.

"What is it?" She asked without looking up.

"Is this a different film?"

"Yes, Alphonso told me he was going to work on another film. That one didn't work out."

"You are sure the script is the only change and nothing else?"

"I've read the script once, and I trust him. Besides, it's nothing to be concerned about, it's a good movie."

"I'm sure it is. I'll be outside, just knock on the door if you need me." I came out of the trailer and stood guard at the door. Even though not much needed, I attempted to maintain my importance by being there as much as I could around the people and a place that didn't want me.

The shooting for the film had started and I watched Marilyn perform lingering in the shadows and corners of the studio. She followed directions from Drake submissively and meticulously, but there were other times when she wouldn't feel comfortable doing certain things but was compelled to do. I don't think anyone on the sets discerned or even suspected her discomfort, or even if they did, they were not in a position to contradict their employer. I couldn't help but notice it all, but I was bound to the word I had given her. Whether in sickness or health, grief or happiness, joy or despair, I was to remain silent, and silent I was. Marilyn had what she always wanted, the warmth of limelight upon her, a circle of applauding admirers even if they faked their true intentions. The sound of a person yelling lights, camera, action. The action was full on from that point. I visited Marilyn's film sets every other day and didn't find anything changing in terms of content of the shoots. It was almost similar every time I watched. Marilyn was hesitant in doing some scenes in which she had to abandon her comfort and disrobe in front of a crew of fifty strangers and a lead actor who would stare at her from head to toe with a reprehensible grin. As she stood naked, I noticed Drake consuming a lot more time to initiate a scene and calling it a cut, repeating the takes multiple times unnecessarily. Marilyn tried her best to cover her vulnerability as Drake approached from one take to another elucidating the needed expressions that were suddenly vacant from her performance. He even tried a hands-on approach, much to her dislike, but anything goes for that few moments of fame.

I was back in the company of my friend with whom I would spend most of my evenings and nights. I actually looked forward to seeing her, or I must say, devouring her. My quarter of whiskey that stayed where I left it off the last time I slept with her. Didn't ask for anything, didn't demand much out of me, except a word or two in its laud. Was always willing to give me as much as I wanted, even if it meant draining the last drop out of her. It was all good. Sometimes I would spend hours just watching the clock sucking time from my life, one minute after another. Sometimes, I would visit the Durdawk Theater to see old friends and acquaintances. I would sit there for long hours discussing their new plays, actors, prospects. I also visited them on their premiere night with a new lead replacing Marilyn. I wouldn't say she was better or worse than Marilyn, but she did amazingly well with her given work. After the play, I was introduced to her by Mr. Durdawk who referred to me as the doctor who resuscitated this theater to life. Much to my embarrassment and denial of the analogy, she willingly accepted that and appeared very amicable in nature. But the pleasant times were short-lived and I had to return to my misery after all the laughs, the talks, the living.

It was a restricted shoot which only lasted seventy days, but I was certain a director with such laudable experience in the field of cinema would definitely know about his craft more than anyone else. Things were exciting for a couple of weeks that followed after the shooting ended and Marilyn went through the whole process of post production with re-recording and voice over. As days passed, I heard Alphonso Drake felt the need to re-shoot some parts of the film which delayed it even more. I didn't know if the news was a rumor or an actuality, but after seeing Marilyn upset for a couple of straight days and finding her extremely exhausted at times, I believed it was true. About seven burdensome months had passed since Marilyn had left the theater in hopes of encountering stardom in films, and I assumed there were many more to intervene until she actually did acquire it. I was quite sure it wouldn't come to her through Drake's venture. The film finally released that November after ten excruciating months of wait and it was a limited release so only graced a few theaters nationwide. The audience response wasn't any different than what I had predicted before any of it even started. Though, I would hate to say, after so much had happened just because of this film, it was a complete failure at the box-office as well as with the critics. The only reception to this movie came from personal acquaintances that were directly or indirectly related to the making of this picture and some handful Alphonso Drake fanboys who loved to watch gratuitous nudity on film without any necessity or meaning to it.

I didn't accompany Marilyn on the promotional campaign for the film, which hardly made a difference. I did not attend the premiere with her. Therefore, I hadn't watched the film. I would stay home by the bar and watch time fly as Marilyn's late night meetings continued to stretch past midnight and even further. I wasn't invited to these parties or social, business gatherings and I didn't make an effort to be a part of them either. But I could tell the character of these meetings by the condition of Marilyn's return. I didn't want to eavesdrop on her, but sometimes I would listen to the faint sounds of her whimpering inside the bathroom where she pretended to take a shower and even left the water running. I could feel her cowered in the corner and crying out her rage, her emotions, her feelings. As much as I wanted to alleviate her pain with an embrace or a kiss, I feared doing both. I could have taken her in my arms and told her that nothing has changed and everything will be all right, but I wasn't sure if I'd be talking to someone who would listen and be comforted by my words, by my support, by my presence. It was the fear of losing the last bit of what I was left with that made me stay away from her.

I conjured enough courage to go to a theater and watch the film, as much as I hated to, but that was the only theater in all the county that still had it running. I sat in an empty theater hall and watched the last day last show with two more spectators ahead of me. One of them, evidently drunk, emptied a six-pack within an hour and went off to sleep. While the other would flutter and pulsate whenever a provocative scene would come up on screen. After a while I realized the man was masturbating in the empty hall with no care of being caught. But that wasn't what aggravated me while I sat in the theater, it was the revelation that rattled my temperament. I had just watched an hour and forty-three minutes of a film that had only about twenty minutes of Marilyn on screen. A film that was suppose to launch Marilyn as one of its leads, made a pinup girl out of her. Twenty minutes of sex scenes and that's all she was in it for.

It eventually dawned upon me what had happened in all this time since the shooting halted. Drake was done with Marilyn and her part in his film as well. A new face was brought in, given the same specious hopes and lies, ensnared just like Marilyn. She wasn't the female lead anymore, but just one of those insignificant substitutes to exploit. In fact the picture was just a collection of scenes featuring six women who were filmed unclothed for the pleasure of the viewers. I was infuriated as I smashed my fist upon the arm rest and stormed out of the hall. Suddenly all of Marilyn's sorrows and heartaches played before my eyes and troubled me to the core. I headed somewhere I did not intend to, but I was too outraged to be stopped now.

Chapter Thirty-Nine

ço·ço·ço

After some time I reached home, my expectations to find Marilyn were close to zilch but I still went up the stairs in search for her. I found the bedroom door ajar and peered through finding her at the vanity staring at herself, devoid of any superficial persona, any embellishment, any fabrication, any emotion, any make-up. She just sat silently and gazed at her reflection. A knock on the door stirred her from her deep pensive state and made her look at me in the mirror as I entered. There was a certain longing in her eyes I could feel, but she kept quiet.

"You're home early." I attempted to begin a conversation.

"I've been home since… you're the one who's been missing." Her voice exhibited signs of recently ended, continuous sniveling.

"I was… I was at the theater, watched your film tonight. They were going to take it down tomorrow, so I thought why not see it before they do. It was… not bad."

She gave a smirk and shook her head. "You here to make fun of me, George? Because if you are, let me help you a little bit. Well, of course I wouldn't be able to excel at it, I still have some dignity left in me, but I'll try. And first of all I'll commend you and your efforts and all you did for me. But being a senseless whore that I am, I just ruined everything you worked for. I destroyed my career with my own hands. You know you aren't the first one to laugh at my face tonight and you wouldn't be the last either. But maybe you're here to do something better." Marilyn fidgeted around the room deliriously.

"Marilyn…" I tried to mollify her, but to no avail.

"No, no let me speak. I finally find the moment to be honest about me, about you, about every fucking thing that's been going on since this circus started and you're trying to take it away from me? You warned me, didn't you? You cautioned me, you protected me from all this. And what did I do? I stepped right into it and now I'm knee-deep in that shit with nowhere to go. Oh, I'm such a dumb slut surrounded by geniuses of all kinds, aren't I?

"I'm not here to talk about the past."

"No? Why wouldn't you? Is it because you'll have to admit that what I'm saying is right? Wouldn't you want to wallow in triumph and gloat about how right you were and how stupid, crazy I was not listening to your advice? Alphonso Drake, the great filmmaker, he was going to put me to the top of the list, the peak of the mountain. It's the second week of our release, people are hardly seen at the theaters, critics haven't even bothered to review the film and theaters are already taking it down. Isn't that enough? I'm the clown right now. I'm the talk of the humiliation town. You should laugh at the sight of me. You're happy, aren't you? This is what you wanted, right?" She took a swig from her wine glass.

"Do you think this is what I wanted? Or that is why I'm here, to mock you?" I advanced closer to her and looked into her eyes. "Right now, all you said, all you did, you reminded me of someone. Someone I personally know. And to tell you the truth, that person went through the same phase of hostility towards the people who loved him the most. He suffered. And you know what he lost? Everything. He lost them all. To a point where he had to start his life over. Don't let it happen to you. You wouldn't be able to endure, trust me. Don't."

She hurtled her glass into the mirror shattering it to fragments. "Then what do you want me to do? Ask for your forgiveness? Beg you to take me back, or the people at the theater, plead for a job?"

"No one is asking you to do that." I went on and embraced her tightly in my arms. She rested her head against my shoulder and cried.

"I'm sorry George, I'm sorry for everything. I didn't know there are so many bad people out there. The kind of life I've had, I should have known. But I... I failed. I failed to understand that everyone out there is a liar and an asshole. I thought I knew everything there was to know about men, but I was wrong. They treated me like an animal and I allowed them just to get that one chance, one chance that would change my life and I didn't even get that. All the time you've been away from me, they used me like a dummy, a living, breathing dummy made of flesh and in the end I have nothing. I was just another idiot who trusted his lies. Why did you leave me? Why did you leave me, George?"

"I didn't leave you. Look at me," I held up her face and wiped away her tears, "I'll never leave you. As long as you want me here, I'll never leave."

"Can we make everything go back to the way it was before?"

"We'll make everything right, together."

"We will?"

"Yes, and listen to me. I have accepted a film offer for you."

"No, no George, I want to go back, away from all this. I want to go back to our little town, our poor, little lives. I can live with that."

"Marilyn, you can't go back now, after coming so close to what you want. You're meant to look forward, don't step back. There are many good opportunities out there. Not just this, better than this."

"I don't need any opportunity, all I want is you and me living in a small home for the rest of our lives together. A little bit of happiness and sadness and joy and everything regular people go through, but not this."

"You have taken your chance, Marilyn, now let me take mine. If this doesn't work out, we're off to where you want to go. But just one last time, believe in yourself."

"I believe in you."

"And I in you. So, trust me with this. Don't give up on me, don't let me down. We're going to go a long way."

"I won't let you down."

"We will come through just fine, together."

"Together, never to part. I love you."

We kissed and began to forget the past troubles, suddenly the phone rang. Marilyn went up to answer it. "Hello, yes... what? Really? Well, good for him. You tell him that and to take all his threats and shove it up his holes, I know he has more than one. Goodbye." She hung up and walked back to me with a titillating smile. "Did you punch him? Did you punch Alphonso Drake in the face?"

"Yeah, I gave him a little visit before I came here. I couldn't help myself after what he did to your part in that film."

She laughed and clung to me and I rejoiced in her laughter which I hadn't heard this close in a while.

Chapter Forty
❧❧❧

It wasn't anything extraordinary, the film offer I had accepted on Marilyn's behalf. But it was certainly something to begin with after her recent fiasco that was partly deliberate and self-inflicted. This decision that I had made wouldn't qualify for being entirely out of desperation, though, it was to some degree. But there were some calculated anticipations attached to it. The film was not a grand project. It wasn't a high-budget, star ensemble, big studio production, but the story and the people involved in this film possessed the most rare and exquisite quality that wasn't easily found these days; heart. An attribute that could only originate from profound passion for the work being done. The moment was exhilarating when Marilyn and I had finalized her contract with this production company as we sat in their office and went through the paperwork. I could sense Marilyn's excitement was immeasurable just as she began to place her initials next to the clauses and finally signed the last page of the agreement while I clutched her sweaty hands under the table for no one to see. Long conversations took place following the completion of the agreement and Marilyn was gradually familiarized with everyone and every protocol that were to follow.

I had taken note of what Mr. Durdawk had told me some months ago that when it all comes crashing down, Marilyn will need me one last time and he was right. Hence, I didn't have to go far to seek another beginning to Marilyn's career but Mr. Durdawk's office. And he was kind and benevolent enough to overlook the past transgressions and give her another chance, this time through his contacts in the film industry. I was deeply grateful for his favor. The initiation of the project was simple and subtle with the entire crew and cast meeting for the first time for a reading and it was a gathering in which even I was made a part of. There were a lot of script readings before any shooting processes commenced, where I could sight some great performers seated around a table with just the way they gave life to their assigned characters. I could feel the ardent drive behind all minds and all talents as each one of them went on to work avidly on the script chipping in with suggestions, recommendations, changes of all sorts and the finalized work was a combined effort and not arbitrary. I could tell Marilyn was equally happy and enlightened by this experience. She grew with this group as days went by and when shooting began, it was a whole another level of contentment. There were no personal trailers to deceptively wow the actors, but were given green rooms inside the studio to prepare for their performances. Stage eleven was all set to begin filming and the first time I saw Marilyn in her costume and make-up ready to impress the world of cinema, I closed my eyes and expressed my gratitude. A prompter stood by the camera and the director announced the most precious word at a film set; action.

৯৯৯৯

Time rolled faster, days and nights flew past as the schedule spanning eight months wrapped the shooting of her first film and in two more months of post-production, the film was released in selected theaters statewide and gradually permeated neighboring states as its acclaim aggregated coming from one critic to another. Marilyn was being applauded for her character role which was short but impressive and just as good as a lead. This laud brought her myriad attention from Hollywood giants and she was being offered three film, five film contracts by many studios. I waited for a little while to give her more options as I went around town, especially Mr. Durdawk, asking for advice and assistance in making a decision that would impact her life the most. After a long consideration we finalized a deal with Glasgow Productions for a five film contract. Though, I hated for Marilyn to be stuck with any one company for a long period of time, but at the moment there was no other choice. But I did add a clause to that agreement stipulating the five films to be completed over a period of five to seven years, and if not, Marilyn would be liberated from the conditions of the contract and permitted to seek other employments at her own behest. It was a just and reasonable statement and met with no contradiction or resistance from the administrators of the company. Her earnings were ascertained and appeared to be quite competitive with the standards of the industry.

The times were changing for Marilyn and me, our lives became meaningful and purposeful. Marilyn's work management was in my hands as I tried to avoid any distressful scheduling and overwork. I was also responsible for her daily routine, making sure she doesn't stay up late, doesn't consume alcohol in extreme amounts, appears personable at all times. I was just like a parent to her, burdened with her guardianship. Her first film with this production was completed in which she played a supporting role and did exceptionally well living the character on screen. This film was a medium-budget film with mostly fresh faces in the leading cast as well and it did accordingly average at the box office. The second film didn't take much time to begin after the release of the first one as Marilyn was continuously shooting for two more upcoming productions. She was playing a love interest of her male lead in the next one in a story that revolved around a love triangle.

Introduced to one of the most scintillating actors of that era, Marilyn couldn't keep herself from shivering with nervousness and pleasure and turn erubescent as Bradley Stewart walked onto the sets and stole hearts of many young spectators who were simply awe-struck by his debonair charm. He was a sight to look at with golden locks, light blue eyes, a square, chiseled face, creases when he smiled, tall and dusky and well muscular built. He was intent on driving the women insane with his craze and his resplendence altogether. Marilyn was no exception to his allure and magnetism, but she held her ground as they talked and discussed their parts together.

The shooting of their new film had gone past the expected period and extended about three months over the allotted time frame. Marilyn and Bradley had formed a bond of friendship over this course of time. After all they were working together for the past year, it was bound to happen. I wasn't disturbed, or I thought I wasn't to encounter their proximity day after day as any two actors, though not of the same celebrity, but the same age and level of effulgence would undoubtedly be drawn to each other. Nothing was deliberate at that time, neither their companionship nor my jealousy, but as it grew, it eventually consumed all of us. The filming finally ended after fourteen months of continuous shoot and the release date was set for Christmas. Marilyn began spending her upcoming days on the promotional campaign for the film which brought them even closer as they traveled together to different cities, states and internationally twice.

The premiere of the film was to happen in ten hours and Marilyn had just arrived from New York after an exhausting trip to four different cities with Bradley. I welcomed her back and made her rest for a while to erase the look of weariness from her face.

I awakened her at seven and asked her to get ready for the premiere as her personal cosmetologist and hairdresser waited downstairs. I stopped by the bar for a drink before going out to the limousine that stood parked in our driveway and a driver next to the vehicle. He nodded to me as I appeared and was just reaching for the door when I gestured him to hold and stay. Half an hour later Marilyn stepped out in her shimmering, silver evening dress that outlined her body perfectly with her hair set up in a bun and diamond crested clips holding intact. Subtle jewelry coruscated and her radiating smile mesmerized my heart. I took her by the arm and helped her into the car and made our way to the theater which was a good twenty minutes of drive.

As we came to our destination, luxury cars and limousines were queued up on the street and emptied the dignitaries inside at the entrance of the theater. Marilyn and I exited the car when our turn came and joined the crowd of tailored personage and their adorned spouses. There were long files of photographers and journalists held behind a security line as they captured these moments in a flash. I effaced myself from all this glory and allowed them Marilyn

McLord's single shots. A sudden cheer erupted from the crowd as Bradley Stewart walked up to me and shook hands and proceeded to Marilyn landing a kiss on her lips as the photographers thrashed their cameras with incessant clicks and flashes. Marilyn laughed at his impish act and posed with him as they continued to whisper to each other and smile for the cameras. There was a roar of approval around them, journalists clapped and showered them perpetually with questions about their relationship and they kept refusing to comment but continued an enactment which forced all of them to believe their speculation.

The crucial part of the premiere was over as now the roaring spectators and flashing cameras were hushed and prohibited inside the theater. The cast of the film along with the director, the producers and other investors including some influential guests were seated in the first row and the crew followed perched until the seventh, while the rest were given seats in the back which included second unit workforce and other related labor. I was in the twelfth row amidst some pleasant faces who were excited to see their work for the first time, or perhaps catch a glimpse of themselves on screen somewhere in the extras or stand-ins. The film began and ran a good length of two hours and eleven minutes, which I thoroughly enjoyed and even if I did not rank it amongst the best pictures of all time in my opinion, I definitely rated it among the best I have seen in terms of performances and writing. I swiftly went over by the exit door and watched the crowd enkindled with exhilaration when the end credits began rolling. There was mayhem in the hall as people began to congratulate and compliment each other on their work and impending success of the film. I saw Marilyn surrounded by admirers and she received commendations just like the day she began her career on stage. She was completely engrossed in the moment, happiness and gaiety. I stayed there for some time observing an eyeful of her, then receded into the dark passageway that led outside and away from all the glitter, the glamour, and the revelry.

I reached home in a taxi, loosened my tie and unbuttoned my shirt and stretched out my weary self upon a recliner and laid my worries to rest. I reached out for the bar, poured myself a drink and enjoyed the moment of peace and tranquility. But a number of thoughts began shuffling in my mind once more. I was content that after a substantial debacle of Marilyn's first attempt in films, she was finally able to reclaim the celebrity she had always desired. I realized my work was almost over as she had done couple of films now, all critically acclaimed projects. The most recent of them a box office boon that will keep her in the public eye for very long. I didn't know when my mind had drifted off to sleep as it must have been so relieved of all the burdens and responsibilities that it finally gave way to a long respite.

When I woke up it was close to 2 a.m. and the door had just been opened and Marilyn walked in still looking beautiful as ever. Her face expressed delight blended with a questionable frown. She quickly got closer and sat by my side.

"Where did you go, George? I was looking for you all around, everywhere. The person I wanted to see the most tonight was the least I got to see." She asked objectionably.

"But I saw you, I saw every moment of your happiness as it went by. You were so glad, so happy. You were surrounded by so many people, so many admirers. I didn't want to step in and ruin all of that for you."

"How could you ruin it?" Her eyes sparkled.

"If I had stayed, I would have ruined it. But the important thing is that *they* loved it. Everyone in that theater loved you. Didn't they?" She nodded with a soft smile. "They praised your work, they praised your beauty, they affirmed your place in Hollywood. They applauded in the end, cheered for you, congratulated you. It happened, right?"

"Yes." She said gently.

"See, I know everything. I'm so proud."

"But you left."

"I wasn't about me tonight, it was about you. It doesn't matter if I did. You came through just fine. Now, go get changed, we will sit all night long and talk about it, unless you're tired and want to sleep. You might have other engagements tomorrow."

"No, I'm game tonight."

"Then I'll cherish this night."

Marilyn smiled and headed for the stairs.

"I love you, Marilyn."

"You know I love you too." She responded. She continued up the stairs and into her bedroom.

"I hope you do," I whispered to myself and went back to my placidity.

Chapter Forty-One

∾∾∾

A lot of changes came into our lives that gradually altered the conditions of our living. Our lives became my life and her life. Our paths digressed. Our thoughts incompatible along with many other aspects that made our relationship just a professional one, nothing more nothing less. After the success of her last feature, Marilyn's wealth and celebrity was immeasurable. She was the talk of the tinseltown, fans and fame trailed her wherever she went. In the next two years, she had landed lead roles in three big studio productions working with esteemed names and receiving accolades and awards for her performances three different but distinguished ceremonies in a row. Her paychecks grew hefty day by day and to accommodate that extreme renown, she decided to move into a more suitable setting for a home.

The first day I had laid my eyes upon her new home, I was just utterly beguiled and in a way frightened of what might happen. Her life was reminiscent of my own and it became so right in front of my eyes and I feared the moment it would all come crashing down upon her which might break her never allowing her to reconstruct. Even though, I had never mentioned the details of my previous life to her, it was obliviously reenacted with same meticulous details that I had regretted for so long. The mansion wasn't any different in luxury and affluence than what I had seen before, once when I was a child and again when I was just an ignorant, boastful, stupid young man. It was nestled at the tip of a peninsula with open private access to the beach, all eleven hundred feet of it. The lands that surrounded the grand structure were lush and green and finally the brick and concrete wonder stood ground, unyielding and prodigious.

The intimacy between Bradley and Marilyn intensified as time went by. He wasn't looking to let go of her and all Marilyn wanted was to have an illustrious man by her side. She had continued to personate her relationship with me for all this time, desirably or undesirably I couldn't say, and I betrayed myself by not trying to find out whether her intentions were true or not. For the second time in my life I was afraid of losing someone, the first time I had such a feeling it was too late for me to return, but now I wanted to hold onto whatever I had. I knew she was slipping away from my grasp like sand slips from a furled fist, but I clung to her and clenched my hand as hard as I could. I didn't want to lose her, not again. And in that longing, I had begun to overlook her faults and connived at her mistakes of living an objectionable lifestyle of revelry, fornication and drugs. But I would always look forward to seeing her by nightfall and welcome her into the silent mansion late hours at night, half drunk, half naked and tuck her into the bed hoping for a new day tomorrow, which never came. I would wait for her sitting idle in the back lawn of the baronial property, looking at the poignant streaks of crimson across the skies while the sun sank behind the horizon and gradually it would all become dark leaving me forlorn with my despairing thoughts. Sometimes I would hear her dulcet voice in my sleep, calling out my name.

"George... George." But when I would awaken from the heavenly dream, she would be absent.

Tonight she was there again, maybe a figment of my imagination that I saw her perching at the edge of my easy chair smiling back at me.

"What are you doing George?" It was her, she was there in reality right by my side. I rubbed my eyes and sat up on the chair. "Now don't tell me you were sleeping?"

"I was, that's what I usually do when I'm alone, waiting for you."

"I'm sorry, George, I was with Mr. Cooper and he mentioned a little bit about the picture he's working on next. He started giving me the outline of the story and I couldn't help but hear it out till the end. It's a wonderful story of a woman who goes through her life thinking her husband truly loves her, but discovers it was nothing but a lie. She spends her whole life trusting and believing him, but as she comes to know the truth, she isn't strong enough to leave him after spending years as a housewife and having no friends or relatives. But in the end she strengthens and encourages herself to be confident enough to leave him, to give him what he deserves. Don't you love this story?"

"Yes, I think I do. It's more than a story. It seems real, that's how good it is."

"I knew you'd like it. And what are you doing outside? You know what George, you've become boring now. I think you should get involved with some people of your own interest, invite them over for drinks, for dinner. Enjoy your evenings. You used to do that, why not anymore?"

"Times change, people change. I expected you home sooner."

"Really, why is that, anything important?"

"No, nothing of that sort. Just thought you might remember."

"Remember what, George? Don't play riddles with me."

"That's okay. As I said, nothing important." I got off the easy chair and began to walk away from her.

"Tell me."

"Six years ago on this day I met a crazy, demented, still lovable woman who demanded my attention with authority and stole my heart in the process. An insane girl, who cursed more than she made sense, but somehow I liked her. This day marks the sixth anniversary of our first meeting. I thought you'd remember that, happy anniversary."

I placed a small jewelry case on the palm of her hand and left for her to listen to the sounds of the waves in the silence of the night, have her feel what I've felt every night for the past two years or longer.

I had spent the next day wandering the streets of Hollywood, trying to find a place in there somewhere. I failed miserably and returned back home. It was late in the afternoon when I came back and expected the place to be vacant as usual, but I was in complete shock when I entered the hall and found about seventy people leaping out from their hide behind furniture and walls and shouting simultaneously - "happy birthday." I stood like a stone in the doorway and watched their faces one by one. I didn't recognize most of them, but the elation on their faces was pleasing. To receive wishes from people you don't recognize is sometimes gratifying.

"Happy birthday, George! You seem like you've seen a ghost?" Marilyn embraced and took me by surprise this time, wrapped her arm around taking me further into the group of her acquaintances. Bradley being one of them came over for a hug.

"Hey man, isn't this a pleasant surprise? Happy big day. Hope you have a good one."

"Well, I think I did two weeks ago."

"Hey, better late than never." He laughed and nudged Marilyn teasingly, to which she responded in equal playfulness.

Marilyn retrieved a small velvet lined case from her handbag and offered it to me. I took and opened it to reveal a gold band with my initials engraved intricately in the middle of the ring. The few people around sounded impressed at the gift, Bradley was one of them.

"Do you like it?" She asked.

"Very much."

Marilyn excused herself and took me closer to the bar. "You don't look happy to me, George. What's the matter?"

"Are these people here for me or for you?" My words expunged her smile.

"I invited them, for you to have a good time and celebrate."

"With all of them? If you really wanted me to celebrate, you alone were enough for that."

Her eyes pierced my gaze. "Okay, we will celebrate alone later, if that's what you want."

"Then I'll wait upstairs until they're gone."

"George, I called all of them here so you could enjoy a bit. Talk to some people, get out of your misery for once."

"You think talking to them can get me out of it?"

She turned to a bottle of bourbon in aggravation. "I don't know what's gotten into you, George. I have no resolution for this."

"What's gotten into me is called loneliness, the resolution is you."

"I am here." She slammed her glass on the countertop, alcohol splashed the granite. She quickly concealed her anger.

"Are you?"

"What do you want me to do? Tell me what makes you happy, I'll do it." She kept her voice down to whispers.

"Only if you remembered what makes me happy, just like you did once." I took a deep breath. "I am very happy. Doesn't it please a man to remind someone to remember him? I'm very happy."

Marilyn shook her head in displeasure and walked away from me. And soon I was joined by two other men who were in awe of my partner and had great admiration for her.

"Isn't she a beauty?" The first one exclaimed.

"Sure is." The second one endorsed that.

"And this man right here, George Bailey, a man we've heard highly of. How do you do, sir?" The first one addressed me.

"Suddenly better." I retorted.

"He's just modest, that's all." The second one joined the party.

"No, that's a virtue I've never come across my whole life." I poured myself a drink.

"So you are indeed honest, a man of his word. I like to see that, you know, that is a lost quality these days. And all due to those mundane troubles and issues, men have forgotten the true meaning of comradeship. You do something for me, I do something for you, easy as that." The first one took a glass of scotch I offered him.

"And you are?" I questioned with converged brows.

"It doesn't matter who we are, but what we do. Meet Mr. Hank, the owner of the most prestigious film magazine in USA today, Celebrity Foremost. I'm his assistant Jeffrey. Nice to meet you, sir."

"I wouldn't be too sure if I am equally thrilled. I thought I had finally met some people who wished to speak to me without any personal gain or expectation. Evidently, I was wrong. Now, if you two would excuse me." I began to leave the bar, but they held me back.

"Oh, Mr. Bailey, you've mistaken our friendship for some selfish motive, though, I wouldn't lie to you and confirm your suspicion as true. But I will make sure that you are equally rewarded for your assistance and those rewards are not just monetary."

"What exactly do you expect me to do for you, Mr. Hank?"

"You hold the key to our success, Mr. Bailey. The key to the vault of profits."

"You would need to be a little more precise for me to understand."

"A mind's comprehension is an enigma. Sometimes it grasps even the most inexplicable things of all and other times it surrenders even to the simplest of matters. We want Ms. McLord to be the centerfold special in the next issue of our magazine. We do an exclusive interview, a photo shoot, and a video shoot for promotional campaigns which will benefit both the ends of the deal. It is going to be her first interview after the awards and we aim to seize this opportunity. How does that sound?"

"That sounds amazingly exciting, but I think you've got the wrong person to talk to about it."

"Oh come on now, I know it is hard for you at times, but please, try to fit in an hour long session somewhere in that haphazard schedule of hers and I will personally make sure that you are rewarded for your kindness. And just to let you know, there are some wannabe actresses on the lookout for good managers and agents and would do anything, I mean anything to bag one. I know you have good taste in women. I'll have my last month's featured model up and here whenever you're ready to take her on. You help me out, I keep you happy."

"Happy?" I marveled at his perception and wondered how using a woman to your pleasure and advantage could make someone happy?

I glanced beyond him at Marilyn and found her with Bradley leaning into her and gently kissing her neck and whispering into her ears which elicited laughter from her.

"You will not regret this friendship." Hank strengthened the offer.

"I'm really sorry folks, but I'm not what you think I am."

"Are you not her manager, or perhaps her personal secretary?"

That tipped my temper closer to the red marking on the dial. "I was never her manager, or personal secretary."

"Well, let's forget about our ranks for a while and focus on what we're capable of getting done. I'm certain you're close enough to get her agreement with a request."

"To tell you the truth, it would surprise you to know I'm not close to her at all. My requests are of no worth to her."

Marilyn sighted this conflict and quickly excused herself from a conversation and headed my way.

"Well, it does come as a surprise to me. I suppose there must be some reason why she is celebrating someone of no worth. And if that is the truth, then who are you and why are you here?"

"I apologize to have wasted you precious time, but here she is. Marilyn why don't you tell these gentlemen who I am and the reason you've thrown this grand party for?"

Marilyn prevaricated and smiled, tried to alleviate the situation. "Gentlemen, I'm sure this conversation is headed towards a humorous arc. This man here has a great sense of humor."

"And I wish it did work with these serious businessmen who are here with an intriguing proposal to have me convince you for an exclusive interview in exchange for some handsome rewards. What do you say?"

"I'll be glad to discuss that."

"Well, there you have it. But you still haven't answered their question, Marilyn. And believe me, I'm equally curious to know the answer to this one. Who am I, and why am I here?"

"George..."

"No, no, no, tell them. They should know. After all, if our relationship is not clear to the people, how would they expect us to live together?"

"I think we should leave." Hank abandoned his glass at the bar.

"Not just your thought, Mr. Hank, I think so too. Before I break your jaw right here in front of all these people." I smashed a glass on the marble floor. There was utter silence in the hall with all eyes fixed on me. I headed up the stairs flaring in anger.

After a good half hour the door of my room opened and Marilyn appeared indignant and infuriated standing in the doorway. She stepped in and glared at me as I sat on the bed.

"I'm getting sick and tired of this, George. Everything that I do, trying to make you feel better, you just go up in flames about it. Those were some good, honest people just trying to do their business. There was no need to insult them like that in front of everybody? They are reputable contacts."

"You're worried about their reputation? What about the way I was insulted? And don't talk to me about honesty, they just offered me their last issue's featured model to sleep with if I get you to say yes. Good people, yeah right."

"They were trying to make a friend out of you."

"By using another woman? I don't know what kind of people become their friends with such tactics, but I'm not one of them."

"You're not one of any, George, that's the problem. No one can please you, not even me. I don't know what you want."

"You once did, Marilyn. But for the past couple of years, I have seen you forget a lot. Forget who we are, forget who I am. And that has somehow made me forget myself. It has made me forget my place here in this house, in your life. A man takes you up in his arms and kisses you in front of everybody and I just watch? He treats you like his woman in front of me, and you expect me to pat your back for humiliating me? It is not a shoot every day, Marilyn. Don't use it as your excuse. Today wasn't a shoot when I saw him nibbling at your neck, and you enjoying that? That premiere night wasn't a shoot when he kissed you in front of all those cameras."

"It isn't what you think, Brad isn't my boyfriend."

"I don't give a fuck who or what he is. I need to know who I am. I'm not your manager, I'm not your secretary, I'm definitely not your boyfriend, then who am I? And if I'm nobody, why am I here? I've spent six years with you for what? For what, Marilyn?"

"I didn't ask you for that."

I stood stunned at her response. I delayed speaking and waited if she would realize her mistake and try to correct it with an apology. But she was rigid as a rock with her words.

"You didn't ask me? That's right, you didn't. So, for all these years and all that I've done was out of my own interest? Oh, I was under the wrong impression then. Forgive me."

"You just know how to make things turn your way, don't you?"

"No, that's all right. I was wrong all along."

"Goddamn it, what do you want me to do, get on my knees and worship you. Make songs of your praise? Put my lips on your feet and kiss them? What do you want?"

"No goddamn it, kiss me. That's what I want. I want the love we had for each other. The times we would spend together, the moments I still remember, that's what I want again. I want the same Marilyn who was gladly ready to go back to our poor lives in a small town as long as I stayed with her."

"I can't go back. If that's what you want, then you can't have it. I've tried my best to keep you happy here, but if that's where you need to be, then you must return alone."

"Keep me happy? If you really knew me, you would know how. This is not my idea of a celebration, Marilyn. I would rather have you alone, sit by my side and talk about everything that's gone wrong in the past. Make it right. This... this was just another reason for you to entertain people, your people. I would rather spend time with you. I don't even know them, who were they? Can you give me back the years I've spent waiting for you? Can you give me all that time back? Do you even know how it feels when people whisper behind your back? When they point at a man who's living off a woman's wealth?"

"Then why did you, George? I never stopped you from doing anything."

"I was right by your side, Marilyn. I'm sorry if you didn't see me, but I was right behind you all this time."

"To make me feel bad for it? That's what you intended?"

"I intended so much more that what we are right now, Marilyn. So much more."

"I'm doing my best to make it work."

"Will you marry me? Will you marry me, Marilyn? You want me on my knees? I'll get on my knees. Here... now will you marry me? You gave me this ring, let me put this on your finger and make everything right this very instant. Will you marry me?"

Marilyn was silent watching me kneel before her. It dawned upon me that my proposal was going to be unanswered no matter how long I stayed, and I needed to stop embarrassing her and insulting myself anymore.

"I'm sorry." I got up and left the room and to the back of the mansion, sinking into my easy chair and solitude that had become my only companion now.

Chapter Forty-Two

 So So So

The next morning I sat upon the wide stretch of the stairway in front of the massive portico entrance and waited for Marilyn to come out. I glanced at the watch when I began to hear the tapping of heels against marble floor and knew she was descending the steps behind me. I stood up and straightened my suit and just as her attention diverted towards me, she stopped.

"George?" That name wasn't said in any other tone but surprise, and then she confirmed it further. "I thought you weren't home."

"I'm not. I just came to say something to you."

"You know I have to get to the studio and I'm already late."

"Aren't we all? Late? Well, I don't want to keep you from anything important. If you don't have time we can talk later. I'll wait right here."

"You have the whole house to yourself until I return, George. Why would you wait here?"

"I can't call it mine now, because you're no longer mine. The house is yours."

"There we go again, woke up in a bad mood just as any other day. I don't have time for another fight, George."

"The moods are fine, it's time that's cheated us."

"What'd you want to say?"

"I'm sorry for everything that happened yesterday. I know I was wrong in asking you to leave... asking you all that I asked. I'm sorry."

"You don't have to apologize to me."

"Partings are best when ended with apologies and good wishes. There shouldn't be any resentment, because if there is, even the warmest memories seem bitter."

"Parting? What are you talking about? I don't understand." She took off her sunglasses to get a better view of my solemnity. She was suddenly shaken to the core, the first time I had seen her concerned in years.

"Some people are hard to understand. Anyway, I wanted to return this to you. You gave it to me once."

I handed her a ring she had once gifted me. A long time ago. She pushed away the case which jumped out of my palm to the ground.

"I don't need it back, I gave it to you. And you're not going anywhere."

"When I woke up this morning I was suddenly reminded of something. Something you said a long time ago. If we could leave everything and go back to our little town, our little lives, and I refused. But today I ask you, is that possible now?"

Marilyn's silence was vehement.

"I have my answer in your silence." I said smiling at her. "It was nice to know you and being with you for all these years, Marilyn. I hope I wasn't a disappointment."

I turned to leave and went down a couple of steps, she came after me.

"Where are you going?"

"I don't know. Somewhere far from here."

"What do you mean far from here? You can't leave me like this."

I took her hand and led her down the stairs toward her limousine that waited.

"Don't do this, George. We can-"

"We can't, Marilyn. That's the root of all our problems, we can't. The only relationship we can have anymore is the one you're not ready for, that you won't accept." I opened the car door and helped her step into its luxury.

"Can't we talk about this?"

"That's all we've done for so long. Talk, and talk, and talk. Have we gained anything out of it?"

"But George-" I shut the door close and she rolled the window down. "There's so much more left to be done, I can't do all of that alone."

"You're not alone. There are hundreds behind you."

"George, I wish-"

"The things we wished for, the things we ended up with. What did I wish, what did I get? It isn't always that simple, is it? Driver, take her to the studio."

I tapped the roof of the car and stood back while Marilyn was transfixed with her eyes at me and tears almost about to trickle down her face. She took it all in swallowing her emotions and tightening her jaws, a deep breath followed. She turned away to the front hiding her teary eyes behind the designer sunglasses.

"Driver." She commanded and the car began moving and rolled down the long driveway and gradually faded from my view and it was the last I heard or saw Marilyn, the second love of my life.

ᏇᏇᏇ

Louise looked away and moved somewhat to stir my attention toward her. As I looked, she quickly came back to face me with a conjured smile on her face. I think she just wiped away under her eyes but attempted to conceal her emotion from me.

"That was the end of it?" She asked.

"That was the end."

"You know George, fault-finding is in human nature. They almost take it up as a birth right when they hear some story to side with the person they feel most connected to, which in turn they feel is right. And I don't know if I should say this to you so bluntly, but from my aged experience in life, I think both of you were right... and wrong. She had the glint of fame in her ambitions, and you had the light of love in your intentions. And these two never go well together. One must lose. In your case, the greater one lost."

"If you had to choose a side, would you?"

"A man's wisdom differs from a woman. But wisdom of both differs from one instance to another. If we stay with our decisions, errors are bound to happen. And sometimes if we don't stick to them, errors still happen. It is quite subjective, the human reaction to each given circumstance. Others are never fit to judge your choices, only the two involved may ever know if they were right or wrong."

Our stop time was almost over, so was my sandwich. We joined the queue of other passengers as they began boarding the bus one more time. We took our seats and in some minutes, the bus began to roll out of Kansas City stop.

"I never tried to blame her for anything. Maybe it was just plain and simple time that separated us."

"Well, then the aspect of gratitude comes into play. All that you did, was she supposed to end it this way?"

"She couldn't just leave everything and come after me, could she?"

"No, it was wrong of you to ask it of her."

"You know, you're a very difficult person to talk to."

"Yes, my husband used to say that. But he talked to me right to his grave. That's what love is, you hate but you can't let go."

"I did let go."

"You couldn't hold her even if you tried. But you held on to life, didn't you?"

"That, I did."

"How did you get started again?"

PART III

Chapter Forty-Three
❧❧❧

It was exactly four months after I had left Marilyn that I found myself navigating the streets of Charlotte, North Carolina. I did not understand how I'd gotten here as I had left LA with one simple intention of traveling as far as possible from Marilyn and the city that reminded me of her. After ruminating on this matter for a while, I finally realized it must be due to the fact that this city was located completely opposite to Hollywood, California on the map and was probably a decision of my subconscious reasoning that I resolved to arrive here. Although, I hadn't actually settled here yet as the only material thing I possessed was a small luggage bag that had some clothes in it, some cash and a lot of empty space. But my plans were not any different from a vagrant who travels in search for shelter.

I glanced around sitting on a street side bench near the bus stop and watched people commute. An unending stream of bobbing heads one after another, in hundreds, in thousands. All this haphazard commotion forced me to invade the feelings of some people I could look at and prolong that gaze just enough to get through their eyes and peek into their souls. I found an ocean of sadness at the verge of inundating their courage to endure and this wasn't just one, but all who passed before my eyes. Through the obstructions and struggles of survival and a ceaseless but futile attempt to overcome all odds, there was nothing they could derive out of life but yet lived in hopes for a better tomorrow. Escaping the past, the experiences that led to grief and anger, loss and heartbreak, no matter what life brought into their existence or took away from it, people still lived. Their courage encouraged me in a way as I had placed my wrist at the mercy of a razor twice in the past week. Just as I sat in my bathtub half submerged in cold water looking down at my wrist that was already afflicted with a scratch, not deep enough to harm me in any way, the razor pressed against my vein, but somehow I didn't have the valiancy to confront the scorching environs and relentless torments of hell for the rest of my afterlife. I was suddenly reminded of the basics of a far forgotten creed known as religion that I hadn't considered in a long time, in fact never in life. I hadn't been religious, but suddenly it became the reason that compelled me to swerve from the path of destruction and out of a lifelong misery, or more precisely the afterlife-long misery. Or maybe I just surrendered to a weak will to die, and live a little longer.

I stood up and brushed away the depression from my conscience and propelled myself across the street into a liquor store and bought myself a quarter of some inexpensive scotch as I was broke and couldn't afford a branded whiskey, but not broke enough to not drink. He packed my purchase in a brown paper bag and handed back three quarters in exchange for a bill of ten. I nodded to him and as I exited the shop I wondered why I'd always find the cashiers at all liquor stores with an undying tendency of concealing a bottle of alcohol in a brown paper bag. A plastic bag could work just fine. Was it due to the fact that they felt guilty of selling something detrimental to the health of mankind and attempted to hide their business? Or were they just trying to be more considerate towards the people affected by habitual drunkards like me who leave a horrid example for the youths and children to follow? Or maybe it was just a way to save the drunks that they may be delivered from subtle culpability and hateful glares from the crowd around if they can't resist but unseal the bottle and avidly devour some of it out of addiction in front of the rest? Though, I doubted it was any one of the three, I definitely suspected that all three came together to have the impact of the brown bag. But then I thought maybe it was just a simple tradition that commenced since the time a brown paper bag was invented, that all store owners followed suit to imitate the first who introduced it. Whatever it was, I did not trouble my mind any further on the matter and refrained from drinking until I got home as I did not prefer multitasking while on the road. I had heard drinking and driving was a crime and deadly in most cases where liquor could obstruct your ability to follow road rules and cause you to miss street lights, but I also knew that drinking and ambling was an equally destructive act where similar hindrances can occur that, if not causing you to run someone over, can definitely have you run over by someone.

I walked my way back to my humble dwelling that was a single room in a deplorable motel that charged its customers according to its merit, eleven dollars a night. The room was painted ages ago, walls were deteriorating due to a pipe leak overflow somewhere in the ceiling. The bathroom was intentionally neglected and made to stand out in all this desolation and the best part of it all was the continuous cacophony of loud music, children crying, couples debating and altercating and finally making fervent love to each other by the end of it. All this and more resounded around this room all night long and disabled my sleep without any deliberate attempt at it. Now, I could have objected to it, if I didn't fear being locked out of my room the next night, or probably coming across a nice and protracted tirade riddled with expletives and profanity from the neighbors, the kind I haven't heard in a long time and neither wished to. So, the best way to go on was to take it all in and lie down drunk on the bed and try to make it through the night with a profound susceptibility to insomnia caused by external factors. Apart from the consternating misery that surrounded me, everything else was just fine, or I made myself falsely believe so. When I couldn't sleep after trying every other course of distraction for two hours, which included counting till hundred where I ended up at two sixty, or singing myself a lullaby, or even arousing myself to exhaustion, I finally gave up when nothing worked and surrendered to the good old television watching resolution that probably worked the best for a majority of people. I kept on flipping channels and the volume was kept medium high as I intended to fall asleep listening to the dull, tedious sounds of people speaking needlessly on television rather than my loud neighbors, but suddenly the screen displayed something I was instantaneously drawn to. Marilyn stood nervously staring back at me, and then smiled. I thought that change of countenance resulted due to my presence before her, but I was quickly corrected when I saw another man proceed before me and between us. He took her into his arms and kissed her and she rejoiced in his embrace as the screen faded to black, I was yet again left alone in the darkness. I looked away transported back to the disconcerting thoughts that I had endeavored vigorously to remove just a little while ago. The screen reappeared with an airing of a special interview of Marilyn McLord and Bradley Stewart.

"Good evening viewers, this is your host Beth Granger here with the famous stars of young Hollywood and the equal contributors to the recent box-office success of Yours and Always, a Glasgow Production presentation that you all just enjoyed the first television premiere of. We welcome Bradley Stewart and his leading lady, Marilyn McLord. So nice to have you folks on set tonight." The television host shifted her microphone to Bradley.

"It's great to be here. Wonderful to be here." Brad and Marilyn responded in unison.

"I would like to begin with my first question to Marilyn here, as I have had the pleasure of speaking to Bradley a couple of times before. Marilyn, all of a sudden this freight train of celebrity and fame coming toward you, how do you intend to handle all this? What are the plans?"

Marilyn laughed and licked her lips before speaking out in a soft voice, and I was extremely delighted to hear it. "I don't believe it has arrived in such great measure, but if it has, I plan to take it naturally with time. I think fame is just a part of success but success does not necessarily emerge from fame. The key is to keep yourself under control. Let those who surround you shape your personality, and fortunately I have so many good characters to look up to around me. Take Brad for instance, he's helped me through a lot."

"That's great, Mr. Stewart is no stranger to renown, let me ask you a question, sir, do you think Ms. McLord has what it takes to be the front runner in Hollywood?" Beth gave a twisted smile as she asked that question.

"She already is." Brad replied confidently.

"That is a wonderful answer, Brad. Now moving to our viewers' questions, I have one for Marilyn here. You have done two romantic dramas in the past two years, so love is the focal point of discussion in both movies. Here is a personal question to you, have you ever been in love before?"

Marilyn swallowed some time. "No, it hasn't happened to me yet."

"But we have heard rumors of you being linked to someone in the past?"

"Let it stay a rumor as long as it is remembered, but there was no truth to it, just an assumption."

"But there was a spark though?"

"No, nothing like that, just a professional relationship, that's all."

I laughed at her response and pondered my errors of the past.

"Very well," the hostess receded. "Then tell us how was it going through the process of working together, this whole project and finally the completion of the film."

"It was a wonderful experience going through such a didactic journey filming this movie. Very difficult initially, but once we got used to it, it gradually subsided into a beautiful feeling. Brad has been a great person and actor to work with-"

I switched off the television and reached for my almost empty bottle of whiskey, drained another mouthful and fell flat on the bed beginning the process of a vain attempt at sleep all over again.

කකක

I had found temporary employment at a supermarket after a brief interview with the manager of the store. My job duties were quite uncomplicated and entailed unloading every box and crate of supplies to the last one at the loading bay from all incoming eighteen wheelers and storing them safely into the warehouse. The tractor trailers kept coming in one after another with groceries, from fresh fruits and vegetables to meats and poultry, to bath tissues and batteries and books and electronics. I travailed an eight hour shift six days a week and managed a marginal paycheck by the end of every two weeks. The only advantage of working at such a massive establishment was that you could split the leftovers between co-workers and carry home what you could use every night. By the end of the day all of us would gather inside the back room and browse through the salvaged, defected, damaged and unintentionally abandoned merchandise and groceries and determine who needed what and distributed accordingly. Our shift was a group of forty-two people with seventeen women and twenty-five men, and were fortunate in terms of having the last shift before the store shut its doors to customers, as the two previous day shift workers couldn't possibly share the leftover goods among themselves. But they did make some requests to reserve an item or two to be able to pick-up the next day and our supervisor was kind enough to grant.

My shift began at five in the afternoon and lasted an hour past midnight. We would get a lunch break around eight at night and even though we had dinner during that hiatus, it was still referred to as a lunch break. I would go up to a diner at the corner of the street for dinner and two coffee breaks in between along with few of my peers. And as I would pass a couple of shops on my way down, I would sight a public accounting firm shuttered closed every day. With the curiosity of discovering if this office ever opened its doors, I went around the neighborhood during daytime and saw the small office open and a receptionist inside bored to the point of sleep with barely any work to do, and it all came to my view from outside a glass door that also had a sign dangling askew from a suction cup hook reading Help Wanted.

Chapter Forty-Four
๛๛๛

I was doing a double shift that day and had my lunch break around noon. Drinking from a cup of black coffee and ravening my order of a cheeseburger combo, I would always contemplate on giving this accounting job a try. Even when I wasn't sure whether it really was an opening for anything related to accounting or just simply janitorial work, I still assumed I could learn a little just by being there. Though, I had no experience in accounting of any sort, yes I had done bookkeeping in my days of sales and ownership, but I never imagined that experience would suffice for a job application in that particular field of work. It wasn't that I was running low on capital or desperately needed to extract myself from the kind of work I was doing. I liked my job. It was just simply an urge to do something else, hopefully part-time, and if not then I could work two schedules just to learn and improve my knowledge. I had thought of stepping into that office inquiring about the job several times in the past three weeks, and luckily the sign had dangled there for that long as well. I made up my mind, sitting on it for almost a month, I decisively cut my lunch time short and went for the CPA's office fifteen minutes before my break was going to be over. As I approached the door, I neatened my appearance and took off my work jacket to not give them an impression of my circumstances. I straightened my hair after a glimpse at my face in the glass and pushed open the door to a new possibility. The door bells chimed at my ingress and I looked around at the small, crummy, clustered interior of a stifling office. The receptionist looked up at me and managed a half smile.

"Mr. Ackres is out for lunch if you came to see him."

"Mr. Ackres?" I asked wondering if I knew him.

"He's unavailable right now."

The woman spoke in a mild accent through which I presumed her roots to be Latin American. She had a pleasant look on her middle aged face, glasses to cover her sunken eyes.

"I came about the sign at the door that says help wanted. I came to apply."

"Oh, I took you for someone else, just a second. Ned-" she shouted out the name at another closed door, "someone here to see you."

A harsh voice, initially faint behind the door, grew in volume as the door was swiftly opened and a man appeared in the doorway lambasting the receptionist. "I have told you so many times not to let these people know I'm here. Just wasting my time, they are."

"That's Mr. Ackres." The receptionist gestured at him.

"It doesn't really matter to you what I say, does it?" He asked a bit more nettled.

The man who stood before me was indeed jaded, exhausted to the core due to overwork or perhaps no work at all, as a man is rendered unsociable in both cases. He would be around the age of 45, bald as so his work would have inflicted upon him, stout, wore wrinkled brown pants that did not compliment his plaid green shirt and an incongruous blue neck tie. "What can I do for you, now that you are here and know I'm here as well?"

"I'm not here to sell anything, sir. I came to inquire about this sign I saw outside that you needed another employee?" I asked politely.

"I don't need an employee. I can hardly afford my paycheck, how am I going to pay someone else?"

"Mine too." The receptionist cut in.

"Yeah, her neither."

"It says help wanted outside." I was embarrassed.

"It does? Who put it there?" He asked.

"You did." The receptionist replied.

"Oh, yes I did. I need someone to manage my paperwork. Are you here for that?"

"Yes, sir."

"Okay, come with me then. Paola, no more useless people in here, alright?"

"You got it, Mr. Ackres."

Ned Ackres took me into his office that hardly accommodated a desk and two chairs amidst a clutter of filing cabinets and towers of documents and paperwork shoved into corners up to the ceilings, tipping to one side at the verge of tumbling into a disaster. He took his chair and offered me one across from him and cleared the mess on the desk to make space.

"Do you have a resume?"

"No sir, I don't. But I'd be able to do any kind of work you might have for me. From cleaning to bookkeeping, I can do it all."

"Do you have any experience in bookkeeping?"

"I do sir. I used to work in sales a long time ago and owned my business for couple of years following. I haven't forgotten any of it."

"You owned your place?"

"Yes, sir. I used to do all account management there, as well as financial statements, assessment of assets, inventory, everything."

"If I hire you, you would be responsible for all transactions completed in and outside this facility. Accounts receivable, very important, accounts payable, not too much unless it's the IRS. Archiving, filling and some assistance in remembering clients and appointments. I can't do much of that anymore."

"Not a problem, sir."

"I can only pay monthly and it won't be much. It is a salary based work so it isn't hourly wages, but you must be available any time of the day or night."

"Yes, sir."

"Do you really need this job so much?"

"To be honest with you, sir, I do work presently. But I've always had this interest in the field of accounting for all these years and what better way to advance myself by learning and furthering my knowledge in the profession starting at this office with a small job in hopes of becoming someone in near future."

"Hmm... I didn't need that speech and I dislike ambition itself as much as I like ambitious people. But I think I'll give you a chance. Hope it can change your life working here, it surely didn't change mine."

"Thank you, sir. Thank you so much."

"That's all right, you can start from tomorrow. We open at nine thirty and close at three thirty. The hours are not very tough, so I expect to see you arrive on time and leave on time as well. I hope it wouldn't be much to ask."

"Not at all, I would be glad. I am glad. Thank you, I will see you tomorrow."

I shook hands with him and left the office. The receptionist waited outside tapping a pencil on a notepad in ennui. She looked up at me as I exited the office with a grand smile.

"Did you get it?"

"Yes."

She stood up to welcome me. "Welcome to Ackers Accounting Services Mr.-"

"George Bailey."

"George, my name is Paola Castillo. I'm the receptionist, slash personal assistant, slash secretary, almost everything but the owner here. And I'm the only staff, so welcome."

"Thank you, Paola. I start from tomorrow, so see you in the morning."

She smiled and sat back behind her desk and before I left, I glanced at her again and gathered her to be a woman in her early 50s, seasoned face with creases of experience around her eyes. A healthy pear shaped body, blonde hair tied up in a bun. A cotton dress outlining shapely stature and an amicable personality. I waved to her and she waved back as I opened the door and joined in a crowd of pedestrians with a common purpose to return back to work on time after 30 minutes of respite.

The next morning I had woken up at seven and calculated the commute time to exceed no more than 40 minutes even in case if I encountered heavy traffic on my bus route, which I knew I will today as a light drizzle had just escalated to a downpour. But I still had enough time to prepare and depart around 8:40.

I traveled along fifty other passengers packed in a bus and it took me exactly thirty-eight minutes to reach my destination, which was just bordering the estimated time of travel in extreme traffic. I grabbed myself a cup of coffee on my two block walk to the office and stood outside the shuttered glass door. I was early.

"Good morning, George."

I flipped around to see Paola walking towards me holding up an umbrella and rummaging her bag in search of something.

"Morning, Paola."

"Oh thank you for that, George." I held the umbrella for her, freeing her right hand for which she thanked me. She finally removed a key ring from her handbag and unlocked the shutters. I pulled up the chains as the shutters rolled up for her to step in and unlock the door.

"You know, a co-worker is always welcome. I have been doing this for twenty-three years and the day Ned hires someone else, I feel relieved and it makes me feel I'm not alone."

"You're not. Anymore."

"Come on let me show you around."

We stepped into the office and took off our rain jackets and hung them in a corner behind a water fountain machine.

"Twenty-three years?" I asked her.

"Yup, Ned was just a young man when I first started with him, and I wasn't old either back then."

"You're not old."

"If you say so, but I feel old now. I'm fifty-two, old enough to admit that."

"Same office?" I inquired some more.

"Yes, right here where he began all of this." She went towards another door at the far end of the room. I followed. "It doesn't seem such a long time. But when you pause to think about it, twenty-three years, that's almost one third of a lifetime, isn't it?"

"It's a long time."

"This is the bathroom, I supervise the supplies as Ned is quite stingy with them. And I clean it every other day. Now, I will clean it two days a week. Why? I hope you get the drift."

"That isn't a problem at all."

"All right, this you see right here are my filing cabinets. Any record or documents more than sixty days old are archived in here." She slid open the first drawer and it was almost all airy. "Last names, then dates. Nothing much to fret about, after you've dumped them here once, Ned hardly ever gets his clients to return. And some that do come back, mostly from the neighborhood who can't afford bigger companies, they end up paying the IRS instead of getting a check back."

"Do you have him do your tax returns as well?"

"Oh God please, I try to make it downtown for that. I depend on it. You already saw his office. That's the water cooler, deliveries come every month between fifth and eighth. Vacuuming twice a week, I'll do that, you don't have to worry about it."

"Nope, once a week from now on for you."

She smiled and took a seat at her desk, offered me to sit at a customer chair temporarily.

"What made you come here, tell me honestly?"

"Honestly? I don't know."

"You don't know why you came here for a job? Running out of cash maybe?"

"No, I work an evening shift at the supermarket three blocks down."

"You do?"

"Not a bad job, an okay paycheck with free stuff here and there. Who wouldn't like it? I'm not here for the money, but maybe a feeling that drew me in. I knew an accountant once, had the pleasure of calling him my friend. I owned a business long ago and he used to manage every single thing for me, even my personal life. I just wanted to sense how he must have felt working for me, as terrible a boss as I was."

She listened intently. "But that feeling could be done and over with in a couple of months, does that mean you're here only for a short time?"

"I have never stayed at one place for very long. I don't know if that is a blessing or a curse, but all my life I have traveled. If it happens again, I wouldn't be surprised."

"Hmm... well, as long as you're here, I think I'll have a lot to talk and share."

"I hope so too. Tell me about Ned, what is he like? What should I expect?"

"Ned Ackres, he is a good man. A good man at heart, caring if he really gets to like you. Doesn't need much from anyone but simple attentiveness. He does like his work finished on time, though, he wouldn't restrict himself much to that principle. He's a loner, that basically gives him an edgy side. Work is the only thing he has, and that's all he cares about. He might not be good at it, but he goes after it with all his strength and all his brains. Many times I have spoken to him about settling down with a nice girl, but he never listens. Being a couple of years older I've tried advising him, but nothing. Apart from that, he's always going to be there for you, that's one thing about him. He will stand by your side even if you're about to get sentenced for murder, he will be there. That's him. Yeah, one more thing, in the past he's developed this illness of forgetting things he does, so you'll have to be extra careful around him and mind his things as well, because he's going to come at you if you don't."

"Sounds like a fun environment to work."

"Party's just started sweetheart. There he is."

Ned stumbled into the office mumbling at the floor mat he just flicked on his way in.

"Who put that mat in the door?" His annoyed voice exclaimed.

"It's not in the door, Ned, it's at the door, for people to dry their feet when they come in." Paola responded with a wry smile.

"No one's coming in. Remove that."

"You just did."

"You can be very annoying at times, you know that? And who is this?" He gestured at me.

"Your new employee. You hired him yesterday."

"Yes, you're on time."

I joined the conversation. "Yes, sir. You told me to be here at nine thirty sharp."

"I did? I've never been here that early." He seemed confused.

"You aren't, but I am." Paola remarked.

"Oh yes, she told you then?

I was just about to correct him when Paola tapped my forearm, silently signaling me to stay quiet. I comprehended. "Yes, she did."

"Okay, can I have my coffee?"

"You have it in your hand, Ned." Paola pointed to a cup of coffee he held firmly.

"Oh, yes I do. Then let's get to work. I'm in my office, see me there." He stormed into his enclosure and shut the door close.

Paola glimpsed at me and shrugged. "See what I told you? Suddenly, I need my coffee now."

"Does he want me or you?"

"You better find out." She left for the coffee machine.

⋙⋙⋙

After eight months of satisfactory employment at the Ackers Accounting, the peak time for our business was imminent. April approached and the open season for CPAs began in full bloom. Our office wasn't bound to be as bustling as our competitors', as I had intuited that in all this time working here, but there were customers, more than a handful, enough for us to endure another year of operations. I had done a certification program in a local school in financial accounting and just graduated with a diploma a week ago. It was certainly not a random, impulsive decision to do that course, but persistent encouragement and long hours of lecturing from both Ned and Paola which propelled me into that classroom. I had reduced the days of work at the supermarket from six a week to four as I still needed the extra paycheck to defray the costs of my tuition and other expenses including rent. Yes, I was renting a small apartment in the neighborhood now where I could actually enjoy a seven hour sleep every night without being bothered with encompassing dissonance. It was a small place, a one bedroom apartment with a view of the street down below from the windows. The living had an inbuilt kitchenette which was just three steps from my couch, a comfortable sight on the days you're really down with exhaustion and have no reason to toil. Life was running smooth. I would refrain from saying good as it wasn't in any aspect, but it was unwrinkled and unfluctuating which it hadn't been in a long time. But a change was about to happen, and it happened soon.

Chapter Forty-Five

☙☙☙

Another year had passed and snow had just ceased. It was a cherished day that I attempted to relish as long as it lasted. It was finally my day off from both jobs, the weather was cold but the day was bright and it forced me to take a stroll out in the open. I gave in. I walked and pondered life, what it had given me, what it had taken from me. I was sporadically reminded of Audrey and then Marilyn, but wasn't certain if they were ever reminded of me. Sometimes I wanted to return to her, my wife, and ask for her forgiveness. But I was weak to face her once more, to bear all that culpability again and hear her grievances. I was afraid to return. On the other hand, Marilyn wouldn't have liked it much I returned to her. So, I was alone, all alone. I had begun a four year degree program at a college for working adults doing my degree in accounting. And yes it was mostly due to Ned and Paola's pestering nudges impelling me into the gates of that educational institution that I finally surrendered. Ned had promised me to assist in learning everything and he claimed that half of things in the curriculum would be what I already knew and he wasn't wrong. The program could be expedited if the student was able to complete certain milestones and pass examinations. On top of that I worked at an accountancy firm which gave me an edge over the studies. Ned knew his people who could help me to sit in for the CPA license exam as soon as I was done with the degree, and experience requirements were no problem at all. It was all set for my future, down the path there were no encumbrances, no hindrance.

It was a random thought that came to my mind and I took the closest bus and planned to travel to its last stop not knowing where and what it was. After a good long ride for about two hours, I had reached some residential area in the outskirts of the city. The bus dropped two other people along with me and took off to the station. I glanced around to scan my surroundings and found it to be a small town-like setting of a place with some quaint shops lined up on the street. The pedestrians were scarce due to the frigid breeze, but enough cars passing down the road. I sighted a small school playground across the street with some children making snow figures and shapes, some just joyfully tossing around. I scampered across the street and perched on a bench right at the entrance of the playground. I don't know why I enjoyed watching children in their playful mischief and impish giggling, but I did this a lot. Maybe it evoked a feeling of fulfillment that I was unable to observe my own child bustled in such activities and took solace in being able to watch other children. Maybe it just gave me a visual of how my own child would have been like, would have acted like, would have smiled like. Children are alike in all aspects but one, their parents. And that's what shapes them into different people, good or bad, upbringing and circumstance are the two deciding factors.

I looked at some children playing in the snow as their mothers cautiously followed them around. I stayed there for a good half an hour at which point I decided to return back home. Just as I was thinking about it, a woman came and sat next to me going through her cell phone. She intermittently eyed her daughter who was on the slides with two more friends and were all leaping off landing into a pile of snow.

"Don't catch a cold now!" The mother exclaimed hardly leaving the screen of her phone to watch her child.

I nodded to the fact that people who yearn for specific things and might go to any extent to obtain them, can't have them. And the people who do have those things, take them for granted. Luxury, money, love, age, vanity are a few examples of these things, in my case it was a daughter which I had, but still didn't. I got up and began walking straight back to the bus stop.

"Come on baby, we have to leave now." I heard the mother call on her daughter again.

I ambled further down the sidewalk and heard some footsteps following close behind, especially tapping of heels against the concrete.

"Who's going to race me to the car?" I heard someone challenge another just a few steps behind me and within a moment a woman and a child hastened down the snowy sidewalk. The woman held a cell phone in one hand and a designer handbag in the other and cantered right after her daughter who kept glancing back at her mother and her face flashed with excitement at her increasing distance. It was the woman I had seen before next to me on the bench and her daughter who played at the slides.

Just as the race went on the woman suddenly stopped dead in her tracks, her phone had just riveted her attention once more. Her daughter had continued some ten kid steps ahead of her when she reached the intersection. My eyes were wide in abrupt shock as I anticipated the impending threat that approached the child. The street light went green for the vehicles going across and the child had no idea how to interpret the signs above her. She simply retained her pace and continued into the arms of death. I knew calling out to her mother would be a disastrous option as it would just waste time. I lunged from my lethargic stride to a forceful, dashing sprint and went past the woman reaching for the child closer and closer every crucial second. Just as she came in front of a moving SUV which blasted the horn vehemently, I leaped for her and snatched her away from death with just inches to spare.

I reeled backwards and stumbled to the ground with the child still safely clutched in my arms in arrant daze. The SUV stopped and uttered a nice long string of insults at me, but witnessing I was in no condition to respond, he drove away. The woman was next to kneel by my side in tearful trauma as she claimed her child and made her stand up before herself checking for injuries.

"Honey, look at me? Oh God, you're not hurt, are you?"

"I'm fine mommy, just this-" the kid showed her mother a small bruise on her palm.

"Oh sweetheart, I'm glad it's just this." The mother arose and looked into my eyes as I had just straightened my numbed legs and brushed off the sidewalk filth from my pants. "Are you all right, sir?"

"I'm all right." I responded taking my time to adjust after the stunning event.

"You're not hurt, are you?"

"You should be more careful. You know that phone isn't as important as her. Its worth is far less than her tears let alone her life." Some people gathered around as the woman lowered her eyes and I eschewed making another event out of her. "Take care of her." With that I walked away moving towards my bus stop.

I crossed the street and stood in the queue for the bus and saw the woman coming to a chauffeured Mercedes limousine with the door opened for her by a suited individual whom I gathered to be her chauffeur and she instructed her daughter to stay inside. She came down to the bus stop and approached me with a contrite soul.

"Can I please talk to you for a moment?" She pleaded.

I slipped from the queue and separated from the people joining her next to a storefront.

"I'm really sorry for what happened. I know I don't have to clarify things to you, you'd think I'm crazy or something, but you've saved my daughter from... from something horrible and I need to thank you for it. You don't know what you have done for me. She is my life, she is everything I have left... now. That phone is never more important than your child, but when you receive news of your husband or rather ex-husband now getting married that's a whole different story. It just drained my senses out of me for one second and this happened. I'm sorry and I thank you."

"That's okay. Actually, I'd like to apologize as well for what I said back there, I shouldn't have said that. Obviously, your daughter means the world to you. I went too far."

"No, that's all right. You at least took an initiative to make me realize what a split second diversion can cost. You're waiting for a bus?"

"Yes."

"Can I drop you off somewhere?"

"That's okay, I live way far-off from here. I'll take the bus."

"Please, that's the least I can do, and it doesn't matter where you live. My driver knows his way around town."

"I live in the city. It's about two hours from here."

"Then it will give us some more time to talk. Besides, I work in the city. I travel up and down every day. Please, I insist, Fiona would love to speak to you."

"Fiona?"

"My daughter's name is Fiona. I'm Winona Warren. The names rhyme."

I was invited to the limousine and led into the warm, cozy interior of the vehicle which was a welcome change in the freezing cold. I shifted to the opposite row of seating across from Winona and her daughter and the car began to glide down the road.

"Thank you mister, you saved my life." The little angel spoke. I was surprised at her perception as well as her mannerisms. Both the adults in the car laughed and I shook hands with her.

"It's all right, but from now on you have to make sure you check the street lights in front of you before crossing. If it says walk, only then you cross the street and make sure you always look over your left shoulder for the incoming traffic, okay?"

"Okay." She answered.

"How old are you?"

"I'm seven, I'll be eight in-" she counted on her fingers, "six months."

"Oh, you're keeping good track of your birthday. That means you're a big girl."

"Yes. See mommy I'm a big girl." She laughed proudly.

"Fiona, you don't call somebody mister just like that, you have to be more polite and ask them their name." Winona pushed her further.

"What's you name, mister?" Fiona obeyed her mother's instructions.

"George, George Bailey."

"Nice to meet you, George."

I smiled at the child, "you too, Fiona."

"He knows my name already." She got excited.

"Yes, he does." Winona secured her right by her side. "Where do you live in the city?"

"Up on South Mint Street."

"That's very close to the city itself, the business hub. What do you do, Mr. Bailey?"

"I am an assistant accountant at Ackres Accounting. I also work at a supermarket. Both jobs are quite close to each other."

"Ackres Accounting, have I heard of this name?" She tapped her forehead trying to recollect any memory of the firm.

"I don't think so, it's just a small private office. We only handle local customers."

"Hmm..."

"If you want a nice house my mom will make one for you. She makes houses, you know." Fiona giggled as she spoke.

"Fiona, your mom does not make houses. Well, partly she does, doesn't she? I work at Bender Realty. We deal in private properties a lot."

"The Bender Group Real Estates?"

"Yes, you know about our company?"

"Who doesn't? I mean it's one of the most successful and prestigious corporations in the city. Even in the times of financial collapse, your company exhibited great resilience to external pressure and recorded a sales hike of thirty-two percent last year. That was in papers for a very long time."

"We managed to get through. Actually, we were challenged unnecessarily by our competitors so we had to step it up a bit. It isn't always the same."

"It was commendable what you did there."

"Thank you. Were you brought up in this city, George?"

"No, I came here from California three years ago, been here since. You reside in the city as well?"

"No, I live where we just met. This little princess goes to school there and today was her playground day. It's close to the house and a very nice school."

"Then you're driving all the way to the city just for me? I could have taken the bus, didn't want to trouble you. You're making me feel bad."

"I told you, it's no trouble. Busses take such a long time to get to the city, I know that. We'll be there in less than an hour."

We sat there in silence for a few moments.

"What brought you all the way from the city to that antiquated hamlet? You're a long way from home."

"A long awaited holiday. Maybe a longing for some time away from a banal routine. I haven't had a day off in about five weeks. I finally got one, so just a spontaneous decision to board a bus and see where it leads to. Then thought of tagging along a little longer to the last stop. This was it. Sat down in the park, watching others live, laugh, love."

"And then we happened."

"Yeah, finally something exciting, but I would rather not have her be the cause of such excitement ever again."

Winona gazed into my eyes and didn't say a word for a long time. I grew uncomfortable with her intrusive stare and looked away.

"Life is harsh, but it always gives you a reason to live. Here is my reason and a beautiful one. I think you would have one too? Do you have a family, Mr. Bailey?"

I stayed quiet and didn't answer her.

"I'm sorry I was too inquisitive, didn't mean to make you uncomfortable."

"I don't. It's just me."

"Well, then I hope you find a reason to live, laugh and love soon."

"That's what I have been looking for all these years, came close twice."

"It isn't always their fault, you know. Sometimes the fault is our own to not see what is in front of you."

"I'm the perfect example of that."

"I'm sorry, I shouldn't have said that."

"That's all right, I don't mind the truth. It is what it is."

"Then you're as guilty as I am."

"But not as fortunate." I gestured toward her daughter who was now dozing off by her side.

"Yes, the best thing that's happened in my life."

The car came to a gradual standstill after another twenty minutes of drive and I had my signal that my destination had come.

I skittered toward the edge of the seat and glanced back at my host. The little sweet was fast asleep as I kept my voice to a whisper.

"I don't like it a bit that I made you travel all the way here."

"You don't have to like it, I do, and I do." Winona responded in a similar hushed voice and smiled.

"Thank you so much."

"Thank you. You leave me in a greater debt that just an hour long drive. What you did, people hardly do."

"Good night."

"I hope to see you again, good night."

I stepped out of the limousine and was introduced to the cold and snow once again as it had just begun to waft. I waved to them as the door of the car was closed by the chauffeur and moved up on the sidewalk seeing them off. The car began to pull away and the rear window slid down. Fiona's face emerged from the window smiling at me and her arm waving a goodbye. I laughed and waved back as they faded down the road and took a turn. I crept back to my humble abode and the hackneyed life once more.

Chapter Forty-Six

୨୭ ୨୭ ୨୭

I had gotten so accustomed to the warmer weather of the west coast that acclimating to this colder climate was taking a bit of time. I had fallen to the ailment of cold every winter since the last two I had been here and this morning was the beginning of my third. Though, I usually got sick when winters started, this time it took its toll twice in the same season as I fell sick while winter waned. It wasn't severe enough to account a day off from work, but strong enough to hold me from working if untreated. I reached for the telephone and dialed the only number I knew or could remember in my condition. I was already late and presumed that Paola might have reached the office and she had as she answered on the third ring.

"Ackres Accounting, how may I help you?"

"Paola, this is George." I spoke in a nasal tone.

"Oh George, telecommuting, are we?"

"No commuting at all. Paola, I need your help. Can I be late for another hour? You've got to tell Ned for me."

"Why do you sound like Quacker from Tom & Jerry?"

"I have a cold."

"Oh, yeah I'll take care of Ned, don't worry. If you want the day off, I think I can get that out of him as well."

"No, I'll be there in a while, two hours tops. Thanks Paola."

"No worries, you do know what medicine to take, right?"

"I think I do."

"No, I mean you're not allergic to any fever reducers or pain killers, are you? Because they add those to every cold and allergy medicine."

"I don't think so. I'm going to have some more sleep."

"Because if you are, some people are to ibuprofen, aspirin, antibiotics. You never know."

"I'll figure that out."

"If you are allergic to acetaminophen, don't take tylenol or aleve, or if it's aspirin, forget about Bayer."

"Paola, I'll take care, thank you."

"Don't overdose on any of them."

"Paola, I'm not trying to kill myself."

"You have to be very careful these days with medications, George. My sister-in-law's niece who has a 14 year old daughter and she slightly overdosed on aspirin and they had to take her to the emergency. She just took one extra pill, can you believe that, one extra pill."

"That's terrible. I think I wouldn't make that same mistake."

"And make sure you take it with warm water."

"Paola, why don't I come there and you can demonstrate how to take a pill in person?"

"No, no, no, don't come here. I'll catch it from you."

"Should I hang up then? Thank you, goodbye." I hung up the phone quite vexed and drowned into the folds of my bed again.

I woke up at half past ten and felt much better as I had harnessed an old remedy to my colds which was just a simple process of sleeping with my head buried between two pillows that warmed the space quickly and breathing in that contaminated air somehow ameliorated this particular ill.

I took the bus to the office and entered the door around eleven finding Paola in an everyday commotion of sitting idle in boredom.

"Hey," she exclaimed, "you feeling better?"

"Kind of, yes. Thanks for all that input on the phone."

"Glad to help anytime."

"Ned in there?" I just reached for his office door and was about to open it.

"He has some clients in there."

"Oh," I stopped and traced my steps back to a chair. "Important clients?"

"I don't know, but look intimidating."

"Really? He's not in trouble, is he? IRS?"

"Nah, I know those guys. They know how to take your money, but don't look as good as much as they swipe out of you."

I looked at her with a confounded gaze. I didn't quite understand what she just said right away, but made sense out of it by repeating aloud in my brain slowly.

After a moment of desperate brooding about Ned's future and safety inside that room, I saw two gentlemen professionally suited and groomed with unyielding stern faces stepping out of Ned's diminutive office and they strode in a perfect line towards the exit door nodding to Paola on their way out.

Following them Ned emerged and appeared befuddled and disoriented due to some unknown reason.

"Ned, what happened?" He was silently confused still. "Ned, what's the matter, who were they?" Paola and I arose in concern.

"I am..." Ned attempted to recall the conversation.

"Now, don't forget, all right? It will be very hard for us if you forget what happened in there, so take your time, deep breaths and try to remember." Paola eased him up.

"What did you do?" Ned came towards me flabbergasted. I receded.

"I... I didn't do anything. I called Paola and told her I'd be late."

"What did you do?" He persisted with his enigmatic accusation.

"I had a cold, I'm sorry, I'm fine now. I'll be on time from tomorrow. It's the first time I've been late in years."

He lunged at me and squeezed me in a hug and kissed me on my cheek. "We did it. You did it." He scrambled to Paola and embraced her tightly. "He did it."

"Did what?" Paola questioned.

"Do you know who these men were?"

"If you'd tell me about it I think I will." Paola uttered.

"These were private accountants from Bender and Bronsky.

"What's Bronsky?"

"'The Construction company' in all North Carolina. The biggest contractors in the entire city and business partners as well. They want a reliable, registered CPA to manage their accounts from now on. On a regular basis, permanently. Not just the annual auditing, or financial reports and statements. They're ready to sign a ten year service agreement. We've got ourselves a permanent client and we've got them by a hook."

"By a hook?" I inquired.

"Recommendation, a personal recommendation. That's referred to as a hook in our vernacular. You son of a gun, whom have you been seeing lately? They mentioned your name and some Winona Warren putting in a good word for us. I think she's one of the partners in the realty."

"I met her some time ago." I was deep in thoughts.

"So we're back in business, Mr. Ackres?" Paola was delighted.

"Back in business with a bang. No more of these despisable conditions to work in, no more of that tiny office, no more of that creaking desk for you. You get a cabin of your own in our new office on the thirtieth floor of BOA plaza. And here is my business partner, Mr. George Bailey, you have changed my life. Such a short time you've been with us and you've done something I couldn't do in years. Thank you, George."

"There are no thank yous in friendship."

"Yup there aren't and on that note I give you two a day off, paid of course. Go home, drink and celebrate, it's our big night."

"Oh, I better leave before he changes his mind." Paola began gathering her things into her handbag. "See you guys later." She hastened out of the office.

"What's the matter, George? You don't look as happy as you should be."

"No, I'm happy. It's just that I was thinking of the woman who did this. She hardly knows me."

"She doesn't know much about you, but at least knows an honest man when she sees one. Now go and have a blast."

"I have nowhere to go, Ned."

"Sure you do, you have someone to thank for this massive favor. It isn't something every person would randomly do. And then you're coming over to my place, we'll order some food and watch a movie together. Okay?"

"Okay." I laughed.

"Now go on."

I collected my jacket on the way as Ned pushed me out the door.

It took me half an hour to get downtown as the midday traffic was at its acme. I was afraid I was going to miss Winona Warren as the clock ticked close to three, but I hastened into the expansive facade of a massive commercial building and inquired at the reception about her office floor.

The elevators opened to the twenty-second floor and I entered a commodious space divided into various sub-sections of a work facility and sighted a company directory upon a wall with embossed name plates next to their corresponding suites. I found Winona Warren listed as a partner and member of Board of Directors, which completely astonished me as I had only imagined her as an employee of the company, a significant one, but an employee. It led me into more hesitation whether to see her or not and a series of questions arose in my mind. I didn't know if it would be appropriate of me to visit her just out of the blue. I didn't know if she would like to meet me at her workplace divulging our contact to all her peers and colleagues. But just as I had made my mind to drop the idea, I was approached by a young lady who appeared most benign and courteous.

"Excuse me, sir. Are you looking for someone? Maybe I can assist you to the right office." She asked with a welcoming smile.

"Winona Warren."

"Oh, right this way, sir." She walked down the hallway leading me further into a beautiful maze of doors and passageways. "I don't know if I'd had the pleasure of speaking to you, sir. Do you have an appointment with her?"

"No, I just stopped by to see her."

The lady paused her strides and wavered to take me any further.

"She gave me her card and asked me to come see her." I presented her with her personal visiting card which assured her I wasn't lying.

"Oh, very well. Allow me." She opened a glass door to another spacious part of the floor made to look like a reception where a couple of women worked on their desks minding their computers and phones that were ringing off the hook. This lady reached for a phone at a side desk and dialed a number. And after a few smiles and submissive nods and affirmations she led me further into the main office. The doors were opened for me as I saw a massive, luxurious office space abundant with high-class furniture in a contemporary setting. Glass walls that gave a view of the front of the building, and a large L-shaped desk lined with multiple computer screens that displayed the stock market with its ups and downs.

"Ms. Warren asked me to have you wait in here, she is on her way to the office. Just a couple more minutes."

"That's all right." I responded still in awe of view before me.

"Is there something I can get you, sir? Some coffee perhaps?"

"I'd be fine, thank you."

She nodded and left me alone in that monolithic den. I sat upon the couch in the corner and waited. Approximately ten minutes later the doors were opened again as it stirred me up to my feet. I saw Winona, followed by three men and the same lady who had brought me in, storm inside in urgency. One of the men held up a file in front of her wanting her signatures which she did, and a phone tucked under her cheek.

"Tell him I need preliminary estimates on our investment returns. If he wants the dough he has to work for it. And I'll personally get in contact with Hamilton about the revisions in the agreement, get him on the phone for me."

Though, it was hard to tell when and whom she was exactly talking to because as much as I could gather, she had spoken to one of her male managers, the person on the phone, and the lady secretary in that one discourse. The secretary whispered something to her that riveted her attention to the corner where I was standing stiff anticipating her.

She took a moment to recollect my name but came up with it quick enough. "George?"

"Hello Winona."

"I can't- leave us for fifteen minutes."

Her staff obeyed her command and left the two of us in the room. She stepped closer to me and offered me to sit. I did.

"I can't believe you're here."

"Now, that is not true. Considering what you have done, I was bound to come over."

"What? Did I do something? Hope it wasn't anything wrong."

"Don't mean to sound haughty, but you possibly couldn't go wrong with that decision."

She laughed at the remark. "Said like a true gentleman. I hope to see more of that confidence in the coming years of our relationship. Professional relationship."

"I hope to serve your company well."

She arose and went to her desk inviting me over and phoned her reception to send in some coffee and snacks.

"I hope I'm not taking your time, I just..." I went over to her desk.

"You're not, I could use a little time-off occasionally from all that infuriating business context. I'm glad you remembered my invitation."

"I held onto your card."

The receptionist came in with a platter of edible stuff and coffee. She poured us both our cups and left the office swiftly.

"I feared I would miss you today, there was a lot of traffic coming here. I reached here after three."

"Three is quite early for us to close."

"Yes, but rich and successful people have shorter work days."

She laughed. "What makes you think I'm rich and successful?"

"Apart from this grand setting, this office, the staff outside, I also happened to come across the company directory on my way here."

"Really, you read that?"

"Yes, and I caught your lies. You told me you worked here."

"You're calling me a liar, to my face, in my office." Her face grew stern and irate.

"I didn't mean to offend you in any way."

But then she burst into laughter again. "I'm sorry, I couldn't resist but see that look on your face. Guilty as charged, but that doesn't make me any more clement towards faults and mistakes, if that's what you're thinking."

"No, I was just being appreciative of your kindness."

"It isn't kindness, George. It's business. You interest me, I give you a chance to prove yourself. Now it's your turn to help yourself.

Somewhere down the road, you can return the favor. That's life." She gazed at me with her poignant hazel eyes, followed by a long hiatus.

"How is Fiona?" I began the talk again.

"She is doing very well, thanks for asking. She does not completely understand the consequence of the incident that day, but thinks fondly of you."

"She is a sweet child."

"I couldn't thank you enough for what you did that day. You saved my life, not hers, mine."

"I think you did thank me, more than what it deserved. This opportunity is more than a conventional expression of gratitude."

"It's nothing. I believe in chances and in all these years of working and managing businesses, I have seen people in need of a chance work more ardently than people who are simply given them out of nepotism."

"Isn't this the same?"

"You are in need, aren't you?

"You have done your research."

"That I have. It was an honest referral, I mentioned your accountancy name in passing and they probably took me too seriously. Nothing exaggerated or unnecessary. After all, you have endured the competition for twenty-five years in such economic cataclysm. You do deserve some high-end clients."

"That's nice of you to consider, my employer wasn't any less excited when he shook hands with the people you sent over. This gratefulness comes from him as well."

"He is welcome."

"I don't want to hold you unnecessarily, I was timing myself. You said I had fifteen minutes, I have four more minutes to go after which your staff is going to come barging in here and probably throw me out that window and shower you with more work and files."

She laughed again. "It's good you keep track of time, it'll come handy in future. But the windows back there don't open up."

"Oh boy, you just saved my life there. Thank you once again." I stood up and shook her hand, just as I turned to leave.

"George, I wanted to ask you something. Fiona's birthday is coming up in a couple of weeks, I was wondering if you could come and join us. She'd been asking about you lately, you've made your impression on her as her new best friend. She'll be happy to see you again."

I contemplated, then nodded. "I would love to."

"Thank you, I will send you the details."

"Good afternoon."

She smiled and nodded, with that I took her leave.

Chapter Forty-Seven
ఞఞఞ

I called Ned after some more hours of sleep and elucidated the content of my conversation with Winona to him. He then persuaded me to come over to his place to celebrate the night together to which I conceded and informed him that I shall be arriving shortly. It was well after seven that I reached his house in a cab and stood at the sidewalk glancing at the neighborhood. It was just another private residence in a sea of similar structures lined up and down the street as far as the eye could reach. An ordinary neighborhood with an average lifestyle which Ned Ackres was a part of. I hadn't been inside his home ever in the past years of working for him. Though, I did get close to this door twice only to drop off some papers at late hours.

I stood at his door knocking and in a few second he appeared behind the mesh screen door with displeasure spread across his face and a bottle of Wild Turkey 101 in his hand.

"Now who is that knocking my door?"

I was taken aback presuming he might have forgotten his recent invite. "Hey Ned, you um... you asked me to come by, you remember?"

"No, did I? Or you're just making that up?" His brows were converged in confusion. I began to trace my steps back to the sidewalk.

"No, that's okay, I can leave. I didn't want to bother you."

"Got you there, didn't I?" And then he exploded into laughter that revealed signs of clear inebriety, but he had gotten me this once. "I'm sorry, I was just trying to play with you a little. Come on in, join me inside my humble abode."

He welcomed me into his home and took me down a hallway into his living room. As I passed the other rooms, I felt an archaic air lurking around the residence, untouched, undisturbed. The furniture, the draperies, the belongings were the same as they had probably been twenty years ago, maybe longer. All buried under a shroud of dust and memory.

"You didn't have any trouble finding the place, did you?"
"No, it's easy to get here."
"Yeah, make a habit of it. We're going to get together for many celebrations from now on."
"I hope so."
"I know it. So what did she say? Tell me everything."
"Well, it wasn't a long conversation, I was there only ten minutes."
"She gave you that much? Usually these rich folks have no time for the poor."
"I don't think she's like others. Maybe, I can't say for sure, but she seems different."
He smiled. "Yeah, they all look good in the beginning. They reveal their true selves at the utmost necessity and then it's not pleasant at all. Can I get you something?"
"Nah, I'm good."
"Come on, it's not that you don't drink."
"All right, just one drink."
"There you are, my boy. So, what else did she say?"
"I told her how much we appreciated all this, and she said she looks forward to working with us. Then she invited me to her daughter's birthday."
"Now, how in the greenest of all the fields and bluest of all the oceans did you manage to impress this lady to the point of such a great favor?"
"I saved her daughter."
"Her daughter?"
"Yeah, she was about to get into an accident, I stepped in and saved her life."

"Oh, so you have her where it hurts the most?"

"Nothing like that."

"No, no, no, I know how it is. You are a very lucky man, you'd be a fool to let this opportunity go."

"What opportunity, Ned?"

"She has a soft spot for you, take advantage of that."

"I'm not taking advantage of anything at the moment."

"You'll learn it the hard way then. You'll allow a great opportunity slip from your hands just like that?"

"Let's start working for them and take advantage of that opportunity the right way, the way we're supposed to."

"Not all things are done right the right way. You'll come across that truth one day, and you'll remember me for telling you. So, what else is going on these days?"

Just then his phone rang in some other room. He got up and went over to answer it giving me the chance to probe his past by observing the pictures on the mantle. They were mostly from his youth, and the surprising fact was that he used to be quite athletic in his days of prime. There was a woman next to him in many pictures that were taken on various occasions but all pertaining to sport or traveling activity of some kind.

"Twenty-five years ago." I turned and found Ned at the doorway again. "That's twenty-five years ago, maybe more. Paola was on the phone, she was just making sure if everything was actually happening, or maybe it was just a charade."

"She's such an adorable character, isn't she?"

"Yup, she is. And has been like that since I've known her. She's loyal as well. There aren't many people who'd stick around an office that hardly compensates them for the work they put in. Sometimes, she'd even go without a paycheck for weeks if she sees I'm tight. In fact, she hasn't had a raise in seven years. But she's always been there, shows up every morning."

"Hard to find people like that."

"Yes. Hey, you're not that bad yourself. You've gone a couple of weeks here and there without pay."

"I'm still new."

He laughed and came over to sit back on a couch and drank in silence, as if a memory had inundated his mind, his thoughts. It was awkward for a minute, then I had to break it.

"You were quite fit at that time. Well, you still are-"

"Sans the pot belly." We both laughed.

"Who is that girl next to you, if you don't mind my asking?"

"What if I do?"

"Then I'll take another drink and spend the rest of the time with my mouth shut."

"You will have another drink," he got up to pour me one. "Because you'll need one to listen about her."

He handed me the glass and joined me on the couch, reclined back and took a deep breath. A long moment passed and I grasped his disinclination to talk.

"This is a very nice house, not a bad neighborhood either."

"This is a crap house, I've lived in it since I was born. It's old. Everything about it is so old. I don't even remember most of the things about it that's how old it is. My father bought it way back in the 50s, when he'd just gotten married to my mom. I did have an apartment of my own when I was in college, but then..." he choked to speak any further. "Old things can make you regret. Old memories, old people, old houses, they hold a lot of secrets, a lot of good and bad, smiles and tears. Don't live in the past, if you'd take my suggestion."

"I try not to."

"So do I, that's why I hate pictures. I am a murderer, Josh. I murdered someone."

My mind was suddenly shifted toward that heinous crime I had committed in my past, which sometimes still haunted me at nights. But I kept the frown, which resulted from contemplating that appalling incident, from creasing my forehead.

"It's George."

"Hmm?"

"My name, George."

"Yes, I know. That woman you see in the pictures was the only woman I ever loved, and she happens to be the person who was taken away from me without a reason. For once in my life, I fell in love, and they couldn't see me like that. They... I don't even know who they are. The people, the world, earth, nature or that thing you

- 305 -

call God. Maybe they all came together in this plot, in this conspiracy against me. Past is an evil thing to remember, it makes you cry, makes you crawl, makes you want to die."

I took another long pause which mollified him somewhat. "What happened to her?"

"She died, that's what happened to her. You know when I first met her?"

I shook my head.

"When we were seven, probably eight. At that time love for us was just going into the playground every afternoon and spending hours on the swing together, without a word. We attended school together and even college, though, she was an arts major. You can tell by looking at her, can't you? She was beautiful, inside and out. All those years of friendship that changed to love and more as we grew, it grew with time. Only to leave me stranded, alone, depressed. She died of cancer, lung cancer. And the best thing about it was she never smoked. Even in the dark dungeons of our dorm room, she would never smoke a single cigarette or even a joint. Her father was a chain smoker, though. Throughout his life, and she had to take it all in for the duration of her childhood, until she finally moved to college, but that was too late. And being so delicate, she couldn't fight the disease. These photos show the last months of her life, of us being together. She wanted to do so much, go so many places, live, but she was short on time. I tried to take her everywhere I could, be with her every minute, not leave her for a second. But eventually time ran out, and the last three weeks of her life I would see her on a hospital bed, fighting a battle she knew she couldn't win, I knew she couldn't win and we were moving towards the end, end of her, end of us, with my hands tied bound to watch her die and to hear her last breath, her last words, her last wish. She passed away and the last thing she said to me through her tears and pain were 'don't you cry for me, you fool, don't cry for me, I've lived my part.'"

I went on to pour him and myself another drink, then came back to the couch. "But you shouldn't blame yourself for her death. It wasn't your fault."

"It isn't her death I blame myself for."

I remained silent and waited for him to continue.

"I tried to kill myself some days after her passing, came quite close. My mother didn't take the incident sportingly and suffered a heart attack. She died, I survived. Life is worse than a devil at a card game. At least when he's bluffing you know he's lying, but life does everything opposite to your plans, every fucking thing contrary to what you want it to be." He guttled the whole glass at once and parted with it with a grimace. "Then my father couldn't bear the sudden separation and he died. Death after death, tragedy upon tragedy, would you believe I lost everything within a year of losing her. Claire, that was her name. The sweetest name I ever uttered in my life. The sound of her laughter still echoes in my thoughts sometimes, but it's beginning to fade now. It's been twenty-five years. I guess I shouldn't have trusted the over-the-counter sleeping pills for the job." He began laughing, and I followed suit suddenly exhumed from the inky pits of sorrow. "Don't ever take those."

"No, I tried a better option. A razor to your wrist, half an hour of wait and you're good to go."

Ned turned and looked at me with a peculiar stare which was neither contemptuous nor sympathetic, but rather more questionable to the action or the reason that caused it.

"Hey, life is cruel, it can't see people happy. That's why we're given it for free and it doesn't like being given out for free. It's always on the lookout to get itself back, wherever it can, from whomever it can. And we're about to go and look for some eatery that might still be open. Businesses around here close earlier than the city's. There's a Chinese place at the mall nearby. Let's get some overeating done tonight. Come on."

Ned led me out of the house to his car and we drove down the street towards the mall. The distance was short and I had almost suggested that we could have walked our way here. But contemplating Ned's euphoric condition, I refrained from getting anywhere near that proposition. The mall was partially closed with only select stores open and a food court in the cellar of the building. There were just two counters open in the food court, a pizza place and the other was Ned's everyday favorite Chinese stall. He went over and ordered the "usual" and the order was surprisingly understood by the benign mandarin speaking woman at the counter, who also greeted us in her own language. That indicated Ned being a routine customer at this place.

"What are you having?" He asked.

"I wasn't looking for Chinese tonight, but whatever they make good."

"How about from that over there. They have pizza, burgers."

"No, I'm fine here. I'll have some teriyaki chicken. That's all."

"You sure?" He questioned, I nodded. "You heard the man, give him some teriyaki."

We collected our platters and went over to a table in the corner. I was surprised to see the amount of food in Ned's platter and curious to see if he could fit all of that somewhere down his throat. The "usual" was a bowl of boiled rice and shredded beef, a side of wonton soup, two chicken wings, two egg rolls and a big bucket size jumbo slurpee. We sat down and began consuming the steaming food as we spoke about the imminent responsibilities and expectation of our new clients. We then shifted back to some family talk as it was unfair of me to intrude upon his past life and not tell him anything about my own. He listened intently to a brief recollection of my past and gave me some encouragement for my failures as well as advice on my mistakes down that memory lane. Though, I eschewed elaborating any of those past instances but I told him the basics.

We stayed there for at least three hours or so, until the janitors had to begin turning off the lights and the owners of Chinese stall were packing their stoves and stuff. Finally, we were urged to leave and Ned waved to the Chinese woman at the counter a goodbye and staggered to the exit. I followed him making sure he doesn't trip or stumble. As we reached the car, he insisted on dropping me to my apartment, but I bluntly refused and demanded of him to sit in the passenger's seat and allow me to drive. He was adamant at first, but then quickly gave in and just as he was put to place on the passenger side, he drifted off to sleep.

I drove him back to the house and carried him inside with great trouble as I had never dead-lifted in my whole life, but had my first experience that night. I put him in bed in one of his rooms and took the couch myself. It had been a long night, a long but exciting day indeed. A lot of revelations about lives had been uttered from both ends, and I was satisfied to acknowledge that it wasn't just my life that was wrecked by fate over and over again. It was all around me. There is a story to each one of us waiting to be told. With that thought alleviating my soul a little, I gave way and drifted off.

Chapter Forty-Eight
ళళళ

Two days later we visited the Bender Realty office again but this time officially in response to an appointment with the board of directors. The meeting was short and concise with a lot of esoteric jargon that I wasn't too familiar with, but Ned on my side was keeping his pace with the company professionals. That day was just the beginning of what was to come our way as in the following weeks, we were introduced to the accounts and finance department located on a separate floor in the same building and their private accountants who were permanent employees of the company amidst myriad others who bustled on the workfloor. We were given past company log books, expenses, tax documents, financial statements and asset summaries, and every other paperwork that was required for us to get familiarized with the company's finances. After a superficial review of their record which took some more days, Ned's request to carry some of those documents back home was granted after some discussions. I met with Winona only a couple of times during my visits and also introduced her to my employer. Though, our meetings were quite short, but she never made me feel like her employee at any point in our conversations. She even remembered her invitation and told me about Fiona's birthday party that was coming in a few days being held at her residence and I was earnestly asked to attend along with Ned and any other guests I wanted to bring. I promised her I would be there and took her leave.

As our obligations developed, Ned told me how I needed to step-up with more responsibilities being handed down to me as I was required to manage the office along with Paola from now on and assist all local customers arriving for service there because Ned needed to attend to the matters of our new high-end client and was estimating to spend at least six hours a day at both companies. I was nervous and hesitant to take his place at first, but as he constantly reminded me that it wasn't anything Paola and I couldn't handle and was the first step to success and money for all three of us, I had to accede. This deluge of work also posed as a cure for Ned's forgetfulness, which Paola and I had managed for a very long time and were glad to see the change in him.

ৡৡৡ

It was half past six that evening and I was riding in a taxi cab towards the outskirts of the city. I was dressed in a rented tuxedo and held onto a present nicely secured in shiny gift wrapping. I had timed my travel to get me there on time as the invitation was for seven thirty. In an hour my taxi pulled off the road and into a gated estate with a long driveway leading under the portico of a grand mansion. The property was formidably large and wasn't inferior to the looks of the White House in any manner except the concentration of security around it. The door was opened by a valet and I was taken inside the mansion. As I entered I saw an immeasurable crowd of rich folks which made me feel strongly inferior to the majority of the attendance. I hadn't felt such a way in my life, but suddenly realized that I was short on confidence as well as self-esteem at the moment. I hardened my jaw and will and went down the hallway into a large gathering space where a horde was presently bustled in conversations, compliments and commendations for each other. There was a group of children in the center of the hall surrounding a large table which was topped with a grand birthday cake and a variety of snacks for the kids. The adults made their way to the far end of the hall to grab their drinks and eatables, a few waiters traversed around with drinks and platters as well.

My eyes fell upon Fiona as she looked beautiful in her blue fairy dress and had busied herself with her classmates. Gazing at her, I was reminded that I might have hosted a similar occasion for my daughter if I had raised her, stayed with and seen her turn eight. But I was unfortunate in that aspect of my life. Just then a hand rested on my shoulder and I flipped to see behind me.

"Hey there! I don't know if I should address you as an acquaintance, a business affiliation, or the savior of my daughter." Winona smiled at me and I was suddenly blinded by her beauty in a glistening gown that corresponded to her gilded locks. The dress outlined her lean figure with immense pleasure and rendered her a divine aura.

"I prefer being referred to as a friend. Business associate looks too formal and savior is a difficult word to define."

"That's an honest answer, I like it."

"I brought this for her. It's not much, I know it doesn't matter, she has everything she needs. But coming to a birthday party empty-handed is not appropriate. And she's not that age to be gifted flowers."

"Oh, you'd be surprised to see how many people showed up with exactly that." We both laughed. "Why don't you give it to her yourself?" She waved to Fiona, but the children were all around her. She leaned to a stewardess and whispered something to her. The stewardess nodded and went into the hall.

"She is happy today, thanks to you."

"You have to stop saying that. It was once and it doesn't need to be mentioned more than once."

"Some things last a lifetime, George. There she is."

The stewardess brought Fiona in her arms to us and handed her over.

"Hello little one, you're finally eight years old."

"Yes I am."

"Happy Birthday!"

"Thank you." She accepted my present, kissed me and ran away with it.

"Hey, come back here." Winona called after her, but she was too far gone to hear her.

"She's a sweetheart."

"Come on, make yourself comfortable. Let me get you a drink."

Winona took me further into the crowd and introduced me around to her business partners, some I had already met. We went to the bar and had a drink together, and when she saw me assimilating into the crowd more freely and mingling with them, she went on to attend other guests. After a while of frivolous talks and rubbing elbows with new people, we were all convoked to the other side of the hall where Fiona performed a solo followed by a duet with her piano instructor on the grand instrument and happened to be quite good at it. The crowd erupted in applause as she finished and she bowed in acceptance while Winona wiped away tears from her cheeks and lifted her daughter in her arms kissing her. It was a happy moment for all present there but there was in inkling of sadness in Fiona's eyes that kept watching the threshold as if awaiting or searching for someone. The cake cutting ceremony followed that sweet recital of some Mozart tune I wasn't too familiar with, and the dinner was served. I saw Fiona leave the circle of admiring adults and walk over to the hallway and leaning by the wall keeping her eyes fixed at the front door. I went on her trail but halted a few steps behind her, perusing the restlessness in her actions to see something or someone come through that door.

"She's waiting for her father." Winona joined me by the stairs. "She doesn't know yet. Most of the people in there don't know about us, except the ones who know him as well. She doesn't understand why he's always late and I'm running out of excuses." She headed toward Fiona. "Honey pie, what are you doing here?"

"Daddy isn't here."

"I know honey, he's probably running late again. Let's go in, there are people waiting for us inside."

"What for?" She folded her arms in sheer annoyance.

"Well, it's your birthday and they're here to celebrate with us. How are they going to do that if the birthday girl is missing from the party?"

"I don't want to go in there."

"Neither do I, but we have to, right? For mommy, please?"

"No." She stomped the floor.

"Okay." Winona arose in utter failure and looked back at me. I went forward and attempted to try my luck.

"Hey, how's the little princess?"

"I'm okay."

"What brings you out here, away from everybody? You don't like all those people in there?"

"No."

"Yeah, me neither. It's too stuffy, right? Sometimes I can't breathe when I see so many people in one place. But what I like is this blue, um... fairy dress."

"It's not a fairy dress, it's Ariel's."

"Oh, you rented it from her?"

"No silly, mommy bought it for me."

"Ariel is the name of a movie character, from The Little Mermaid." Winona came to my rescue.

"Oh right, Ariel is wonderful, isn't she?"

"She's beautiful."

"Yeah, and I think daddy has gone shopping for little Fiona to buy her something else Ariel has."

"What is that?"

Winona silently made hand gestures behind Fiona to help me a bit. She pointed to her ring finger and the gold wedding band she still wore.

"Um... Ariel's princess ring, that's what he's going to get you."

"Really? But I'm still going to be very angry with him for being late."

"Me too."

"But it's not his fault. He works too much, just like mommy. He has so many people to see." She empathized with her father and astonished me with her superior understanding.

"Hmm. How about I stay here and wait along with you? Or how about we play your favorite video game?"

Winona shook her head.

"I don't like video games." Fiona confirmed.

"Oh, then..." Winona swung her arms and I interpreted as best as I could. "Baseball. We'll play baseball."

"No!" Fiona expressed.

Winona beckoned negatively, then continued to swing her arms.

"Golf?"

"Eww, that's for old people."

Winona thumped her head in vexation and was almost about to give up.

"We'll play tennis!" Fiona exclaimed to the relief of her mother and my surprise.

"Tennis? You can play that?" My surprise was sublime.

"Yes, Come on-" She began dragging me away.

"Wait, only on one condition. That you spend just fifteen more minutes in there with those boring people until they've had their dinner. They are your friends and your mother's friends. You don't want them to go home hungry and sad just because Fiona didn't talk to them, do you?"

"No."

"So just fifteen minutes, then we play as long as you want. Agreed?"

"Okay, but fifteen minutes."

"You have my word."

"Let's go." She held onto my hand and took me inside. Winona watched all this seemingly impressed with my ability in the art of persuasion. I winked at her on my way in.

As the guests lingered on after dinner, I had managed to hold Fiona in that hall for more than half an hour keeping her occupied with her little friends, opening of her gifts and some conversations with close family friends that unnecessarily involved her as a subject in which Winona and I equally abetted each other. As the guests began to diminish, it was time to finally give in to Fiona's badgering and I was led to the rear of the property into a mini tennis court that was specifically designed for her size of play. She also had junior rackets for her and was evidently quite deft with her moves and skill.

"Come on, you aren't even trying." She yelled from the other side of the court.

"I'm trying my best to keep up here."

I was sweating profusely within ten minutes of play and within ten more I was done for the night. I fell to the ground and breathed for my life. Fiona joined me and giggled at my condition.

"What are you laughing at?"

"You play like my grandma."

"Anybody who's playing with you will turn into a grandma within ten minutes. You're making me run all over the court."

"Mom is better than you."

"Of course, she is. She is your mother. Have you ever thought of going pro?"

"Mommy says she wants to see me as the world champion one day. I even have my own coach."

"Well, the way you're playing, she will see you as one soon enough."

"Then get up and we'll play more."

"Oh boy, just ten more minutes."

"Oh, you're just too tired."

"Yeah, I'll ask you thirty-five years from now, when you're my age. Let's go."

I began the run-around again as every trick I tried was answered with such an adept prowess that I couldn't counter. My surrender was imminent when a voice called up for her and saved me the humiliation of defeat from an eight year old.

"Fiona, your mother's calling you." A caregiver stood at the stairs of the patio.

I jumped in before Fiona could request a delay. "Okay, finally. Let's go, you should never ever keep your mother waiting. Let's be quick."

I was in more hurry to answer her mother's request than she was and we both headed inside, with me employing all the effort I had left just to make it away from that tennis court, while Fiona followed lethargically disappointed with the short duration of play.

Chapter Forty-Nine
❧❧❧

Fiona and I came back into the hall and saw Winona in a heated confrontation with a man who was equally attractive in looks as her, but a few more years of experience in life and perhaps business. He was groomed but casually dressed in a jacket and khakis. Just as Winona sighted us coming in, she conjured a false smile on her face. I stopped in my path giving them their space and privacy, but Fiona hastened over to that man and leaped into his arms.

"Daddy." She cried.

"My dear baby." He responded and picked her up and kissed her. "How is my little princess?"

"Daddy, why didn't you come sooner?"

"Oh, I'm sorry honey, I was delayed. I got caught up with work. But I'm here now."

"I waited for you to cut the cake with me."

"I'm sorry I missed the cake."

"You missed a lot more than that." Winona joined in but left right away fading into the hall inside and reaching for a drink at the bar.

I lingered in the hall as I didn't know whether to leave or stay. I didn't want to interfere with the family and personal matters of the house, but it would unmannerly of me to depart without taking leave from my host. I saw Fiona was delighted to be with her father, so I kept my distance. Then following a couple of minutes of rest, I decisively approached Winona to say goodbye for the night. The guests were gone with only the workers of the mansion remaining in the hall beginning the long, tiresome process of cleaning and stowing the leftovers of the gathering.

"Give me another scotch, Benny." I heard Winona order another drink as I came closer.

"Right away, ma'am." The butler complied.

"It's quite early for three shots in row. Especially when an eight year old is around."

"Now you're going to give me lessons on how to raise my child as well?"

"Okay, not a good time to talk, I suppose. Was that recently done?"

"You see that man over there? That's my husband. And I can't say ex, because he's still mine according to the paperwork. Do you know why he's late? Because a nineteen year old cheerleader wrapped in the folds of his bed wouldn't let him go after a long weekend of fun at his beach house. He remembered to take care of her, but forgot he had a daughter. And when he was reminded of her birthday party, it caused him an inconvenience which he was very unhappy about."

"Your daughter looks quite happy with him."

"So was I until I realized what kind of a person he is. I still gave him time, but some things never change."

Her husband joined us at the bar and released Fiona to her governess.

"Winona, I need to talk to you about some things." He demanded.

"John, meet George Bailey, our new accountancy associate."

"Hello."

I shook hands with him.

"And this is my husband John Bender. The primary owner of Bender Realty."

"Nice to meet you, sir." I greeted.

"You too." John was in a hurry to leave.

"You're going to see a lot of him from now on." Winona added.

"Okay, now can we talk?" He ignored.

"What do you want to talk about?"

John eyed me repeatedly and I understood his tacit requisition and separated myself from them.

"Are you drunk?" He asked her.

"Not drunk enough to not smell that scent off of you. Who is that? You've had a keen interest in college soccer, right? Who's the girl? Or better, how old is she? Twenty-one, twenty, nineteen? The numbers keep going down the more you age. Blonde? Oh no, you already had a blonde, a brunette this time, or a redhead. She must have a tight little-"

"Will you stop it? Your daughter is right there listening to you."

"She's just listening to all of this. I've watched you do it for all these years."

"Well, now that you want to be explicit in front of your daughter, I'll try my best to keep up. I was thinking we could discuss our divorce sometime next week with our counselors but you probably want it done sooner. So, how about tomorrow?"

"How about tonight?"

"Other people have families and children to attend to. They don't do this kind of stuff at night."

"Yes, and you have some young girls to attend to, so you better run off to them before they find someone younger."

"I'm leaving. I have a flight to catch. My attorney is going to get in contact with you from now on."

"Aren't you going to kiss your daughter goodbye, or she's too young for you to kiss?"

"You disgust me."

"Welcome to the table you made me sit for the last three years."

John shook his head in disbelief and began storming away. Winona followed him to the door.

"How about your daughter? Your attorneys are going to contact her from now on as well?"

"I love my daughter."

"Say that to me one more time and I'll know it's not true."

"I'm going to get her, you know that."

"Yeah, try your best. I'm not the one sleeping around with girls half my age."

"I'm working."

"I'm sure you're working very hard to keep up with all of them. For once in your life, you never gave me anything, at least give her something to remember you for. Make her your priority just once."

"I can't ignore work."

Winona laughed through her tears. "No, of course you can't."

"Say goodbye to her for me, if I stay she won't let me leave. Make up an excuse, she'll understand."

"I'm sure she will. That's one of the things she does better than me."

John dashed out the door leaving Winona in misery of loneliness. I watched this from the doorway of the hall and felt sympathy for them both. Winona turned and walked back to me.

"I'm good at making excuses, aren't I?" She went past me as she remarked.

"Winona, I think I should leave now."

She stopped and turned back. There was certain sadness in her tearful eyes and her forlorn soul needed help. "Stay for a little while. Just a little?" She asked, almost pleading.

I smiled and nodded.

After an hour of my promise, a lot had concluded and the employees of the mansion were beginning to retire from their ranks. I stood by the door to Fiona's room as her mother tucked her in for the night and sang happy birthday to her in her whispering voice that sounded as mellifluous as a lullaby. She left the door ajar allowing a tenuous shaft of light to enter the room. We both went down to the living room and sat down together. The butler being the last one to leave approached her.

"Any further instructions for me, ma'am?"

"No, I think we're all done for the day. Thank you. Good night."

"Good night to you and you, sir."

He walked away leaving the two of us alone in the ten thousand square feet concrete structure. Winona drew in some oxygen and exhaled her weariness reclining back on the couch.

"I think I should leave as well, it's quite late."

"Have you ever been married, George?"

"I was, a long time ago."

"And it ended?"

"Yes, but it was entirely my fault that it did."

"All of you men are like that. You make it look so good in the beginning. It's all about us, how beautiful we are, how nice and polite we are to others. Eyes are the way to the soul and your soul is so pure. You all say that, right? It's kind of like a process that all men follow, a recurring cycle which resets with every new woman. And then you lure us into believing you love us like nothing else in the world. The most important person in your life, or rather, someone you can't take your eyes off. You put a ring on us to claim us as your own. Then a couple of nights later we begin to get a little boring, a little usual. And then the ecstasy of finding someone new, someone else, someone younger takes over and marriage finds its way to the threshold of marriage counselors and divorce courts. Isn't that the story of all of us?"

"You're right."

"Did you just agree with me? You're a man yourself, I just insulted your kind."

"I am guilty of that, for me it is the truth. If I disagree with you, I'd be lying. Though, not all men are like that, sometimes women take advantage of men as well. I have seen that. So, rather than generalizing men into that category, we should keep it simple by saying people. Some people are loyal, and some are not."

"Why are you so honest? It almost makes me fear you."

"It's not honesty you should fear, the lies is what frightens me."

"How did you become like this?"

"Life makes you into a man you never were. Or a woman you never were. Did you imagine raising a child on your own? Running a business on your own? But you are, and you're good at it. You changed with time, I changed with time. I have seen a lot of people in my life, a lot of mistakes I've made. But if I can't learn from them, they shouldn't be called mistakes. If I'd be intentionally repeating them over and over again, it'll be more like a proclivity, not mistakes. That's what changes you. You don't put your hand on a hot stove ever again after getting burned when you were four, do you? You learned not to from that mistake. Life is the same. It burns you a lot and teaches you every time it hurts you."

"Why did you leave her then, conflicts, irreconcilable differences?"

"I had become a different man. It didn't have to be that way, but time made it so. We loved each other, but somewhere down the road something went wrong with me. When I look back at things I want to go back and change that man. Talk some sense into him, smack him across the head and let him know what love is. But that man is long gone. Marriage is coming together of two people, two souls, two perceptions. I failed to understand that it isn't just me anymore. I, that's what I was. Me, I, mine."

"But if you have changed now, why don't you return to her?"

"I shouldn't. She's happy now."

"Without you?"

"Even more without me. I have no complaints." I took a long pause. "I don't know if I should say this, but when I saw Fiona, I saw my own daughter in her."

"You had a daughter?"

"Yes. She would be ten by now."

Winona wiped her tears that had just slipped from her eye. "Fiona has seen a lot, I wish no other child has to see that much. Since the age of five, she'd been waiting for her father to come by and spend time with her, love her, at least show up on her birthdays. But it doesn't matter to him. At that age a broken family is the hardest thing to endure, but she went through it. She's my angel, she's held my hand through so much. I was so emotionally lacerated, I could have died. But when I looked into her eyes, her innocence, her strength gave me strength and I fought if not for myself, for her. She made me live, and now everything I do is for her. I can't see anybody hurt her anymore. When you saved her, you saved me." Our eyes met and she held that gaze. "I need someone to help me, with her, with work, with myself. Someone I can rely on, someone I can talk to, relate to, someone I can feel. I can't go on alone forever."

She leaned in for a kiss, but I receded. She stopped and looked away.

"There, I just made a fool of myself. I'm not worth it, right?"

"Winona, it's not you. Trust me if I were the man I was some years ago, I wouldn't hesitate to kiss you back. But then I was a greedy man. Now, I only search for love, nothing else matters to me. And I can't trust love anymore, I'm not ready for it just yet. There are things that have passed in my life that have made me what I am. I can't forget them so easily. I don't know if I'd be able to relate to someone, love someone, be there for someone. I don't want you to be disappointed in me like someone else was. Don't get me wrong."

"No, this is what I precisely understand. If this had happened to me three or two years ago, I would have done the same. I did not trust anyone at that time. Trust comes but gradually. But loneliness stays, and believe me, I'm not the one to be going around and kissing other men for the same reason. With you, I felt different, I felt myself again. I don't want just another man for time being, I want someone for all times. The men who surround me, I know are not very different from him. And I can't have that anymore."

"I know."

"But we can still see each other every now and then, right?"

"That we will continue to do."

"Excellent."

"I have to leave now. It's past midnight, I don't think I will get a bus at this hour."

"Who said you were taking a bus?"

"I did, because your drivers are off to sleep by now. And let them, they've worked enough for the day."

"Can't do. He's waiting outside, go."

"You had him wait all this time?"

"Yes."

"Poor guy. Why did you do that?"

"I could answer, but you don't want to make him wait any longer, do you?"

"Me? Oh no, well then without wasting any more time, good night, ma'am."

"Good night to you, sir."

I laughed on my way out of the dwelling.

Chapter Fifty

ৡ৽ৡ৽ৡ৽

Two winters had passed since the time I was made familiar with life once again. After a long time it would suffice for me to say that I was indeed doing well. I was doing well in terms of work, in terms of relationships, in terms of social status as well as living conditions. None of it happened overnight, but took a long, persistent, enduring effort to accomplish, to achieve and sustain what had been gained in the past years. Our three prominent clients, two of which we had gained after brandishing our undisputed diligence at Winona's corporation, were more than adequate to nudge our wheels up the mountain of success and get our careers rolling to our satisfaction. Besides, Ned and I had decided to stick with only a few high-end clients and make them our priority which allowed us to work resolutely and sincerely to their gratification.

As far as work was concerned, Ned was the one who began maintaining accounts for all these companies, as I was given the responsibility to man our office meanwhile. It was our big concern initially to impress our clients and elicit a long working relationship with them, which Ned had done wondrously and managed to secure a contract with all three of them. I, on the other hand, was kept from all the onerous paperwork and had little part to play in our endeavors. I continued to work with our local, individual clients on their tax preparations for the past two years, had eventually gained my degree in accounting and was helped through the licensing process by Ned and his associates and was finally able to put the coveted initials next to my name commonly known as CPA. But also had an inappropriately lewd, secret expansion to those initials that Ned and I joked about, which I refrain from saying out loud, but was probably more widely known to people who were related to this field. Ned would spend most of his day away from the office and only return to see us a couple of hours a week. That gave Paola much needed time off, as she would excel in luring me into giving her days and hours off earlier than her usual time, and I didn't mind to that as she would leave no pending work on her desk or mine by the time she left. We even had a little celebration the day my license came in mail as we popped a bottle of bubbles and ordered food from a big Italian restaurant at the corner of the street where neither of us had eaten in our lives. Ned, unfortunately, didn't make it to that feast, but gave me a surprise of a lifetime when he proposed a fifty percent partnership in his accountancy which meant I would be sharing all his profits from our clients as well as a six figure salary, bonuses, perquisites, and vacations. I would be a fool to refuse to such a proposition and shook his hand on the agreement and thanked him from the bottom of my heart. In a couple of months following that partnership, Ned and I both were making six figure salary, though he was on the higher end of it. He had rented his parent's house and moved to a 2-acre estate in the suburbs, but I was required to stay a lot closer to our office in case if circumstance needed someone to answer. Therefore, I bought a penthouse apartment in one of the most prestigious residential buildings in the city and loved every square feet of my dwelling. Paola was given a company paid house in the city and tripled salary with two receptionists working under her wing. Oh yes, I almost forgot, our office wasn't the same anymore, it was a seven thousand square foot office on the seventeenth floor of another prestigious commercial building. Our lives had changed dramatically in the past years since coming in contact with Winona. Her coming was like a welcome blessing that had entered our lives with intent to shower us all in rewards for an unknown deed, grace for an unknown supplication. She was the person who turned everything into gold with her touch and I was one of the few fortunate souls to have the pleasure of knowing her personally, too personally.

ꗞꗞꗞ

Louise put her hands together in a hushed applause. "So you were right back on it? And rich, I might add."

"Rich? No, it was just the beginning. But I was well-off, you could say."

"And this woman?"

"I don't know what drew her toward me, I wasn't even that appealing."

"Well, she had already figured out what going for a shallow relationship based on physical appearance over something deep as intellect and emotion meant. She just came out of a good-looking marriage, now she needed someone to love her not compliment her standing by her side."

"But the way she surprised me, I didn't expect her to be so vulnerable."

"You were married once, you loved again, and you still don't know what a woman really is?"

"Do you think I'd be here if I did?"

"Hmm... let me tell you. You must have heard so many things about women. The way they want to be complimented every time they try a new dress or fit into an old one they previously couldn't. Or to commend their efforts they put in to make your home, to make you feel special, to cook food for you and that they want to be recognized for all those things. You might have also heard how they want you to remember special days, like the first time you two met anniversaries, or the first time you two kissed, or birthdays, or even their family's important dates. Sometimes it's even material things, you buy her gifts, jewelry, take her out to dinner, candle light even better. But there's one thing that you haven't been told yet, I am going to tell you that. If you want a woman to love you forever, love her child. And if she doesn't have a child, give her one. If she is true at heart, she can never hate you after that. You might leave her, but she never will. Because when you love a woman's child, you love the most precious thing she's ever brought to life. A woman is capable of giving life, that's her gift. If you love that gift, she will love you."

"Forever?"

Louise smiled. "Time will tell. So, where were we?"

Chapter Fifty-One

୬ଡ଼ ୬ଡ଼ ୬ଡ଼

My relationship with Winona grew deeper as time passed. It was a strange relationship to begin with, as the only object that brought us closer was the unconditional love of a child. It was her right to love her daughter, but I was given the permission to love and cherish Fiona equally. There was a certain compassion I felt in Winona's eyes when she would see me, when she would talk to me, which initially wasn't as frequent as we both would have liked, but random enough to bring us closer. And that commiseration of two ruptured hearts was ample to cover the crevices of our suffering and anguish and bring forth one desire of love for each other and the one who brought us together. It was just a few months after my official declaration as a business partner in our firm that we began dating each other publicly. I had delayed any furtherance to our relation and avoided being seen in public together prior to that partly to save myself from the embarrassment of being called an opportunist, but mostly to save her from the humiliation of being attached with an insignificant nobody. I was honest with her in telling her clearly what I felt. She did not concur with me at first, but agreed and trusted my judgment in the matter. But these reasons weren't the only ones that persuaded Winona into acceding, it was also due to a fact that she had finalized her divorce from John just recently and managed to win sole custody of Fiona with visitation rights granted to the father. I believed Winona's silent surrender to delay our rendezvous was also pertaining to a latent fear of losing her daughter's permanent guardianship to John if such matters surfaced or even appeared as nebulous as a rumor for his attorneys to harness.

But that fear was over and with only two weekends a month visitation schedule permitted to John, which he hardly kept due to conflicting work hours and other matters, Fiona was her mother's. As we all drew closer to each other through love, affection and dedication, though, sometimes my personal dedication towards Fiona's well-being would be considered overprotection, but it wasn't noted so by either of them and we were beginning to form into a family. We all needed each other, we all wanted each other and we all protected each other, and it gradually became my life to be there for them. Maybe I wanted to compensate for the mistakes I had committed towards my previous family that would have looked the same if I stayed. But the past does not allow itself to change, it only gives you the future to fulfill your lost desires. And this was the only way I could redeem myself from the guilt of being absent, of being away, of being selfish.

The three of us would travel to our lake house near Gaston and spend weekends there in seclusion, in tranquility. I would sit upon a garden chair watching a ten year old Fiona tiptoeing upon rocks waving back at times, discovering the fissures of nature, swimming in crisp waters of the lake, chasing after her pet dog named Gr unts, with her mother relaxing at the pier. It was all good, life seemed better now and I was happy.

ഏഏഏ

A chance came and I received an opportunity to meet with Winona's mother who lived in another grand estate up in Hot Springs, Virginia. It was Winona's 40th birthday and her visit back home was a long awaited one as she had spoken about it to me for quite a while but never finalized, and I initiated that surprise trip to her hometown. Her excitement was not very profound compared to Fiona's, but rather angled towards certain nervousness and apprehension to meet with her mother after three years of separation. They both couldn't sit still or silent for a minute throughout the two hour journey up the hills while I drove. But I enjoyed all of Fiona's laughter and her pestering attempts to steer me off-road, which was altogether dangerous, but the elation in her eyes compelled a smile on my face. As well as her mother's uneasiness and distressed words that gave me a hint of her mother's personality and temperament as they both sounded alarming to my understanding. We began our ascension up the hill on a winding road that took us well into the mountains at a considerable altitude from where the town could be seen a good couple hundred feet below. The view from the road was scenic and picturesque and we finally arrived at our destination which was another lavish property nestled amidst the cool folds of the hills.

We dismounted our Cadillac as a valet approached and opened the doors for us and a doorman welcomed us into a commodious as well as stately residence which was extremely well-kept and regarded even with its age nearing a century.

Fiona ran forward and clung to a woman who came down the stairs with laughter and trails of tears down her face. She wrapped the child in her arms and endeavored to lift her up, but failed due to Fiona's increasing weight and size and her own age. She parted with more tears of joy and kissed her numerous times.

"My child has grown so much. Last I met you, I didn't have any problems carrying you all day long and look at you now. I can't even lift you up. You're so big." The lady kissed Fiona again.

"I'm a big girl." Fiona confirmed.

"Indeed you are. But I'll still try to put you up here." She managed, with great effort, to cradle her up in her arms again. "Here we are. See, after all you're not that big for your grandmother. And it also reminds me that I haven't lost my practice at handling children since your mother's time." She joked as Winona and I stepped closer to greet her.

"I can see you haven't." Winona kissed her mother. "But if you'll be but a little more considerate of your back pain, maybe you'd do better next time not trying to lift her up."

"Oh, that you can't have. That's a secret pact between a grandmother and a granddaughter. I'll pick her up in these arms as long as I breathe, every time I see her."

"That's great. Adamant, just like your daughter you are." Winona commented.

"Well, she does get her genes from someone." Grandmother retorted. "And who is this young man here?"

"Good afternoon, Mrs. Warren."

"Good afternoon. Warren was my husband's name. Unfortunately he left us twenty-five years ago, that indicates I'm not a missus anymore."

That was an awkward situation she had put me in and I was almost about to apologize for my ill use of expression but Winona cut in to my rescue.

"That's usually how she greets people. She's grim in nature and always on a lookout for young men, young blood. She feasts on their fear, you know. Be afraid of her, very afraid."

"If I had known prior to our departure, I would have carried a stock of garlic and wore it around my neck. I hope you haven't ensnared me into this fortress to have life sucked out of me."

"That's a good one." Winona approved and began laughing. "Mother, this is George Bailey. I had told you about him in our conversations."

"You had mentioned him vaguely."

"I hope I meet your expectations."

"Expectations are sky high, young man, it requires a lot of travail to satisfy them. Just an introduction wouldn't suffice." She released Fiona from her arms and came in for a hand shake, but I pecked it instead of shaking it. "A true gentleman. Call me Esther."

"The pleasure is mine."

"Okay, enough of that eighteenth century Hungarian etiquette. Can we get back to normal, please?" Winona objected.

"Normal is boring, sweetheart. Life is only fair when improvised. By the manners of this young man, I'd be very watchful of him. You never know whom he might lure in."

"Mother."

"I'm certain he wouldn't mind the truth. He's already made an impression on you mother, child. It is my age that gives me wisdom and lack of, what should I say, endurance that I resist. The young won't. It wouldn't come as a surprise when a man's tongue has gained him many favors."

"Mother!" Winona objected.

"Now, who wants some hot chocolate granny style?"

Fiona jumped at the sound of it and followed her grandma further into the house. Winona leaned into me.

My brows were still raised and almost dried to concrete right there. "I'm a philanderer already."

"Don't mind her, that's her way to probe into our relationship. That's how she would intimidate all my boyfriends since I was nineteen. She'd plant the seed of infidelity in them so they could commit to it, and she would triumph. She is full of tricks."

"I like that. What did she find out?" I asked.

"Right now, that you're capable of handling a spontaneous remark, have a courteous demeanor, and probably that you're not going to fall for her sometime down the path."

"For her?"

"It's an old memory. I knew a man once, boy I should say. We both were maybe twenty-four or five. My mother claims to possess an ability to interpret people's brainwaves or more like their intentions, thoughts by gazing into their eyes, clairvoyance."

"Is she good at it?" I added.

"She is. So, when she saw this guy I was dating, somehow she knew he was there for two things. She was quite explicit with her terms, but I'm going to keep it down to euphemisms, that he wanted to get in my pants and my purse. She suggested a proposal to get the truth out of him and had him invited for the weekend. I didn't realize she could be right until I received a call from her room around two at night asking me to come over. When I did, I opened the door to my naked boyfriend duct-taped to a chair, being welted with a little whip she had and quite intensely. I came to know after some persistent effort at seducing him, it wasn't difficult to have him end up in her room at midnight with an offer to... He was hurt, physically and mentally, to a point that he left this town and never came back."

"That's interesting. Has she done that to every man you've come across?"

"Except one, John. And I dearly wish she had."

"She believes love does not exist anymore. She says true love has ended along with her generation. Now it's just a necessity that accompanies a reason. She's right, actually, most of the times. So you better buckle up, she's going to test you as well."

"Here we go!"

Winona walked into one of the rooms ahead, while I stayed there and pondered the ramification I was about to encounter behind that kitchen door.

We had arrived there after half past noon, so lunch was immediately served. But the surprising fact about lunch hour was that it was extremely silent around the table as long as it lasted. Even in the hours that followed the lunch, I was anticipating to be a part of hour long talk sessions around the kitchen table and laughter and happiness of a reunion everywhere in the house. But it turned out to be quite contrary to my expectations as there were no such conversations, no hushed gathering and no recollections of old times which usually is the core of a mother-daughter relationship. And as the day progressed I understood that the diurnal functioning of this house was very peculiar to my understanding and very formal as well. Esther preferred to spend the day in isolation of her bedroom except for fixed sequences of meetings at time of meals and snacks in between. I literally did not see her until three hours after lunch when we gathered in the green house for afternoon tea. Winona and Fiona seemed surprisingly accustomed to that procedural living as they would strangely isolate themselves in unknown activities for the intervening hours, imitating their elder perhaps, and suddenly show up at the designated place of gathering precisely on time. I was even more astounded to see such behavioral pattern in a ten year old, let alone her mother. I, on the other hand, was quite upset at this prosaic routine and objected to such living. Of course not verbally to anyone present there, but the question rotated in my mind over and over again. As I sat down to share another twenty minutes of tea time, that's all that was permitted, I looked at the distaff members of the family and marveled. Marveled at their willingness to concede to this formality, marveled at the sudden change in their character as if a fake persona was required to please one another. But that was the end of my wonderment, as I was here just two more days and be gone by Sunday noon. It was a short-lived visit, but it was more than enough to familiarize with Mrs. Warren. Dinner was given at seven and wasn't any different than the previous two occasions where the family gathered. It was just as formal and mute as lunch or afternoon tea. The settlement of our stay in the house was amusingly strange as Winona and I were given separate rooms with Fiona's room in between ours. I was used to sleeping alone but not for the past couple of months as Winona and I shared our lives, we shared our room as well some nights of the week when I would visit her. But neither of us complained as it was just a matter of two nights and as long as we could watch Fiona drift off to sleep together, it was just fine.

Chapter Fifty-Two

The next morning I woke up to a knocking on the door and just when I answered it, I was enraged to the point of eruption after hearing the message that was brought to me by one of the ushers coming directly from our hostess; the breakfast would be served in five minutes. The mistress of the house doesn't care to wait for her guests, and neither does the table as it is quickly folded as soon as she's done. Out of this message, one indication was clear as crystal. If I didn't want to famish myself for the next couple of hours, I better hurry to the dining and grab the leftovers.

Twenty minutes of noiseless nibbling came to an end and with it the time allotted for breakfast as I reached late and could only stuff my mouth for a short while before they removed the plate before me. The family dispersed once more scattering into different parts of the house and I was yet again surprised at their demeanor that comprised nothing but silence and isolation.

An hour later, as I relaxed in the garden, Winona approached and took a chair by my side.

"So we are allowed to see each other outside of that dining, I didn't know that." I commented as she approached.

"I wanted to ask you something."

"Are we cutting this visit short?" I sparked with excitement.

"Nope, it's a bit leaning on the bad side."

"Don't tell me we're staying here longer than Sunday."

"This is even worse. Mother wants to take me and Fiona out to meet her friends, some old people I met years ago. There's a new freak in town, recently divorced, has a miserable life and an abject daughter at the verge of a nervous breakdown. Mother doesn't wanna miss that chance to flaunt me around."

"No, I don't think you should worry about them. If they're just the same as your mother, I can assure you there wouldn't be any sounds to be heard but cups and saucers. They're just going to sit there on the couch, sip black tea without milk without sugar, and stare the hell out of you like there's no tomorrow."

"Ah, so you finally get the drift. Do want to come along and share the experience?"

"Oh please, spare me. Besides, your mother wouldn't like it at all if I came."

"You're right. Mother doesn't want you to be discussed at all. She has given me her clear instructions, Fiona as well. "

"Well, take your time and don't forget to share the strange remarks and condolences you receive from your aunts and uncles when you return. I'll enjoy out here meanwhile."

"Lucky you. See you later."

I lay back on the easy chair and watched her go back inside the house.

It had been hours since I had spoken to anyone, four hours to be exact and to kill time I began a self administered tour of the house and walked a complete circle around the peripheries of the estate in which I saw a pool, a tennis court, a detached garage for five cars, a garden attached to a small maze which was probably made for the amusement of the kids, if there were any and a clearing that led into the woods which I didn't explore in fear of straying. I returned to the house after forty minutes of expedition and came to know they still weren't back. It was lunch time and the attendant reminded me that food had been set on the sideboard but I was going to eat alone as I was the only one there. So, I took the liberty of overfilling my plate and bringing it out into the garden to finally enjoy a meal to my liking. Another hour passed and I heard sounds of a car pulling outside the house and some chatter that was primarily Esther speaking. But from this distance if I could discern the content or nature of that chatter, it didn't sound too pleasant. I collected my plate from the table that was still there while I relaxed because I had refused to hand it over to the attendant when he came to take it. But now I feared the reaction of the tyrant to such a forbidden and punishable crime of having lunch out in the garden and hurried with the plate to the kitchen. As I entered the house, I heard Esther storming toward the stairs and mumbling reprimands that were evidently directed toward Fiona and probably her mother. Esther saw me and stopped as I quickly hid the plate behind me. She glared at me for half a minute and then ascended the stairs entering her room and slamming the door behind.

"What happened?" I asked.

Winona massaged her temples walking closer to me. "She was with her important acquaintances and Fiona mentioned you. They all began asking who she was talking about and who you are and I had to tell them about us."

"And she apparently didn't like that?"

"She was very upset at Fiona for it." She confirmed.

"Fiona, could you go out and play by the pool? I'll be right there in a few minutes." I asked the little one.

Fiona nodded and went straight out.

"Winona, I think you should have been clearer with her about us, about me. I don't entirely blame her as she was misinformed about the status of our relationship. Maybe she didn't expect me by your side, maybe she didn't expect me here at all. You should have told her everything."

"I know, but I never thought she would react so aggressively to our relationship. I was going to tell her, that's why I came here."

"It seems it's quite late now. She thinks you've shattered the house rules by bringing me here without asking her. If she wants, I can leave."

"No, please George, stay with me. I will need you, I always do. I'll speak to her."

I went closer and kissed her. "Are you all right?"

"I think I made a mistake coming here, I can't possibly live up to her expectations. That's why I left in the first place."

"Hey, it was my idea remember? You know what? Take some rest, go to your room lie down a while and take a nap. I'll stay with Fiona."

"Thanks." She kissed me back and took my leave.

Fiona sat in the garden near the pool bored to exhaustion, as I joined her and spent the entire afternoon keeping her company. After a while of play and run around, we were called in by an attendant to the garden for afternoon tea at four. Fiona asked for my permission to skip tea and stay by the pool, as they had already eaten much at the gathering and she wasn't hungry. I didn't see any reason to refuse and I agreed, then followed the attendant down the path into a larger adjoining garden and saw a greenhouse amidst lush motley of outdoor flowers and plants that spanned the whole acre. I entered the warm interior of the greenhouse and sat down next to Winona.

"Good afternoon, everyone." I greeted.

"Good afternoon, I hope you are enjoying the crisp, cool air of the mountains, Mr. Bailey?" Esther asked.

"I am, it's quite nice here. Though, I would say I'm enjoying the long hours of seclusion more than the air."

"Good. Didn't I ask you to bring everyone to the table for tea?" She addressed the steward this time.

"My apologies ma'am, but Ms. Fiona was given permission to skip tea and continue her play."

"And who, may I ask, gave this outrageous permission?"

The steward hesitated but I spoke up. "I did. I'm sorry if I offended anyone, but Fiona wasn't too hungry and I thought she didn't need to come. Besides, she dislikes tea."

"Gathering here on time does not concern the issue of likes or dislikes. It is an obligation, an essential one to each member of this family and has been so for years. Fiona is a part of this family and she needs to learn how to share table with the rest. Bring her here, right now."

"Yes ma'am." The steward nodded.

I looked at Winona while she remained silent as the steward walked out of the greenhouse and returned with Fiona a moment later. Fiona ran to her mother and leaned into her, placing herself on her laps.

"Take a chair Fiona, you do not see anyone else here leaning into your mother's laps, do you? It's not an appropriate place to sit. Take a chair."

"Sorry grandma."

I was instigated to a point of eruption and could have said a lot at that moment, but I contained my wrath to save the dignity of this visit. I watched Fiona sit dully with a dampened spirit and chafe away the paint from the armrest of her chair. She grimaced while she sipped from the cup of black tea. I waited for this time to end and just as it did, I called Fiona along and stormed out of there with her in my arms not caring what the other two might have thought about my actions.

We both sat together at the terrace outside our rooms lost in a game of checkers. When it became tedious after the third reset, I suggested a proposal.

"How about we go for a drive and explore the town a little? What do you say?"

"Yes, let's go. I'm bored with this anyways." Fiona was exhilarated at the thought.

"Okay, you stay right here, I'm going to ask mommy if she wants to come. I'll be back, all right?"

"I'll wait right here." She saluted and I dashed off inside looking for Winona.

As I searched for her inside the house, I came across a library with its door ajar and some disputing voices emerging from the interior.

"I still do not understand your decision to leave your husband. It is the first time in our lineage that someone has been divorced. I don't know what you wanted to extract out of that marriage or what you thought you could. Love is just a small part of a relationship, if it begins to diminish that doesn't mean you're going to abandon every other positive facet for that one insignificant thing. Marriage is not just happy endings and love stories, it has a larger meaning than that." Esther was tyrannical as usual.

"What does it mean, mother? Because in all those eight years of mine, I didn't see a single thing that could have made it more bearable for me." Winona implored for her faith.

"It is your life and your child's life. Her whole upbringing depends on its outcome. If you didn't wish to preserve intimacy with your husband, that's understandable. But it doesn't necessarily mean to divest yourself of a future. I spent a lifetime married to your father, forty-five years. I know all there is to know about that relationship, and if I stayed with him it was because of you."

"Father loved you."

"That's for you to say. You do not know the kind of sacrifices I made to hold this family together. I knew I had to make it work for you, not for me, for you. And you just went ahead and ruined it for the both of you. If you have no concern for your own future, at least think about your offspring."

"Do you think I don't care about my daughter? Do you think I would do something to hurt her?"

"Well, I wouldn't commend you on your maternal skills either. The child is losing formal mannerisms as well as her speech. I don't want to see her turned into one of street smarts who can't complete a sentence without profanity. What is all with this mommy and mom, you never addressed me as such. It was always mother, a proper term. And the omission of 'g' at the end of words, incomplete pronunciations, what is all this? You better keep her chained to propriety, or you shall regret it."

"She is my... your granddaughter, not a hound to be chained next to a doorpost to guard your threshold. And what convinces you that I am raising her to be like that?"

"I do not trust your discretion after your divorce from John. And especially the replacement you've brought in his stead. Have you even looked at that man? Do you know of his family, his background, where he comes from or what his character is like? A joke of a companion, no features of royalty in his blood, misbehaving in front of the help. A man who doesn't know how to discipline a child knows nothing of noble traditions. And what does he mean by carrying Fiona around all day like that? She is your daughter, not his."

"And I thought you would be glad to see a man who treats my child as his own. Yes, I do not know his family, or where he comes from, or what he did. But I know he loves me and will do anything to protect us both. Even if it is from you."

"You think I would harm you in any way?"

"No, why would I? Since I've arrived, you've done nothing but shower me with love and happiness."

"It is your happiness I'm concerned about. I'm not a fool to be tossing around words without matter. John was your future, your life would have been prosperous if you stayed with him."

"Future? Is that all you care about? There wouldn't be a future if there isn't a present. Who do you think I am? Sleep with someone because he pays my bills on time? Mistresses do that, not me. I can live life on my own, and I can take care of Fiona myself. You taught me to be independent, what happened all of a sudden?"

"A woman's independence is in the confines of her husband's arms. I never taught you to give up on your domestic problems, your personal relationships. I never taught you to surrender."

"I did not surrender, I fought. I took my daughter from a man who did not have time for her, and still doesn't. You think he comes to visit her on weekends when he's supposed to? You think Fiona loves to wait for him all day long and finally give in to tears by bedtime? He did not deserve her, he did not deserve me. And I'm not someone to give up my happiness for money, maybe you did, but I can't."

"How dare you say that to me?"

"How dare you don't support your daughter in her decisions, in tribulations of her life? I thought no matter what happens, my mother would understand me, stand up for me. But I can see I was wrong. Wealth means more to you than love. And that man you just insulted is someone who's held my hand through everything for the past two years. He did not come to me asking for my favors or my money, I fell in love with him first. I want him and I need him."

I was delighted to hear this declaration, but equally furious about Esther's comments involving Fiona. I didn't feel the need to stay there anymore because if I had heard anymore out of her venomous tongue, I would either admit guilt of eavesdropping by entering that library and possibly trouncing the old crone, or I was going to collect Fiona and her belongings and leave this wretched witch house never to return. So, to mollify the aggravation, I decided to take Fiona out for a ride around town without anyone else's permission. But just as I moved away from the door, a towering pendulum clock sounded the time with seven strikes. I stayed and after a moment, Esther emerged from the room and began to walk away.

Winona followed her to the doorway. "I'm talking to you," she said.

"It is dinnertime, we can continue this contestation at a later time."

"So you're just going to walk away?"

"I've never kept the table waiting. The rules of this house will not change unless you get rid of me and hang my picture on that wall next to your father's, which isn't going to be anytime soon. You will uphold my laws in the house as long as I breathe. So, you better make it to the table quick with your little one and your man."

Esther walked away and Winona just watched her in disbelief, then receded into the library giving up on her end. I went to the library door once more and peered inside. Winona caught me there and managed a smile.

"Hey." She waved.

"Are you all right?" I asked.

"I'm fine, just a little talk. Been a long time since I've had one with mother. Almost forgotten how fun they are. It's dinnertime, we should go. Where's Fiona?"

"I'll go get her."

"Okay, thanks."

Minutes later I had the privilege of seeing her majesty again and the family gathered for supper around a large dining table that was set in the middle of another massive hall with crystal chandeliers and wainscoted walls, with gold plated candlesticks and flatware ornately placed upon ebony dinner table that seated eighteen guests. The mistress of the house was so far away from the three of us, sitting at the far end of the table, that I could barely see her without my glasses. As the main course was served at the table, we all sat mute and watched the attendants fill our plates. We began eating with no disruption to our silence until I heard a familiar voice come up with more corrections on Fiona's conduct.

"Fiona, my dear, you do not necessarily place yourself into your plate to eat out of it. You sit back and allow the spoons and forks to come to your mouth." Esther commanded.

"Sorry." Fiona straightened her slouched posture and sat back barely able to reach the plate with her small arms.

"And similarly, if your hands are doing all the work, you do not need your elbows on the table at all, do you?" She hinted towards Winona and me.

"No." Fiona took it upon herself. I struck a glimpse at Winona and then at her mother. We both slipped our elbows off the table.

"How is work, Winona? Any troubles after the divorce in handling a shared ownership?"

"I'm thinking about selling my shares at the Realty. I'm going to let go of it."

"Hmm... I think I might not be hearing right at the moment, what did you say?"

"I'm going to let go of my stake in the company. I can't continue there anymore."

"So, I did hear just right. Have you lost your mind? You own thirty percent of shares, basically you own that company along with John and you'll just sell your ownership?"

"Well, there's your reason mother, I don't want anything to do with John anymore. This is the final connection between us and I don't want it to last any longer than it should."

"It is a multi-million dollar company, Winona. You'd be a fool to release yourself from it."

"At least I'd be a happy fool."

"Happiness is a whole another issue to converse upon. The revenue derived from that business is more than enough to gratify you."

"I wish it could. But money never brought me happiness, mother. Most of all, you should know."

"I would expect you to be courteous when speaking to me, at least while others are around."

"I'm sorry, mother. But George and I have talked about it and we've both decided to start our own company, our own business."

"And what nature of business, if I am permitted to ask?"

"I suggested something I was more familiar with, so a construction business."

"Hmm, how much of this decision comes from you and how much of it comes from your left?"

My fork halted halfway to my mouth as I sat left to Winona at the table. She was equally indignant at the remark her mother just uttered.

"It was entirely my decision. I wish he had more to say, but he gives me my independence to work as I please, to live as I want."

"Then this relationship is short-lived, I can assure you of that."

My fork clattered into the china and I left the table.

Chapter Fifty-Three
ఴఴఴ

I was a stranger to this house, so the only place where I could attain peace was the pool that adjoined my room. I sat by the water and looked up at the moon in all its glory and shape. It glistened white against the inky pool and I submerged my feet into the cold relaxing for a bit. After a while, Fiona came over and joined my side dangling her feet into the water next to me.

"Grandma is always upset. I don't know why."

"Me neither. Where's your mother?"

"They went for a talk. I think they are going to fight again. Mommy was upset."

"They won't fight, they'll just disagree on things."

"Why do they disagree so much and we don't?"

"It's good that we don't. I wouldn't want to see the day we do."

"I'm sleepy. I'm off to bed, good night."

"Good night, sweety."

I gave her a night kiss and she strode away into her room that was right next to mine. I took another fifteen minutes to calm myself down, then retired into my bedroom and decided to sleep the anger away.

The next morning was just as usual and I had outslept the breakfast hour, but lethargy wasn't the reason why I skipped on breakfast. Even when I had just pretended to sleep but stayed wide-eyed all night long, I still wouldn't have gone to the dining this morning. I left my room around noon and was relieved to find Winona and Fiona together by the pool. I relaxed on a teak pool chair and watched Fiona splash around the coruscating surface in snorkel gear, while Winona completed three laps around the pool and then joined me under the canopy.

"Where were you, we were waiting for you at breakfast? Then I came to your room and you were sleeping like a baby." She spoke as she put on her sunglasses and lay back revealing her long legs in a black one-piece which suddenly beguiled me. I had never seen her in a swimsuit before but only suits and dresses and the sight of her long legs, even when she only stood around five seven or half an inch shorter, was enchanting. "I didn't want to disturb you."

"Are you sure I was sleeping?" I responded.

Her smile faded. "I'm sorry for what happened last night."

"Winona, your mother not liking me I can understand that. But her own granddaughter, that's strange."

"I overheard your talk last night, the supposed talk. I'm sorry, but I did. And the only thing I heard in that room was your mother telling you how to live your life and have Fiona stand in the queue next. Not once did I hear her talk, she just spoke, complete pontification, that's all. And if you'd take her suggestion, train the little one to stay on a leash, that's what she would like. I thought we were coming home to a grandmother who's going to go berserk at the sight of her granddaughter she hasn't seen in years. It doesn't look like she's happy at all. Chain her down, that's what she said, right? She's a ten year old child goddamn it. You can at least show her a little love, and then she instructs you on how to raise her? Does this look like a family to you? It surely does not seem anywhere close to me."

Fiona came to my chair and leaned into me kissing on my cheek, I retaliated with a peck on her forehead.

"I've decided something. I'm going to be an Olympic swimmer one day." She said.

"Your ambitions change like the weather, sweetheart." Winona replied.

"I'm sure about it this time."

Winona sat up and smiled. "Really? Then show mommy how you do your flip jump into the pool." Fiona instantly darted and did an amazing flying cartwheel into the water. Winona turned back to me after applauding her.

"You shouldn't encourage her to do all that stuff, she could get hurt. It's all concrete around the pool." I was concerned.

"Come here," she landed a kiss on my lips. "My mother has a different perception of life. She's old now and old people don't change for the young. That's how she's been for ages. I'm surprised how I lived through my time. I guess it was different when we were young. Times have changed, but she hasn't. I try to keep her... rules, if you may, around this house because it's hers. I know you were expecting something different out of her, out of my family, but this is how we've been. That does not mean I'm the same. Does it?" She held my hand and caressed it. I smiled and agreed. "She had raised me like this, but I never complained. She chose and decided everything that went on in my life. But in exchange for my liberty, if she gave me the courage to survive on my own without any help from a man, I'm grateful for that. In exchange for my laughter if she gave me a future that secured my tomorrow, I'm thankful for that as well. I am what I am because of her, and she expects to do the same with Fiona. Maybe she's right, maybe I'm not strong enough to lead her-"

"You are a good mother and Fiona is a wonderful child. Being a mother is the best quality about you."

"Thank you. I'm proud that you said it. Her definition of love is somewhat different than ours."

"For me that definition is to not hear a single word against the people I love, no matter who says it."

"You know what I wish sometimes? I wish I had found you earlier, when I was younger. I wouldn't have made as many mistakes as I did if you were by my side."

"You have me now."

"Yup, so we keep it cool and we keep it simple, it's just a matter of hours now. And I hope she doesn't try her charm on you in this while."

"I'm all prepared for it."

"You better be, it's inevitable." She ran off and dived into the pool splattering all around.

After dinner I went for a stroll trying to fatigue myself for a good night's sleep before our journey back home the next noon. I came back into the house and found silence in every corner. Then I decided to go for a drink of brandy in hopes of a relaxed sleep. I walked to the bar and poured myself a drink and as I sat down, I was suddenly reminded of Winona's earnest longing for love which she claimed to have found in me before her mother. There is nothing more arousing for a man than to be claimed by his woma n. I was just in deep brooding when I heard footsteps approaching my way. I imagined them to be Winona's as I prepared to fervently kiss her until kingdom come for what went on in that library last night, but it wasn't her.

"So, you are an alcoholic as well?" Esther came up and took a seat on the couch near the bar. I remained quiet.

"That is a childish way to hold grievance against someone, refuse to talk, to answer. You seem quite combative, go ahead give your lips a chance."

"What makes you think so?"

"Well, your chivalry must be at sleep to have overlooked the civility of offering the lady a drink, while you go at it like a horse."

I got up my chair and poured her scotch and kept the glass on the coffee table next to her.

"Thank you. Though, I dislike that particular brand you seem to be very fond of, but I'll still drink it."

"I will be so very pleased."

"You need not patronize me, I meant no harm when I said what I said at the table."

"Yeah, none was taken."

"You are a man of character, I will give you that."

I turned and looked straight at her, there was a veil of an elusive personality that she wore over a hardened shell, but I intuited a strange core inside it.

"I have survived numerous days, many years and several decades of this thing called life. I know all there is to know about it. You might not think so, my daughter definitely doubts that I could possibly speak in her favor. But, if I've learned something from all these years of living it's this; there's one thing in the world that does not come with an attached price tag, and that's character."

"Well, thank-"

"Don't thank me yet, you have a lot to listen to tonight. I have seen many young men come to sit at our table on the left hand side of my daughter, seven to be precise. My daughter might have forgotten the correct number, but I still remember. From the eve of her High School prom date when she was seventeen to her ex-husband, seven. And none of them had the courage to leave that table like you did. And I can assure you this isn't the first time I have derided someone at my supper table. I have had millionaires take my insults like a baby sleeps to a lullaby. You just changed that, and it shook away the foundations of the grounds upon which I stood. The last man I saw with such valiance was my husband and he was a rock of a man. You can take my word for it. He could take on anything, anywhere and there were only two other people who mattered to him his whole life, one stands in front of you and one behind you."

I turned to see if anyone was there, but there wasn't and then the figurative meaning of her remark dawned upon me.

"I have seen that strength in you, and somehow I'm inclined to put my faith in it. But I fear, more than my daughter, your love and your attention grows vast for *her* daughter. Don't take it the wrong way, I intend for it to remain as simple as it sounds. You love the child more than you love Winona, and I do sense a strange longing in your eyes when you're with her. As if you mean to denounce the splendors of the world for her one brief smile. There is something you hide in that heart of yours that I do not need to probe, as I know what it might be. A past that impels you to cover your mistakes, to conceal the grief of separation by involvement in someone else's child. My daughter has no objection to it, neither do I. But I caution you to confine your love to certain limits. I have seen aging teens take advantage of blind devotion and make use of it in their favor no matter how selfish or foolish their intentions are. Fiona, after all, is a girl. She will be a woman one day. You might regret the times you failed to restrict her liberties if she masks a mortal sin with a justification. I know you might not endorse my perspective on things as you are city people of the new generation, but the novelty of the present generation is archaic and stale for the next. As far as my daughter is concerned, she does not need you to continue her life. She wants you for the fact that she is suddenly alone, and she hasn't been in a circumstance of solitude in her life.

This house has been like a haven to her for twenty-eight years. Under my wings she has educated herself to independence without second thoughts. She is having some now, second thoughts on the things she had missed out on in her younger years, and you have forced her to assume my protection for incarceration. Which is untrue. She is what I wanted... her to be. I have nothing to gain from her success. I have never claimed any part of her triumphs. She is what she is because of me, and there's no doubt about it."

She paused to take a deep sigh, which was long enough for me to grasp her true inner feelings.

"I know men like you, I know all kinds of men. I chose John for my daughter because I knew what he was capable of. Winona thinks I did not know of his insatiable sexual appetite or late night escapades with school age girls. But I still approved of that marriage because I knew by the time it is over between them, my daughter would be one of the most influential names in the city of Charlotte, North Carolina, and by my word she is. But now she has brought you and with you... It's not that I can't point out foibles in this relationship, but I don't wish to."

I waited if anything else needed to come out of her.

"Well, if you must listen," she continued, "I know where you come from, what type of life you have lived and all that you intend to do. I know your kind that originates from poverty, some of you might sell your mother for a price, but there are just a handful of you who hold their souls intact. I have no faith in your kind, but somehow I trust you. You men don't want women for love itself, but you always have some dark, obscured reason to be with us. Whether it is money, fame, influence, or sometimes even our beauty, there's always something down there that you keep hidden. I do not trust your type, but I think you do love my daughter without reason and more than her, your daughter unconditionally. But then your true colors are demonstrated when you gain our trust and financial matters make their way into your hands. You're free to utilize the yield of our toil, the fruits of our efforts and expend our wealth at your own will. No wonder womankind is still referred to as a counterpart of a superior creature called man, as we give away our faith, our love and our bodies without ever questioning your intent. We are the inferior ones, aren't we? Gullible, foolish, waiting to be taken advantage of which eventually happens and then we're left all alone in misery and shadow of an unscrupulous ex-husband, who made it with everything we had to give."

She took another pause, this time a softer one.

"I believe you are different, and I sense you will not deceive my daughter in any manner that I can think of."

I took a moment before I spoke. "Can I thank you now?"

"No, I'm not finished. You have given my daughter strength to stand on her own. Something I thought only I could do, and I was incensed at the sound of her imputing her courage to you and not me. I hated you for that while. I have never seen her stand against me for someone else, you're the first. Even though, you're the eighth man in her life, you're the first. Two years ago, if she wanted to she could have dreamed about commencing her own business and her husband would have turned that into reality, that's how rich he is. But if that had happened, I wouldn't call it courage, I wouldn't call it strength, I would call it dependence on my daughter's end and riddance on her husband's. She has never managed a business on her own ever before. Now she will, with you, without me. So this is what I'm going to ask you; do not leave her or betray her in any way, because if you do, you'll have a lot of me to deal with. Love her as much as you can, love her daughter as much as she needs, stay with them as long as you may, but protect them at all times."

She stood up and began to leave, but suddenly came back.

"And yes, if it's construction business that you two have planned to enter, convince her to carry on her father's company. It is a small business, nothing too fancy, earns enough to pay for this house, which is not bad at all. If she is looking to venture, a new profile would be useless. We already have a loyal customer base, all she would need to do is take it further. That's what her father dreamt for her to carry on after him. It's not that I need help, not at all. But I'm gentle and loving enough to consider her progress even when she mistreats me and wounds my feelings. I am her mother, that's what we do. So, if you may be able to talk to her about this proposal, I would be pleased."

"Do you know what the biggest problem with you is? You are not the person that you try to be. And inside that chrome steel hull, there's a different woman who is a mother and a grandmother at the same time. Maybe a little old-fashioned, but it's still in there. You just carry on that fake, seasoned personality to uphold your terror, that's all." I finally give her the truth that probably no one had in years.

"Uphold my terror? That's a first. I don't think I have that problem, but you can keep your opinion to yourself. In this house, I'm the only person allowed to speak, the rest listen. And yes..." she came closer and stood inches away from my face. "It is believed that a woman is most beautiful after the age of sixty and I don't disagree with this common belief. When I disrobe at night, I have a habit of standing out on the balcony all alone under the direct light of the moon which washes upon every square inch of my naked body. You can even get a clear view from the area around the pool while I'm there. Then I go to bed refreshed and revived, ready for anything, but still au naturel. And... I never lock my bedroom door. You have an open invitation."

I was beguiled at the intimation for a moment, but then I remembered Winona's warning of this entrapment. I simply smiled, which I think made her believe I was going to give in. She walked away and up the stairs fading into one of the rooms above.

The next morning was altogether pleasant for reasons I did not know. Maybe it was an inner understanding of what this family was all about, or perhaps coming to terms with someone as tempered as Winona's mother, or maybe just a simple fact that we were heading back home. I watched the doorman load our luggage into our car with Fiona leaning by my side. Winona and Esther came down the stairs and joined us under the portico. Their eyes were tearful as well as delighted. Esther kneeled next to Fiona and embraced her, as they parted Fiona wiped away the tears from her face.

"You are crying grandma?"

"No, it's just happiness that flows from my eyes."

"You're happy that I'm going?"

"I'm happy that you will come back." Esther looked up at me. "And I hope it will be soon."

"I'll come back on my birthday."

"You shouldn't make promises you can't keep, Fiona." Winona remarked.

"I think she'll keep this one." I chipped in.

Esther embraced her daughter and parted with a kiss on her forehead. "Take care of yourself, and the ones you love."

"And you as well, you need to rest more and work less," Winona said politely, as Esther kissed her once more.

"Only you can make that happen." Esther shifted her attention to me. "Thank you for bringing them here, I heard it was your idea."

"You're welcome." I took her hand and kissed it.

"Formalities are for strangers. In our family we embrace each other."

With laughter and rejoice we hugged and she whispered in my ears. "I place all my bets on you."

We parted and nodded to each other. Stepping back into our car, all three of us waved back to Esther and slowly drove out of the gates.

Some hours later we arrived at our residence and were all of us equally exhausted to continue with any other activity as we had faced a lot of traffic coming back. After an early dinner, Fiona went to sleep and Winona pleaded me to stay to which I agreed as another hour long drive back to the city would obliterate my energy reserves. As night approached, we both went into our bedroom. Winona took a shower and when she emerged from the bathroom she found me working on some reports as my hand flew from one estimate to another.

"Really? I thought all you wanted to do, after such a long day, was go to bed." She crawled up the bed toward me in her lace-trim nightie.

"That's correct, and by going to bed I meant sleep." I smiled.

"Oh, I had a different idea."

"Well, what did you have in mind?"

"This." She leaned in for a kiss and removed the reports from the way and straddled me.

"No, don't crinkle the reports, these are important."

"More important than this?" She unbuttoned the front of her nightdress.

"Our future depends on them."

Winona stopped and dismounted. "You just quoted my mother."

- 352 -

"She is an influential one."

"What did she do to you?"

"She made a proposal. Actually more like a request to you."

"Request? From her? You're kidding me, right?"

"I wish I was."

"What did she say?"

"Look Winona, I'm not going to take from her that she is quite right in this matter."

"What matter?"

"You told her we're looking to get into construction business."

"Oh no, she didn't say that."

"She hinted on it, I'm saying it to you. She wants you to continue your family business, and I say yes. Grow with it. Expand to a new office in the city here. Get new clients, a new profile, a new visual, we already have a ground to stand upon, it's only going to go up from there. There is no tumbling down."

"No, I can't do business with her." She cried.

"It wouldn't be all hers anymore. You are going to be an equal partner in that company, you already are with fifteen percent stake. She wants you to take over. I'll handle the paperwork if you want me to. It is a good investment with a lot of return. She gave me these reports to see, these are your father's company documents."

"George, I wish I were capable of handling her on my own. I couldn't do it in personal life, how am I going to do it in professional life?"

"Winona, she's old, don't mind my saying that, but she is. She might not admit to you, but she needs to give up now. Now, who doesn't desire a life away from all this stress, especially at her age? She hasn't been able to retire so far, think about it. She wouldn't have mentioned all of this to me if she wasn't looking to let go. It is going to be yours after her, why not familiarize ourselves with the company while she's still there to guide us?"

"She said that to you?"

"Yes."

"She wants me to run her business?"

"Yes."

"Did she do something to you?"

"Um... she tried last night, said she would be at her terrace in all her glory standing under the moon for my viewing."

"Yup, that's been tired before. But you were with me all night."

"You thought I was going to go?"

Winona smiled and kissed me again. "If you're with me, I'll take on anything there is. Even if it means to face the Devil in flesh."

I laughed. "She might wear that mask of wickedness, but she's not evil inside. She just has a different way of showing her love, which is many times too severe to handle, but right. Right in many ways."

"Well, you like my mother more than I do."

"I know you love her. In a heart like yours, there is no place for hatred. So what do you say?"

"If that seems right to you, I think I'll consider."

"You come here." I flipped her under me, caressed her hair and softly kissed her neck, she quivered with pleasure.

"But we're not living there with her." She cleared any suspicion on the matter.

"Not in a million years."

Chapter Fifty-Four

ၐၐ

It wasn't exceedingly difficult to have Winona bring the matter of adhering herself to her family company under consideration, and it was even more effortless after a genuine affirmation of gains and profits coming from Ned. It's not that I was eager to deliver on my word and blindly compelled her to raise her stake in her mother's business. But we had taken our time, about 5 months to be exact, to assess and evaluate the business's profitability, network and supplier accountability, and finally confirmed its credibility amongst the community it has served as well as satisfaction and work quality levels with its previous customers. The data we had gathered through SWOT analysis in this time period was unbelievably impressive. Not a hundred percent, but that was the nature of this business as all fickle expectations can never be fulfilled which was more than enough for Ned and me to place our approval without reserve.

And it happened, the day was auspicious already as it was Fiona's eleventh birthday and we had celebrated the occasion at Esther's residence which also kept the little one's promise to her nana and the night following the event, the papers were signed. It was a joyous day for many reasons, but the most important was the fact that Esther finally decided to give up her supremacy to the next generation. She had signed over her ownership of seventy percent share in the company under Winona's name and had only kept fifteen percent for her remaining days. Winona objected to the fact that she had retained a very small ownership in the company, but was countered easily by her mother's reply in which she said she believed in her daughter and trusted that under her ownership this business could only grow. Hence, bringing her more than enough fortune to live her life, or what's left of it, in peace and tranquility of this home. And it was in just under a week that Warren Constructions saw its new, eighty-five percent shareholder step into the main office and begin her management of the closed corporation for the first time.

We had temporarily extended our stay in town to familiarize ourselves with the operation of this business and gradually proceeded to handle the decision-making, planning and management of the business. Winona had a novel perspective to construct this business to an unprecedented magnitude and outgrow its competition, and so for the next six months she and I were able to implement new corporate strategies, contingency planning, crisis management and other important structural changes as well as new changes in departmentalization, span of control and authority. She had even surprised the most seasoned line managers with her radical approach to increasing the company's capacity and production with each contractual assignment that came our way. In a short time, Winona had proven her skills to be inimitable as the company was able to produce an increased amount of output with a similar workforce and materials supplied without any compromise in quality. It was becoming quite famous around town as well as the neighboring vicinities where our work was more prominent that if a construction needed to be done before time, it must be through Warrens. We were bidding tenders for many government projects in adjacent areas that were ITT, and secured many contracts in the process. As our work escalated, the current local suppliers and affiliations to the business were ineffective in satisfying our surging need for materials, hence we were forced to seek fulfillment from new suppliers from neighboring areas. Though, running stable for the past thirty years, the business had never encountered an increase of two hundred and thirty-seven percent in revenue within a year. But it did and it was a dulcet surprise to everyone, except me as I was well conversant with Winona's aptitude and knew she could do lots more. We were heading uphill on a roll, but everything that goes up must come down.

We faced an intrinsic part of a business cycle when the demand for work decreased and an inevitable downturn occurred. It wasn't as dreadful as to diminish our value in terms of service or prominence, but it severely affected our operations as there were fewer contracts and work orders heading our way. I did not mind trudging through this slump period as I had already gained knowledge of this decline from the reports I had studied and was very much prepared for it. Our supplier loyalty was undisturbed through these trying times, but Winona didn't take this sudden debacle placidly and probing deeper into this quandary, she came to realize that some weeks before and after Christmas leading into New Year were referred to as a roosting period in the local vernacular and admitted this fall in business to be related to that factor only after corroborations from Esther, Ned, me and two middle managers.

She was quite restive in this time but I had an entirely different reason to be impatient with our prolonged stay in the town. What I thought was going to be temporary, maybe lasting for a couple of months, had quickly elevated into a year in matter of days, or so it seemed, and the biggest fault I imputed to myself was neglecting Fiona in this whole process. It only began as separation for a few days which was equally undesirable and painful for both of us. But as work and wealth took over our minds, we were completely oblivious to Fiona and her needs and sorrow resulting from this year long separation. We had left her back in Charlotte under guardianship of a governess to avert any disruption to her school year and made plans to visit her every weekend or even during the week as much as we could together. But as the obligations toward the business grew more requisite and imperative, Winona was falling behind with her responsibilities toward her daughter. I would even quarrel with her on her forgetfulness toward Fiona, which would make her feel culpable but then I would feel empathy and comfort her recognizing her intentions in building this business were only in favor of her daughter. I would travel alone some days back to Charlotte and spend time with Fiona, attempting to pacify her suffering of staying away from her mother, from me. There was nothing I could do to end her woe unless I was going to discontinue her school and take her back to Winona. But there is always a way to cease each adversity and time paves the path for it.

The idea of expansion was sown in Winona's mind and the yearn for more of everything imbued her reasoning. Her primary reason behind this impetuous determination was simply more wealth, success and prominence of this corporation. My primary reason to abet this decision was to be able to fortify a heartbroken Fiona in our love once more, as I knew if this arrangement of expansion was implemented, the first undertaking would be a definitive relocation of our principal office to Charlotte. With the initiation of this concept, I could at least imagine us reuniting with Fiona some time in the future. Ned had arrived from the city and took full responsibility in executing all necessary paperwork. With new possibilities in sight, greater opportunities to advance, and higher earnings in return for travail, it was just a matter of weeks within which all legal formalities were completed and a new setup welcomed us in the familiar environs of the city. After a while of sulking and frowns and glowers, Fiona forgave our negligence and our family began living together again. But as time went on and the business commenced to thrive in the pool of new competitors and challenges, I found Winona drifting from her responsibilities toward Fiona once more. I was caught in the middle with ambivalence confounding my standing whether to raise a twelve year old with proper care and love or to dedicate myself to a woman who needs me every step of the way. Time was slipping away, the choice was daunting, but I tried to manage both of my accountabilities to the best of my capability. Fiona was growing up without the comforting shelter of her mother and I couldn't take her place. I was afraid of losing them both, one by one.

In one year Ned had directed the business into public trading through our first IPO. The investments were accumulating in large numbers, the company soared through the charts as work and fame equally outgrew the previous state of this privately owned corporation. At one time, our business had more government building contracts than the rest of businesses in the city combined and we had eighty one simultaneous multi-million dollar deals lined up at our threshold. Our revenues skyrocketed beyond expectations, as our projects grew statewide so did our suppliers. Our operating expenses crossed the mark of six hundred million dollars a year, our net profit doubled. The workforce was steadily increasing nearing five thousand full-time employees. The line managers were working hard and honestly, labor wages were boosted along with perquisites and insurance benefits. Tricks like job enrichment and participative empowerment were triggered, work sharing and flextime programs were introduced for higher job satisfaction. It was classic case of Hawthorne effect, and the people were putting over time and extra time working efficiently to our contentment. Everything Winona and I touched turned to gold. It was a happy life for each and every soul that was directly or indirectly connected to Warren Constructions.

Our family grew apart as a couple more years passed. Winona and I were living in the same house just as any other married couple, but barely able to gather time to see each other anymore apart from work related meetings. Fiona was moving through a tough time of coping with our absence. Esther had reconciled the differences and visited us every now and then in addition to special occasions keeping Fiona company. But a fifteen year old has many other issues that need to be addressed.

But something might have happened that triggered a concern in Winona's mind towards her forgotten responsibility. She proposed to me a ten percent partnership and the position of CEO which would replace her in the company, but she assured it was a collaborative decision of the board of directors. I knew she was just trying to involve me into the governance body as I had only been a field manager since the commencement of the new Warren constructions. I didn't disapprove the kind of work I did as I managed and supervised all construction projects our company executed in the city as well as the ones in proximity. But had just one regret, that I was unable to spend as much time with my family as I would've liked. This was her way of thanking me for the work I've put in.

I refused at first as I didn't want to claim unnecessarily what was built on the foundations laid by the Warren family. But Winona persisted and surprised me with the reason why she had decided to give up her position as the CEO of the company. It was simply so she could suspend herself from work and commit to her daughter more than she had in the recent years. I couldn't decline the offer anymore after witnessing her earnest aspiration to care for her daughter, to love and rear her. I accepted the position but I still turned down the stake in the company. I was happy with my promotion and the fortunes that came with it, and they were plenty. I had already left the accounting firm way back when I became an employee of Warren Constrictions, as I was told I couldn't be a partner in the accounting firm that conducted annual auditing of the company I was employed at. I had no dealing with the accounting or finance department of the company since I trusted Ned and Winona with their respective responsibilities.

But out of this whole ordeal, the most commendable achievement belonged to Ned Ackres. He had a team of twelve accountants working under his wing and had promoted Paola as the executive administrator in his firm. And the most surprising event of his life was yet to take place. He was getting married!

Chapter Fifty-Five
❦❦❦

Paola had requested Ned a job for her cousin Jennifer about ten months ago, and being a provider that Ned is, the job was swiftly made available. Jennifer began working as a secretary to Paola and managing her daily chores. She was a sweet thirty-eight year old, recently migrated but with excellent verbal skills and grasp of English language, soft-spoken but well educated, shy but confident and got noticed for her exceptional administrative skills and especially her punctuality. I had the pleasure of witnessing her work firsthand and wouldn't hold back my recommendation. Ned eventually came close to knowing her personally when he had asked Paola to accompany him on his business trips back and forth between Virginia and Charlotte, but Paola was unable to travel that frequently and requested if Jennifer could replace her. Following those trips Ned was barely able to converse without mention of his new found attraction. They had gradually fallen in love and were tying the knot in three weeks. It was a special Thanksgiving Day ceremony and we were in abysmal preparations for it as I had taken full control of the provisions needed and forced Ned to take at least three days off before his wedding day. But it was the day of the wedding when I went to his house and was informed by the housekeeper that he had gone off to work that morning.

I drove back to the city in frustration and stormed into his office yelling out at him.

"What the hell are you doing here, Ned?"

Ned looked up from behind a heap of files on his desk. "George. I was just going to go back." He shut the open file before him.

"I told you to stay home. What is so important that you had to come all the way here on your wedding day?"

"Nothing much, just a little bit of um... overview of statements."

"Overview? Really? Who are you auditing, the president that couldn't wait?"

"You know I handle your reports personally."

"I know and that's great. But not as much to leave your bride waiting on you. I'm going to ask Paola to take these reports to my office and we're not working on them until you get back from your two week vacation in Belize. Now get up and come with me. You know you have to get dressed. People might have started arriving by now. It's almost four, the sun would set in an hour or so. You don't want to get married in the dark, do you?"

"No, the files stay. In fact, I'm taking them with me. I'm not going to leave them here, it's not safe."

"Okay, take your files and move it."

He collected the stack of files. "Winona there already?"

"No, I have to pick them up after I get you in that tux."

"Oh boy, we better hurry up then."

In moments we were flying down the highway back to Ned's residence as the ceremony was taking place in the massive courtyard within the walls of his property. I had set up every thing from decorations to catering and the union was taking place in a gazebo which looked wonderful an hour ago when I went to inspect. I got Ned home in time and slipped him into his tuxedo. The guests were already coming along and I welcomed them into the celebration area. The drinks were being served, the appetizers were sizzling on the grill. It was all set for the big moment.

I found Ned with the parish priest and borrowed him for a moment.

"Ned, I got to go and get Winona and Fiona. I'll be right back."

"Yeah, I'm waiting."

"Alright." I was skipping away when he called out to me again.

"George, thanks for everything."

"You thanking me? Think again."

He shook his head and I scrambled away to my car.

I reached back home and found no traces of Winona or our daughter inside the hall as I expected them to be waiting by the time I got there. I ran up to the bedroom and sighted Winona sitting morose at the dresser trying to hook an earring to her left lobe. She looked back at me solemnly.

"Winona, I thought you two would be ready to leave. What happened?"

She got up and strode closer. "Fiona isn't home, I tried calling her but she hasn't answered her phone in two hours."

"What do you mean she isn't home? Did she come back from school?"

"I was at the office and I left early, when I arrived, she wasn't here."

"Did you tell her about the wedding?"

"She knows. She knows we were going together, we spoke over dinner last night."

"Let me call her." I left the bedroom and hastened down the stairs as the phone rang a bell.

Just as I reached the hall I saw Fiona enter with a boy almost the same age as her, maybe a bit older, hand in hand, giggling as they walked in. He pushed her against the wall and attempted to kiss her.

"Go, my parents could be home." Fiona requested.

"I'm not leavin' without a kiss." He demanded.

"No, you had all the kisses for tonight, now go."

"Okay, okay I'm goin'."

"Fiona?" I disrupted their titillating chatter.

She quickly shoved him away and snatched her hand from his. I walked closer to the door and got a good look at this young man. He was obviously a part of some boy band as his attire and demeanor delineated. Skinny jeans, with ankle boots, chains of some sort dangling by his knees that were hooked to his belt and back pockets. A rolling stones t-shirt, aproned plaid shirt and sundry bracelets on both of his wrists, a spiked neckband, effeminate facial structure or made to look like it, and dark, shiny hair. I eyed him lividly from head to toe.

"Why weren't you answering your phone?" I questioned.

"My battery died on me, I didn't have a charger."

"I thought you were given that phone to be able to call and answer calls from your mother. The rest is unimportant."

"It is actually my fault, I-" the boy began to defend Fiona.

"This is the matter of our house, speak when you're spoken to." I interrupted. "And I think you need to leave now."

The boy glimpsed then waved to Fiona and scrammed. Fiona began walking inwards.

"Who is that?" I followed her as I asked.

"Bony, he's a friend from school." She was infuriated.

"A friend? Since when did you start making friends with that kind of boys?"

"What's wrong with him? I like his music, and he's a good student. We've known each other since junior high."

"And he doesn't even tell you his real name? Boni, that's probably what his homies call him."

"There's nothing wrong with that name. Besides, you don't have to throw insults at everybody I know. You didn't have to treat him like that."

"Throw insults? That guy disrespected this house, I saw him coming down the stairs, what he was doing. The way I treated him was the best he would be treated for his actions, young lady. You should be happy I didn't punch his face in."

"I should be worried about that the next time, maybe? You acting like a savage?"

"So, you are going to bring him here again?"

"Yeah, why not? Do I have to get your permission?"

Winona came down the stairs and joined in the conversation. "Fiona, what's the matter?"

"Nothing's the matter, but he's trying to create something out of nothing."

"Not coming home when your school ended hours ago is not nothing. We're worried here about you. You didn't call, you didn't care to inform us where you were. You have no sense of responsibility toward your mother? And then you show up holding hands with a boy and bring him inside the house, what kind of behavior is this? And watch your tone when you talk to us, you're still under our roof." Winona went harsher with every word.

"Well, you don't have to listen to that tone if you stop asking me those stupid questions."

"Fiona." I thundered.

"You two always treat me like that. Always. I can never have my friends over, and when I try to spend time with them or go out, you still have a problem."

"When have we ever stopped you from bringing your friends over?" Winona questioned.

"Right now, didn't you just see him? He acted like I killed someone."

"What's the matter with you, why are you acting so strange? What happened all of a sudden?"

"All of a sudden? No, I've been seeing this for too long. I can't take it anymore living like a prisoner. I hate you."

"Watch what you say to your mother, Fiona." I added.

"I don't even want to talk right now. I'm going to my room." Fiona protested.

"You're not going anywhere," Winona cut in. "You're coming with us."

"No, I'm not."

"I told you last night we were going to a wedding today. I've been waiting for you to get home since last two hours."

"I don't want to go anywhere right now."

"What do you mean you don't want to go? It's Mr. Ackres's wedding. He would love to see you there."

"He's your friend, you're the one invited. I don't have to tag along to make anyone feel better."

"How could you even say that, you've known him for such a long time?"

"Not me, mom. You've known him for this long, not me."

"He is a family friend and this wedding is a family event. You spend hours with your friends after school, I never interfere with your personal life. But if you expect to be a part of this family you have to participate in our lives as well."

"Family? You call this a family? If you don't know the definition of the word, it's not my problem."

"I am not going to take this kind of shameful argument." Winona advanced at Fiona.

"Winona." I stopped her before this got out of hands. "We can talk about this later when all of us can reason with each other. If she doesn't want to go, that's fine. But Fiona, you should understand your mother is just upset because she was worried about you. She's just concerned about your safety, that's all." I pleaded with Fiona to acknowledge her mistake, stepped closer and tapped her shoulder.

"Don't touch me. Stay away from me." She jolted away.

"What is wrong with you?" Winona yelled at her.

"God, you finally realize there's something wrong. Thanks for noticing, ma. Thanks for noticing after years of staying absent on me. You just woke up and all of a sudden there's other life around you. Welcome back to the world where other people exist and not everything revolves around you. And yes there's something wrong with me now, maybe because nobody cares about me. No one loves me anymore. If you thought that one month of our vacation in Hawaii is going to fix everything, then you need a reality check. You can't change things like that, not people. You need to wake out of that false dream. I was alone for far too long, because you left me that way, that's your fault. Now, when you finally return, I don't need you because I have him. Bony was the one who was there for me while you were busy stuffing your vaults with money. So thanks for your concern, but keep it. I'm not going to need it anymore. And for you, you're not my father so stop acting like one."

Fiona burst in tears and stormed up the stairs wailing on her way. Winona was heartbroken and gazed back at me. I was shocked as well as dejected. I went to Winona and gave a comforting tap on her back.

"I can call him up and tell him we can't make it."

"No, you've done so much for this ceremony. It would be unfair for you to miss it. Ned will never forgive you. We'll go, the two of us."

I nodded slowly and led her out of the house. I had Winona sit in the car and sent the driver to fetch the governess while we waited. He returned after some time and I explained the governess the sudden change of plans and if she could supervise Fiona until we returned. She quickly agreed and sent us off with one less worry to trouble our minds.

Chapter Fifty-Six

❦❦❦

We got back to the wedding as the celebrations were in full bloom. As we reached, Paola hurried up to the two of us. "Come on, they're waiting to start the ceremony. You're late already."

We followed her right up to the gazebo as people were all seated in the pews, the orchestra playing music, the priest attired in his cassock guarding his holy book in hand. As I walked through with all eyes set upon me, Ned came to my aid whispering. "What happened? I thought you were-"

"Don't worry, it's nothing. I got the ring right here. Go."

I stood right behind him as the best man and the bride walked down the open aisle clutching onto her father's arm. She was both excited as well as nervous which gave her face an aura of beauty and innocence. Jubilation turned into blushing as she walked closer to Ned and just as she left her father's arm, took one step ahead into the gazebo, she entered a new life. The priest began his blessings on the couple as they exchanged rings and vows and finally kissed each other to strengthen their love. They turned to face the assemblage of well-wishers and we all applauded this union throwing rice at them as they made their way amongst us. It was a wonderful sight, but my mind was set on a different matter.

While people began enjoying the feast and drinks, I found Winona sitting alone at the far end of the courtyard all by herself. I got myself a drink and shuffled the possibility of interrupting her state of dolorous isolation, but I resisted, maybe to give her time to think about what went wrong, or maybe to give myself time to conjure words of comfort that I could offer her. We were both disconcerted as we had never expected such revolt from someone we've loved more than each other. But then I contemplated Fiona's situation in all this and coming to understand her circumstance, she wasn't wrong in saying that she had been abandoned by us for the past couple of years, and it happened at the most destructive time of her age. As I rummaged the past pages of my life, I found very little mention of her. Maybe we were to blame in all this, our lust for wealth, for success, disregarded her happiness in the process. But the biggest wealth of our lives was nothing but spent now.

"I thought you weren't coming." I turned and found Ned behind me.

"No, I was just..." I had no answer to his question.

"Where's Fiona, I didn't see her?"

"She just couldn't make it. She was tired after school and all."

"I understand." Ned smiled. Someone called out to him from one of the tables. "I'll be right back."

I nodded and sauntered back into the house trying to find a corner of silence and peace as everywhere outside was loud revelry and celebratory pandemonium. As I walked down the hall I saw Jennifer coming down the stairs with Paola and few of her bridesmaids as they had all just changed their gowns to bit less formal ones. She stopped by the mirror to reflect on her looks. She was a beautiful woman, though a bit on the heavier side of the scale, but beautiful and pretty indeed. But those few extra pounds were enough to make her conscious of her body weight, especially at such an event with a large audience of evaluators. She found me in the mirror and turned toward me.

"How do I look, George?"

I went to her and took her face in my hands and kissed her forehead. "Better than everybody else. You're beautiful, and you're the only one who doesn't know it."

Her eyes almost slipped tears.

"Now go out there and make this night your own. No one else's, your own."

"Thank you."

She walked out with a revived confidence and the rest of the women with her. Paola winked at me for that booster she couldn't provide.

I ambled through the hall into the living and found the door to Ned's den. I entered a nice, comfortable setting to work in, or relax at the same time. The cacophony faded substantially in here and only sounded like a humming of a tune. A few files were piled on the side of his desk that I remembered were the same files that he brought with him earlier in the day from his main office. I took a chair close to the desk and fell back closing my eyes, taking a moment or two of alleviation. I kept my glass on the table. The top file on the heap slipped and toppled the glass spilling the drink all over the desk. I quickly reacted and wiped the tabletop with a roll towel and dabbed the wet file and papers inside to soak the smell of whiskey from them. As I patted the papers, I saw the files belonged to Warren Constructions and contained current financial statements and audit reports. I went through the first sheet and my eyes squinted suspiciously at the computed figures. I flipped page after page and creases on my forehead deepened as I had just come across something that swirled the wind out of me.

I hastened over to Winona and slammed these falsified documents upon the table in front of her.
"What the hell is this?"
Winona looked up at me in surprise, then at the reports. She arose and held on to my arm and took me back inside the house.

I was made to wait in Ned's office as Winona went to fetch him from outside. As they both joined me in the room, their intentions were simply to convince me to connive, but I was hell bent on the contrary.
"What is all this?" They hadn't even taken seats when I began. "Every document in this file is falsified. Look at this, inflated receivables, assets, revenues, every section is fake. There's not a single thing true in there."
"George..." Ned tried to assuage me. "It's all right, that's nothing."

"What do you mean it's nothing? This is a crime to manipulate the statements like that. It's not all right."

"It's common practice in all businesses, everybody does that. It's not just you or me, we're all a part of it."

"George, he's right. Look, the competition out there would tear us apart if we don't do these kinds of beneficial changes to our standing, and there's nothing wrong with that." Winona added.

"You knew about this?"

"Yes." She answered taking her time.

"This is criminal in nature, Winona. What are you talking about?"

"We know the people we need to address in case something happens. But it wouldn't, because everyone is involved in this, they all get a share."

"What if there's an inquiry?"

"You don't have to worry about that, we know our way out of it."

"This is a violation, Ned. You should be aware of that. They could implicate you if there's an investigation. They could revoke your license for fraudulent reports. And that's the least they'll do."

"No one will find out, how would they? You think I'm a rookie at this? I've been doing this for almost thirty-five years now, I know it like the back of my hand, trust me. And what do you think, George, they don't know about it? The SEC, FMS, IRS you think they don't know? They know, they know way before we get to do it. They have a permanent funding program financed by these corporations. Half of their lives they live off of these perks. Who do you think pays for their homes and properties by the size of acres and millions worth? Who do you think pays for Yale and Harvard education for their children? Who do you think funds their leisure time, world tours and all the fucking vacations in the Caribbean? There's nothing here that hasn't been done before, trust me."

"I can't believe the two of you." I shook my head in disbelief and barged out of the office.

Winona and I reached back home as I had driven in rage and hurry. I slammed the door open and stormed into the house, making my way straight to the bar for a drink. I picked up the bottle and headed for the kitchen, gulped the whole glass before sitting down and catching my breath. Winona entered the kitchen and stared at me standing at the other end of the table.

"I sent Maria away. She said Fiona went to sleep ten minutes ago."

"Don't try to change the subject. I'm still not done with our previous conversation."

"What do you want to talk about?"

I dashed and hovered inches away from her. "You seriously believe we can get away with this? This is a fucking crime goddamn it."

"Then what do you want me to do?" Winona yelled at her highest vocal capacity. "Business is the last thing on my mind. I have a daughter who says she hates me. A little up and down in the financial statements is the least of my concerns right now."

"But what was the need to do all this, Winona? We are going perfectly fine, why did you have to take such a risk?"

"May I enter if permitted?"

Both of us turned to a domineering personality walking toward the door. Esther was here. "My apologies if I startled you, but I just couldn't resist."

"Mother, what are you doing here?" Winona was indeed startled.

"That is a very interesting question, but an unimportant one. The important question is; what is going on in this house?"

"Mother we were just-"

"I will not hear the kind of language you just uttered." She addressed me this time. "My daughter is your companion not your servant and you are inside a home, not a barracks or a corner tavern."

I turned away and went back to my bottle of scotch.

"Drinking does obstruct a man's mannerisms, but shouldn't to such a lowly state where you use profanity in a house with a fifteen year old. She has cried enough for today, I will not see the disputes amongst the two of you squeeze anymore tears out of her."

"How do you know what happened?"

"She called me, she said she felt alone in this house and if I could come and take her. I stayed on the phone with her for the duration of my travel all the way from my place to here. I just put her to sleep and thank goodness for that. I asked the maid to not mention my arrival, as I hoped we could speak in the morning. But, I believe that might not be possible as your temperaments are out of control and need to be managed right away."

"There's nothing important to talk about, mother."

"Yeah, there isn't." I cut in. "Except that you could just go ahead and plan another business because this one is going to into closure sometime soon."

"What is he talking about, Winona?"

"Why don't you let me explain? Your daughter and her accountants have faked every single thing on their financial reports from profits to losses, every fucking thing. Oh, sorry, I thought I was allowed to speak freely in this house."

"Freely, yes. Loutishly, no. And all this ruckus is because of some financial statements that have been changed to seem better on paper?"

"Some financial statements? It is legal document that binds us under law not to misrepresent any parts of it. It's called fraud."

"You uncivilized man. No wonder you haven't conducted business on your own or you wouldn't have said that. Fraud? The correct nomenclature you would use here is creative accounting. And I don't believe we're the ones who have originated this practice. It's been done since you were still swinging in your cradle snickering to you mother's lullaby."

"It's against the rules."

"New businesses obey rules, old ones oblige relationships. And the people you fear are all related in this transgression one way or another."

"Mother, I can take care of this, please. You don't have to worry."

"You mean to say, I do not have to interfere? Hmm, I will go and check upon Fiona. There are more important matters at hand than some papers."

Esther left the kitchen. Winona stepped closer to me and held my hand.

"What you're worried about is a normal part of business, that's how they're run. I've been doing this for twenty years, every company manipulates their statements. Don't worry about it, please, trust me. There's nothing more important than our relationship, and it's meant to last. This can't be the end of our family. I need you. But right now our daughter is much more important to me, and I know she is to you as well. She's drifting away. I don't want to lose her, or even lose her to my mother. I need your help in bringing her back to us, to our lives. Please, can we do this? Please?"

I thought about it for long then gave in to my desire of seeing them all happy and together as a family again.

"Yes."

Chapter Fifty-Seven

ᑫᑫᑫ

The next morning I walked down the stairs and into the dining for breakfast. I usually was the first person to wake up in this house due to an old habit, but I was soundly defeated by Esther today as it seemed she was done with her breakfast and now enjoyed her morning tea. As I scratched my head while entering the room in pajamas, she glared at me up and down.

"There was time when men would dress up early in the morning to impress the ladies of the house and set a good example for their offspring. Now, I see it changed somewhat. Men these days like to undress to impress women."

"I don't go to bed in a tuxedo."

"According to your appearance, you aren't out of bed yet. But at least you're in control of your faculties to reason with. Last night was a different story."

"I know I shouldn't have behaved the way I did last night."

"The people of this age, they can't even apologize. But it isn't your fault. A heartfelt apology takes a lot of courage to admit. Gone are the days-"

"I'm sorry."

She looked at me blankly.

"Well, I'm not the one you should be apologizing to, but I'll still accept. What I won't accept is the way you two have treated my granddaughter, tantalized her to the point of seeking refuge somewhere other than her own house? The moment she called me, whimpering and crying out to me, I thought something worse had happened. But this is bad enough. She wasn't much concerned or aggravated against you, but I suppose you must have some part to play in this rift, this detachment between mother and daughter."

"If I have done anything so far for this family, it is bringing all of you closer. You know that, Winona knows that. The last thing I want to see is Fiona getting hurt for any reason. If I were to begin blaming, a lot of people would be involved, but I don't play that game."

"Why don't you try your hand at it?"

"You suggested for Winona to join your business, you knew if she was going to work there she will be away from her daughter. That is what turned Fiona against her. She thinks she wasn't cared for, she thinks we don't love her."

"Welcome to my world, darling."

"You knew this will happen."

"Operating a business does not mean you will disregard your children. You were there only for over a year. What do you make of the time since you returned? How much have you gained on the time that was lost? How much better or wanted have you made her feel since?"

"I have been there as much as I could."

"Well, 'as much' did not suffice apparently. There is reason why a family is made up of two parents. For one to work for their children's living, and the other to work for their children's lives. Earning a living is easy, building a life is the hardest job there is. What have you given my daughter in return for her favors upon you? She has given you authority over her business, over her life, over her house. And you haven't even given her daughter the right to call you her father. What are you doing in this house?"

"Mother." Winona stood in the door and was raging with fury. "I have listened to you talk about him, against him a lot. I will not take that anymore in my house. If you want to stay here you stay away from him. If I hear anymore negativity out of you, you're not welcome here."

Esther smirked. "I'm not welcome in my daughter's house. Well, I did not come here to see you. I came here to comfort my granddaughter whom you have done your best to wound emotionally. If you'd heard her cries last night, you would have murdered the people who caused it. But then again your ways of expressing love somewhat differs from mine."

"She doesn't need you. I'm her mother, I know how to take care of her."

"The kind you've exhibited for the past couple of years which boiled down to yesterday?"

"If you think she's going with you, you're wrong. She's not."

"That is for her to decide. But if you ever want to win her back, try and be her mother. Not a father, she doesn't need that. Remember, you were raised without your father after a certain age as well, but even before that he was hardly there for you. But your mother never left."

Esther walked out of the dining after that. Winona stood helpless and began to weep.

"Is it really my fault, George? Is it?"

I went over to her and wiped away the tears embracing her firmly in my arms. "The past is over, there will be no faults from now on."

෯෯෯

For the next couple of months Winona and I had taken our time and attention off from work and began to invest ourselves into our daughter's life. We would wake up with her and drop her off at school, we would pick her up from there as well. We would spend weekends with her and go out for movies, shopping, sight-seeing. At first, she didn't take all that too well and began to think that we were sheltering her and confining her independence, but we had no intention of doing that. We began to give her permissions to spend time with her friends whenever she wanted, sleepovers at her friends' with needed precautions. Fiona's outlook toward our relationship started to alter. I knew it wouldn't take much to make her realize our true feelings for her, as her anger was just an impulsive reaction to our absence. The effect of absorbing too much heat from our failure to dedicate ourselves to her, resulting in an outburst. But she was loving and gentle at heart, and she slowly began to understand.

As our routine continued of driving her to and back from school, having movie nights, dropping her at friend's and picking-up after, she started with smiles and small exchange of words. It gradually grew to full sentences and laughter and we had her back again. Took us a good six months to accomplish this, but it did make me realize one thing that a child is never lost as long as you're willing to bring them back. The mistakes committed were corrected, life was made possible again. The blessing in all this was that Esther actually restrained from inflicting any more trouble by taking Fiona with her. It would have been very hard on both of us if that had happened.

Winona would take her out on Friday evenings to socialize with her friends and their daughters over dinner on a ladies night out. It was a formal event that aggregated a couple of rich wives with their rich daughters discussing rich men and their businesses. Fiona would return from these gatherings exhausted to end of her hairs listening to all that relentless chatter lasting more than three hours in duration. Winona herself would only have enough strength to crawl onto her bed and doze off after such protracted garrulity. And that night was no different, but it was different in one aspect. After a very long hiatus that maybe lasted for months, Fiona initiated a conversation with me. Maybe she searched for that moment when she could talk to me alone in the absence of her mother. She came into the living room and sat by my side on the couch as I had just closed my eyes after watching television for an hour or more.

"Are you asleep?" She whispered.

I opened my eyes and sat up. "Oh, you guys are back? How was your night with the ladies of the town?"

"Boring, as always." She rolled her eyes.

"Hmm... your mother enjoys their company. Well, that is the only company she has."

"She hates them all. I don't know how she tolerates them. At least one of them could have a different personality, a different subject to talk about. But no, they're all the same. From the oldest to the youngest, men, money and jewelry, that's all they talk about. That's all they know."

"Aren't you the youngest there?"

"No, there are twelve year olds there who behave like their mother. I just met Mrs. Gaskins's youngest daughter today and she couldn't get over her blue diamond earrings her father imported from Angola and gifted her on her twelfth birthday. She was so fake and superficial."

"That's an expensive birthday gift."

"It's useless when you're twelve."

"How about when you're sixteen? That's not too far."

"Still not worth it. I won't be able to look after them the way I should. I'll only lose it."

"Okay, my little one talks wisdom now. That's nice."

"I don't want expensive birthday gifts."

"What do you want then?"

"I just want the two of you to stay with me."

I turned and looked at her. There was longing in her eyes for the love she missed in the past.

"We're always with you, don't worry about it ever. Nothing will change that."

"You promise? Because if you two leave me again, I won't be able to live. I will run off somewhere and never come back."

"Don't say that. I promise we will never leave."

"I wanted to tell you something. I know I should have said this earlier, but I didn't get the chance. I'm sorry. I'm sorry for what I said that day. It was stupid of me to say all of that to you."

"It's okay, sweetheart."

"I will only forgive myself when you forgive me."

"I can't forgive you for something I can't even remember. Whatever happened that day wasn't you, it was anger, it was all emotion. But the good thing that emerged from that event was a realization, an understanding of where we went wrong, why you were hurt. There's a first time for everything right? But it doesn't mean it would be repeated again. I'll make sure it isn't."

She hugged me with tears in her eyes. "You know what nana said to me before she left? She said you were the only person in this house I can trust with everything. She said not mom, you. And she told me why, because you have nothing to gain out of us, but only to give."

I smiled and kissed her forehead, holding my own tears. "Never ignore advice from your grandma, she's very good at that. And love your mother the most, she will always need you. Promise me that."

"I promise."

"Don't ever break your word."

"I won't."

"Good. Now, what else did I have to say? You just made me forget. Oh yes, your friend Bony called. He said he wanted to talk to you urgently and you weren't answering his calls on your phone. I told him to try back."

"Don't even talk about him. He's a jerk."

"Aren't they all?"

"They are, absolutely."

"So, is it over between you two?"

"It never even started between us? And that part where I said he was there for me while you both weren't. I lied, I was actually all alone."

"Come here." I embraced her one more time and stayed there for a long moment just when we were interrupted.

"What's going on here?" Winona entered in her night suit and a golden mess on her head. She came in scratching her belly. "I couldn't sleep, had too much to eat."

"Come here, you. Our family hug isn't complete without you. Come on." I roped her in.

We welcomed her into our family embrace and stayed there until death do us part. But the never ending troubles of life can be overlooked for some time, not forgotten.

Chapter Fifty-Eight

❧❧❧

I was on my way to the office when passing across the elevators I gazed at my reflection in the mirrors and realized that I was beginning to get old with graying hair and traces of creases around my eyes and face. That thought lingered in my mind for some time as I sat inside my office thinking how much time it has been since I began my life back in New York. How much time it has been since I left Los Angeles. But my reflective state was disrupted by Ned who came barging inside and locked the door swiftly before approaching me at the desk. I glanced at him and found him distressed and sweating due to some cause.

"Are you all right?"

"George, I think we might have a problem."

"What's the matter?"

"Look at this." He put a clasp envelope in front of me and waited for me to read its contents. I went through the papers inside and discovered a court notice.

"What the hell is this?"

"One of our recent clients is suing us for payroll fraud."

"Payroll fraud? Now how is that possible, we're not guilty of any..." I piercingly glared into his guilty eyes. I had my answer. I swung at a glass pitcher in my office and it crashed to smithereens upon the floor.

I remained speechless following that revelation as Ned fidgeted from one end of the office to other. He had called Winona into the office and she was equally shocked to hear the unpropitious news. She read the notice and sunk into the chair.

"I'm not worried about this client taking us to court, we can handle anyone right now without breaking a sweat. What I'm worried about is if there's any further investigation into our financial records and government contracts, we'd be in big trouble." Ned confirmed.

"I told you not to tamper with those financial statements, Ned. I told you. How long have you been doing this?"

"Since we started. How do you think we got to this position in the market? These alterations were essential to our growth. We didn't have a lifetime to progress."

"We wouldn't have a lifetime at all due to what you've done."

"I consulted with Winona for every little change. She permitted that along with the rest of the board."

"What else have you done? And what is exactly this payroll fraud?"

"It's giving false payroll statements to your contractees. Creating fraudulent, ghost employees, if you will, who never existed and getting reimbursed for that."

"How much?"

"In the past four years? Twenty million, maybe more."

"What else are we guilty of?"

"There're a lot of things, George. You better not ask me about it. And it's common practice in all companies."

"Do not say that to me again. Don't. Just tell me what else?"

"Show a consistent profit, profit smoothing. Inflated receivables, overstating assets, revenues, decreased liabilities for a higher market capitalization. It wasn't a big deal at the time we started doing all of this, George."

"Our careers are at stake here."

"That's not all. Tell him Ned." Winona finally spoke.

I turned to him expecting a more grievous divulgence.

"There's a supplier we purchase lumber from at regular intervals, remitting timely payments to them by check. It actually doesn't exist, it is a dummy corporation. We created it. And because of that there's been some money laundering in the past and false tax returns."

"You just keep getting better, Ned."

"It's not his fault, George. I made him do that." Winona took on the blame.

"Well, if you made him do that, you might have a better idea on how to get us out of this quagmire. I told you guys to stay away from all this, less than a year ago I said that. We would have done just fine with an honest, reputable business that didn't need any fallacious misdeeds to its name. But the greed of getting too much too soon is going to take all of us down. We're going to be in a worse situation than we are in right now."

"I won't let that happen. We have built this business from nothing, not to have it investigated and consequently shut-down in the process. I will not lose my reputation, not this soon."

"What are we going to do?" Ned questioned.

"Get to them before they come to us."

"What?" I was confused.

"The less people are involved the better it is. We go to the IRS, the SEC, Department of Justice and the State before they could even think about conducting an investigation. We stop and seal any attempts for an inquiry."

"How do you plan on doing that?" I asked.

"I know the right people, I know the right amounts to divert their intentions. They wouldn't be too hard to influence."

"I like that, bring the giants in the picture, who gives a damn about the little people." Ned added.

"You're going to go to them yourself and tell them the acts of fraud you've committed in all these years?" I took a drink of water.

"There's no other way. If there is an investigation, a lot of people are going to enter the process. It gets exceedingly difficult to control a crowd as opposed to a handful. We satisfy the leaders, the rest just follow suit."

"And who are these leaders?"

"That you can leave to me. I know just the people to invite for this kind of transaction."

"What about this, what are you going to do about this notice?"

"Out of court settlement, it's nothing to worry about. I got this, George, look at me. I got this, trust me." Ned tried to reassure me.

"I did, Ned. I did. I don't care what you do to resolve this, but I don't want any part of it."

As I left the office and walked the hallway, it dawned in my mind the amount of life that was depending on the survival of this company. I saw an endless stream of employees, from secretaries to managers, field officers to all those five thousand laborers. The possibility of losing their jobs and hopes for a better future hadn't even crossed their minds and we were dallying with this corporation and deciding its fate like we were the only ones affected. I went straight home from there and in the seclusion of my bedroom I contemplated the tomorrow of our lives and the thousands that were connected to us professionally or personally. I spent the entire evening in isolation as I knew Winona would not return home anytime soon as she needed to arrange herself to successfully deal in this exchange to emerge triumphant over all ills and plights. I felt bad at some point for abandoning her in the time of distress and during moments when people usually need all the support they can get. Someone she needed and depended upon the most wasn't with her. It reminded me of the time of my past life, when I abandoned someone at the time when she needed me the most and continued to curse myself for years following that error. Would I repeat the same mistake again? Would I go on living in regret and hatred for many more years to come? The first time it happened, it could be a mistake. But if I repeated it for a second time, it would be intentional. And I wasn't a man who would intend to wish harm upon someone or abandon them in the times of need and trouble. I had made up my mind. I had left someone before, I wasn't going to leave this time.

The forthcoming days were very engaging and bustling as I saw Winona and Ned toiling at the office incessantly hour after hour. Many reports were made and changed, many accounts closed and expunged. At times a sense of foreboding filled my heart to the fullest as I feared losing everything that was garnered in the past years. But then somewhere I trusted their judgments. It was after weeks of consistent efforts and flattery that the meeting with the executives and authorities of the main departments involved finally came into existence. It was a serious business in gathering all of these people into one conference room, but Winona and Ned had done it.

That late afternoon Winona was all prepared to leave when I stepped into the bedroom and looked straight at her. I saw no fright in her eyes and no disdain for me either. She smiled back.

"Is Ned going to be there?"

"He is. I couldn't do this without him. I couldn't be here without you."

"I was thinking if you need me for anything, I'm always there."

"I know."

"Even if you need me tonight, I will come."

"George, have you ever seen a young redwood tree? When it is newly planted, it is supported by a stake on either side secured by a cord so it doesn't fall in a storm. You have been that stake for me for a very long time. If you don't come with me tonight, I still wouldn't think of you disapprovingly. But I would be proud to have you by my side when I enter that room and stand before all those men."

We came down the stairs and sighted Fiona in someone's embrace. As we got closer, Esther turned and looked back at us, parted with her granddaughter after a kiss and stepped toward Winona.

"You might have forgotten you have an elder most useful in such time of asperities, but I haven't forgotten I still have a daughter to take care of."

"Mother?" Winona was surprised.

"Did you think I wouldn't stand by you in your troubles even though you threw me out of your house the last time I was here?"

"Actually, I did."

"Well, then you know very little about your mother. If such affrays would begin to distance us apart, I would be living somewhere in Somalia by now."

We all laughed at the remark. "But how did you know?" Winona asked.

"I have my ways, but this time the tip came from someone in this house."

"And it wasn't me." Fiona added.

They all looked up at me and I raised my hands in surrender. "I hope I didn't do anything wrong."

"Do you ever?" Winona commented.

"Don't you always?" Esther added. "Now, where are we headed?"

Chapter Fifty-Nine

ೀೀೀ

The meeting convened at The Regency Hotel some miles from the city to keep it under a cover of secrecy. We arrived outside the conference room as Ned waited impatiently with two of our counselors.

"All right, you're finally here."

"Are we late?" Winona questioned.

"No, no, I guess I'm just too excited. Now, I have them all in there warmed up and a bit drunk. I think we're ready to tackle."

"You make it sound like a football game." Esther commented.

"It's worse than that, ma'am. Worse than that."

We entered the conference room and found a group of aging individuals huddling in the corner over the bar with glasses of scotch and brandy in their hands. Their laughter was disingenuous, their talk was insincere and superficial as if a cloak was around them that prohibited one another from invading their true intentions, their evil thoughts.

"Gentlemen, allow me to introduce all of you to my employer. Here is Ms. Winona Warren, her mother Mrs. Esther Warren, and our CEO Mr. George Bailey. Our counselors here are Mr. Levinson, and Mr. Barnik. And here are the gentlemen we have trying to bring together for many days, the Commissioner of -"

"Please, Mr. Ackres. The nature of this conference is quite peculiar as well as surreptitious. Hence, it would be better if we kept our identities implicit. In my profession, the walls are known to have ears and we cannot be too careful every time." The man who spoke came forward, probably around sixty-five, stood very well poised, calm and relaxed.

"Understood Mr... sir." Ned corrected himself.

"Very well. It is a pleasure to meet you Mrs. Warren and it would excite you to hear that I have had a lot of dealings with your husband in the times of his supremacy around the Springs area. Oh, those were some days."

"Please, I would love to hear more." Esther's tone was very ingratiating.

The man took Esther by the arm and led her to the bar offering her a drink. He seemed to me like the chieftain of the faction the way he presented himself. The rest were a bit reserved in their demeanor, or perhaps deliberately acted that way to shroud their true positions and ranks. Winona and I glanced at each other. So far it wasn't going against our advantage and that was a wonderful start. The men inside the room were very well groomed, suited, mannerly, most of them over the age of sixty, balding and creased with time.

After sometime of obsequious talk and a lot of drinks, we all gathered around the conference table. Men from the departments on one side of the table and the people of Warren Construction on the other.

"So, Mr. Ackres, here we are at your summons. Now, if you would enlighten us with the reason behind such urgency that required you to cumulate these reputable gentlemen together here, I believe we all should be taken out of the dark."

"You embarrass me, sir. Out of your graciousness have you answered my request, who am I to summon you?" Ned answered.

"Oh, come now, we are but public servants. This is the least we can do."

One of the other gentlemen leaned in to join the conversation. "I think we all know the purpose for which we're called here. Mr. Ackres was quite unequivocal in articulating the misappropriations and misdeeds of his employers at Warren Constructions and I do not see any reason as to why they shouldn't be indicted and tried before a court committee following necessary investigations."

"Excuse me, Randall." The leader of the pack spoke again. "You of all should be aware of how to address businessmen of such caliber, you do it all the time. You shouldn't forget your paycheck is derived from their taxes." The chief spoke.

"Fraudulent taxes." The dissident added.

"Well, that is why we have gathered here to correct what was made wrong. Isn't that right Ms. Warren?" This time the leader turned to Winona.

"Look, I have my granddaughter's birthday to attend in an hour. So, the quicker we're done here, the sooner I can leave. If we get to the point of discussion without any delay, I would be very pleased." Another aging man from the group spoke. He was much leaner in structure but more seasoned in endurance.

"I'm honored to be in the company of such luminary individuals. And I apologize if any of you had to abandon vital engagements to be here. But I will certainly make sure this is worth your while." Winona assured them.

"See, that's what business does to you. It gives you a delusional supposition that everything out there is up for sale." The leader was incisive this time.

"Is it not?" I spoke out of my silence and aggravation.

There was a silence following that in the conference room for about ten seconds.

"You tell me, sir?" The chief smiled and disrupted that awkward hush.

"This is ridiculous, what about-"

"Randall, just stop your fretting now. If you're trying to intimidate them, it's evidently not working."

"Why is everybody taking my name, I thought you said no names."

"Then shut your mouth. Ms. Warren, please. We're all ears."

"Thank you, sir. As we know what dire situation brings us all together, and I trust Mr. Ackres with his categorical explanation of the matters. But what has been done cannot be erased now. I think we will agree to one fact that the outcome, call it a consequence, conclusion or the aftermath as your companion just suggested, is not beneficial or preferable to any of us present in this room. It will not benefit you in any way, perhaps some personal pleasure maybe, and it will definitely not benefit us. So, why not try to change this circumstance into a more profitable, a more gainful experience for all? I admit to some alterations in our financial reports, I admit to money laundering and establishing a dummy corporation in the process. I admit to tax evasion and false reports, but find me a business that isn't guilty of these wrongdoings. This might probably be the first time you've heard someone acknowledge their mistakes before they're even detected. Now we can either discuss an offer I have for you gentlemen which compels us all forget the past faults and leave them buried for the rest of the future, or you could go ahead with the tedious process of conducting an investigation, indicting us and sending us to jail, which gives you nothing but a salutation in the newspapers for a couple of days and a pat on the back by your seniors, which one of you doesn't have. So, do you benefit from you decision, or you regret your decision? It's your call."

"Hmm... it is a tough call, isn't it gentlemen?" There was contemptuous laughter from all of them. "Ms. Warren, I appreciate you taking all that time to familiarize us here on this side of the table with your good intentions. But I don't find myself getting into that game spirit unless I hear that one word which sounds to me as sweet as Nancy Sinatra singing softly in my ears all day long. It's a simple five letter word; money. Now we can talk about tax laws and fraud and laundering and consequences of them all night long if we had that much time, heck I can even cite the Codes and Statutes and what Article and Section you're alluding to. But we're not here to challenge my knowledge on the subject. We're here to test your knowledge in the matter of, for lack of a better word, gratuity. So, do I hear that word now?" The chief's eyes were green by the time he finished.

"Five million each. To appreciate your understanding of the errors made, five million dollars each. Cash, check, transferred to your accounts, as you like."

The groups exchanged glances at each other.

"Have you gathered us here to humiliate our standing, Ms. Warren? Do you think we're going to demean and tarnish the honor of our state and department laws for that insignificant pittance? This is an insult, you try to shame us with a bribe?"

"You have mistaken our gesture, sir. It wasn't meant to sound that way." Ned quickly pacified the intensity in the room. "Please..."

"Maybe we have a penchant for good business people, maybe I'm too gullible. Let me confirm once again what you said. Was it ten million dollars each?"

This time the people on our side of the table exchanged glances.

"Yes. I might not have made myself clear the first time. Ten million is what I said."

"Hmm..." the man got up and walked to our end of the table and whispered. "Then let us shake hands on that word. The dispersal of the incentive can be discussed with Randall, and I'm sure we wouldn't have much trouble claiming it as legit money."

"No, Mr. Ackres will see to that himself."

"Very well."

"I'll have to make sure we agree on the terms before that," Winona added. "What does this exactly put on the platter for us?"

"Look Ms. Warren, a payment is only good for that particular purchase. It can't be redeemed for life. You know this better than anyone else in the room. But if the tokens are recurrent, I could be blind for life or as long as I hold this office. And I can assure you the gentleman succeeding my tenure would be equally tolerant of minor mishaps in businesses. Let's renew this deal every five years and we'll be rolling along faster than a carousel. I hope you understand."

"I do."

"Good, now just a minute detail I forgot to mention before we finalized this bargain. A complaint has been already filed with IRS. I believe someone out there seeks to ruin your reputation publicly. An investigation is inevitable. If this is taken any further, which it will be, there would be some fraud and criminal charges along the way."

"But you just..."

"Ms. Warren, there's hardly anything I can do to make this better as this has been filed with our office some time ago. I can only prevent new graves from being dug, covering the existing ones is not my job. I will have to initiate an investigation in a matter of days. You should be prepared for that. But I will assure you, after this is over you will have nothing to fear."

Winona sank into her chair rubbing her temples.

"Nothing to worry about," the man continued. "Take your time and prepare your defense, your counselors will help in creating one.

Mr. Ackres is quite adept at convincing people to his favor, trenchant as well."

"I thought we wouldn't have to go through all this after our settlement." I jumped in.

"The settlement hasn't been completed yet. Though, I do not doubt your word, but it is still unfinished business. But I will make one provision in exchange for your kind gesture. I will restrict the time designated to this investigation which will limit the nefarious findings, hence less burden to bear. Does that sound fair enough to everyone?"

His side of the table nodded in approval. We had no choice but to concede.

"I think we can manage." Ned nodded to Winona and me.

"Excellent. That concludes our negotiation. It was wonderful to meet with all of you."

The parties arose from their chairs and shook hands with each other, began to exit the conference room one after another. Just as we were to leave, the leader of the pack pulled Winona and Esther into a corner. Ned and our counselors had just stepped out, and I was at a close distance able to overhear their talk.

"When this case is brought to trail, it is bound to generate some publicity as well as media interest. I would need a source to satisfy their hunger for blind justice to rationalize any ruling on the matter and make it seem credible."

"I'm afraid I can't follow?" Winona was confused.

"Have you ever witnessed a ritual killing, Ms. Warren? People sometimes ascribe a religious purpose to it, sometimes a personal belief to attain peace or pleasure or maybe a blessing. But what they fail to grasp is does a ritual killing appease their desire for good or evil? Does taking a life make their lives more forgivable or punishable? That's for you to decide, but I will need a victim to be marked as a sacrificial lamb, a scapegoat that's pulled to the scaffold and is put up the stake. It isn't much to worry about, just around five years in prison and some insignificant restitution would suffice. And in my experience the little people are the ones who take the most heat in such matters, the middle men as we call them. Throw a hefty check at them, the loyal dogs would take on anything for their good master. We'll rope in your accountant, he's expendable. Give him to me, you have yourself a clear road ahead." He winked at them and collected his coat on the way out.

Chapter Sixty

ŷŷŷ

Our drive back home was a silent one. All of us were in a distressing contemplation of the suggestion made earlier, but we refrained from mentioning it to each other. We reached home close to ten at night and dispersed into different parts of the house while I headed straight for the bar. I spent around two hours there, not drinking much but thinking. And when I looked back at the watch it ticked close to midnight. I was exhausted in mind and body and just when I attempted to retire to the bedroom, I saw Winona come into the room still in her business suit, still disturbed. She hadn't changed.

"You're not tired, George? Not going to sleep?" She asked.

"Are you?"

"No, I don't know whether I should or shouldn't. Can we talk about it?"

"There's hardly anything to talk now, Winona. We might be good negotiating deals for our company, but we got duped trying to make a deal for our lives."

"I asked mother to join us, we need to talk about it and decide on things here. I hope you don't mind."

"Why should I? You two are the principal owners of the company, anything that occurs with it should be your decision."

"Did you hear what he said before leaving?" She sought confirmation.

"It would have been better if I didn't." I gave it to her.

"I know how you're feeling, George." She came closer and leaned into me holding my face in her hands. "I don't want to do anything wrong."

"Then do the right thing."

"What is the right thing?"

"You know what it is. We shouldn't even be thinking about doing it any other way."

"Then what should I do? Let it go. Let go of everything we've built? All we've worked for the past years, just close our doors and wait for a lawsuit to come by?"

"This was not a part of the deal we signed for, or maybe I signed for. You told me everything is going to be all right and if we throw money at them they're going to come running wagging their tails. I don't see that happening."

"It's better than an indictment."

"Putting our friend out there for them to prosecute for our greed is better?"

"Then you tell me what to do and I'll do just that. Show me a way out of this."

"I did, some time ago. I asked you to stop, but you didn't. This wouldn't have happened if we corrected the wrong. And what deal did we get today? Those men basically laughed at us and kicked us in the rear with no guarantee of immunity from an investigation in exchange for ten million dollar each. Eighty million dollar is a massive amount, Winona. And we couldn't even buy our peace of mind tonight for that much money."

"Then I call off the deal."

"You'd be the biggest fool if you do that." Esther came into the room. "He isn't wrong, they tricked us tonight. I suppose they saw our vulnerability even when we tried to conceal it."

"Then what would you have me do?" Winona whimpered.

"It is not your fault, dear." The mother supported her. "You're not to be blamed here. It isn't anyone's fault. They had a superior position at that negotiation and they took full advantage of that."

"Well, you were quite speechless for the entire time." I remarked.

"Yes I was, because I couldn't see anything coming out of my mouth that would change what happened in that room. You cannot control such greedy, immoral men who bear no sense of

- 394 -

understanding, no sense of integrity. There are men you can change with time, with words, with compassion, but not these creatures. They sit in decay and grow only in age, not honesty nor wisdom. They are unscrupulous fools who do not know the meaning of honest corruption. There's no honor in them, not even to keep their word for the money they've taken. But if this is how we emerge from the black pool of depravity, so be it. It wouldn't be the first time someone is paid to take the blames of others. Ackres is clever enough to know that. If they want someone to stand before the people and admit the mistakes, I don't see any harm in this."

"Have you considered what he would go through?" I questioned.

"He's getting paid. We will double the amount."

"You can keep your goddamn money. He doesn't give a shit about it. He has enough of it already. The man just got married less than a year ago. What is wrong with you?"

"Keep your tone in check when you speak to me, George. I will not hear that kind of language used in front of me. And if it's not him, then who? Would you do it? Or would you rather have them put Winona in jail? That sounds fair enough, why don't go ahead and declare yourself guilty of everything Winona and have them put you away for years? By the time you come out of prison your daughter would be so far gone you wouldn't know where to begin looking for her. I doubt I'd be alive by then."

"The sentencing is never that long."

"Shame on you, you foul man. You are considering it, aren't you? You say you love her? You do? Ruin their lives, that's what you will. That girl who sleeps soundly in her bed right now, you think she will be able to bear life if she's separated from her mother again? You just saw what the recent years did to her, imagine her living alone for another five. No, I will not see it happen as long as I live. She's only done this for her daughter and I would have done the same for mine. We only blunder in our lives for the sake of our children, maybe you don't know that, but it's the truth. If we lived for the sake of our own survival, I wouldn't have left a shred for her to cover her body with. Our generations need to endure and we must continue to make sure it does. The rest are unimportant, unless they become a part of it."

"Mother." Winona interrupted.

"You and your society, the others are just animals to you."

"We are all born animals, refinement comes through virtue. The sooner you understand the better it is for all of us."

"You conspire to betray him, and expect me to understand? It's useless talking to you about it, but you Winona. You've known him just as long as you've known me. Would you have done the same to me?"

She remained silent.

"If we are going to betray him, he needs to know the truth and I will tell him that." I began to leave.

"You will tell him nothing." Esther objected.

"Try and stop me."

I stormed out of the house and drove in the dark of the night straight to Ackres residence.

It was way past midnight when Ned came wrapping himself in a robe to answer the door. "George, what's the matter?"

"I need to talk to you, Ned."

He took me into his office as all that shuffle had woken Jennifer up and she came downstairs to check on her husband. She knocked at the door and slipped inside.

"Is everything all right? Hey, George."

"How are you Jennifer? Did I wake you up?"

"Not really, I could hardly sleep these days. And you haven't been around to check up on us lately. Your friend here blames me for you skipping on your visits since I came into this house. He tells me you were very frequent before our marriage."

"No, it's nothing like that. Work, it's gotten way out of hands now. He can tell you about it better than me."

"That's all right, I understand. Mr. Ackres, now don't you go around blaming me for it, he just gave you the real reason. And I believe it's actually your fault."

"He doesn't listen to me, that's for sure. I keep telling him not to exhaust himself." Ned punched in.

Jennifer smiled and shook her hear at us. "I'll keep the coffee on the stove in case you need any. And George, we wanted to tell you something."

"What is it?" I turned to Ned in surprise.

"I think it's better if you hear it from her." Ned gestured to Jennifer.

"We're going to have a baby!" She exclaimed.

"What? When?"

"Not anytime soon, I'm due in March next year. Still a lot of time to go."

"Oh boy, so the baby celebrates birthday with Winona then?"

"Yeah. We'll have a joint celebration."

I got up from my chair and kissed her, blessing her womb. "May you stay happy just like this, always."

"Thanks."

"Now would you let us talk, please? And give the baby some rest." Ned interrupted.

"I'll leave."

"Thank you." Ned shook his head then turned to me. Jennifer walked out closing the door behind.

"What is it, George?" Ned was anxious. "Anything wrong? You have me worried."

I waited to answer, then smiled and looked back at him warmly. "Nothing." He knew there was something that I hid, but couldn't guess. "Nothing. I just came to see you guys."

I got up and took off from there.

"George... George..."

Ned attempted to follow and kept calling me as I ran out of the house and back into my car and drove away.

ço·ço·ço

After approximately eight months, as I was beginning to lose count of our days spent in distress, we had finally reached the last phase of proceedings which was a hearing set before the U.S. District Court. We were tackling both SEC and IRS with multiple counts of fraud against our defense to begin with, and criminal charges were like cherry on the pie. The investigations had lasted more than five months and consequently instituted the trial after a series of hardships. We had a couple of more surreptitious conferences with the same group of "inside men" from the departments and abided by their recommendations and instructions. They had roped in the judge for some clemency on our part, and a hefty reward in return. It seemed like a devised setup not just for us but the endless number of cases, to go through and walk out in the end with a marred reputation and a lighter wallet, with the exception of some dispensable pawns, in our case a head staff accountant and three top line executives. I wasn't happy with that settlement but I had no other choice but to contain myself and keep my lips sealed.

It was the night before the beginning of our public hearing that I found myself all alone in the house as Esther and Winona had other important matters to attend to and prepare for tomorrow. I navigated the dark, hushed emptiness of the opulent home but still couldn't locate a moment of peace anywhere. As I sat in the hall thinking of what may come I saw a figure moving toward me but then diverting to the light switch and illumining the room.

"You shouldn't sit in the dark, grandma always says that." Fiona commented and took a chair by my side. "It's inauspicious."

"Don't take your grandma so seriously."

"Yeah, I know." She laughed. "That's not what you said last time we spoke."

"It's been a long time, hasn't it?"

"You're never there."

"I know, and I'm sorry."

"I understand now, sometimes work is more important than people."

"Don't say that. There's nothing more important than you, for me or for your mother."

She nodded then sat silently. A long hiatus passed.

"Can I ask something of you, Fiona?"

"Yes?"

"What if I asked your forgiveness for breaking a promise?"

"Breaking a promise?"

"I made a promise to you some time ago that I will always be there with you. I have to break that promise now. I have to go somewhere, and I can't say I would be returning soon."

She was slightly perturbed, but held her composure. "Where are you going?"

"I can't tell you right now, but I have to."

"Send someone else, whatever it is that needs to be done."

I smiled. "No, it has to be me. If it's someone else, it will defeat the purpose for which I must go. See, you need to understand."

"Understand what? Should I be okay with you leaving me, once again? And why does it have to be you? You said you'll be right there whenever I needed you," she began to whimper. "It's a promise, you can't just run away from it like that. Take me with you then, take us all with you."

"I'm afraid I can't do that. There are not many people allowed where I'm going."

"But you promised." Her soft whimpers altered into a loud cries and sobs.

"I will miss you a lot."

"You can't do that to me."

"You have your mom, your grandma with you. What else can you ask for?"

"I don't care, I want you there too."

"We don't always get what we wish for. Please Fiona, try and understand."

"But at least tell me where you're going, I can come see you."

"You will know that, you will know soon enough."

"Why can't I come?"

"You can't, no one can. But we will meet one day, when I return. Would you remember me then?"

She clung to me like a baby and stayed there soaking my shirt with her tears.

"I won't forget you. Never."

"I know you won't."

The court building was teeming with officers, reporters and spectators of all sorts as we made our way to the security check the following morning. Our team was almost as vast as any committee ever devised for a court proceeding. The stage was set, the instructions were passed and interpreted. The courtroom was brought into order as the judge made his ingress and took his Bench after a proud gait. The presence of the parties was duly noted and the hearing began as we each took an oath and answered the state counselor's questions one after another. As I took the witness stand I stated my name and relation to the company in question and fortified my oath again. The counselor stepped out to the stand but just before he could revise a question to begin with, I stood up.

"Your honor, could I have permission to address the court before any questions are asked?"

The judge considered for a few seconds, then nodded. "You may."

"Your honor, I accept all charges brought against our company." A sudden burst of mumbling swept the pews. "I declare knowledge and responsibility of all and every decision made to alter our company records. From tax fraud to fake entities, I am solely responsible for all fraudulent acts committed by our corporation and my principal shareholders did not partake in any of these dishonest and deceitful procedures. As far as my accounting department is concerned, they had formulated these statements at my behest and under my full supervision against their will. I stand guilty and ready for justice."

The courtroom erupted into chaos at the sound of this confession. Esther, Winona and Ned were stunned to the core. Our counselors began flipping pages of their defense files and whispering to the Warren ladies. The judge struck his gavel. "Order in the court, order."

Winona held my gaze with a torrent of emotions glinting in her eyes. There was compassion, there was hatred, there was love and there was pity. Tears slipped down her eyes. I tacitly explained to her why I did this. She understood, understood well enough.

Chapter Sixty-One
 So So So

I had ultimately found my peace that I had searched for quite some time inside the confines of a solitary prison cell. It wasn't going to be a short stay so I had to make myself comfortable and accustomed to such restricted living. But it was something that I wasn't afraid of; isolation and loneliness. I was very proficient at handling both living conditions as I had confronted them in my past. My trip to this side of the steel bars was a long and tiresome process which didn't happen right after my explosive and astonishing confession in the courtroom. A lot of days passed since and after shuffling between state and federal courts and jury and committee convictions, I was finally sentenced for a total of six years in prison. I was unhappy with this verdict, but my embitterment wasn't due to the fact that I was sent to jail for such a long time, it was for three other people who were convicted along with me and were sentenced from ten to eighteen months in prison. My intention in taking all the blame upon myself was only to secure the rest from any incarceration, but that was too much to ask I suppose. I thought if they had the big shark, they wouldn't go after the small fish anymore. I was wrong. The officials of the corrupt system needed to somehow impact the media with their moral, honest, law-upholding character and found three victims from our management willing to imprison themselves in exchange for a couple million dollars. Their departmental integrity was conserved and Warren Constructions didn't lose its shareholders. I was content that Winona and Ned were safe and back to their homes with nothing to worry about in the future except monetary fines and penalties that were in excess of thirty-four million dollars. But that was something that didn't require much effort as Winona and Ned both had enough to compensate these dues. My desire was to save them from prison, and that I did, as there wouldn't be any denser stigma to bear in life than being a convict. Fiona would have her mother by her side always, and Ned would be able love his child after it's born.

I was going to be here for six years, a lot changes in six years. I would alight on the berth thinking of the days that were to come after my release, or any positive thoughts that might shift my attention from this bleak prison cell, but I couldn't imagine a moment of that time as I had no power to visualize or imagine anything good anymore. I didn't know what would happen, how life will be. But for some reason I felt much safer and invulnerable behind the bars than I ever did out in the open. At least I knew the people here were honest in their untrustworthy deeds and all of us were in there for some reason which was evil in some way. There could be handful innocent souls here as well, but I hadn't found any so far. Out there in the open you could never know who would turn out be how wicked, how much more evil. The alleged good people of a respectable society are much more scarier than the evil ones in here, as they could go around with masks of deception to cover their malicious faces all the time. But I was not a saint myself. I had spent years on the loose after killing someone. Maybe this confession was my attempt at redemption, to come full circle. The guilt of that crime had lingered on my conscience for years, and penitence could only be derived through punishment. Six years wasn't enough time, but who says I had lived my life in happiness since I committed that crime? Maybe some scattered contentment here and there, but never in its whole.

Winona visited me after a long time of silence from her end. It wasn't a surprise as I expected her to limit our contact once my name was counted amongst inmates. But I was glad to see Fiona accompany her. Winona said she didn't want to bring her daughter to such a depraved setting, but she surrendered to her imploring. When Fiona saw me enter the visiting room, all she did was embrace me and cry irrepressibly for an hour. I tried to alleviate her pain with words and laughter, but it didn't impact her seething emotions. When she finally parted, she just said two words to me and ran away.

"Thank you."

I had never been so satisfied in my life with just two words as I was that day. Winona stayed another thirty minutes explaining to me how she had managed to make Fiona understand the reasons I was in prison. She also gave me news of how they were coping with degrading publicity and scandalization of the company and planned to move further after the case. Ned was still with her every step of the way and according to his resolute assertion, their lives were going to revert to its former standing and everything was going to be fine. I couldn't be any happier. She also conveyed a message that came directly from Esther's lips which was stated in simple words that if I expected a verbal expression of gratitude from her, I was very much mistaken. We laughed at this remark for a good five minutes, but our delight swiftly dwindled into sullen thoughts. It was time for her to leave, and leave she did.

I was back into the isolation of my enclosure as days changed to weeks and weeks into months, the recurrence of her visits became more distant with time and gradually came to a halt. The only contact I had with the outer world after spending seven months in jail was with Fiona as she would write to me every week telling me about her school, about Winona and Esther and how they worked to rebuild their lost business and stature. She also spoke to me about her future plans as she was going to graduate from high school in a short time and had myriad option to choose from for further education. She said she would only decide once she has my permission and advice on the matter and regardless of what Esther and Winona had to recommend or enforce upon her, she would only honor my opinion. Maybe it was her way to make me feel special or wanted and she might have noticed her mother and everyone who knew me once beginning to forget me now. But I advised her to follow the guidelines set by her mother and suggested that she would have a better and more relevant guidance on this matter as Winona had been through all of this. I had never attended college in my days and it was quite different back then, also I wouldn't know much about education locked in a prison compared to the family she had locked outside of it. It was very challenging as well as pleasant making her agree to things, as she still acted like an eight year old when I saw her for the first time on the street. I, on the other hand, always pictured her so. But eventually that exchange came to a stop and it wasn't a surprise as Fiona had mentioned in passing how Esther and Winona both compelled her against writing to me and kept her from replying to my letters. Though, she vowed to be persistent, I guess our letters never actually reached each other after a while as I continued writing. But when there was no response from her end for a long time, I stopped as well.

But then something came to pass that I had never imagined in my wildest dreams. It was a Saturday and I was supposed to see some visitors that noon. When I was given the names of those visitors, I was in sublime shock. I could barely walk as my legs were numb with excitement and my body trembled with nervousness. I entered the visiting room and saw... for the first time in my life I had cried, cried with tears streaming down my face. I had always thought I never had any emotions in me, or tears to let go of. But I was wrong and realized that no matter how hardened your outer shell is made to be, how impervious your emotions and hostile your heart is, there are moments in everyone's life that turn you inside out.

I saw Audrey.

Chapter Sixty-Two
❧❧❧

Audrey stood there in front of me with yearning in her eyes and sadness on her face trying to break through the subtle smile that still remained on her lips. She had aged, but not lost the resplendence of her soul and beauty of her benevolence. There were traces of white on her hairline and creases of overwork around her eyes and mouth. She appeared jaded and emaciated enduring years of rigorous survival. She stepped forward and welcomed me into an embrace which I quickly accepted and wept on her shoulders and she equally responded in likeness. I kissed her, again and again, like I had never kissed her before. I embraced her one more time and then kissed her some more. Our reunification was filled with tears and laughter, and love that was long forgotten but rekindled by fate and time. Our intimacy was checked by one of the officers standing at the door as he commanded us to sit down and take it easy. Audrey took me to a table and had me sit down, but we couldn't begin talking due to our ceaseless wailing.

"Stop crying, everybody is looking at you." I demanded of her.
"They're not looking at me, they're looking at you." She smiled through her tears.
"No, I'm not crying at all."
"Really?"
"Well, let me cry then."
"I didn't know there were tears in there somewhere."
"I've held them inside for too long, Audrey. Let them go today." I cried for some more time just holding her hands.

"George, how are you?" She finally broke through the awkward whimpering.

"You tell me. Oh God..." I had never called out to God or spoken his name ever before except when cursing, but somehow it slipped out of my lips unknowingly. Whether it was comfort you felt in saying His name, or perhaps the gratitude for the circumstances in life and how the game of fate turns out in favor or against you time after time. I said it. "You have changed so much."

"But you haven't changed a bit."

"No, I've grown old. A lot older. Hair's all white." I pointed out to my head.

"And that's almost about it." We chuckled.

"How did you know where I was? You don't know how much I... I can't believe you're here."

"I'm here. I'm right here." She spoke gathering herself.

"I love you so much."

Her smile faded and I felt her receding into unease.

"I'm sorry I said that, I didn't mean to-"

"You don't? Even now?"

"Audrey, you have no idea how happy I am to see you."

"You don't know how happy I am. Eighteen years. Eighteen years since I last saw you. You never came back, George? What did I do to deserve that?"

"Audrey... I thought you were better off without me there. I didn't want to repeat anything that happened. I knew if I stayed, something even worse might come upon you."

"Can you tell me anything worse than a wife waiting for her husband for eighteen years? Or rather anything worse than a daughter waiting for her father?"

"Our daughter?"

"Yes, your daughter, our daughter."

"But I thought Harry and you-"

"Please don't say that, George, please. You left Harry a responsibility and he did his best to make sure we lived. He's been like a brother to me that I wished I had. Your best friend wasn't going to betray you. How could you think that?"

I closed my eyes and didn't know what to say. The mistake had been committed, four lives had just paid the price for the fault of one.

"I came Audrey, I came and I saw you and our daughter. But just when I looked at her innocent face, I didn't want to enter your lives and... and cause anymore pain to her or to you. I'm sorry, Audrey. I was wrong all my life, I was wrong to begin with. It's all my fault."

"I waited for you all these years. Your friend waited for you, your daughter waited for you. In eighteen years she'd only known her father through pictures. I wanted to bring her along today, but I-"

"No, don't do that to me. I don't want her to see her father for the first time in prison. I won't be able to bear that. How is she? I'm sure she's just like you."

"I'll have to disagree with that, she has your temper."

Audrey showed me a picture of our daughter and she was indeed a spitting image of her mother, but I think she had my eyes. She was beautiful.

"I want to look into her eyes and ask for forgiveness."

"She had always waited for you, George. For years. And it was my fault that I kept giving her false hope that you may return one day. She's a grown lady now, knows my sadness at the mention of our separation. She doesn't ask about you any longer, but I know deep within, she still waits."

"I am the most unfortunate man in the world right now. Fate has just defeated me. The things that I longed for were right there back home and I never returned."

"I looked for you everywhere, George. I saw you on TV with some famous actress some years ago and I went to California searching for you. I managed to speak to her, Marilyn, but she said you had already left. She didn't know where. I begged her to tell me where you were, but she didn't know."

"How did you find me here?"

"Harry found out about the case you were involved in. He brought me here to you."

"Is he here?"

"He's outside. He wanted me to see you first. He's done his part."

"Can you ever forgive me, Audrey?"

"I was never angry with you, George."

"But I am." Harry was behind me and looked down at me furiously, a feigned countenance.

"Your friend is an idiot, stupid moron who doesn't know what to do with the good things given to him. All I can say is I'm sorry for everything I've done. And a friend never denies forgiveness."

"Don't give me lessons on friendship, you should take some."

I lowered my face and stood there hopeless but he suddenly hugged me and patted my back.

"It's wonderful to see you once more, buddy. You look terrible."

"So do you, and what's with this beer gut blowing up like a balloon?" I commented.

"Hey you never know when you might wanna impress the girls, besides it helps me stay afloat on the beach."

We cackled at that and sat down.

"No seriously, George, where were you for all these years? We waited. Audrey is a strong woman to take on all she has been through for the past years, raising a child on her own, taking care of her mother until she passed away. She was all alone, and you were nowhere in sight. She couldn't handle all that you left behind by herself, why didn't you come back?"

"I was lost, Harry. I didn't know where I was going or what I was doing. And when I finally returned to my senses, it was too late."

"It's never too late, to take on your responsibilities, to care for the family you left. It's never too late." Harry comforted me.

I held Audrey's hand and her gaze.

"I'm sorry."

"How long will you be here?" She asked.

"Six years. A little less now."

"It isn't over then. It still continues."

"I deserve this punishment for my actions, for my faults that hurt so many people. But I finally have this chance to repent for my sins. Maybe by doing this I would be able to forgive myself."

"If that is your decision, then I will stand by it. But when you've forgiven yourself, you might want to see your daughter once. Of course I can't force you to do that, you might have some other place to go, some other people to live with, maybe a family of your own now."

"Audrey, when I come out of here, I don't think I will have anywhere to go."

"Then I will wait."

She got up and kissed me on the cheek and left the room.

"I'll be there in a minute, Audrey." Harry stayed. Audrey nodded and left the hall.

"I can't even ask for her forgiveness, I've caused so much suffering. Harry, tell me everything that happened?"

"It was very hard, George. Very hard for her and your daughter. After she was born I went looking for you when you stopped all contact, from Ohio to New Mexico, I looked everywhere. I knew it was useless, but I tried. She wanted to come along but I said no. I managed to bring everything together and found them a home in a nice neighborhood. And it has been all about the wait since then. The wait that ended today. She went to California to ask that Marilyn McLord if she knew where you were. We saw you on TV, but she couldn't help us. Then I saw you in the papers about this case and I knew I had to take her to see you. If you had come back none of this would have happened, George. She is all alone now. Her mother lived with her, she passed away some time ago. Her sister is living in Miami. She doesn't have anyone but her daughter now. Come back to her."

"That's what I intend to do, Harry. But the thought of coming back brings memories of that dreadful night. I have blood on my hands."

"Don't even say that, George. He died of an accident, you didn't kill him."

"I don't know."

"You know, and I was there. You're not a murderer. Even the police didn't suspect he was murdered, it was deemed an accident. There were traces of alcohol everywhere as well as in his body. It wasn't difficult for them to get over it."

"It's been difficult for me."

"Come back to them, they need you. Forget about everything else. The only thing that matters is your family. Think about them."

I returned to my chamber and countless emotions were roiling inside of me. The contentment of uniting with my wife and friend after many years estrangement, but also the accompanying frustration of separation for such a long time. The result of this one foolishness had inflicted so much suffering and pain into our lives, but I had no right to complain as it was my own fault but the anguish was greater on them than it was on me. As night and time grew on me, I was forced to contemplate the true reasons why I escaped domesticity. What was I searching for? Was I right, or wrong? I had a lot of time to ruminate on the issues that lay before me, and I promised myself that if I were to find the answers to these questions and if I truly found myself culpable, I would leave this world and relieve the people associated with my existence once and for all. I had more than five years to think, and that was all I did for the duration of my sentence that remained.

Chapter Sixty-Three

The time of my repentance came to an end. Though, as short as six years seemed against the counts and measure of my faults, I couldn't make myself stay within those walls another moment as I was too eager to meet with the people who waited for me outside. I collected my belongings and signed the release forms and headed across, waving to many officers who had made acquaintance with my benign personality in the past years, and finally reached the last wire-fenced exit before I could step out into freedom. I stepped into freedom beyond the gates of the prison, but just as I came out, the delight that soared in my body and soul suddenly waned.

I stood upon the road that welcomed me to choose whichever direction I wanted to turn, but I saw no one awaiting that choice. No one had come to welcome me back into the free world or their lives. I was hurt at the sight of standing there all alone by myself. Was I not needed anymore? Didn't I exist for anyone? I stood amidst the nothingness of a single road that stretched miles both ways and asked me to choose the side I wanted to go. There was one side leading down south which would draw me away from everything I had before entering this prison and take me once more into the dark of loneliness, of sorrow and it could as well be my bane this time. I waited a little more hoping to see someone arrive, late perhaps. I feared being renounced yet again in life. But why wouldn't I? If this were true and done to me, it would be a just comeuppance for my acts against many. Did I expect Audrey to stand there with open arms to welcome me back into her world? After what I had done to her, could I expect anything different? But then whom shall I turn to, Marilyn? Who cares not where I am and what I have been through, who didn't even bother to search for me once I left her. And why should she? I had no place in her life, in her fame.

But Winona should have come. After all, I took this trouble upon myself for her. Well, not entirely for her, it was for Ned's safekeeping also, but she was a part of it and her honor was conserved. But did I really expect her to be there? Didn't I already have my answer some months into my prison time when she stopped visiting me? We weren't even married to begin with, for the sake of which relationship could I ask her to be mine? Weren't all my motives derived out of personal gain and pleasure? If I took the plight of prison upon myself, didn't I get rewarded for it equally in wealth and fame for the past years? I didn't do anybody a favor, or did I? The women who came in my life after Audrey, it was in my own selfishness that I stayed with them. It didn't solve any purpose for them to shelter someone like me. I wanted to be with Marilyn because I needed someone to share my days and sorrows with. I went with Winona because I had failed miserably and wanted some stability after all that had happened. They didn't come to me, I went to them. I then realized that I was wrong in expecting anything from anyone anymore.

But then I looked at the other side of the road that led north and back into the prolific environs of life and happiness that I was a part of not too long ago. And I was tempted to make one final endeavor at living again. I wanted to be amongst the rich, in company of an influential woman by my side and her mother to back us up. What difference does it make if we weren't officially married, not all relationships are contingent on such terms. When I shall return to their surprise, their delight would overcome their emotions and our lives would commence from newer beginnings. I shall be happy once more with them until the end.

But I felt my feet getting heavier as I trod that road. If my return in the lives of the people I wanted to go back to was just, then why did I stop to reconsider? Was there something wrong that needed to be contemplated, maybe a slight injustice? And even if I did decide to return, which family would I choose to be part of? The exuding wealth of the Warren family and the assurance of luxury and repose for the remaining days of my old age? The beauty of a rich woman, the restraints of a privileged mother, but also the love of a young daughter who had always treated me like her father?

But then there was another family, my own family. The only woman who had loved me unconditionally. The woman who was there with me in the lowest of my poverty and the acme of my affluence. The woman who had aged with time and troubles, but gained in love and kindness. The one who forgave me even after eighteen years of hardships, and our own daughter who had never seen the face of her father. Through the times she needed him the most, she lived in his absence. Now twenty-four years old, would she accept a man who abruptly appears out of darkness to put a claim on her mother, on her house, on her affection? Would she forgive a man who abandoned her for worthless mundane temptations that never lasted more than an eyeblink? I curse that I had brought these circumstances upon myself. It is human nature to falsely impute the blame for their mistakes to others, but I had no one I could reproach but myself. But is it really true? When we ascribe our faults to others, do we honestly justify ourselves? Could I, or any other person in my situation, blame others for all that was done?

What did I search for? If I said love, it wouldn't be true. I had love, I had true love. In the arms of Audrey I would have found everything if I didn't go mad with pride and wealth. If I said family, wouldn't I still be lying? The foundations of a family were laid, it was something I had to build, but I never stayed to construct. A child, the biggest lie I could tell myself was that I need a child, the love of a child. I knew I was going to have a child, my own daughter, but I still ran away. What for? To escape responsibility perhaps? Wasn't I too afraid to create a life or a family, didn't I ruin everything I had?

Friendship, loyalty, peace, I had it all. Harry, a man who kept his word for twenty-four years, that's almost a lifetime and he didn't even flinch the last time we met. What is loyalty if not the courage of a woman who endured loneliness for years, raised a child all on her own and never frowned in the process? What is peace if not the satisfaction of a home that shelters love, dedication and serenity under one roof? The content heart of an aging couple at the sight of their daughter who begins her own life, her own family. What is peace if not a restful life that has nothing more to accomplish, nothing more to prove, and is spent alongside your true love until the end of days? If I had desired of all of this and if I couldn't achieve it with what was given to me, then all the desires of my heart were false. My acts of altruism were a lie to veil my evil intentions to keep moving from one house to another, from one woman to another, from one love to another. I said I had gone in search of love; I already had it back home. I said I had gone in search of peace; have I found it yet? I was a liar and if I hadn't walked away from life in the first place, none of this would have happened. I would be a settled man now. Maybe not as rich and lavish as I wanted to be, maybe not as profoundly desired by others, but that isn't what I seek now. The folly of a young mind, the ruin of a whole life. The brevity of our inclinations is laughable, but we advocate them like our creed, to discover in the end how wrong we were. But what is more merciful and compassionate than your own conscience that forgives, and that one last want to live just once more. To love or more than that, be loved. To care, but more than that to be cared for. And I surrendered to my decision of going back. I had to make many things right, I had many people to apologize to. I had to return.

But then came the question of where. Who shall I return to? I couldn't just run off to New York abandoning everything I had here. What about Ned, the custodian of what I owned? He had fulfilled every responsibility I left him with. The least I could do was to return and thank him for his tasks. And Winona, the person who helped us through a difficult stage of work and life. Though, she might have forgotten about me, or wouldn't want to associate with an inmate anymore, still her motives were not at question here but mine. And what about Fiona, her love was true, her intent pure, would it be fair of me to leave without ever seeing her again? I was standing at the crossroads and this wasn't the first time I had encountered such predicament. I had good practice at tackling such situations. But the choice I faced this time was much more grave and daunting than any before. I guess even six years of prison weren't enough to answer these questions I had in my mind, so I had to leave it all to the good old thing known as time.

I started for the city and my first stop was Ackres Accounting. Yes, it was still there and I couldn't be more delighted to see my old friends again. I waited in the lobby as the receptionist informed the office and after some moments I saw Paola and Ned heading out the elevator with cheerful smiles. Paola had aged gracefully while Ned seemed almost the same as I saw him last at the prison. He hugged me and stayed there for quite some time and Paola waited her chance.

"That's enough of you two, there are others in line." Paola exclaimed. We parted with tearful laughs and I embraced Paola with a kiss on her cheek. "How are you, George? It's been ages."

"I'm back from the dead."

"Thank god for that." She smiled. "Now brush off that dust from your shoulders and change your clothes. It's about time."

"Let's go inside." Ned took me inside his office and we sat down together upon a couch.

"I see your office expands with time, Mr. Ackres. New faces, more space." I teased.

"Not just space, buddy, worries as well. I'm still knee-deep in the business, you know what that means." Ned lit up a cigar.

"I think I do, now. But I see you haven't cared for our most treasured asset right here. Has he been treating you well, Paola?"

"He's an average boss and I don't mind as long I get my measly paycheck." Paola joked.

"Oh yeah, go ahead and talk behind my back. Only, I'm still here."

"How are you, Paola? Tell me about you?" I turned to her.

"Oh, I'm still the same. Just gained a little weight around the belly and lost a lot around the house."

"Around the house?"

"The kids are all gone, all four of them. Moved out to the last one, all grown up. Now it's just me and my old man. Life changes so quick, it snaps right in front of your eyes."

"I know what you mean."

"The youngest one got married, last June. You missed it. I wish you could be there. Now I'm a grandmother of seven. I don't look that old, do I?"

"Not at all."

"Yeah, you go on with your lying. I'm thinking of retiring now. Have spoken to your friend right here about it many times. But he doesn't want to let me go."

"What can I say? I'm used to seeing old, idle people pestering me all day long." Ned taunted.

"I hear that, how about I don't show up tomorrow and see who sits idle then?"

"Oh, don't break his heart." I added.

The intercom rang in the room. Paola answered and was called out to the front.

"He doesn't have one, even the doctors couldn't locate it. You guys continue, I'm going to send in some coffee." Paola headed out while continuing the banter.

Ned looked at me and smiled. "It's so good to see you again, so good. I can't wait for us to get started. But as much as I would like you to step back into the ring again, I think you should take some time off. How about a vacation? I arrange everything, no worries."

"Nah, I'm too old to drain the troubles of my mind with a vacation. They're all in there, adamant as ever."

"Don't worry about anything. It's going to be just as before. Everything awaits you, George."

"I have to start from the beginning. A lot needs to be done, a lot needs to be said. Tell me everything that happened in these six years, Ned. What did I miss?"

"Well, everything would be a long story. But if we come to think of it, you didn't miss a thing, but you missed a lot."

"How are they? How is Winona?"

"Winona? You haven't met them?"

"No, I came straight to you. They haven't visited in a long time, five years to be exact. Fiona used to write to me, but she stopped as well shortly after six or seven months."

"Then I think you should see them. It's better that you do."

"Right."

"How about we go together? You are coming to my house, that's done and final. How about we stop by on our way?"

"Ned, you don't need to do that."

"Do what?"

"Take me to your house, I'm fine."

"You think Jennifer's going to let me sleep tonight if she finds out you're released and I didn't bring you over? You think so? George, she knows. And she knows well enough if that house still remains, it is because of you. Her son has seen his father for all these years because of you. I have cherished my son's childhood because of you."

"How old is he now?" I wiped away something that had just slipped down my eye.

"Your nephew is six. He would love to meet his godfather."

"What? I am?"

"Surprise, surprise."

"You are..."

"An asshole, right?"

"Not exactly what I was aiming for, but close."

"Good, let's go."

Chapter Sixty-Four

❧❧❧

I said goodbye to Paola and Ned drove me to the Warren residence. He stayed in the car as I approached the gates of the mansion. The concierge was surprised to see me but respected me enough to let me in with a joyous greeting. I asked how he was and his response was subtle and short. I walked the length of the driveway and reached the main entrance where I was greeted by more house attendants. I was ushered inside to the living room and I waited for Winona or anyone from the house to be called. After some delay, I saw Winona come down the stairs with a strange uneasiness and met me with evident discomfort.

"George, so nice of you to come." Her greeting was filled with an awkward oddity. I leaned in for a kiss and she hindered that gesture to a handshake. "Come, let's sit down." We went to the hall again and sat by each other.

"I wasn't expecting to see you here. The doorman let you in?" I struck a piercing look at her which she dismissed with a laugh. "I mean he usually calls in for permission to allow people in, he doesn't let everybody come in like that."

"Everybody?"

"Anyway, so you were just released from prison?"

"Two hours ago. Everything looks so different here. The house is changed."

"Many things are changed, many things will be. What are your plans now? What's next?"

"Is something wrong, Winona? Did I do something wrong in coming here?"

"It depends on how long you're planning to stay. Depends on what you're expecting of me."

"I don't know, Winona. I thought you were going to tell me."

"There's hardly anything I can tell you now, George. I don't think I can make decisions for you. It's your life."

"It was mine all this long, and I thought it was ours. Well, you only come to know the truth about people in good time. But for me that time happened to come quite late. Better late than never. How is Fiona? I'd like to meet her, if you don't mind."

"She isn't here anymore. She is studying abroad now."

"Abroad?"

"She had excellent grades in school, you know that. She found her interest in some subjects and had to travel in search for the right school."

"Abroad where?"

"Would you like some tea?"

"I don't want any tea, Winona. Where is she?"

"You don't need to know that. It's just some school. She's been there for quite some time now. She'll be coming back soon. But George, I don't think you should..."

The words were too big to be uttered from those lips.

"See her anymore?" I completed her sentence.

"You're wise enough to understand why."

"So are you."

"I am, that's why I don't want you to have anything to do with my daughter now. It doesn't matter why you were there, but you were in prison. That could hurt us in many ways. In fact it would be better if you-"

"Do not come here at all?"

"Yes." She lowered her eyes.

I arose from the couch. "She stopped writing to me some time after I left. Did you have anything to do with it?"

"I wasn't going to drive her into this correspondence, if that continued I don't know what she would do. Your opinion mattered to her more than ours. Do you think it would make me happy to hear her talk about you, write to you in all her free time? Everything else was just secondary to her. I stopped giving her your letters making her believe that you didn't write to her anymore. I had to make her forget you."

"I wasn't gone forever, Winona. I was going to come back."

"What for?"

I looked down at her and she held my stare.

"Now, I don't know what for. I don't see anything here that reminds me of what this was six years ago. Or anyone. At least your doorkeeper remembers and thinks of me better than you do. Well, I believe I'm done here. I loved you once, Winona. I really did. I had heard time changes people, I had even seen it once. But I thought everybody else was better than me. You proved me wrong, thanks for that. But if you have any emotions, any compassion left in you, tell Fiona that I came back to see her. Not you, her." I began to leave but I heard her call me again.

"Wait, George."

I turned and saw her whispering to her maid. The maid quickly ran up the stairs. She returned with a bundle of envelopes and handed them to her mistress.

"The letters you wrote to her. The ones she had, she wouldn't let go of and still has them. But these are the ones that never got to her."

I took the stack of envelopes. "I'm grateful for what you did. Really." I left the house and abandoned the memories of a past that had her in it there at the doorstep.

Just as I made my way back down the treelined driveway through the surrounding lush gardens, I heard a voice speak out of somewhere.

"Love is strangely foolish, you know. It makes you do silly things."

I stopped and glanced around and found Esther in her gardening attire. She brushed off the dirt from her covers and took off her mitts as she ambled closer.

"Love isn't anything but love, but you can't blame anyone if it isn't there. If it never was." I answered.

"Well, then I'd say it makes you blind. To see what's never there, and not see what is. I have seen you ruin a life for it, your life. What for?"

"For..."

"Admit it, you're wrong. We live in a world where respect is a legend, honor a myth and love a necessity. And it's been that way for ages. People who are too naive to misconstrue need for that thing you call love are hurt the most. And I see a living example standing before me. So look around you, young man, you still have a lot to learn."

"I wish I was given this wisdom six years ago."

"The need back then was different. But I warned you, if you would have listened, you would know better than to just give away yourself like that. But there's another question that needs answering. Was that your own conscience or love for the people who surrounded you that forced you down the path?"

"I'd say both."

"And so the consequence stands before you. A long road upon which you must travel alone."

I looked at the long driveway that waited before me. I started walking away from Esther and to the gates.

"She's at Cambridge. She's an honor student, quite renowned in her campus. It wouldn't be difficult to find her."

I turned. "Thank you." I continued on my way.

"Untie your blindfold if you will, so you don't fall... again."

I waved to her without looking back and kept going.

Ned drove me to his home as I spent the entire thirty minute trip brooding and resenting the time I had spent looking for compassion and love in a woman who had but an indifferent, insensitive heart. As we reached Ackres residence, I decided to deluge the past away and its effects from my mind and look forward to the novelty of life and what it held for me in store. I had the pleasure of seeing Jennifer again who hadn't changed in her congenial and kind personality and was also introduced to their six year old son who fidgeted around attired in a superman costume with a red cape dangling by his shoulders and leaped across couches and coffee tables. After some while of family talk, Ned excused himself from his wife and took me into his office. He poured me a drink and offered me a seat.

"What's the matter, George? You look disturbed." He had read my eyes very well. As much as I attempted to veil my dismay, he was able to surmise.

"Nothing's the matter, Ned."

"There's something bothering you and if you think you can get away without telling me then I'm footsteps away from locking us both inside the office until we talk it through. I have the whole night."

I still remained quiet.

"If you think I don't know what went on in there, you're wrong. I knew what was going to happen. I just wanted you to see for yourself."

"What did I see, Ned?"

"You saw deception in flesh. That's how it looks like. I have seen some selfish ingrates in my life, but this one beats them all to the dust."

"That's all right, Ned."

"It isn't all right. Hey, I'm no saint myself. I'm equally guilty of using you, but at least I'm here. You go in there and spend six godforsaken years in that prison for what? To hear all that shit when you return? I don't know what exactly she said to you, but I know it wasn't pleasant. Why did you go to prison? For her, for me, someone was going to take the beating, and you took it for all of us. I know what was brewing up there, I was the marked man. But you did me a favor even my own brother won't. If you ask for my life in return, it still wouldn't suffice. But that ungrateful woman, she's worse than a streetwalker, at least with them you know what you're buying."

"That's enough." I stood up in anger.

"You know that's your problem, the reason why you were hurt today. Because you don't know when to let go of your feelings for someone. Do you know why she didn't want you there anymore? She's back with her ex-husband."

I was shocked to hear this. I looked into his eyes and saw nothing but truth.

"Surprised? Well, that's the truth and thank mother wisdom for her trickery in it. Warren Constructions was acquired by the Bender Group. That's the best deal Winona could land under given circumstances, a small price to pay for more wealth as she still retains her stake in the company. It was a clever and a sensible deal, I'll give her that, to save the company from losing any more money or reputation in the market by selling its name. The Warrens got a new life. So, they now live happily ever after upon the remains of a man who suffered for them. I regret the day you stood in that court and took the blame upon you. It should have been us, I really wish with all my heart, it should have been us. We should have been punished for our greed. But I still thought she might have a little bit of humanity left in her to at least give you some respect when you come back. But I was wrong. They stopped the little one from writing to you, both of them, mother and daughter. Fiona told me that before she left, she used to give them her letters that never reached you and she never received yours. I pity that poor girl."

"When did you last see her?" I asked.

"She didn't tell you about her, did she?"

"No, her mother did."

"I saw her two years ago, maybe. That's one kid you should be proud of. But the differences between the three women of the house made her change countries. She couldn't stay with them anymore. After you left, the house wasn't any different than a lodge for her. She transferred to Cambridge about three years ago. Her mother didn't approve of your interference in her life, not even you writing to her. The way she asked for your counsel in everything, their differences just grew vast. One day it was one argument too many and she decided to leave everything behind. So, Europe it was."

"She returned the letters back to me that I wrote to her."

"It was a disaster while you were away. But that's over now and we have a lot of work to do. Start working on getting back, making you a businessman again."

"That's over, Ned. I'm done with that life now."

"What do you mean you're done?"

"I want to live in peace, all of that once again is too much for me."

"Don't do that to yourself, to me. You're giving up because she's not with you anymore?"

"I didn't have her when I started with you. I don't need her. But there comes a time when life becomes more important than work. I think I've reached that point now. I haven't told anyone this, but I will tell you. I have somewhere to go, someone to seek, and if it works out, I would be the happiest I've ever been in my entire existence."

"If it works out?" He raised his brows.

"Someone I've hurt, someone I loved."

"That's hard to believe, you hurting someone."

"We aren't born the way we die."

"If there's anything I can do for you?"

"You have, so much."

"But I'm still in indebted to you. And everything that you put in my care is still as you left it. It all awaits you. Your apartment, your cars, your bank accounts, although slightly declined in numbers, but enough for your desired future."

"Then hold onto them for a little while longer. I will ask for your help regarding all that one more time."

"I'm always there for you, always."

"Thank you, Ned."

"There are no thank yous in friendship. You taught me that."

I hugged him.

"Wouldn't you stay for the night?"

"I don't want to be late. It is a twelve hour trip."

"But tell me something, will you find peace and happiness there?"

"That's why I intend to go."

"Then go and I hope you never come back here."

Chapter Sixty-Five
ৎৡৎৡৎৡ

I wasn't interested in going to the bank and reinstating my accounts yet, so whatever money I had in my pocket I used that to purchase a train ticket to New York. I was going back to see my family once more. The splendor of my excitement was unfathomable. A wordless delight that filled my heart as long as that twelve hour overnight trip lasted. I disembarked at Penn Station, New York around one thirty in the afternoon and straightaway headed for the address in New Hyde Park that Audrey once handed to me to come find her if I wished. The cab ride was another forty minutes but when I reached my destination with a bouquet of flowers that I had collected on my way here, I was reminded of a similar circumstance that changed our lives years ago. But I was adamant this time not to deviate from my decision, hence, wrecking everything once again.

I stood at the door, rang the bell and waited. The door opened and a shocked woman stood there wrapped in her Christmas apron and her hands daubed in some chocolate mixture.

"Audrey."

"George, oh goodness." She almost stumbled back at the sight but then smiled nervously and began to welcome me inside and we kissed. She had grown a little older now but the mesmerizing smile always remained unscathed. "I'm sorry I was just about to bake some Christmas cakes."

"That's all right, actually I'm sorry that I didn't call before."

"You don't have to call to come home."

I just gazed at her.

"Come on in, would you shut that door please for me." I did. "I'm making you do chores already."

"I'd love to."

"Make yourself comfortable, I'll be right back."

I entered a small living room to the side of the foyer and found a lot of memories inside of it. Loads of pictures that hung on the walls and filled the mantle along with every table top in the room. I looked out the window at the street outside and began to perch on the couch that was right in front but stopped as my eyes fell upon something. I went closer and saw a lot of accolades and certificates of excellence in great numbers. Student of the year, junior high state synchronized swimming championship, high school volleyball state winners trophy, all belonged to one engraved name; Hope H. Bailey. Tears slipped down my eyes and I couldn't stand there anymore as I felt weak in my legs and sat down. I looked around the house and I saw nothing but peace, and contentment. Even in marginal conditions and meager earnings, Audrey had made a home that drew me towards it. It did not have the cold of the opulence that massive halls and mansions possessed, but had the warmth of scarce, but satisfactory living. It did not offer the luxuries of wealth brought to your disposal on command by attendants, bu t it had the devotion to keep the members of the household together and engaged in helping each other.

"George, would you like to drink some coffee? I know it's cold out there."

"Thank you, I'll have some." I wiped off the tears from my face and found Audrey coming towards me with a cup of coffee. She kept it on the table.

"I'm sorry for all this mess. It's Christmas time and things get a little out of hands during."

"That's all right. It looks like a home."

"Hope is very enthusiastic about festivities. She actually conducts all these celebrations. She would invite so many friends and relatives and make it a family gathering. Whether it's Thanksgiving or Christmas, she's always on the lookout for a reason to bring everyone together."

"Hope, that is her name?"

"Yes, I couldn't think of a better one than this. She is my hope. Hope that kept me alive, kept me breathing."

"She is a family girl then?"

"I made her that way. I don't know if it's good for her or bad, but I didn't want her to feel alone the way I did. I used to do that when she was little, just gather close friends and family and make her feel good."

"I wish I could be here to see all that."

"Me too."

"So how's everybody in your relations?"

"My mother passed away a long time ago. And Grace lives in Miami now, she would be coming over for Christmas with her family."

"Hope invited her?"

"Who else?"

"That's nice. She takes care of you?"

"She is the reason I lived after you left, George. I had no other purpose."

"It's all my fault, everything that happened."

"Hush, don't say that anymore. It's over, forgotten." She held my hand and I smiled.

"I see she is into sports as well."

"Oh, she's a darling. Never gave me any headaches growing up, especially from school. Good grades always, sports, science, maths, she's very good at maths. I guess she takes after you on that." We laughed. "She's in college now, NYU. I couldn't afford it, but your daughter is so good at studies she received a scholarship for further education."

"What's her major?"

"English and Comparative Literature."

"Oh boy, she way ahead of us then."

"Yes, she is. It's the law of nature, I suppose. To steal happiness from you in one relationship and give it back to you in abundance through the other."

"Maybe she wouldn't have turned out to be so good if I stayed."

"George, a child is a responsibility most difficult to handle. But together we would have reared her the same way she is."

"No Audrey, I am not as good as you are. And I don't even need to prove anything in argument, it's all there. You and I both know it."

"Let's forget about it."

"You have a heart of gold, Audrey. You may forgive me, but I can't."

"Then what do you mean to do? Curse yourself to death? If you keep on living in the past, how will you look at the future? You're done with everything now, you've spent time in jail. There couldn't be any greater self-punishment. I know why you took on the blame upon yourself, to save others. You have cleansed your soul, your sins."

I began to weep, she took my face in her hands. "Look at me, let it go. It will only hurt you, let it go." I nodded and embraced her. My strength gained space inside of me and I felt better, we parted.

"When is she coming home?"

"Maybe in a couple of minutes. You can't wait to see her, can you?"

"I have waited for all this time. Not anymore."

We conversed more about our past lives and she showed me around the house. After a while we decided to take a stroll out on the street while we waited for Hope. I came to know that Harry got married some years ago and adopted a son named Curtis, also nicknamed Junior. He was thirteen and the delight of their lives.

We had just gotten inside the house and into the kitchen for another cup of hot coffee when the doorbell rang.

"That must be her." Audrey began to move to the door. "Aren't you coming?"

"I think I will..." I was frozen with excitement.

"Okay."

I heard her opening the door and someone entering inside. I heard sounds of their voices.

"How was your day honey?"

"You know there's no service between Times Square and sixty-first. I had to get a shuttle bus."

"What happened?"

"Track work, what else. It's been a lifetime and they still haven't figured out what to do with the subways. Anyway, guess who's coming for Christmas to our school."

"Who?"

"Frestonaye DuPont."

"Who is that? That's a tough name to pronounce."

"She is one of the most famous fiction writers of all time, ma. Don't tell me you haven't heard of her."

"Well, you know me. All right, come into the living room, I have something to tell you. Have a seat inside and stay there."

"Okay. Now I'm not going to get the keys to my new car, am I?"

"For that you need to wait a little longer. Just stay there."

"Okay, okay. I'm going."

Audrey came to the kitchen and held my hand and took me towards the living. I stopped just before entering. I didn't have the courage to see her.

"Hope, I want you to meet someone."

Hope arose from the couch and looked at her expectantly, her eyes were brightly wide and a smile spread across her face. She looked at me and suddenly went dull.

"Hope, this is your father."

Her breaths grew shallow and heavier. She stood there like a stone and glowered. A long pause followed.

"Nice to meet you." A fake smile quickly vanished from Hope's face. "When are you leaving?" She uttered in a somber voice.

"Hope." Audrey reprimanded.

"No, you didn't ask him the last time he ran away, I'd rather like to know and be prepared to wake up and not find him one morning. What's the harm in that?"

"Hope, he's returned to us now." Audrey confirmed.

"Returned? Why? Because all of sudden we've come across a phase in life that we're in such a direful need of him? What is it that we don't have, ma? You need money? I can get a job and bring money to this house. You need love, I can assure you I can love you way more than he can. At least I wouldn't betray you like he did."

"He's your father, you waited for him once."

"Once. I did, I was what? Four, five, six, seven, eight, you want me to keep going? I'm going to be twenty-four now. You know, sir, in life you get used to things. You get used to people, you get used to seeing them there for you and you get used to not seeing them there at all. I've gotten used to my mother being there for me, and she's all I need. No one else. So, please don't try to change anything now, it's too late for me. And yes, I'm not going to call you dad or papa, you're a stranger to me and that's how it will stay."

Hope shoved through and began ascending the stairs.

"Don't walk away from us, Hope. I didn't raise you to behave like this."

Hope turned and was in tears by now. She came back down.

"Don't you see it, ma? He has nowhere else to go now that's why he is here. He wouldn't be here if he had a younger woman to return to or a luxurious house."

Audrey slapped her on the face.

"Audrey." I objected.

"Don't you say a word to my mother." Hope thundered at me then held her cheek and began crying. "You're going to hit me because of him? Who never took a moment out of his rich, important life to ask whether you were alive or dead? Let's forget about you, how about me? I am still his daughter, right? Or you slept with someone else?"

"Don't say that Hope." I interrupted.

"You stay out of this, it is between me and my mother. No stranger has the right to interfere in our matters. So, if I am really his daughter, did he ever take a moment to ask how I was, how I lived, how I grew up? He hated you, okay fine. But he hated me as well? He didn't want to come back, fine. He could have at least written, called, or messaged me. He knew I was alive, didn't he? Or you thought I died at birth?"

"I'm sorry, Hope. I'm sorry I came here."

"No, you're not. I'm sorry that I actually spent years of my childhood waiting for a man like you. I waited, I waited long enough, and I watched her die day by day. The way she worked, three jobs at a time, seven days a week, sixteen hours every day, to make me what I am. Where is your participation in all that? I didn't see you chipping in anywhere. It's supposed to be a family. I don't think you know what it means. And now you come barging into our lives and expect us to gather around and worship you, accommodate you in our house, our hearts, why? There must be a reason? You got kicked out of your fancy home in Charlotte and can't find an open door anywhere else? And let me tell you something, if we can get by twenty-four years of our lives without you, we can do just as well for the next twenty-four. She was alone back then, but now she has me and we don't need anyone else. So, go back to where you came from and even if she allows you to stay, this is her house, she may have anyone come live with us if she wants. But if that happens, don't expect to see me here ever again."

She ran up the stairs and slammed the door shut.

"She doesn't mean that, George." Audrey was embarrassed as she held my arm.

"I know, I know, she doesn't. She is your daughter."

"I'm going to speak to her."

"No, wait, let her be. She's angry right now, don't upset her more."

"She isn't like that."

"I know, but I'm glad about one thing. She loves you so much. I wish I could share a little part of it, but... if I am the reason why she loves you that much, I'm happy to stay away from both of you for her to love you even more."

"No, George. She's just confused right now, to see you all of a sudden. She doesn't know how to accept it, how to react to it. She's shaken to the core."

"She's young, Audrey. At this age every impulsive decision she makes will seem right to her. I cannot see her leave you, I can't see her leave this house because if she steps out of that door, there is something that will keep her from returning, always. I know that, I've been through it. You know what blood runs in her, she's my daughter after all. If that happens I will never forgive myself, and we would never find her again. Let her calm down, it may take days, maybe months. But the day she asks to see her father again would be the happiest day of my life and I will wait for that day."

"I'm sure that will happen. I will talk to her and make her understand."

"I will wait." I receded to the door.

"Where are you going?"

"Some place I could wait until she accepts me, for you to come and bring me home."

"Don't leave, George. Not now, not again."

"This time I leave to keep this home together. I will see you again."

"Yes, you will. Definitely."

I kissed her and left the house, took the LIRR from the station nearby and came back to the city. I was quick to leave Audrey but I hadn't really thought where I was going to go, and just as I strode the streets of Midtown thinking about my next few days, the night prevailed around me and light snow caressed the length of my topcoat. I had traveled some distance from Midtown in search for affordable lodging and rented a room at a corner sublet which was quite a tall building at first sight, but the deplorable interior was disgusting enough. Well, I wasn't planning to stay very long, so I took a room and requested it to be on the top floor so I could breathe, which was made possible with a twenty dollar surcharge. I collected a to-go order of spaghetti and meatballs from a small Italian restaurant across the street before I went up to my unit. And there I stayed the night.

Chapter Sixty-Six
ç§ç§ç§

"And that was, if I'm not mistaken, two days ago?" Louise inquired quite certain in her conjecture.

"Yes."

"So, this is what it all came down to?"

"Yeah, right back where I started. All by myself. I blame no one but myself for all that happened. It wouldn't be fair. I have matured enough to accept my faults. But I'm pleased with one aspect in all this mess. The people I've encountered so far and been a part of their lives, all of them are happy. In their own way, in their own lives, they are content. Even those I had left miserable through my errors, they have gathered themselves together and built their lives. No one is alone anymore."

"Except one." She added. I laughed. "You know George, I thought I had seen it all. The sorrows, the joys, the tears and smiles, but in life you sometimes come across people who just shock you with their stories. You are one of them. And I don't say this out of commiseration or empathy for you, I say this because you simply surprised me with what you have endured. I cannot judge whether your decisions in life were right or wrong, but you have survived a lot and this makes me want to, I don't know, congratulate you or commend you for what you've seen and done for others or even yourself. You are a strong man to yet be alive after all and so much of it."

"Thank you."

"I know you haven't heard this from any of the people you've helped in life, but I will say this to you on their behalf; *thank you*. As far as your wife and daughter are concerned, they will forgive. I give you my word."

"I am alive only to see that day."

"Where are you going to go from here?"

"One last promise needs to be taken care of."

"The theater?"

"Yes."

Just as I finished, an announcement sounded on the speakers. We were about to reach Grand Junction, Colorado in 10 minutes. Louise was about to depart my life as well.

"Well, that's my stop."

"It is, isn't it?"

"You're a strong man, I know you can handle it well."

I laughed. "Yes, I hope so."

"You know when I entered this bus back in New York and I saw you sitting there with a solemn look on your face, I knew I had to sit with you. And I intentionally exchanged seats with this young couple so I could talk to you. Make you smile, maybe I didn't know if I'd be successful, but I wanted to try. And boy, I did."

"Well, you excelled at what you intended."

"Did I?"

"Yes, I didn't even notice this long journey in all that time we spent together, and now it seems it ended too soon."

"Then I'm glad."

The bus pulled into the parking and passengers began stepping out for another respite. I assisted Louise in gathering her belongings that were taken out of her handbag for usage which included her glasses, pack of peanuts, handkerchief and an asthma inhaler. I collected her small luggage bag from the compartment above the seats and followed her out of the bus. She went on to the public phone and ringed her son as she didn't have a cell phone. She returned after a moment.

"He says he's on his way. Not more than five minutes."

"That's good." I was a little down to watch her leave.

"Here." She extracted a little note from her handbag and gave it to me. "If you ever come back to New York, I hope you make a trip to my home. Maybe you can tell me how it went after this."

"I hope I have something to tell."

"I'm sure you will."

"You know, I have something to say to you as well."

"What is it?"

"When you first sat by my side on that bus, I hated it. I hated you and I hated the fact that I'll have to share this ride with a cranky old woman. That's a basic belief that all old people are quite irritating and annoying, we all think so."

"Oh, the younger you mean?"

"Yeah."

"I understand, and sometimes we are."

"But, you changed that. I think no matter how steadfast we are in our beliefs, somewhere down the line there's always someone who can change our thinking completely around. This trip was that for me, you were that person for me. And I can't say I have enjoyed a three day bus ride more than this ever. I loved your company, and I wish it could last longer than this."

A car horn sounded in the background. A man stepped out from a black metallic Dodge Challenger. He was suited, tall, groomed. He waved while Louise looked back at him.

"Well, that's him. That's my son."

"It was wonderful to know you, Louise."

"It was wonderful to know you, George. And I believe I can say that with utmost certainty. Take care now."

We embraced and parted. I handed her small wheeled luggage over. She began to move away. Stopped and came back one last time.

"Do not lose hope. I read this somewhere or maybe heard it, the expansion of the word Hope. Hold on, pain ends." She left after that and met with her son with great emotions. I waited and watched her reunite with her beloved son once more, the family awaited. He loaded her luggage in the back and they both got inside the car. She rolled down the window and waved, I smiled and waved back. The car moved further and went onto the road and faded from my view.

I shuffled back to the food court bought my lunch for the last four dollars that I had left and continued on.

જ્જ્જ

I had reached Los Angeles Bus Terminal forty minutes after ten and it was dark and cold outside with a slight drizzle that soaked everything lustrous. I was still ten-twelve miles from my destination, from the magnificence of Hollywood. But I was out of money to travel in convenience any further, so I troubled the most trusted part of my body to carry me there, my lower extremities. I began walking in the dead of the night, taking local roads one after another as I was quite familiar with navigating that part of the county. About three miles down the journey, I began to feel weary and attempted to hitchhike. Cars, as scarce as they were at the time, rushed by without a second look to my signal and I continued to trudge. Finally a construction ram truck came to stop a little further and flicked his beams to indicate. I scrambled up to the pick-up and got in the passenger side. I thanked the man, who seemingly returned from a night shift as his sleep laden and squinting eyes delineated, so did his jacket that had spots of fresh white paint all over it making it almost seem like a pattern. He asked my destination and informed me that he lived uptown but could drop me on the way there. And he was true to his word as we arrived in the area within minutes and I got off at Hollywood Boulevard. I waved to him as he drove away and I went further up the road to that one promise that was left unfulfilled. I knew when I reached my destination, I would definitely encounter the person I yearned to see as it was too early to be in bed, and it was Friday night so probably it would be lights and dazzle still. I walked a couple blocks and turned a few corners and finally stood before the place.

It was a grand edifice but just as I left it years ago. I glanced at the flashing lights heartily and presented the usher with a battered visiting card that I held onto for so long. He allowed me inside, I didn't exactly know why, but somehow I felt he recognized me. I made my way inside and traversed the familiar halls, corridors and passageways and finally reached the door. I knocked twice and waited. The door opened after a pause and a face appeared that was equally surprised to see me as I was to see him.

Mr. Durdawk, now years older, stood with a string of expressions across his visage. He was delighted, he was startled, he was smiling, he was astonished, and it all occurred at the same time. I embraced the aging man to save him any further shock fearing his weak heart and frail health. But he was stronger than I expected as he squeezed me with the strength of a twenty-five year old.

"How are you, my lad?"

"I'm all better now."

"It's wonderful to see you, and I mean it."

"You too, sir. I'm so glad to see you."

"You gave me a surprise of a lifetime."

"I hope it's a pleasant one."

"In my age, a visit from an old friend is always pleasant. You will understand this twenty years from now."

"You don't look a day older than... than forty."

"Oh there, I caught your lies. You should never think twice when trying to flatter an old man about his age. A compliment with a pause, is always false. But I am worse inside than what I look on the outside. Have a chair, let me pour you a drink. Oh, I can't believe you're here."

"I made a promise to you once, I had to come back."

"Well, you might have to remind me of that promise as my memory isn't as sharp as my looks, but we'd have a lot more time to discuss that. First, tell me how you have been, and where for all these years?"

"Around. Definitely not stationary. It also includes a duration of six years in prison."

"Prison? What for?"

"Mistakes. Yes, I'd say mistakes now, as I came to learn it wasn't love. The people I thought would stand there for me were only there to push me off, and then leave."

"I think I am familiar with what you intend to say. I have seen it happen more than once in my life as well."

"But that's me, tell me about you, sir. How is Mrs. Durdawk?"

"Oh, the old woman wouldn't listen to anybody. Didn't have anything to blame but herself for not heeding her doctor's caution. Paid for it after all."

"I am so sorry to hear that. When did it happen?"

"When did what happen?"

"She..." I stood there in perplexed silence.

"Oh, you think she died? Oh no, not that old vamp, she's a fighter. Though, bedridden now, but she still breathes. She already had asthma, now mingle that with high blood pressure and heart trouble. What do you have? A sick old woman. But she still hasn't abandoned her dictatorship around the house. She still subjugates the help right from her king size bed in the room, howling at and afflicting the poor people."

"You're just saying that, she was such a sweet person."

"Oh, you haven't lived with her, or you wouldn't speak so cordially of her. No, you're right. She is a sweetheart, but can't do much now. If you wish, come and see her one day. She'd like to see you again."

"I will definitely come."

A knock on the door brought someone inside with a message.

"Mr. Durdawk, we're almost finished with our third act."

"Yes, I'll be in there. Handle the rest of the show, will you?"

"Yes, sir."

The man exited and I turned back to Durdawk.

"How is the theater going?"

"I wouldn't complain at all. Your coming here was like an avalanche of success which never stopped sliding down the mountain. I still haven't reached the bottom yet."

"May you never."

"Marilyn somewhat triggered a revolution amidst performers to undertake stage, as they finally realized that there is renown in theater as well. I have also used the capital and influence gained from that success to lure some a-list movie stars to grace my stage randomly. It has been quite amusing since you came in our lives, George. I wish we had remained the way we began, with you, with Marilyn. But good things are meant to fade."

"Isn't that the truth?"

I rummaged my bag and found a sheaf of papers and I placed it upon his table.

"And this is?"

"You asked me if I had something to say, I should write it down. My father was a true storyteller, you believed I couldn't be any different. Well, this is my life on paper. I wrote it for you. I fulfilled my promise."

"Marvelous. I knew you would one day follow your father's footsteps. Then it is good and final, we get to work once again, you and I, together?"

"This time, it's just you, sir. I will watch from the back."

"Oh you, I will draw you in. I will make this play the best of my life and I will force you to come and join us. I am going to make this the production of the year. You just wait and watch."

"Wait, I will, Mr. Durdawk. Wait, I will."

Chapter Sixty-Seven
৯৯৯

As a few months passed and I began the term of painful anticipation which was harder on my soul than the jail sentence I had served recently, I suddenly had a realization that made me consider the act of disregard and neglect I had committed against someone who was one of the few who never abandoned me. Fiona had just come into my thoughts and her innocent face reminded me of all the things we had promised each other. It would be unfair of me to simply ignore and not even see her once after my prison term. I called up Ned and questioned the possibilities of visiting her university and seeing her. He assured me he would make all possible arrangements for me to travel abroad and visit. I waited for his call and within three days he had me setup with a flight, a hotel to stay overnight and also messaged Fiona about my visit. I was elated at the sound of that news and packed a little luggage with a few belongings to leave at once.

Two days later I found myself flying off to Heathrow Airport without any difficulties or hindrances as Ned had taken care of the passport and a temporary entry visa with the help of his attorneys. For the ten hours of flight time, I could only think of the things I wanted to discuss with Fiona and speak to her about the past six years that had changed so much of the Warren family. And in those thoughts, the travel seemed brief as I landed at the airport and took a taxi to Cambridge University right away.

I met with a campus administrator in her office and requested to see Fiona Warren. She initially questioned me my relationship to the student and was quite unwilling to grant the meeting, but as I explained to her the gravity of my visit, she conceded. I was told to wait as Fiona was in a lecture class and after twenty minutes of excited expectation, I saw the door of her office opened once again and an eight year old made her way through. She came to a sudden stop finding me inside, as her face went from shocked to jubilant and then all emotional. She rushed forward into my arms and embraced me. I just realized that my eight year old Fiona had grown into a twenty-two year old lady now. She was taller, stronger, wiser, but had the same heart that I left her with years ago, giving into tears even at the most smallest of things. But this meeting was no small thing for me, and I guess it wasn't for her either.

Fiona and I walked out of the building to the green, expansive campus ground and found a bench to alight upon. She had cleaned up her face of her tears, so did I and we both were finally able to speak.

"You've grown so much. Coming here I was just imagining how you must have changed. But I find you just the same, a lady now, not a teenager anymore. But just as I last saw you years ago."

"Were you mad at me that I didn't come to see you in prison more often?"

"No. That's no reason to be mad at someone. A prison is supposed to make you feel separated from the people you love. It never fails to do that. Besides, I never wanted you to come there at all. That place wasn't for someone so young."

"Not even to see you?"

"The day you did was the happiest I'd ever been in all the six years I spent there."

"Sometimes I wish I could just turn back the time to the way we were. If I could stay the same age, I would. But I want to relive that time over and over again, to see us back together."

"We are, aren't we? Both of us, just as we were?"

"But there's one missing."

"It gets increasingly difficult to bring some people back no matter how hard you try. They're so far away, you can hardly see them."

"Can't we do anything to change it?" She was sincere in her longing.

"Maybe, but that will require me to degrade myself to a very lowly state. To go back into a house that doesn't welcome me anymore."

"I can never ask you to do that."

"I know you won't. And there's no use in trying to go back where you're not needed. What made you think I would be mad at you?"

"You stopped writing to me."

"Do you really think I did?"

"She didn't want me to write to you after you left. I came to know my letters weren't being sent when I found one in the trash. The last of the letters I wrote I would secretly mail them out with the help of some friends, but then you stopped. Did you forget about me?"

"Forget you? I couldn't do that if I were to stay in that prison for the rest of my life. I wrote to you almost every week, kept writing for a very long time, but I stopped receiving your letters. I knew someone didn't like that we wrote to each other. My letters couldn't reach you, and yours couldn't reach me."

I retrieved a pack of envelopes and handed them over. She took those letters in surprise and sifted through the bunch. She looked up at me and tears filled her eyes again.

"I could never forget you." I wiped away the tears under her eyes.

"I hate her for this."

"No, Fiona. I will not hear that word from your lips. I know in rage and anger you say those things, but I will not have you mean it at all. Your mother has done a lot for you, her whole life she's just thought about you and no one else. Not even me. You cannot hate her even if you tried. It is a very difficult word to hear, not many people can live with that. You wouldn't know the way it hurts the one who hears it, has to live with it. It might just be a way to express anger for the one who says it, but... don't say it again, to your mother or anyone you've loved. There is no place for hatred in that heart of yours, I know."

"I never thought mom could change so much in so little time."

"You shouldn't have left home."

"It was difficult for me to breathe that air. Everything that went on in that house was strange, I never thought she would do all of those things just for money, business, reputation. Ungrateful, that's what they were for everything you did. One instance after another, they just wanted to eradicate your memory from that house, from me. But I couldn't, and I ran away."

"Running away is never the answer, Fiona. Believe me because I know all about leaving everything behind."

"Then why did you leave? Why did you ruin everything we had?"

"I needed to. If I hadn't, another family might have been ruined. And living with that guilt would have destroyed me inside."

"I don't care. At least we'd be together."

"You can never build upon ruins, Fiona, whether it's yours or someone else's. You know this better than I do. You must have an even surface to build something that lasts a lifetime, right? I couldn't do that to a friend. Do you think I was wrong?"

She began whimpering, concealing her face in her hands. "Why do you always have to be right? Why do you always have to look out for others and not yourself?"

"Because that's what we're meant to do. I wasn't like this, Fiona. I made my mistakes, but correcting those mistakes is the only answer to your guilt, your anger. And that's what you're going to do."

"Me?" She looked up.

"You made me a promise once, do you remember?"

"I don't want to remember." She frowned like a child, then spoke softly. "That I should love them no matter what?"

"So, you do remember."

"I remember everything you told and asked of me."

"Will you keep your promise then?"

Fiona remained silent for a long pause.

"If I asked you to?" I added.

"You broke your promise."

"I did, but I'm happy that I did. Life would have been worse if I didn't."

"Are you sure about that?"

I kissed her forehead. "You are pure at heart, Fiona. I know you can't hate anyone. What your mother did is forgotten. I forgive her, I ask you to forgive her too."

"Then come back with me, we'll make our home together, all three of us. I'll forgive her."

"Forgiveness is unconditional. It should be absolute or it'll be incomplete. Your mother is happy now, I believe she is. And your father is back, you should be there with them."

"He wasn't there when I needed him."

"Please don't say that, he is still your father and nothing can change it. Will you forgive them for me?"

"Will you come with me then?"

"Fiona, my path is changed now. I look for forgiveness myself. Will you keep me waiting as well?"

"I don't understand."

"I told you the day you came to see me in prison was the happiest day of my life. There was just one other day a similar thing happened, when my wife came."

"Your wife?" She gazed into my eyes and I wanted them to appear as honest as they could.

An hour had passed and I kept the truth of my life before her. In honest words I narrated how I had left my family before and abandoned them and that I now waited for their forgiveness so we could be together again. She was in tears by the end of it.

"I never imagined you could have a family of your own, your own daughter."

"I have two daughters, one who's not forgiven me yet and the other who will because I asked her to."

She smiled. "She's mad at you?"

"She is angry with me," I continued, "and she is right. I have made many mistakes against her and my wife. But I cannot see this repeated again, Fiona. Will you give me that part of peace I desire? Please..."

She took my hand in hers, "I will do what you've asked. In fact, I will return to them if it makes you happy."

"I want you to be happy in your decision as well. Fiona, no one can attain true contentment all alone, there is a reason why families were created. And no matter how much you fight with each other, or are mad at each other, or even if you don't speak to each other at all, by the end of the day we all sit down and thank someone for bringing us together. That is the strength of a family, of people who are united. You separated yourself from them because of me, now I'm with you. That anger has no place now, it has no substance. The reason behind it is over. And if I'm here with you, why would you deny them the delight of having their daughter with them? You don't know how happy it makes us parents to see our children there, close to us."

"But you're not there."

"For that I have already given you two reasons; a house where I cannot return and my past. If I come with you, the purpose of my life which I seek now would be defeated. And I have no place in that house, you should understand that. I will remain yours even when I'm gone, but I can never be hers."

She took some time to grasp that, then agreed. "You're right."

"But I would be the happiest man in the world if you return home. For me."

She didn't answer, just held on to my hand and wept. I embraced her and kissed her forehead. I knew she wouldn't refuse.

Chapter Sixty-Eight

With Fiona's promise to return home once her semester ends and make amends with her mother, I finally had peace from their end. Returning from that visit I waited for the other half of peace I desired, waited for something I hoped to recover somewhere down the road but never trusted. Recover the lost love of a daughter, recover the longed-for companionship of a woman who was more than a wife to me. Time went on as I slept with my despair every night and breathed it every day. I was yet again afraid of hearing a denial that might come from Hope if I tried reaching them again and so I procrastinated contacting them for many months. But in this time I found Mr. Durdawk descend upon his word and for the next five months I saw him prepare and develop into production the play that I wrote for him. Just as my life was being transmuted into dramatic reality of stage, I incurred a thought to write another account of myself which would be much more truthful, answering the verisimilitude of life and free of any superfluous fabrications. This will be one truth that I would want to leave my daughter with and implore her to read thoroughly, if she may, and understand her father, the man who searches her forgiveness. I intend to be honest in these writings and bring memories into words to the best of my ability. I will admit to my mistakes, I will concede to my faults and I will state sincerely every important phase of my existence that somehow shaped my life before this point and brought me here today. I do not plan to influence or convince her to love me without reason, I leave that to her own discretion. I do not try to impress her by writing about myself, being that she is a Literature student and might have read hundreds of autobiographies and liked and disliked them. I just wanted her to have something to remember me by. Maybe years from now when she wonders about her father and what kind of a man he was, this would make a good read and probably make her realize that her father wasn't too bad after all.

I took a couple of months to write my life on paper as I watched the preparations for my play furthered into production during that time. And it was just about one day when it premiered at the theater on Friday night and saw a crowd of enthusiasts come to witness it. I sat in the last seat of the back row and watched people react to every minute of that three hour long show. I saw them content, I saw them cry, I saw smiles, I saw sorrow, I heard cheers of joy and grunts of disgust, all emerging from that one set of crowd. Mr. Durdawk once told me that the best plays are those able to elicit every kind of emotion from the audience. I think I had managed to do that. The play continued for seven months at the theater making it a successful run, and I had ample time to finish my memoir, though, I knew it couldn't be finished until the last breath I drew. It was the final day of the run, Sunday night, and the theater still saw a good amount of people in pews. I took my regular seat in the darkness of the rear and saw the years of my life depicted in three acts of a stage play. There couldn't be a better time or opportunity to delve into the past and consider the seminal faults of my life as my actions were enacted before me.

The first act was the puerile and impetuous phase when I didn't know what to do with the things I had. I had love, I had loyalty and friendship, and there couldn't be a bigger fool who would let it all slip away in fervent madness of greed, lust and anger. But I did, and in the quick rage of my actions I didn't even realize that these would finally prove to be the things I would long for later in life. I was wrong to run away, I was wrong to abandon my wife and my child. If I wanted love it was right there for me, but I didn't see it. If I wanted a stable, settled life, it was still there but all gambled against an uncontrollable want for women and money. I regret that now, and that man who's committing all these mistakes right there on stage, I want to go to him and shake him out of his belief that everything will eventually turn out to be in his favor. It never does, fate and time does not allow that and we're slaves to both. I want to tell him to stay and love his wife, find a way through all troubles together and not seek affection elsewhere because sooner or later it will always surface to be nothing but carnal, delusive, conditional and false. That woman right there, that friend who means nothing but loyalty, both love you. Do not leave.

Then came the desperation and the repercussion of a decision that would haunt him for a very long time. The second act was simply a dire search to collect the shattered pieces of a life and bring them together. That abject man grasped onto anyone who came to his aid in the time of misery and what he thought was going to be another chance at love, was nothing but fictitious and unrequited. But the fault wasn't hers to begin with. The passion that he bore to create a star out of her was bound to retaliate somewhere. And in that process of accomplishment, if she drifted away from him, she wasn't the only to blame. It wasn't something unprecedented and she reminded him to take her back and away from that celebrity, but that man was too eager to see her succeed. Their separation wasn't novel to this field of industry, and it would continue for times to come. He didn't understand what could happen and how it could change everything he's worked for against his own will. It demanded the sacrifice of their relationship, if there ever was one, and the outcome of their separation could only mean loneliness for one of them, and it was him again.

And the final act was just as someone once said, the realization of need. The need to belong to someone, to have someone belong to him. He realized the hard way that love comes in many disguises, and need is one of them. He was blind to see the true intention behind that conditional affection, but it will all be revealed to him in time. In that blazing desire he just kept drowning deeper and deeper into the ocean of dependence. And when he surfaced, life was right where he started and he was at the mercy of the people he once abandoned. It had come full circle.

And then considering a life that was exhibited before me in form of a stage play, I suddenly realized that I finally had the answer to the questions that lingered in my mind for ages now. And the answer was simple, I was wrong indeed. Wrong in my acts, wrong in my assumptions and wrong in my decisions. If I had never left home, I wouldn't be in such misery today. I was wrong to cheat on a revered relation such as that of a husband and wife, I was wrong to leave her. I was wrong to not return, and continue my life as a vagabond searching for love and affection in other women and homes, where it could never be genuine and true. And now when I realize my mistake, it is too late. Too late to ask forgiveness, too late to ask for a small little space in the hearts of those whom I should had never emotionally lacerated.

I pity myself and all those who have been in situations as I have. And I am certain in their lives they must have contemplated their faults, their weakness at least once if not more. I pity my life, and I feel for everybody who's gone through their years without hope and without faith, without love. People who have searched for love elsewhere, when all they needed to do was to be strong and come back to one they truly loved and were loved by. But I have seen many lives just go on, not belonging to where they are, not accepted by the people they call family and that is a terrible feeling. If I could talk to them, if I could talk some sense into me, I'd say stay if you've found that one true love. No matter what troubles come your way, no matter what hardships attempt to tear you two apart. Stay. Stay with the one who loves you the most. Because once you step out of that door, you may never find peace of a home and warmth of true love ever again. Not all souls are that fortunate the first time, and it is good for them to move on. But how can I forgive myself when I *was* that fortunate, when I made grave mistakes that brought about the darkest debacle of my existence. A search for true love, that was my excuse, but I was dumb enough to leave it in the first place. I believe every single person in the world had used the term true love somewhere in their lives. But what is it? We're all searching for it, but who has found it? Some yes, but the majority of us don't even know if it is true or not. I know it is not a pack of cigarettes that you can find at the corner store on every block. It is not your favorite meal that you can order whenever you feel the need for it. It's a bit more complicated than that. If I'd say I never found love I'd be lying because I did find it once. But I failed to say those simplest of words, and more than that, I failed to understand those words. If anyone ever said it more than once to different people, they'd be lying right to their faces. True love doesn't happen every time, it doesn't repeat once in a while, or a year, or a month, because if it did, our love stories would sound somewhat like an eight year old's. But I guess we're adult enough to differentiate our real world from the fairy tales of the young. Wisdom is not knowing how to love right but to know the right love when it comes your way and preserving it while it lasts. If you've managed to encounter it, you're the lucky one just as I was. Don't let go of it, I made that mistake for which I have paid for twenty-four years. Not all can take that misery for such a long time. Stay and don't let go.

Suddenly someone tapped my shoulder drawing me from the pool of thoughts. I looked behind and found Mr. Durdawk, as he glanced back at me with smile.

"The play is done. Wouldn't you want to meet the people who've come to congratulate the maker of this wonderful thing?"

"Then you're calling the wrong person for them to meet. I just put it into words. The maker is up there, somewhere. Can I ask you something?"

"Go ahead."

"I know this is the last day, last show, but could you do one more for me? Just for me and a few others. Like a rehearsal, nothing too fancy, even at an odd time."

"Can I ask you something?"

"Yes."

"What do you keep writing in there? I have seen you do this for months now."

"This is for my daughter."

"She was in the play, wasn't she?" Mr. Drudawk had seen the world to miss that little detail.

"Yes, she doesn't want to see me. She hates me for the reasons you already know. But I can't let go of a feeling that she might want to know her father one day, maybe years from now, but some day. And I want to keep myself alive in here. I may or may not be there to tell her in person. But she will find me in these pages, alive and talking to her. This is my life, free of drama, full of reality."

"When do you want it?"

Chapter Sixty-Nine

ೲೲೲ

I had asked him to give me fifteen days in which I could send for all of those I wanted to come and see me one last time. I mailed out invitations to the Warrens, Marilyn, and my wife and daughter with tickets for them to come. I also got in contact with Ned and asked him to complete all necessary paperwork to free my accounts and make arrangements to transfer everything I owned under Audrey's name and to come here with the documents. I had also asked him to transfer the ownership of my apartment in Charlotte to Fiona as she might have some childhood memories attached to that place. Then I waited for the day to arrive with anticipation and some cryptic fear within. Anticipation of seeing everyone answer my humble calling, and the fear of hearing an ardent refusal. Just as the day approached closer every hour, every minute, I didn't know what to expect.

Some minutes before it was to begin, I saw Audrey come into the empty hall. She nervously glimpsed around trying to find someone in that faint luminance of the overhead fresnels. I watched her from the darkness of the upper corner of the hall. I was surprised as well as delighted, but even more grieved to find her alone. Hope hadn't come. Then followed Marilyn into the hall with Bradley by her side, still in the glimmer of her fame and renown. And finally it was Winona who stepped inside and found a seat in the middle with Fiona, Esther and Ned in her company. All of them had come but one, the one I wanted to see the most. The forgiveness that I sought was nowhere in sight, the path I would have taken that led back to my family wasn't paved. The curtains were raised and the show began.

I waited there a bit more until the middle of the second act just hoping to see Hope's ingress into the hall, but I failed. She hadn't come. I traced my steps back into the hallway in the rear of the auditorium and went into the empty office locking the door from inside. I stayed there thinking, thinking on a vital matter and did not come out for a very long time. During this time I wrote a letter that I intended to pass on to Hope through her mother perhaps. When I finally exited that office, I heard the last of the third act was being enacted on stage and saw some coordinators hastening up and down the hallway and some actors huddling together. I went back to my seat with my manuscript in hand and a pen ready to determine where I would end the account of my life.

The actor who portrayed me had gotten up an elevation in the final scene of the play, which was made to look like a precipice. The three women stood behind him, turned away.

"And you, the woman who loved me, or was it my mistake; your intent I couldn't foresee. Will you turn away from me and my life, forsake?" He said.

"You are forgotten my long lost man, return to you I never can. For I fly amongst the stars and you crawl upon earth. My love is for the rich, my affection of great worth. The past recollects our affinity no more, those days I do not remember or adore. I leave you to your fate and desolation, may they both serve you well." The second lead responded.

"For she has abandoned me, now I look to you. Will you do the same? Will you forsake me too?" He turned to the next one.

"Love is what but moments shared in necessity of one another? A light that is lit when dark surrounds and doused when dawn smothers. I tread back the way I came, I knew you once, but I know you no more just others. I leave you to your fate and desolation, may they both serve you well." The third lead responded.

"And so is a foolish man defeated in life who's defeated in love? But I still have hope, for I see the truth in it like a light is cast from above. And where shall I find it, if not in the embrace of my companion, my wife, my love." He finally gestured towards the first who stood there with a younger artist by her side.

"Stay away from us, for I know you not. You had left us once, this world we alone fought. Who are you to me and who am I to you? I needed you when I was feeble and your daughter grew. Leave us now that we need you no more. Do not come back, your face I abhor." The woman answered.

"Leave us in peace or you shall see the destruction of this house one last time before your evil eyes. The day you enter our lives, you shall see me exit hers. The choices set, I stay forever, or you leave forever." The younger artist spoke.

My throat went dry as I coughed a little but continued writing the last words of that memoir as I wanted it to be ready and perfect when Hope finds to read it. I just had one unfulfilled desire, her forgiveness. The rest had forgiven me, but the one I sought the most seemed the farthest from me. She has no memories of me, but through this I hope she comes to know that her father wasn't really a miscreant that she thought he was.

"Then I leave and leave forever I will, for I dare not see my house in shreds, my woman in tears, or my child in despair. I leave to find peace and redemption in another world somewhere, may you find it in the one you live here. But if you come to remember, remember me though your delight. Cry not for me, for the rain never quenches the earth, no matter how frequent the heaven cries, the earth hungers more, the earth hungers right. Cry not for me, for your tears are rain and my parting earth. The more you cry the more it yearns. Cry not for me..."

The actor jumped down that elevation and found himself at the cushion of a concealed mattress. The three women dropped to their knees and wept. The curtains dropped.

I have heard the roar of applause at the end of this play many times before, but tonight's silence in tears was the most beautiful sound I had ever heard. But just as the show ended, I saw someone come into the theater. She was swift and panting. She glanced around and found her mother amidst the spectators. It was a sight I had waited for, it was my daughter who came looking for me. Hope, you have finally come. But why did my hand tremble as I continued to write? Was I going away, going away too soon? I was beginning to drift as somnolence started to manifest. What did I do? Yet again, another mistake, another error, the last there will ever be? But my delight was in the sight of my daughter whom I have seen and heard through my dying senses as Mr. Durdawk introduced himself and she inquired about me.

With my eyelids fluttering close, all I could remember was the fondest days of my past. And my final thoughts were to say goodbye to all I've come across in my life and apologize for any transgressions, or any promise I hadn't satisfied. I even wanted to apologize to Louise for not being able to honor her invitation to her home in New York. But then I was content that Hope and Audrey had come to see me. That my daughter had finally come to forgive me. With that wish fulfilled I go in peace now, but remember this promise I ask of you tonight. Just as I wrote in the end of my play, at any point in life when you come to remember me, if you do, remember me through the splendor of your laughter and your mother's smile. Cry not for me, for I have lived my part.

The Letter

ളൗളൗളൗ

Dear Hope,

I don't know how to begin explaining myself to you, and I think I shouldn't as for that I have already scripted the reality of my life and left it for you to read and decide whether I truly deserve your forgiveness or not. But I will not waste the length of this letter to tell you what I want, but to tell you how I feel. You are my daughter. There is nothing in this world that can change that. You are my blood and you are someone I had searched for a very long time in the past years of my life. I know I was wrong to look in the incorrect places for the love of a daughter or a wife, and it's not that I didn't find it. But what I truly sought was you and your mother, our family. It was my mistake that I left you both once, and I can assure you I had received merited comeuppance for those faults. When I returned, I returned in hopes of a new life, but I could never see you separated from your mother as your love for each other was so greater than mine. When I asked you two to come and see me here in LA, I had great anticipations attached. The sight of us reuniting again would have driven me mad, and I do not lie. You may think every word I have put in this letter is false and I wouldn't blame you for taking it so. A man leaves his memories not in reality but in those who survive after him. Those who talk about him, those who remember his words, his actions, his love and laughter. No one dies with the dead, but the dead live through the living. I have written this chronicle of my life for you and I promise every word in this account is true to its happening. You may dislike and love me at times, you may cry and smile at times, but after reading this story I hope you will at last forgive, or more importantly love me.

I can still remember the day I first saw you in the arms of your mother with a pink hat that fitted perfectly around your soft forehead. Your eyes were as big as the sky and your face so precious and pure. Believe me that I wanted to break away every worldly shackle to just hold you once and kiss you, but those shackles were frail when contrasted against the misery and misfortune I would have brought along if I returned. I could be wrong, maybe my suppositions about my ill fate were unrealistic and irrational, but just one glimpse of watching your mother holding you close in her arms against the warmth of her breast, I couldn't risk it. No matter how much I curse myself now, for that one time in life I thought I made a good decision. To walk away from you and your mother and not bring you two under the shadow of my tragic fate. I did come once and I looked at your face, and that angelic face remained with me until the day I saw you again all grown up. No matter what you said to me, I have no complaints against you, because I know you were right. But that day was the happiest of my life to see you all grown up into a lady whose care and love for her mother is absolute and unqualified.

I am about to leave this world. The sleeping pills are going to work their way into my body any moment now. At this point I am left with no choice but to prove my true love for you and your mother, and I don't know any other way to prove it but through my end. No one is to be blamed for my decision in leaving, as it is my time to go. I leave with sweet thoughts and memories of you as a baby and your mother as the woman who has loved me no matter what. I know your mother is weak, you might not see it on the outside as she has been a warrior all these years, but her heart is delicate. She is emotional and easily aroused to tears, only those who are close enough to her might know. You know her better than I do. She will need you for the rest of her life to survive, to hold on. But I can't see her in tears. Enough tears have been shed on my account, not anymore. Stay by her when she finds me tonight and make sure she doesn't cry too much. I am yet again leaving you with a responsibility and a job to finish. Smile if you may, but I cannot bear to see you in tears anymore. I want to be remembered through your laughter, not your sorrow. Take care of your mother and take care of yourself. And remember, I will always be with you and love you. Even when I am not there, my presence and my love for you and your mother will never cease to exist.

Your father,
George Frederick Bailey

www.ingramcontent.com/pod-product-compliance
Lightning Source LLC
Chambersburg PA
CBHW030536260626
47157CB00006B/2051